Dark Voices

The Best from The Pan Book of Horror Stories

Stephen Jones was born in 1953 and is the winner of the World Fantasy Award and seven-time recipient of the British Fantasy Award for *Fantasy Tales*, the paperback magazine of fantasy and terror. A full-time columnist, film reviewer, illustrator, television producer/director and horror movie publicist (*Hellraiser, Hellbound, Nightbreed* etc.), he is the co-editor of *Horror: 100 Best Books, The Best Horror from Fantasy Tales, Gaslight & Ghosts, Now We are Sick*, and compiler of *Clive Barker's Shadows in Eden, Clive Barker's The Nightbreed Chronicles* and *James Herbert: By Horror Haunted*.

Clarence Paget was born in 1909 and gained a degree in History at Oxford. He entered publishing after the War when he joined the A. D. Peters Literary Agency. By the early 1950s he was assistant to the managing director of Cassell, and in 1956 became the Chief Editor of Pan Books. He remained at Pan until his retirement in 1974, but has continued his active involvement in publishing up to the present day – most notably as the editor of the past five volumes of *The Pan Book of Horror Stories*.

Edited by
Stephen Jones
and Clarence Paget

DARK
VOICES

The Best from The
Pan Book of Horror Stories

PAN
HORROR

Pan Books
London, Sydney and Auckland

This selection first published 1990 by
Pan Books Ltd, Cavaye Place, London SW10 9PG

9 8 7 6

© This selection Stephen Jones and Clarence Paget 1990

ISBN 0 330 31565 X (cased)

ISBN 0 330 31100 X (paper)

Phototypeset by Input Typesetting Ltd, London

Printed by Richard Clay Ltd, Bungay, Suffolk

In memory of
Rosemary Timperley
1920–1988

Acknowledgements

Introductory Note © Pan Books Ltd. 1959

Foreword: Dark Voices © Stephen Jones 1990.

Baby's Blood © Alan Ryan 1982. Reprinted by permission of the author. Introduction © Stephen Gallagher 1990.

The Mangler © Stephen King 1976, 1977, 1978. Reprinted by permission of the author's publishers, New English Library Ltd. Introduction © James Herbert 1990.

The Speciality of the House © Stanley Ellin 1948, renewed 1976. Reprinted by permission of the author's agent, Curtis Brown Ltd. Introduction © Clive Barker 1990.

Camera Obscura © Basil Copper 1965. Reprinted by permission of the author. Introduction © Charles L. Grant 1990.

No Flies on Frank © John Lennon 1964. Reprinted by permission of the Estate of John Lennon. Introduction © F. Paul Wilson 1990.

The Streets of Ashkelon © Harry Harrison 1965. Reprinted by permission of the author. Introduction © Brian W. Aldiss 1990.

Lucy Comes To Stay © 1952, *Weird Tales*, renewed 1980 by Robert Bloch. Reprinted by permission of the author. Introduction © Graham Masterton 1990.

The Fly © George Langelaan 1957. Reprinted by permission of the author's agent, Curtis Brown Ltd. Introduction © David Cronenberg 1990.

The Emissary © 1947, renewed 1975 by Ray Bradbury. Reprinted by permission of the author's agent, Don Congdon Associates, Inc. Introduction © Dennis Etchison 1990.

Pornography © Ian McEwan 1978. Reprinted by permission of the author. Introduction © Shaun Hutson 1990.

Ringing the Changes © Robert Aickman 1956. Reprinted by permission of the Estate of Robert Aickman. Introduction © Peter Straub 1990.

The Quiet Girl © Robert Holdstock 1978. Reprinted by permission of the author. Introduction © Robert R. McCammon 1990.

ACKNOWLEDGEMENTS

The Hunter © David Case 1969. Reprinted by permission of the author. Introduction © Ramsey Campbell 1990.

Afterword: Bringing the Horror Back Home © Stephen Jones 1990.

The Pan Book of Horror Stories Index Volumes 1–30 © Stephen Jones 1990.

Title page illustration © Dave Carson 1990.

Contents

Introductory Note

Why do we like reading about torture, sadistic monsters, cruel people? Why do we like frightening ourselves by reading about events which we would hope never to see, let alone participate in? Is it not the memorable and age-long custom that we like 'being taken out of ourselves'? And is there not a slight feeling of smugness, that while sitting in our (we hope) comfortable armchairs we can safely read of the ingenious and terrifying things men do to men?

Despite the so-called advance of civilization, we have witnessed wars, revolutions and crimes that are often more terrifying than fiction.

In short, truth is stranger than fiction. Even so, we feel that the stories in this book are such that if your nerves are not of the strongest, then it is wise to read them in daylight lest you should suffer nightmares, for these authors know their craft, and they have not hesitated to expound it with little thought of sparing you from the horrifying details.

HERBERT VAN THAL

Foreword: Dark Voices

Pull your armchair closer to the fire, check that all the doors are securely locked, and reassure yourself that the tapping at the window is only a wind-blown branch. Listen to the night's *Dark Voices* . . .

The Pan Book of Horror Stories was created in 1959. Edited by experienced anthologist and publisher Herbert van Thal, it was designed to stand as a one-off volume, but sales of the first book exceeded all expectations, and the title rapidly developed into the world's longest-running and most successful horror anthology series.

Over three decades, it has published both new and reprint fiction by some of the greatest practitioners of terror and suspense, and continues to lead the field in short horror fiction.

Dark Voices is a celebration of that success, and some of the best-known names in the horror and fantasy field have agreed to share our anniversary by contributing unique introductions to each of the stories chosen for this volume.

You'll discover such gruesome delights as a restaurant that serves a highly unusual dish; a device that can see into a dark and evil world; a town that celebrates a macabre festival; a hunt for a modern-day werewolf, and the diabolical secret behind a new brand of drink – along with more traditional terrors such as murder, madness and metamorphosis.

Although we've subtitled this book *The Best from the Pan Book of Horror Stories*, such a description can never be entirely accurate. With room only for a baker's dozen of terrifying tales, we have been unable to pay full tribute to many of the writers who have sustained the series with their regular contributions over the years. We are sorry that old favourites such as William Sansom, Martin Waddell, Rosemary Timperley, Rene Morris, John D. Keefauver, Dulcie Gray, Alex White, Norman P. Kaufman, Harry Turner and Alan Temperley, to mention only a few, are not included here.

However, *Dark Voices* boasts classic tales of the macabre that we hope reflect the impressive range of storytelling and talent featured in *The Pan Book of Horror Stories* over the years.

So now it's time to turn the page and prepare to meet some old friends and, just perhaps, several less welcome acquaintances. Welcome, once again, to your nightmares . . .

The Editors
London, July 1989

Baby's Blood
Introduction

*Many of the people that I know in the British horror field –
whether they're readers, writers, editors, or artists – got their
first taste of the grown-up stuff from* The Pan Book of Horror
Stories. *I suppose that I'm talking here mostly about my
own generation, reaching adolescence too late for* Weird Tales
*and with the horror boom of the seventies yet to come; it was
the Pan collections that gave a kind of continuity between the
two eras, and so saved many of us from losing our way. At
a time of flower power, psychedelia, peace, love, and The
Monkees, it was reassuring to know that someone out there
cared enough to give us a book featuring a severed head in a
bucket on its cover. We might have had to climb across racks
of spy stories and Rod McKuen to get to it but once there, we
knew we were home.*

*If you are one of us then, you'll know exactly what to expect
now. And if you weren't, but perhaps you're calling by for
the first time, then all I can say is . . . welcome to the family.
I know you're going to stay. Because the bridge is down and
your tyres have been slashed and we nailed up the door just
after you came in . . .*

You may know Alan Ryan from such novels as Dead
White *and* Cast A Cold Eye; *he's hugely talented, highly
respected, and he knows exactly how to induce that delighted
shudder which is a characteristic effect of the horror story at
its best.*

Here's 'Baby's Blood' to prove it. Enjoy the experience.

Mike the barkeep certainly did . . .

STEPHEN GALLAGHER
Author of Valley of Lights, Oktober *and* Down River.

Alan Ryan
Baby's Blood

"It's called Baby's Blood," the man said. "Taste it."

Mike the barkeep cocked his head to one side, drummed his thick fingertips on the bar in front of him, and looked speculatively at the stranger.

"Go on," the man said pleasantly, an understanding smile flitting across his face. "It won't hurt to try. Just have a sip and tell me if it isn't different from anything you've ever tasted before."

A hard-edged shaft of brilliant sunlight stabbed through the narrow window at the front of the bar, but the interior of the place remained dark and gloomy, as if resisting the onslaught of morning light from the outside world. The heavy wooden tables and booths shone dully beneath dim light bulbs, and the long wooden bar itself glowed as if it was still damp from last night's business. By night, the place offered Mike's regulars and the sometime drinkers a haven of warmth and glowing yellow light to hold at bay the emptiness of these spring evenings; but by day, and especially by morning, the place seemed, almost felt, chill and dark. A night-time place, for sure, and the dazzling light outside succeeded only in peeking hungrily through the window.

It was for this reason that Mike the barkeep had decided seven years ago, when he first came to this country from the other side, that he would not open his place until two o'clock in the afternoon. Sure, many of his countrymen, fellow owners of taverns, opened up at eight in the morning, but that wasn't for Mike, it wasn't his way. If he couldn't keep a bar and make his fortune on it by selling beer and liquor during the hours when drinking was decent and proper, then he wouldn't do it at all, he wouldn't. He'd told that to everyone from the start, and he'd stuck to it. And to tell the truth, besides, he couldn't say that he much cared for the inside of a tavern in the morning hours, his own included. A tavern was too dark, too gloomy, in the morning, with too many alcoholics coming in to drink their breakfast while the missus cried at home.

No, that wasn't the way for Mike. And he was satisfied. He lived like a decent citizen and a good family man in a nice house with a garden over in Riverdale (and wasn't it a crying shame his father, God rest his soul, hadn't lived to see *that*), his two girls were in a good Catholic high school, he seldom had to deal with drunks, and there against the mirror, right over the cash register, was the handsomely painted sign that proclaimed for all the world to see: MICHAEL WALSH, COUNTY CORK, PROPRIETOR. Thank God for America.

But he still disliked being here in the mornings. He wouldn't have been here today, in fact, except that Tommy, his afternoon bartender, had called him at home and said that one of the kids had been taken sick and he was giving the wife a hand and he was sorry but would Mike mind going in himself to straighten up the accounts and check the stock? Well, Tommy was a good man and these things happened. But if it hadn't been for that, this stranger on the other side of the bar would be talking to Tommy instead of him.

"Come on," the man said, "at least you can give it a try. It certainly won't hurt to try. Just taste it and I think you'll be convinced."

Mike let his eyes drop from the stranger's face to the small clear bottle the man had placed on the bar. It was an odd-shaped bottle, he was thinking, a shape he'd never seen before. His trained eye studied it and he guessed it held about a pint and a half. There was no label on it and that made Mike just a bit uneasy. On the other hand, it didn't put him off completely, either. He was an honourable businessman, always had been, and no one could say otherwise, but after all, a businessman had to be watching for the advantages, now, didn't he? It wouldn't be the first time Mike had tasted – or bought, for the matter of that – something offered in an unlabelled bottle with an unusual shape.

"Baby's Blood, eh?" he said. He studied the bottle. Through the clear glass, a thick but bright red liquid seemed almost to glow. Mike's eyes – eyes that could tell one brand of whisky from another, and do the same with scotch or bourbon, in the half-light of evening in the bar – failed to get much information from the bottle of liquid. It stood just a few inches from where his large-knuckled hands rested on the gleaming wooden surface.

"That's right," the man said. "Baby's Blood."

"Powerful name," Mike said. His eyes were still playing over the bottle, his lips pursed.

"Powerful drink," the stranger said.

After a moment's silence, Mike said, "Don't look thick enough to be blood." He glanced up from the bottle to the man's face, a pleasant, reliable sort of a face, he would have said.

The stranger's smile widened slightly. "No," he said. "No, as a matter of fact, it doesn't, does it." He glanced down for a second at the bottle, then looked back at Mike, and his shoulders moved in a shrug. "Babies, you know," he said. "Very thin blood."

They smiled together.

"Well, what do I do with it?" Mike asked. His fingers closed around the bottle, slid it closer to his side of the bar. It was cool to the touch and Mike thought he remembered seeing something white, maybe some kind of insulation, inside the man's sample case when he'd first opened it to take out the bottle. Mike tried again to recall where he might have seen a bottle of this size and shape before, but the memory, if indeed he had it, eluded him.

"Almost anything," the man said. He leaned forward, his arms on the outer lip of the bar, relaxed now that Mike was actually going to taste the sample. "Almost anything at all. You can mix it with anything. Use a customer's favourite mixer – tonic, cola drinks, lemon drinks, whatever. Or splash a little water in it. Or even a *lot* of water. Some people like to use it in mixed drinks, you know, just use a few drops in, oh, say, a Manhattan or an old-fashioned. You'll come up with all sorts of things, depending on your clientele."

"What about straight?" Mike asked.

For the first time in their conversation, it was the stranger's turn to hesitate. "Well," he said slowly, "I'll tell you the truth. We don't recommend it. This is pretty strong stuff. Now that's not to say you mightn't want to serve it that way. God knows, in this business there's no accounting for taste." He looked Mike directly in the eye and they smiled together again. No, that was certainly the truth; there was no accounting for taste, especially in this business. "But really," the man went on, "we'd prefer to see it used with something else. That's what we recommend. Besides, there *is* the matter of price."

"What does this stuff cost?" Mike asked.

The stranger looked relaxed again, confident just this side of smug. "Taste it," he said.

"And you're not going to tell me what it is?"

"Taste it," the stranger said again.

Mike shrugged and figured what the hell, he'd gone this far, might as well give it a go. He slid the cool bottle to his side of the bar, then reached overhead to one of the glasses that hung upside down from a rack above his head. He scooped a few ice cubes into the glass from beneath the bar, then set the glass beside the bottle. The cap required a tight downward pressure and opened with a tiny pop. Mike realised instantly what the bottle was: one of those special jars made for home canning and preserving, with a grey rubber ring around the mouth, the kind that Paul Harvey is always advertising on the radio. Mike lifted it, held it up to the dim overhead light. It glowed red, but otherwise told him nothing. For a second, he thought he might sniff at the mouth of the bottle, but instead he just splashed some of the red liquid over the cubes in the glass. As he set the bottle down, a dime-sized drop of red landed on the bar. Automatically, Mike reached under the bar for a towel and wiped it away.

The red liquid shone bright around the ice cubes. Mike tried to judge its consistency and decided that it was somewhere midway between tomato juice and cranberry juice.

He lifted the glass to his nose, swirled the contents around a couple of times, and sniffed. Nothing. No, wait. Well, maybe just the slightest suggestion of something vaguely familiar. He sniffed again, swirled the crimson liquid over the cubes, sniffed once more. No. No, there was nothing he could recognize.

"This is alcoholic, isn't it?" he asked the stranger. "I have no use for those damned prepared mixes, you know."

"Just add a little water and taste it," the stranger said.

Mike sighed. Might as well get on with it, he thought. This thing will either be something or nothing, so the sooner we get on with it, the sooner I can get on with my work, one way or the other.

He reached for the head of the hose dispenser, pressed the button, and fired a sparkling stream of water into the glass. The mixture of water and red liquid foamed madly for a few seconds, then settled down, leaving a frothy ring of tiny pink bubbles coating the inside of the glass.

"Down the hatch," the stranger said.

Mike lifted the glass to his lips. Lord ha' mercy, he thought quickly. He took a drink, filled his mouth with the liquid, sloshed it around to get the full effect of the flavour. He felt, first, the coldness of the drink, then felt it warming slowly in his mouth, but he could discern nothing by way of a distinctive flavour. He waited a few seconds longer, letting his mouth warm the drink a little more to see if that would release the taste, then sloshed it around again, searching now for the right area of his tongue that would report the taste it found. He waited, but he still wasn't certain that there was any taste at all.

"Have a little more," the stranger said.

Mike, committed to going along with the man's request now that he had started, swallowed the mouthful he had and lifted the glass to his lips to take another. As the first mouthful slid down, he thought he detected, as if at a great distance, a familiar and comfortable warming sensation in his gullet, right down the middle of his chest, but still, he couldn't really be absolutely sure. It might just be an automatic reaction to taking a drink; the mind could play tricks on a man, after all. He filled his mouth a second time, leaving, he noticed, a streak of frothy bubbles, pale pink in colour, up the inside of the glass. As before, he tossed the drink around in his mouth and waited for some sensation to reach his brain. The stuff must have some taste, he thought, it must taste like something, unless the stranger was trying to sell him coloured water. But no, it couldn't be that, he thought at once, the stuff, whatever it was, was certainly thicker than water. He sloshed it around again in his mouth and waited.

The phrase he had just thought echoed for a moment in his mind. Thicker than water. Blood. Baby's Blood.

He swallowed abruptly, hesitated for a second, then cleared his throat and said, "This isn't blood, is it?"

"Baby's Blood," the stranger said, his pleasant, patient expression unchanged. "We call it Baby's Blood. Take some more. You won't have long to wait."

Mike sighed quietly once more. In for a penny, he thought, in for a pound. He took another mouthful from the glass.

This one seemed somehow different. Warmer. Thicker. Richer. He was just barely aware, at the outer edge of his consciousness, of a hint of something metallic. And maybe a suggestion of . . . the ocean? Salt? Yes, maybe a slightly metallic taste. And the warming effect was growing, yes, he could feel that now, not only in his mouth but in his chest and stomach, as if the accumulation of liquid he had so far swallowed was painting the inside of his body, coating it thoroughly with its red and glowing warmth. And something else. It felt good in his mouth, without actually tasting like anything in particular.

"Very interesting," he said, after swallowing the last mouthful.

"Take one more drink," the stranger said.

Mike lifted the glass again, noting – was that a tiny twinge of sadness? – that it was almost empty. There was just a light coating of pink, with a tiny pool of darker red at the bottom, the spot of colour magnified and distorted by the ice cubes. When he filled his mouth this time, the drink felt – tasted? – very pleasantly warm, surprisingly so, because the ice should have cooled it. And then, too, he remembered, the bottle itself had been cool when the stranger placed it on the bar. But this mouthful already seemed warm when it entered his mouth, as if it had been warm all along. Very pleasantly warm. In fact, Mike was beginning to think that he liked it a lot more this way, warm, than he had when it was cool, like that first taste he'd had. Yes, it was definitely better warm. He looked down into his glass and saw that a final drop had collected at the bottom. Oh yes, it was a very interesting drink indeed. He swallowed what was in his mouth and, lifting the glass one more time, drained off the remainder. Warm, the drink was warm now and sending warmth all through his body. The back of his neck felt warm. Mike was feeling by now very confident of his ability to recognize a good thing when he saw it or, for that matter, tasted it. Yes indeed. It was a fine drink, a very fine drink. He was quite warm now, yes, but feeling very, very good. Reluctantly, he let the last of it slip down his throat and looked with mingled regret and satisfaction into the empty glass.

"Baby's Blood, eh?" he said, letting his eyes meet those of the stranger. He cleared his throat. "I'm just wondering," he began, "do you have to be calling it that? Maybe some other . . ."

"Baby's Blood," the stranger said, his voice flat but smiling still.

"Ah," Mike said.

A tiny silence hung between them.

"Well," Mike said, his breath almost a sigh, "it's different, all right, isn't it? Almost like you'd imagine."

The stranger's nice smile never wavered. "Almost," he said.

"The genuine article, I suppose, of course?" Mike said,

raising one eyebrow at the man across the bar. "Or are there added ingredients?"

"Maybe just a little something added," the stranger said easily. "But consider it the genuine article." His smile broadened ever so slightly and he added, "For all practical purposes."

They smiled, understanding each other, businessman to businessman.

"I see," Mike said slowly. "Well." He ran his tongue around the inside of his mouth. The soft and quiet warmth the drink had induced flowed gently throughout his body, bringing a comfortable glow to his stomach, his groin, his legs. The sensation was like nothing he had ever felt before, warmer and somehow deeper. His fingers slid across the smooth surface of the bar and lightly touched the bottle. It still held, he estimated with a hopeful glance, enough red liquid for . . . oh, for quite a number of drinks. The tips of his fingers were tingling pleasantly now, a sensation he hadn't felt since the very earliest of his drinking days. "I see," he said again. Remarkable, he thought, how, despite the obviously potent effect of the drink, it did nothing to impair one's speech. His fingers caressed the cool glass of the bottle. "And just what would you be asking for a bottle of this Baby's Blood?"

"The price is high," said the stranger.

Mike nodded. "I was thinking you might say that. But it's a fine drink, a fine drink indeed." Oh, he felt good. "How much would you be asking?"

The stranger told him.

The price he mentioned was so high that, for a second, despite the overwhelmingly comfortable effect of the drink on his mind and body, Mike wondered if he had heard the man correctly. But in the next second, he knew he had, and in the next second after that, he knew the price was a fair one. Before he even realized what he was doing, his mind was calculating the price of a bottle, the quantity of its contents, the number of drinks that could be made from a single bottle, the amount he would have to charge per drink, and who among his trusty regulars and friends would be willing and able to pay such a price. And, he added to himself, who among them would be worthy of such a drink as this. All the while he stood there thinking, leaning comfortably against the bar, the effect of the drink was spreading even more cosily through his body.

"All right then," he said. "I'll be taking it."

"Have another drink," the stranger said, smiling even more nicely as he lifted the bottle and poured. "This one's on me."

The man let his car roll to a carefully timed halt, the front bumper coming to rest precisely over the painted stop line in the road, as the traffic signal above showed a combination of red and green. He could have slipped through the light, and he knew it, and he knew too that a lot of drivers would have just kept going, or even hit the accelerator to speed up and make the turn, but he was the kind of driver who always obeyed the traffic regulations to the letter of the law. Let the speed demons waiting behind him to make the turn grumble as much as they wanted. The law was the law. He glanced into the rear-view mirror and saw a kid in a green Skylark giving him the finger. The man shifted his gaze away to the traffic facing him on the other side of the divider and the traffic signal swinging overhead in a gentle spring breeze.

He sat patiently until a green arrow indicated he could make the turn, then swung the car left across the road and into the parking lot of the shopping centre. He drove carefully, keeping a wary eye out for less cautious drivers who might back quickly out of the parking space without first checking in both directions. Observing the posted speed limit of 15 mph, he rolled slowly between the rows of cars, following his familiar path along the yellow-painted arrows on the blacktop. He drove to the far end of the sprawling lot, towards the four-storey department store at the other end of the mall. A section of parking spaces here was labelled EMPLOYEE PARKING ONLY. He found a free space immediately, pulled into it, made certain his car was centred between the lines for his space, then shut off the engine and rolled up the windows. When he opened the door to get out, he took great care to make certain that the edge of his door didn't hit the side of the car beside him and chip the paint.

He locked the car, tested the handle, and walked briskly across the parking lot to the employees' entrance, straightening his tie and buttoning his brown tweed jacket as he walked.

By the time he reached the door, he had pulled from his jacket a black plastic card case with a shiny clear window displaying his store employee identification card. He had worked here for quite some while now but, as a security measure, all employees were required to show their cards every time they entered the building for work. The store had a policy of rotating the guards at the door every couple of days, in order to keep them from getting to know too many people by sight and getting too friendly with them. An extra precautionary measure and, the man thought, a good one. You couldn't be too careful these days.

At the door he flashed his card, the guard glanced briefly at it and nodded, and the man hurried inside. He paused at the time clock to punch in and quickly compared the time on the face of the machine with that of his own watch. They agreed. Good. He thought for a second. Yes, he would have just enough time to make the quick stop he had planned before reporting to his post. There were just a few things he had to pick up before starting work today.

He left the employee area and took the escalator to the second floor, standing patiently as it glided upward and stepping aside to let a young stockboy hurry past him up the steps. At the top of the escalator, he stepped off quickly and turned right, towards the toy department.

The salesgirl behind the cash register saw him coming and greeted him brightly. She was a pretty little thing with rich dark hair and bright eager eyes.

"Hi, there!" she said. "Good morning! Got a long shopping list today?" Her smile was warm and genuine and clearly she would have liked to know the man better than she did. She was not the only one who felt that way, and she knew it, so she tried to make her smile as cheery and pretty as possible on the mornings when he dropped in at the toy department to do his shopping.

"Oh, just a few things," he said, favouring her with his own nice smile. "I know where they are."

"We have some new items you might want to take," the girl offered. "I can show you where they are, if you like."

"I just need a few replacements," the man told her. "You know how quickly they get worn out. I'll just be a minute." He stepped away and disappeared down one of the aisles.

The girl hid her disappointment behind another bright smile.

She had time to ring up only one sale for a customer before the man was back, standing quietly in front of her cash register. In his arms he was clutching six bright pink and blue baby rattles and an open box of one dozen pacifiers in shiny clear bubble cards.

"You really enjoy your work," the girl said warmly.

"Yes," the man replied. "I do."

The girl hesitated, trying desperately to think of something else to say that would hold him there. She couldn't. Well, maybe tomorrow. She'd think about it tonight and come up with something for tomorrow.

"I'll write that up for you and put it through myself," she said quickly. "Don't worry about it. And if there's anything else I can do, just say so."

"I will, and thanks a lot," the man said. "This should hold me for a bit. See you tomorrow probably."

The girls' big dark eyes followed him as he walked away with his arms full of pacifiers and baby rattles. Maybe tomorrow she'd have a chance to talk with him, get to know him better, let him get to know her better. Her girl friend in the personnel office had secretly checked the records and told her he wasn't married.

The man walked through the main aisle on the floor, past racks and tables of children's wear, towards his own little space at the other end of the floor. Several salespeople greeted him as he passed. He returned each greeting with a pleasant smile.

When he reached his post, there were two women waiting for him already, although he wasn't actually due for another five minutes. They smiled in recognition when they saw him coming.

Cradling the rattles and the box of pacifiers in one arm, the man pulled out his key.

"Good morning, ladies," he said as he unlocked the door. "Just give me a minute to get these things out of my hands and I'll be right with you." He pushed the door open, stepped inside, and flipped the lights on with his elbow.

"Oh, take your time," one of the women said. "We're early anyway." She hitched the baby she was holding a little higher against her shoulder. The infant was blinking in the bright lights of the store, its chubby little face nestled warmly in the folds of a pink blanket.

"Really," the woman said, looking at her companion, who was also holding a baby in her arms, "he's so good with them, especially the little ones." She patted her baby gently on the back. "Mine is always so sleepy and quiet for hours and hours after he's taken care of her. He just has a magic touch with babies."

The man appeared in the doorway. "All set," he said, smiling warmly at the women and their infants. Directly over his head, just above the doorway, a neatly lettered sign said, COURTESY BABYSITTING SERVICE FOR SHOPPERS.

"Here," the man said, stretching out his arms for the first baby. "Let me have your little angel. And don't you worry about a thing. She's in good hands with me."

"It's called Baby's Blood," the man said. "Taste it."

Nick D'Agostino rubbed one hand across the wiry stubble of beard on his chin, then leaned forward with both hands placed flat against the cool steel of his cart. Hanging from the red and green striped umbrella above his head, a sign offered passersby "*Genuine* Italian Ices". Lined up across the front of the cart were large clear plastic bottles of syrup, all ready to be poured over freshly shaved ice: yellow for lemon, green for lime, white for pineapple, purple for grape. Nick looked at the glass bottle the stranger had placed in front of him, its red liquid shining brightly.

"Go on," the man said pleasantly. "It won't hurt to try."

The Mangler
Introduction

I have to admit I'm totally biased as far as Stephen King is concerned. We were both published around the same time, King with Carrie, *me with* The Rats, *and I think it's reasonable to say that this was probably the beginning of horror fiction's renaissance in the UK and the USA. It was also when I became a solid fan of his work.*

We met a little later when he was in England on a publicity jaunt, and we shared an after-dinner speaking engagement. If not quite hostile to horror, our middle-aged, middle-class audience was certainly not comfortable with it. However, mainly due to King's relaxed and good-humoured manner, together with his special ability to communicate, by the end of the evening we had managed to win them over.

Now, although a relatively small event, it was an important one, for that audience was comprised of booksellers and wholesalers – the "Trade". In their hands was the power to make or break a book (in this case, read "book" as "genre"). To my mind it was a significant step towards the general acceptability of the horror novel in the British market place.

In his work, as in his approach to that evening in Surrey, Stephen King lacks pomp and pretension. He has humour. He has depth. He knows how to strike at the heart.

I've often referred to him as the Norman Rockwell of American literature. Like Rockwell, whose brilliant paintings of 'Americana' were often reviled by certain bloodless critics, King induces instant recognition with his characters and scenarios (but never with his plots – they're unique to him). He introduces us to people who live and breathe, people we can love, like, or very easily hate. He presents images so vivid that one suspects some kind of telepathy between author and reader.

And of course, most important of all (this was what we hand over our money for, isn't it?), he scares the hell out of us every time.

"The Mangler", a short story gleaned from his own early days working in a laundry, is but an indication of his rich talent; nevertheless, the visions therein – a Speed Ironer and Folder that does precisely that to its human victims, a clunking machine that uproots and follows its prey – are magnificently potent. Be chilled.

JAMES HERBERT
Author of The Magic Cottage, Sepulchre *and* Haunted

Stephen King
The Mangler

Officer Hunton got to the laundry just as the ambulance was leaving – slowly, with no siren or flashing lights. Ominous. Inside, the office was stuffed with milling, silent people, some of them weeping. The plant itself was empty; the big automatic washers at the far end had not even been shut down. It made Hunton very wary. The crowd should be at the scene of the accident, not in the office. It was the way things worked – the human animal had a built-in urge to view the remains. A very bad one, then. Hunton felt his stomach tighten as it always did when the accident was very bad. Fourteen years of cleaning human litter from highways and streets and the sidewalks at the bases of very tall buildings had not been able to erase that little hitch in the belly, as if something evil had clotted there.

A man in a white shirt saw Hunton and walked towards him reluctantly. He was a buffalo of a man with head thrust forwards between shoulders, nose and cheeks vein-broken either from high blood pressure or too many conversations with the brown bottle. He was trying to frame words, but after two tries Hunton cut him off briskly. "Are you the owner? Mr Gartley?"

"No . . . no. I'm Stanner. The foreman. God, this – "

Hunton got out his notebook. "Please show me the scene of the accident, Mr Stanner, and tell me what happened."

Stanner seemed to grow even more white; the blotches on his nose and cheeks stood out like birthmarks. "D-do I have to?"

Hunton raised his eyebrows. "I'm afraid you do. The call I got said it was serious."

"Serious – " Stanner seemed to be battling with his

gorge; for a moment his Adam's apple went up and down like a monkey on a stick. "Mrs Frawley is dead. Jesus I wish Bill Gartley *was* here."

"What happened?"

Stanner said, "You better come over here."

He led Hunton past a row of hand presses, a shirt-folding unit, and then stopped by a laundry-marking machine. He passed a shaky hand across his forehead. "You'll have to go over by yourself, Officer. I can't look at it again. It makes me . . . I can't. I'm sorry."

Hunton walked around the marking machine with a mild feeling of contempt for the man. They run a loose shop, cut corners, run live steam through home-welded pipes, they work with dangerous cleaning chemicals without the proper protection, and finally, someone gets hurt. Or gets dead. Then they can't look. They can't –

Hunton saw it.

The machine was still running. No one had shut it off. The machine he later came to know intimately: the Hadley-Watson Model–6 Speed Ironer and Folder. A long and clumsy name. The people who worked here in the steam and the wet had a better name for it. The mangler.

Hunton took a long, frozen look, and then he performed a first in his fourteen years as a law-enforcement officer: he turned around, put a convulsive hand to his mouth, and threw up.

"You didn't eat much," Jackson said.

The women were inside, doing dishes and talking babies while John Hunton and Mark Jackson sat in lawn chairs near the aromatic barbecue. Hunton smiled slightly at the understatement. He had eaten nothing.

"There was a bad one today," he said. "The worst."

"Car crash?"

"No. Industrial."

"Messy?"

Hunton did not reply immediately, but his face made an involuntary, writhing grimace. He got a beer out of the cooler between them, opened it, and emptied half of it.

"I suppose you college profs don't know anything about industrial laundries?"

Jackson chuckled. "This one does. I spent a summer working in one as an undergraduate."

"Then you know the machine they call the speed ironer?"

Jackson nodded. "Sure. They run damp flatwork through them, mostly sheets and linen. A big, long machine."

"That's it," Hunton said. "A woman named Adelle Frawley got caught in it at the Blue Ribbon Laundry crosstown. It sucked her right in."

Jackson looked suddenly ill. "But . . . that can't happen, Johnny. There's a safety bar. If one of the women feeding the machine accidentally gets a hand under it, the bar snaps up and stops the machine. At least that's how I remember it."

Hunton nodded. "It's a state law. But it happened."

Hunton closed his eyes and in the darkness he could see the Hadley-Watson speed ironer again, as it had been that afternoon. It formed a long rectangular box shape, thirty feet by six. At the feeder end, a moving canvas belt moved under the safety bar, up at a slight angle, and then down. The belt carried the damp-dried, wrinkled sheets in continuous cycle over and under sixteen huge revolving cylinders that made up the main body of the machine. Over eight and under eight, pressed between them like thin ham between layers of superheated bread. Steam heat in the cylinders could be adjusted up to 300 degrees for maximum drying. The pressure on the sheets that rode the moving canvas belt was set at 800 pounds per square foot to get out every wrinkle.

And Mrs Frawley, somehow, had been caught and dragged in. The steel, asbestos-jacketed pressing cylinders had been as red as barn paint, and the rising steam from the machine had carried the sickening stench of hot blood. Bits of her white blouse and blue slacks, even ripped segments of her bra and panties, had been torn free and ejected from the machine's far end thirty feet down, the bigger sections of cloth folded with grotesque and bloodstained neatness by the automatic folder. But not even that was the worst.

"It tried to fold everything," he said to Jackson, tasting bile in his throat. "But a person isn't a sheet, Mark. What I saw . . . what was left of her . . ." Like Stanner, the hapless foreman, he could not finish. "They took her out in a basket," he said softly.

Jackson whistled. "Who's going to get it in the neck? The laundry or the state inspectors?"

"Don't know yet," Hunton said. The malign image still hung behind the eyes, the image of the mangler wheezing and thumping and hissing, blood dripping down the green sides of the long cabinet in runnels, the burning *stink* of her . . . "It depends on who okayed that goddamn safety bar and under what circumstances."

"If it's the management, can they wiggle out of it?"

Hunton smiled without humour. "The woman died, Mark. If Gartley and Stanner were cutting corners on the speed ironer's maintenance, they'll go to jail. No matter who they know on the City Council."

"Do you think they were cutting corners?"

Hunton thought of the Blue Ribbon Laundry, badly lighted, floors wet and slippery, some of the machines incredibly ancient and creaking. "I think it's likely," he said quietly.

They got up to go in the house together. "Tell me how it comes out, Johnny," Jackson said. "I'm interested."

Hunton was wrong about the mangler; it was clean as a whistle.

Six state inspectors went over it before the inquest, piece by piece. The net result was absolutely nothing. The inquest verdict was death by misadventure.

Hunton, dumbfounded, cornered Roger Martin, one of the inspectors, after the hearing. Martin was a tall drink of water with glasses as thick as the bottoms of shot glasses. He fidgeted with a ballpoint pen under Hunton's questions.

"Nothing? Absolutely nothing doing with the machine?"

"Nothing," Martin said. "Of course, the safety bar was

the guts of the matter. It's in perfect working order. You heard that Mrs Gillian testify. Mrs Frawley must have pushed her hand too far. No one saw that; they were watching their own work. She started screaming. Her hand was gone already, and the machine was taking her arm. They tried to pull her out instead of shutting it down – pure panic. Another woman, Mrs Keene, said she *did* try to shut it off, but it's a fair assumption that she hit the start button rather than the stop in the confusion. By then it was too late."

"Then the safety bar malfunctioned," Hunton said flatly. "Unless she put her hand over it rather than under?"

"You can't. There's a stainless-steel facing above the safety bar. And the bar itself didn't malfunction. It's circuited into the machine itself. If the safety bar goes on the blink, the machine shuts down."

"Then how did it happen, for Christ's sake?"

"We don't know. My colleagues and I are of the opinion that the only way the speed ironer could have killed Mrs Frawley was for her to have fallen into it from above. And she had both feet on the floor when it happened. A dozen witnesses can testify to that."

"You're describing an impossible accident," Hunton said.

"No. Only one we don't understand." He paused, hesitated, and then said, "I will tell you one thing, Hunton, since you seem to have taken this case to heart. If you mention it to anyone else, I'll deny I said it. But I didn't like that machine. It seemed . . . almost to be mocking us. I've inspected over a dozen speed ironers in the last five years on a regular basis. Some of them are in such bad shape that I wouldn't leave a dog unleashed around them – the state law is lamentably lax. But they were only machines for all that. But this one . . . it's a spook. I don't know why, but it is. I think if I'd found one thing, even a technicality, that was off whack, I would have ordered it shut down. Crazy, huh?"

"I felt the same way," Hunton said.

"Let me tell you something that happened two years ago

in Milton," the inspector said. He took off his glasses and began to polish them slowly on his vest. "Fella had parked an old icebox out in his backyard. The woman who called us said her dog had been caught in it and suffocated. We got the state policeman in the area to inform him it had to go to the town dump. Nice enough fella, sorry about the dog. He loaded it into his pickup and took it to the dump the next morning. That afternoon a woman in the neighbourhood reported her son missing."

"God," Hunton said.

"The icebox was at the dump and the kid was in it, dead. A smart kid, according to his mother. She said he'd no more play in an empty icebox than he would take a ride with a strange man. Well, he did. We wrote it off. Case closed?"

"I guess," Hunton said.

"No. The dump caretaker went out next day to take the door off the thing. City Ordinance No. 58 on the maintenance of public dumping places." Martin looked at him expressionlessly. "He found six dead birds inside. Gulls, sparrows, a robin. And he said the door closed on his arm while he was brushing them out. Gave him a hell of a jump. That mangler at the Blue Ribbon strikes me like that, Hunton. I don't like it."

They looked at each other wordlessly in the empty inquest chamber, some six city blocks from where the Hadley-Watson Model-6 Speed Ironer and Folder sat in the busy laundry, steaming and fuming over its sheets.

The case was driven out of his mind in the space of a week by the press of more prosaic police work. It was only brought back when he and his wife dropped over to Mark Jackson's house for an evening of bid whist and beer.

Jackson greeted him with: "Have you ever wondered if that laundry machine you told me about is haunted, Johnny?"

Hunton blinked, at a loss. "What?"

"The speed ironer at the Blue Ribbon Laundry, I guess you didn't catch the squeal this time."

"What squeal?" Hunton asked, interested.

Jackson passed him the evening paper and pointed to an item at the bottom of page two. The story said that a steam line had let go on the large speed ironer at the Blue Ribbon Laundry, burning three of the six women working at the feeder end. The accident had occurred at 3.45 p.m., and was attributed to a rise in steam pressure from the laundry's boiler. One of the women, Mrs Annette Gillian, had been held at City Receiving Hospital with second-degree burns.

"Funny coincidence," he said, but the memory of Inspector Martin's words in the empty inquest chamber suddenly recurred: *It's a spook* . . . And the story about the dog and the boy and the birds caught in the discarded refrigerator.

He played cards very badly that night.

Mrs Gillian was propped up in bed reading *Screen Secrets* when Hunton came into the four-bed hospital room. A large bandage blanketed one arm and the side of her neck. The room's other occupant, a young woman with a pallid face, was sleeping.

Mrs Gillian blinked at the blue uniform and then smiled tentatively. "If it was for Mrs Cherinikov, you'll have to come back later. They just gave her medication."

"No, it's for you, Mrs Gillian." Her smile faded a little. "I'm here unofficially – which means I'm curious about the accident at the laundry. John Hunton." He held out his hand.

It was the right move. Mrs Gillian's smile became brilliant and she took his grip awkwardly with her unburnt hand. "Anything I can tell you, Mr Hunton. God, I thought my Andy was in trouble at school again."

"What happened?"

"We was running sheets and the ironer just blew up – or it seemed that way. I was thinking about going home an' getting off my dogs when there's this great big bang, like a bomb. Steam is everywhere and this hissing noise . . . awful." Her smile trembled on the verge of extinction. "It was like the ironer was breathing. Like a dragon, it was.

And Alberta – that's Alberta Keene – shouted that something was exploding and everyone was running and screaming and Ginny Jason started yelling she was burnt. I started to run away and I fell down. I didn't know I got it worst until then. God forbid it was no worse than it was. That live steam is three hundred degrees."

"The paper said a steam line let go. What does that mean?"

"The overhead pipe comes down into this kinda flexible line that feeds the machine. George – Mr Stanner – said there must have been a surge from the boiler or something. The line split wide open."

Hunton could think of nothing else to ask. He was making ready to leave when she said reflectively,

"We never used to have these things on that machine. Only lately. The steam line breaking. That awful, awful accident with Mrs Frawley, God rest her. And little things. Like the day Essie got her dress caught in one of the drive chains. That could have been dangerous if she hadn't ripped it right out. Bolts and things fall off. Oh, Herb Diment – he's the laundry repairman – has had an awful time with it. Sheets get caught in the folder. George says that's because they're using too much bleach in the washers, but it never used to happen. Now the girls hate to work on it. Essie even says there are still little bits of Adelle Frawley caught in it and it's sacrilege or something. Like it had a curse. It's been that way ever since Sherry cut her hand on one of the clamps."

"Sherry?" Hunton asked.

"Sherry Ouelette. Pretty little thing, just out of high school. Good worker. But clumsy sometimes. You know how young girls are."

"She cut her hand on something?"

"Nothing strange about *that*. There are clamps to tighten down the feeder belt, see. Sherry was adjusting them so we could do a heavier load and probably dreaming about some boy. She cut her finger and bled all over everything." Mrs Gillian looked puzzled. "It wasn't until after that the bolts started falling off. Adelle was . . . you know . . . about a week later. As if the machine had tasted blood and found it liked it. Don't women get funny ideas sometimes, Officer Hinton?"

"Hunton," he said absently, looking over her head and into space.

Ironically, he had met Mark Jackson in a washeteria in the block that separated their houses, and it was there that the cop and the English professor still had their most interesting conversations.

Now they sat side by side in bland plastic chairs, their clothes going round and round behind the glass portholes of the coin-op washers. Jackson's paperback copy of Milton's collected works lay neglected beside him while he listened to Hunton tell Mrs Gillian's story.

When Hunton had finished, Jackson said, "I asked you once if you thought the mangler might be haunted. I was only half joking. I'll ask you again now."

"No," Hunton said uneasily. "Don't be stupid."

Jackson watched the turning clothes reflectively. "Haunted is a bad word. Let's say possessed. There are almost as many spells for casting demons in as there are for casting them out. Frazer's *Golden Bough* is replete with them. Druidic and Aztec lore contain others. Even older ones, back to Egypt. Almost all of them can be reduced to startlingly common denominators. The most common, of course, is the blood of a virgin." He looked at Hunton. "Mrs Gillian said the trouble started after this Sherry Ouelette accidentally cut herself."

"Oh, come on," Hunton said.

"You have to admit she sounds just the type," Jackson said.

"I'll run right over to her house," Hunton said with a small smile. "I can see it. 'Miss Ouelette, I'm Officer John Hunton. I'm investigating an ironer with a bad case of demon possession and would like to know if you're a virgin.' Do you think I'd get a chance to say goodbye to Sandra and the kids before they carted me off to the booby hatch?"

"I'd be willing to bet you'll end up saying something just like that," Jackson said without smiling. "I'm serious, Johnny. That machine scares the hell out of me and I've never seen it."

"For the sake of conversation," Hunton said, "what are some of the other so-called common denominators?"

Jackson shrugged. "Hard to say without study. Most Anglo-Saxon hex formulas specify graveyard dirt or the eye of a toad. European spells often mention the hand of glory, which can be interpeted as the actual hand of a dead man or one of the hallucinogenics used in connection with the Witches' Sabbath – usually belladonna or a psilocybin derivative. There could be others."

"And you think all those things got into the Blue Ribbon ironer? Christ, Mark, I'll bet there isn't any belladonna within a five-hundred-mile radius. Or do you think someone whacked off their Uncle Fred's hand and dropped it in the folder?"

"If seven hundred monkeys typed for seven hundred years – '

"One of them would turn out the works of Shakespeare," Hunton finished sourly. "Go to hell. Your turn to go across to the drugstore and get some dimes for the dryers."

It was very funny how George Stanner lost his arm in the mangler.

Seven o'clock Monday morning the laundry was deserted except for Stanner and Herb Diment, the maintenance man. They were performing the twice-yearly function of greasing the mangler's bearings before the laundry's regular day began at seven-thirty. Diment was at the far end, greasing the four secondaries and thinking of how unpleasant this machine made him feel lately, when the mangler suddenly roared into life.

He had been holding up four of the canvas exit belts to get at the motor beneath and suddenly the belts were running in his hands, ripping the flesh off his palms, dragging him along.

He pulled free with a convulsive jerk seconds before the belts would have carried his hands into the folder.

"What the Christ, George!" he yelled. "Shut the frigging thing *off!*"

George Stanner began to scream.

It was a high, wailing, blood-maddened sound that filled the laundry, echoing off the steel faces of the washers, the grinning mouths of the steam presses, the vacant eyes of the industrial dryers. Stanner drew in a great, whooping gasp of air and screamed again: *"Oh God of Christ I'm caught I'M CAUGHT – "*

The rollers began to produce rising steam. The folder gnashed and thumped. Bearings and motors seemed to cry out with a hidden life of their own.

Diment raced to the other end of the machine.

The first roller was already going a sinister red. Diment made a moaning, gobbling noise in his throat. The mangler howled and thumped and hissed.

A deaf observer might have thought at first that Stanner was merely bent over the machine at an odd angle. Then even a deaf man would have seen the pallid, eye-bulging rictus of his face, mouth twisted open in a continuous scream. The arm was disappearing under the safety bar and beneath the first roller; the fabric of his shirt had torn away at the shoulder seam and his upper arm bulged grotesquely as the blood was pushed steadily backward.

"Turn it off!" Stanner screamed. There was a snap as his elbow broke.

Diment thumbed the off button.

The mangler continued to hum and growl and turn.

Unbelieving, he slammed the button again and again – nothing. The skin of Stanner's arm had grown shiny and taut. Soon it would split with the pressure the roll was putting on it; and still he was conscious and screaming. Diment had a nightmare cartoon image of a man flattened by a steamroller, leaving only a shadow.

"Fuses – " Stanner screeched. His head was being pulled down, down, as he was dragged forward.

Diment whirled and ran to the boiler room, Stanner's

screams chasing him like lunatic ghosts. The mixed stench of blood and steam rose in the air.

On the left wall were three heavy grey boxes containing all the fuses for the laundry's electricity. Diment yanked them open and began to pull the long, cylindrical fuses like a crazy man, throwing them back over his shoulders. The overhead lights went out; then the air compressor; then the boiler itself, with a huge dying whine.

And still the mangler turned. Stanner's screams had been reduced to bubbly moans.

Diment's eye happened on the fire axe in its glassed-in box. He grabbed it with a small, gagging whimper and ran back. Stanner's arm was gone almost to the shoulder. Within seconds his bent and straining neck would be snapped against the safety bar.

"I can't," Diment blubbered, holding the axe. "Jesus, George, I can't, I can't, I – "

The machine was an abattoir now. The folder spat out pieces of shirt sleeve, scraps of flesh, a finger. Stanner gave a huge, whooping scream and Diment swung the axe up and brought it down in the laundry's shadowy lightlesness. Twice. Again.

Stanner fell away, unconscious and blue, blood jetting from the stump just below the shoulder. The mangler sucked what was left into itself . . . and shut down.

Weeping, Diment pulled his belt out of its loops and began to make a tourniquet.

Hunton was talking on the phone with Roger Martin, the inspector. Jackson watched him while he patiently rolled a ball back and forth for three-year-old Patty Hunton to chase.

"He pulled *all* the fuses?" Hunton was asking. "And the off button just didn't function, huh? . . . Has the ironer been shut down? . . . Good. Great. Huh? . . . No, not official." Hunton frowned, then looked sideways at Jackson. "Are you still reminded of that refrigerator, Roger? . . . Yes. Me too. Goodbye."

He hung up and looked at Jackson. "Let's go see the girl, Mark."

She had her own apartment (the hesitant yet proprietary way she showed them in after Hunton had flashed his buzzer made him suspect that she hadn't had it long), and she sat uncomfortably across from them in the carefully decorated, postage-stamp living room.

"I'm Officer Hunton and this is my associate, Mr Jackson. It's about the accident at the laundry." He felt hugely uncomfortable with this dark, shyly pretty girl.

"Awful," Sherry Ouelette murmured. "It's the only place I've ever worked. Mr Gartley is my uncle. I liked it because it let me have this place and my own friends. But now . . . it's so *spooky*."

"The State Board of Safety has shut the ironer down pending a full investigation," Hunton said. "Did you know that?"

"Sure." She sighed restlessly. "I don't know what I'm going to do – "

"Miss Ouelette," Jackson interrupted, "you had an accident with the ironer, didn't you? Cut your hand on a clamp, I believe?"

"Yes, I cut my finger." Suddenly her face clouded. "That was the first thing." She looked at them woefully. "Sometimes I feel like the girls don't like me so much anymore . . . as if I were to blame."

"I have to ask you a hard question," Jackson said slowly. "A question you won't like. It seems absurdly personal and off the subject, but I can only tell you it is not. Your answers won't ever be marked down in a file or record."

She looked frightened. "D-did I do something?"

Jackson smiled and shook his head; she melted. *Thank God for Mark*, Hunton thought.

"I'll add this, though: the answer may help to keep your nice little flat here, get your job back, and make things at the laundry the way they were before."

"I'd answer anything to have that," she said.

"Sherry, are you a virgin?"

She looked utterly flabbergasted, utterly shocked, as if a priest had given communion and then slapped her. Then she lifted her head, made a gesture at her neat efficient apartment, as if asking them how they could believe it might be a place of assignation.

"I'm saving myself for my husband," she said simply.

Hunton and Jackson looked calmly at each other, and in that tick of a second, Hunton knew that it was all true: a devil had taken over the inanimate steel and cogs and gears of the mangler and had turned it into something with its own life.

"Thank you," Jackson said quietly.

"What now?" Hunton asked bleakly as they rode back. "Find a priest to exorcise it?"

Jackson snorted. "You'd go a far piece to find one that wouldn't hand you a few tracts to read while he phoned the booby hatch. It has to be our play, Johnny."

"Can we do it?"

"Maybe. The problem is this: We know something is in the mangler. We don't know *what*. Hunton felt cold, as if touched by a fleshless finger. "There are a great many demons. Is the one we're dealing with in the circle of Bubastis or Pan? Baal? Or the Christian deity we call Satan? We don't know. If the demon had been deliberately cast, we would have a better chance. But this seems to be a case of random possession."

Jackson ran his fingers through his hair. "The blood of a virgin, yes. But that narrows it down hardly at all. We have to be sure, very sure."

"Why?" Hunton asked bluntly. "Why not just get a bunch of exorcism formulas together and try them out?"

Jackson's face went cold. "This isn't cops 'n' robbers, Johnny. For Christ's sake, don't think it is. The rite of exorcism is horribly dangerous. It's like controlled nuclear fission, in a way. We could make a mistake and destroy ourselves. The demon is caught in that piece of machinery. But give it a chance and – '

"It could get out?"

"It would love to get out," Jackson said grimly. "And it likes to kill."

When Jackson came over the following evening, Hunton had sent his wife and daughter to a movie. They had the living room to themselves, and for this Hunton was relieved. He could still barely believe what he had become involved in.

"I cancelled my classes," Jackson said, "and spent the day with some of the most god-awful books you can imagine. This afternoon I fed over thirty recipies for calling demons into the tech computer. I've got a number of common elements. Surprisingly few."

He showed Hunton the list: blood of a virgin, graveyard dirt, hand of glory, bat's blood, night moss, horse's hoof, eye of toad.

There were others, all marked secondary.

"Horse's hoof," Hunton said thoughtfully, "Funny – "

"Very common. In fact – "

"Could these things – any of them – be interpreted loosely?" Hunton interrupted.

"If lichens picked at night could be substituted for night moss, for instance?"

"Yes."

"It's very likely," Jackson said. "Magical formulas are often ambiguous and elastic. The black arts have always allowed plenty of room for creativity."

"Substitute Jell-O for horse's hoof," Hunton said. "Very popular in bag lunches. I noticed a little container of it sitting under the ironer's sheet platform on the day the Frawley woman died. Gelatine is made from horses' hooves."

Jackson nodded. "Anything else?"

"Bat's blood . . . well, it's a big place. Lots of unlighted nooks and crannies. Bats seem likely, although I doubt if the management would admit to it. One could conceivably have been trapped in the mangler."

Jackson tipped his head back and knuckled bloodshot eyes. "It fits . . . it all fits."

"It does?"

"Yes. We can safely rule out the hand of glory, I think. Certainly no one dropped a hand into the ironer *before* Mrs Frawley's death, and belladonna is definitely not indigenous to this area."

"Graveyard dirt?"

"What do you think?"

"It would have to be a hell of a coincidence," Hunton said. "Nearest cemetery is Pleasant Hill, and that's five miles from the Blue Ribbon."

"Okay," Jackson said. "I got the computer operator – who thought I was getting ready for Halloween – to run a positive breakdown of all the primary and secondary elements on the list. Every possible combination. I threw out some two dozen which were completely meaningless. The others fall into fairly clear-cut categories. The elements we've isolated are in one of those."

"What is it?"

Jackson grinned. "An easy one. The mythos centres in South America with branches in the Caribbean. Related to voodoo. The literature I've got looks on the deities as strictly bush league, compared to some of the real heavies, like Saddath or He-Who-Cannot-Be-Named. The thing in that machine is going to slink away like the neighbourhood bully."

"How do we do it?"

"Holy water and a smidgen of the Holy Eucharist ought to do it. And we can read some of the Leviticus to it. Strictly Christian white magic."

"You're sure it's not worse?"

"Don't see how it can be," Jackson said pensively. "I don't mind telling you I was worried about that hand of glory. That's very black juju. Strong magic."

"Holy water wouldn't stop it?"

"A demon called up in conjunction with the hand of glory could eat a stack of Bibles for breakfast. We would be in bad trouble messing with something like that at all. Better to pull the goddamn thing apart."

"Well, are you completely sure – "

"No, but fairly sure. It all fits too well."

"When?"

"The sooner, the better," Jackson said. "How do we get in? Break a window?"

Hunton smiled, reached into his pocket, and dangled a key in front of Jackson's nose.

"Where'd you get that? Gartley?"

"No," Hunton said. "From a state inspector named Martin."

"He knows what we're doing?"

"I think he suspects. He told me a funny story a couple of weeks ago."

"About the mangler?"

"No," Hunton said. "About a refrigerator. Come on."

Adelle Frawley was dead; sewed together by a patient undertaker, she lay in her coffin. Yet something of her spirit perhaps remained in the machine, and if it did, it cried out. She would have known, could have warned them. She had been prone to indigestion, and for this common ailment she had taken a common stomach tablet called E-Z Gel, purchasable over the counter of any drugstore for seventy-nine cents. The side panel holds a warning: People with glaucoma must not take E-Z Gel, because the active ingredient causes an aggravation of that condition. Unfortunately, Adelle Frawley did not have that condition. She might have remembered the day, shortly before Sherry Ouelette cut her hand, that she had dropped a full box of E-Z Gel tablets into the mangler by accident. But she was dead, unaware that the active ingredient which soothed her heartburn was a chemical derivative of belladonna, known quaintly in some European countries as the hand of glory.

There was a sudden ghastly burping noise in the spectral silence of the Blue Ribbon laundry – a bat fluttered madly for its hole in the insulation above the dryers where it had roosted, wrapping wings around its blind face.

It was a noise almost like a chuckle.

The mangler began to run with a sudden, lurching grind – belts hurrying through the darkness, cogs meeting and meshing and grinding, heavy pulverizing rollers rotating on and on.

It was ready for them.

When Hunton pulled into the parking lot it was shortly after midnight and the moon was hidden behind a raft of moving clouds. He jammed on the brakes and switched off the lights in the same motion; Jackson's forehead almost slammed against the padded dash.

He switched off the ignition and the steady thump-hiss-thump became louder. "It's the mangler," he said slowly. "It's the mangler. Running by itself. In the middle of the night."

They sat for a moment in silence, feeling the fear crawl up their legs.

Hunton said, "All right. Let's do it."

They got out and walked to the building, the sound of the mangler growing louder. As Hunton put the key into the lock of the service door, he thought that the machine *did* sound alive — as if it were breathing in great hot gasps and speaking to itself in hissing, sardonic whispers.

"All of a sudden I'm glad I'm with a cop," Jackson said. He shifted the brown bag he held from one arm to the other. Inside was a small jelly jar filled with holy water wrapped in waxed paper, and a Gideon Bible.

They stepped inside and Hunton snapped up the light switches by the door. The fluorescents flickered into cold life. At the same instant the mangler shut off.

A membrane of steam hung over its rollers. It waited for them in its new ominous silence.

"God, it's an ugly thing," Jackson whispered.

"Come on," Hunton said. "Before we lose our nerve."

They walked over to it. The safety bar was in its down position over the belt which fed the machine.

Hunton put out a hand. "Close enough, Mark. Give me the stuff and tell me what to do."

"But — "

"No argument."

Jackson handed him the bag and Hunton put it on the

sheet table in front of the machine. He gave Jackson the Bible.

"I'm going to read," Jackson said. "When I point at you, sprinkle the holy water on the machine with your fingers. You say: In the name of the Father, and of the Son, and of the Holy Ghost, get thee from this place, thou unclean. Got it?"

"Yes."

"The second time I point, break the wafer and repeat the incantation again."

"How will we know if it's working?"

"You'll know. The thing is apt to break every window in the place getting out. If it doesn't work the first time, we keep doing it until it does."

"I'm scared green," Hunton said.

"As a matter of fact, so am I."

"If we're wrong about the hand of glory – "

"We're not," Jackson said. "Here we go."

He began. His voice filled the empty laundry with spectral echoes. "Turnest not thou aside to idols, nor make molten gods for yourself. I am the Lord thy God . . ." The words fell like stones into the silence that had suddenly become filled with a creeping, tomblike cold. The mangler remained still and silent under the fluorescents, and to Hunton it still seemed to grin.

". . . and the land will vomit you out for having defiled it, as it vomited out nations before you." Jackson looked up, his face strained, and pointed.

Hunton sprinkled holy water across the feeder belt.

There was a sudden, gnashing scream of tortured metal. Smoke rose from the canvas belts where the holy water had touched and took on writhing, red-tinged shapes. The mangler suddenly jerked into life.

"We've got it!" Jackson cried above the rising clamour. "It's on the run!"

He began to read again, his voice rising over the sound of the machinery. He pointed to Hunton again, and Hunton sprinkled some of the host. As he did so he was suddenly swept with a bone-freezing terror, a sudden vivid feeling

that it had gone wrong, that the machine had called their
bluff – and was the stronger.

Jackson's voice was still rising, approaching climax.

Sparks began to jump across the arc between the main
motor and the secondary; the smell of ozone filled the air,
like the copper smell of hot blood. Now the main motor
was smoking; the mangler was running at an insane, blurred
speed: a finger touched to the central belt would have
caused the whole body to be hauled in and turned to a
bloody rag in the space of five seconds. The concrete
beneath their feet trembled and thrummed.

A main bearing blew with a searing flash of purple light,
filling the chill air with the smell of thunderstorms, and
still the mangler ran, faster and faster, belts and rollers and
cogs moving at a speed that made them seem to blend and
merge, change, melt, transmute –

Hunton, who had been standing almost hypnotized, suddenly took a step backward. "Get away!" he screamed over
the blaring racket.

"We've almost got it!" Jackson yelled back. "Why – "

There was a sudden indescribable ripping noise and a
fissure in the concrete floor suddenly raced towards them
and past, widening. Chips of ancient cement flew up in a
starburst.

Jackson looked at the mangler and screamed.

It was trying to pull itself out of the concrete, like a
dinosaur trying to escape a tar pit. And it wasn't precisely
an ironer anymore. It was still changing, melting. The 550-
volt cable fell, spitting blue fire, into the roller and was
chewed away. For a moment two fireballs glared at them
like lambent eyes, eyes filled with a great and cold hunger.

Another fault line tore open. The mangler leaned towards
them, within an ace of being free of the concrete moorings
that held it. It leered at them; the safety bar had slammed
up and what Hunton saw was a gaping, hungry mouth filled
with steam.

They turned to run and another fissure opened at their
feet. Behind them, a great screaming roar as the thing came

free. Hunton leaped over, but Jackson stumbled and fell sprawling.

Hunton turned to help and a huge, amorphous shadow fell over him, blocking the fluorescents.

It stood over Jackson who lay on his back, staring up in a silent rictus of terror – the perfect sacrifice. Hunton had only a confused impression of something black and moving that bulked to a tremendous height above them both, something with glaring electric eyes the size of footballs, an open mouth with a moving canvas tongue.

He ran; Jackson's dying scream followed him.

When Roger Martin finally got out of bed to answer the doorbell, he was still only a third awake; but when Hunton reeled in, shock slapped him fully into the world with a rough hand.

Hunton's eyes bulged madly from his head, and his hands were claws as he scratched at the front of Martin's robe. There was a small oozing cut on his cheek and his face was splashed with dirty grey specks of powdered cement.

His hair had gone dead white.

"Help me . . . for Jesus' sake, help me. Mark is dead. Jackson is dead."

"Slow down," Martin said. "Come in the living room."

Hunton followed him, making a thick whining noise in his throat, like a dog.

Martin poured him a two-ounce knock of Jim Beam and Hunton held the glass in both hands, downing the raw liquor in a choked gulp. The glass fell unheeded to the carpet and his hands, like wandering ghosts, sought Martin's lapels again.

"The mangler killed Mark Jackson. It . . . it . . . oh God, it might get out! We can't let it get out! We can't . . . we . . . oh – " He began to scream, a crazy, whooping sound that rose and fell in jagged cycles.

Martin tried to hand him another drink but Hunton knocked it aside. "We have to burn it," he said. "Burn it before it can get out. Oh, what if it gets out? Oh Jesus, what if – " His eyes suddenly flickered, glazed, rolled up to show the whites, and he fell to the carpet in a stonelike faint.

Mrs Martin was in the doorway, clutching her robe to her throat. "Who is he, Rog? Is he crazy? I thought – " She shuddered.

"I don't think he's crazy." She was suddenly frightened by the sick shadow of fear on her husband's face. "God, I hope he came quick enough."

He turned to the telephone, picked up the receiver, froze.

There was a faint, swelling noise from the east of the house, the way that Hunton had come. A steady, grinding clatter, growing louder. The living-room window stood half open and now Martin caught a dark smell on the breeze. An odour of ozone . . . or blood.

He stood with his hand on the useless telephone as it grew louder, louder, gnashing and fuming, something in the streets that was hot and steaming. The blood stench filled the room.

His hand dropped from the telephone.

It was already out.

The Speciality of the House
Introduction

*Like a juggler who spins plates on sticks, the writer of the
fantastique must sustain a certain speed in his conceits or
else see them break into nonsenses. It's no accident that so
many masterpieces of the genre are in the form of short stories,
where that speed can be kept up without the effort showing.*

*The Pan Books of Horror Stories were, as far as I can
remember, the first collections I bought that contained works
by several hands, and I shamelessly stole and embroidered the
tales for retelling around scout camp-fires and on school treks.
It was one of the few things I was actually good at as a kid;
and I don't doubt that those retellings were the first
experiences I had of the power the teller of horror stories feels
as he holds his audience in a grip from which they might
wish to wriggle but can't . . .*

*I don't think I ever shaped 'The Speciality of the House'
for such a telling; it was too oblique for my oral style to
translate. But it certainly made an impression on me. Here
was – is – a highly distressing idea told with a wilful elegance
that feeds the distress rather than draining it. The lesson? That
you can say just about anything as long as you say it with
sufficient style.*

The things you learn from books . . .

CLIVE BARKER
Author of The Books of Blood, Weaveworld *and* The Great
and Secret Show

Stanley Ellin

The Speciality of the House

"And this," said Laffler, "is Sbirro's." Costain saw a square brownstone façade identical with the others that extended from either side into the clammy darkness of the deserted street. From the barred windows of the basement at his feet, a glimmer of light showed behind heavy curtains.

"Lord," he observed, "it's a dismal hole, isn't it?"

"I beg you to understand," said Laffler stiffly, "that Sbirro's is the restaurant without pretensions. Besieged by these ghastly, neurotic times, it has refused to compromise. It is perhaps the last important establishment in this city lit by gas jets. Here you will find the same honest furnishings, the same magnificent Sheffield service, and possibly, in a far corner, the very same spider webs that were remarked by the patrons of a half century ago!"

"A doubtful recommendation," said Costain, "and hardly sanitary."

"When you enter," Laffler continued, "you leave the insanity of this year, this day, and this hour, and you find yourself for a brief span restored in spirit, not by opulence, but by dignity, which is the lost quality of our time."

Costain laughed uncomfortably. "You make it sound more like a cathedral than a restaurant," he said.

In the pale reflection of the street lamp overhead, Laffler peered at his companion's face. "I wonder," he said abruptly, "whether I have not made a mistake in extending this invitation to you."

Costain was hurt. Despite an impressive title and large salary, he was no more than clerk to this pompous little man, but he was impelled to make some display of his feelings. "If you wish," he said coldly, "I can make other plans for my evening with no trouble."

With his large, cowlike eyes turned up to Costain, the mist drifting into the ruddy, full moon of his face, Laffler seemed strangely ill at ease. Then "No, no," he said at last, "absolutely not. It's important that you dine at Sbirro's with me." He grasped Costain's arm firmly and led the way to the wrought-iron gate of the basement. "You see, you're the sole person in my office who seems to know anything at all about good food. And on my part, knowing about Sbirro's but not having some appreciative friend to share it is like having a unique piece of art locked in a room where no one else can enjoy it."

Costain was considerably mollified by this. "I understand there are a great many people who relish that situation."

"I'm not one of that kind!" Laffler said sharply. "And having the secret of Sbirro's locked in myself for years has finally become unendurable." He fumbled at the side of the gate and from within could be heard the small, discordant jangle of an ancient pull-bell. An interior door opened with a groan, and Costain found himself peering into a dark face whose only discernible feature was a row of gleaming teeth.

"Sair?" said the face.

"Mr Laffler and a guest."

"Sair," the face said again, this time in what was clearly an invitation. It moved aside and Costain stumbled down a single step behind his host. The door and gate creaked behind him, and he stood blinking in a small foyer. It took him a moment to realize that the figure he now stared at was his own reflection in a gigantic pier glass that extended from floor to ceiling. "Atmosphere," he said under his breath and chuckled as he followed his guide to a seat.

He faced Laffler across a small table for two and peered curiously around the dining room. It was no size at all, but the half-dozen guttering gas jets which provided the only illumination threw such a deceptive light that the walls flickered and faded into uncertain distance.

There were no more than eight or ten tables about, arranged to insure the maximum privacy. All were occupied, and the few waiters serving them moved with quiet efficiency. In the air were a soft clash and scrape of cutlery and a soothing murmur of talk. Costain nodded appreciatively.

Laffler breathed an audible sigh of gratification. "I knew you would share my enthusiasm," he said. "Have you noticed, by the way, that there are no women present?"

Costain raised inquiring eyebrows.

"Sbirro," said Laffler, "does not encourage members of the fair sex to enter the premises. And, I can tell you, his method is decidedly effective. I had the experience of seeing a woman get a taste of it not long ago. She sat at a table for not less than an hour waiting for service which was never forthcoming."

"Didn't she make a scene?"

"She did." Laffler smiled at the recollection. "She succeeded in annoying the customers, embarrassing her partner, and nothing more."

"And what about Mr Sbirro?"

"He did not make an appearance. Whether he directed affairs from behind the scenes, or was not even present during the episode, I don't know. Whichever it was, he won a complete victory. The woman never reappeared nor, for that matter, did the witless gentleman who by bringing her was really the cause of the entire contretemps."

"A fair warning to all present," laughed Costain.

A waiter now appeared at the table. The chocolate-dark skin, the thin, beautifully moulded nose and lips, the large liquid eyes, heavily lashed, and the silver white hair so heavy and silken that it lay on the skull like a cap, all marked him definitely as an East Indian of some sort, Costain decided. The man arranged the stiff table linen, filled two tumblers from a huge, cut-glass pitcher, and set them in their proper places.

"Tell me," Laffler said eagerly, "is the special being served this evening?"

The waiter smiled regretfully and showed teeth as spectacular as those of the majordomo. "I am so sorry, sair. There is no special this evening."

Laffler's face fell into lines of heavy disappointment. "After waiting so long. It's been a month already, and I hoped to show my friend here . . ."

"You understand the difficulties, sair."

"Of course, of course." Laffler looked at Costain sadly and shrugged. "You see, I had in mind to introduce you to the greatest treat that Sbirro's offers, but unfortunately it isn't on the menu this evening."

The waiter said, "Do you wish to be served now, sair?" and Laffler nodded. To Costain's surprise the waiter made his way off without waiting for any instructions.

"Have you ordered in advance?" he asked.

"Ah," said Laffler, "I really should have explained. Sbirro's offers no choice whatsoever. You will eat the same meal as everyone else in this room. Tomorrow evening you would eat an entirely different meal, but again without designating a single preference."

"Very unusual," said Costain, "and certainly unsatisfactory at times. What if one doesn't have a taste for the particular dish set before him?"

"On that score," said Laffler solemnly, "you need have no fears. I give you my word that no matter how exacting your tastes, you will relish every mouthful you eat in Sbirro's."

Costain looked doubtful, and Laffler smiled. "And consider the subtle advantages of the system," he said. "When you pick up the menu of a popular restaurant, you find yourself confronted with innumerable choices. You are forced to weigh, to evaluate, to make uneasy decisions which you may instantly regret. The effect of all this a tension which, however slight, must make for discomfort.

"And consider the mechanics of the process. Instead of a hurly-burly of sweating cooks rushing about a kitchen in a frenzy to prepare a hundred varying items, we have a chef who stands serenely alone, bringing all his talents to bear on one task, with all assurance of a complete triumph!"

"Then you have seen the kitchen?"

"Unfortunately, no," said Laffler sadly. "The picture I offer is hypothetical, made of conversational fragments I have pieced together over the years. I must admit, though, that my desire to see the functioning of the kitchen here comes very close to being my sole obsession nowadays."

"But have you mentioned this to Sbirro?"

"A dozen times. He shrugs the suggestion away."

"Isn't that a rather curious foible on his part?"

"No, no," Laffler said hastily, "a master artist is never under the compulsion of petty courtesies. Still," he sighed, "I have never given up hope."

The waiter now reappeared bearing two soup bowls which he set in place with mathematical exactitude, and a small tureen from which he slowly ladled a measure of clear, thin broth. Costain dipped his spoon into the broth and tasted it with some curiosity. It was delicately flavoured, bland to the verge of tastelessness. Costain frowned, tentatively reached for the salt and pepper cellars, and discovered there were none on the table. He looked up, saw Laffler's eyes on him, and although unwilling to compromise with his own tastes, he hesitated to act as a damper on Laffler's enthusiasm. Therefore he smiled and indicated the broth.

"Excellent," he said.

Laffler returned his smile. "You do not find it excellent at all," he said coolly. "You find it flat and badly in need of condiments. I know this," he continued as Costain's eyebrows shot upwards, "because it was my own reaction many years ago, and because like yourself I found myself reaching for salt and pepper after the first mouthful. I also learned with surprise that condiments are not available in Sbirro's."

Costain was shocked. "Not even salt!" he exclaimed. '

"Not even salt. The very fact that you require it for your soup stands as evidence that your taste is unduly jaded. I am confident that you will now make the same discovery that I did: by the time you have nearly finished your soup, your desire for salt will be non-existent."

Laffler was right; before Costain had reached the bottom of his plate, he was relishing the nuances of the broth with steadily increasing delight. Laffler thrust aside his own empty bowl and rested his elbows on the table. "Do you agree with me now?"

"To my surprise," said Costain, "I do."

As the waiter busied himself clearing the table, Laffler lowered his voice significantly. "You will find," he said, "that the absence of condiments is but one of several noteworthy characteristics which mark Sbirro's. I may as well prepare you for these. For example, no alcoholic beverages of any sort are served here, nor for that matter any beverage except clear, cold water, the first and only drink necessary for a human being."

"Outside of mother's milk," suggested Costain dryly.

"I can answer that in like vein by pointing out that the average patron of Sbirro's has passed that primal stage of his development."

Costain laughed. "Granted," he said.

"Very well. There is also a ban on the use of tobacco in any form."

"But good heavens," said Costain, "doesn't that make Sbirro's more a teetotaller's retreat than a gourmet's sanctuary?"

"I fear," said Laffler solemnly, "that you confuse the words, *gourmet* and *gourmand*. The gourmand, through glutting himself, requires a wider and wider latitude of experience to stir his surfeited senses, but the very nature of the gourmet is simplicity. The ancient Greek in his coarse chiton savoring the ripe olive; the Japanese in his bare room contemplating the curve of a single flower stem – these are the true gourmets."

"But an occasional drop of brandy or pipeful of tobacco," said Costain dubiously, "are hardly over-indulgences."

"By alternating stimulant and narcotic," said Laffler, "you seesaw the delicate balance of your taste so violently that it loses its most precious quality: the appreciation of fine food. During my years as a patron of Sbirro's, I have proved this to my satisfaction."

"May I ask," said Costain, "why you regard the ban on these things as having such deep aesthetic motives? What about such mundane reasons as the high cost of a liquor licence, or the possibility that patrons would object to the smell of tobacco in such confined quarters?"

Laffler shook his head violently. "If and when you meet Sbirro," he said, "you will understand at once that he is not the man to make decisions on a mundane basis. As a matter of fact, it was Sbirro himself who first made me cognizant of what you call 'aesthetic' motives."

"An amazing man," said Costain as the waiter prepared to serve the entrée.

Laffler's next words were not spoken until he had savoured and swallowed a large portion of meat. "I hesitate to use superlatives," he aid, "but to my way of thinking, Sbirro represents man at the apex of his civilization!"

Costain cocked an eyebrow and applied himself to his roast which rested in a pool of stiff gravy ungarnished by green or vegetable. The thin steam rising from it carried to his nostrils a subtle, tantalizing odour which made his mouth water. He chewed a piece as slowly and thoughtfully as if he were analysing the intricacies of a Mozart symphony. The range of taste he discovered was really extraordinary, from the pungent nip of the crisp outer edge to the peculiarly flat yet soul-satisfying ooze of blood which the pressure of his jaws forced from the half-raw interior.

Upon swallowing he found himself ferociously hungry for another piece, and then another, and it was only with an effort that he prevented himself from wolfing down all his share of the meat and gravy without waiting to get the full voluptuous satisfaction from each mouthful. When he had scraped his platter clean, he realized that both he and Laffler had completed the entire course without exchanging a single word. He commented on this, and Laffler said, "Can you see any need for words in the presence of such food?"

Costain looked around at the shabby, dimly lit room, the quiet diners with a new perception. "No," he said humbly, "I cannot. For any doubts I had I apologize unreservedly. In all your praise of Sbirro's there was not a single word of exaggeration."

"Ah," said Laffler delightedly. "And that is only part

of the story. You heard me mention the special which unfortunately was not on the menu tonight. What you have just eaten is as nothing when compared to the absolute delights of that special!"

"Good Lord!" cried Costain. "What is it? Nightingale's tongues? Fillet of unicorn?"

"Neither," said Laffler. "It is lamb."

"Lamb?"

Laffler remained lost in thought for a minute. "If," he said at last, "I were to give you in my own unstinted words my opinion of this dish, you would judge me completely insane. That is how deeply the mere thought of it affects me. It is neither the fatty chop, nor the too solid leg; it is, instead, a select portion of the rarest sheep in existence and is named after the species – lamb Amirstan."

Costain knit his brows. "Amirstan?"

"A fragment of desolation almost lost on the border which separates Afghanistan and Russia. From chance remarks dropped by Sbirro, I gather it is no more than a plateau which grazes the pitiful remnants of a flock of superb sheep. Sbirro, through some means or other, obtained rights to the traffic in this flock and is, therefore, the sole restaurateur ever to have lamb Amirstan on his bill of fare. I can tell you that the appearance of this dish is a rare occurrence indeed, and luck is the only guide in determining for the clientele the exact date when it will be served."

"But surely," said Costain, "Sbirro could provide some advance knowledge of this event."

"The objection to that is simply stated," said Laffler. "There exists in this city a huge number of professional gluttons. Should advance information slip out, it is quite likely that they will, out of curiosity, become familiar with the dish and thenceforth supplant the regular patrons at these tables."

"But you don't mean to say," objected Costain, "that these few people present are the only ones in the entire city, or for that matter, in the whole wide world, who know of the existence of Sbirro's!"

"Very nearly. There may be one or two regular patrons who, for some reason, are not present at the moment."

"That's incredible."

"It is done," said Laffler, the slightest shade of menace in his voice, "by every patron making it his solemn obligation to keep the secret. By accepting my invitation this evening you automatically assume that obligation. I hope you can be trusted with it."

Costain flushed. "My position in your employ should vouch for me. I only question the wisdom of a policy which keeps such magnificent food away from so many who would enjoy it."

"Do you know the inevitable result of the policy *you* favour?" asked Laffler bitterly. "An influx of idiots who would nightly complain that they are never served roast duck with chocolate sauce. Is that picture tolerable to you?"

"No," admitted Costain, "I am forced to agree with you."

Laffler leaned back in his chair wearily and passed his hand over his eyes in an uncertain gesture. "I am a solitary man," he said quietly. "and not by choice alone. It may sound strange to you, it may border on eccentricity, but I feel to my depths that this restaurant, this warm haven in a coldly insane world, is both family and friend to me."

And Costain, who to this moment had never viewed his companion as other than tyrannical employer or officious host, now felt an overwhelming pity twist inside his comfortably expanded stomach.

By the end of two weeks the invitations to join Laffler at Sbirro's had become something of a ritual. Every day, at a few minutes after five, Costain would step out into the office corridor and lock his cubicle behind him; he would drape his overcoat neatly over his left arm, and peer into the glass of the door to make sure his Homburg was set at the proper angle. At one time he would have followed this by lighting a cigarette, but under Laffler's prodding he had decided to give abstinence a fair trial. Then he would start down the corridor, and Laffler would fall in step at his elbow, clearing his throat. "Ah, Costain. No plans for this evening, I hope."

"No," Costain would say, "I'm footloose and fancy-free," or "At your service," or something equally inane. He wondered at times whether it would not be more tactful to vary the ritual with an occasional refusal, but the glow with which Laffler received his answer, and the rough friendliness of Laffler's grip on his arm, forestalled him.

Among the treacherous crags of the business world, reflected Costain, what better way to secure your footing than friendship with one's employer. Already, a secretary close to the workings of the inner office had commented publicly on Laffler's highly favourable opinion of Costain. That was all to the good.

And the food! The incomparable food at Sbirro's! For the first time in his life, Costain, ordinarily a lean and bony man, noted with gratification that he was certainly gaining weight; within two weeks his bones had disappeared under a layer of sleek, firm flesh, and here and there were even signs of incipient plumpness. It struck Costain one night, while surveying himself in his bath, that the rotund Laffler, himself, might have been a spare and bony man before discovering Sbirro's.

So there was obviously everything to be gained and nothing to be lost by accepting Laffler's invitations. Perhaps after testing the heralded wonders of lamb Amirstan and meeting Sbirro, who thus far had not made an appearance, a refusal or two might be in order. But certainly not until then.

That evening, two weeks to a day after his first visit to Sbirro's, Costain had both desires fulfilled: he dined on lamb Amirstan, and he met Sbirro. Both exceeded all his expectations.

When the waiter leaned over their table immediately after seating them and gravely announced: "Tonight is special, sair," Costain was shocked to find his heart pounding with expectation. On the table before him he saw Laffler's hands trembling violently. But it isn't natural, he thought suddenly. Two full grown men, presumably intelligent and in the full possession of their senses, as jumpy as a pair of cats waiting to have their meat flung to them!

"This is it!" Laffler's voice startled him so that he almost leaped from his seat. "The culinary triumph of all times! And faced by it you are embarrassed by the very emotions it distills."

"How did you know that?" Costain asked faintly.

"How? Because a decade ago I underwent your embarrassment. Add to that your air of revulsion and it's easy to see how affronted you are by the knowledge that man has not yet forgotten how to slaver over his meat."

"And these others," whispered Costain, "do they all feel the same thing?"

"Judge for yourself."

Costain looked furtively around at the nearby tables. "You are right," he finally said. "At any rate, there's comfort in numbers."

Laffler inclined his head slightly to one side. "One of the numbers," he remarked, "appears to be in for a disappointment."

Costain followed the gesture. At the table indicated a grey-haired man sat conspicuously alone, and Costain frowned at the empty chair opposite him.

"Why, yes," he recalled, "that very stout, bald man, isn't it? I believe it's the first dinner he's missed here in two weeks."

"The entire decade more likely," said Laffler sympathetically. "Rain or shine, crisis or calamity, I don't think he's missed an evening at Sbirro's since the first time I dined here. Imagine his expression when he's told that, on his very first defection, lamb Amirstan was the *plat du jour*."

Costain looked at the empty chair again with a dim discomfort. "His very first?" he murmured.

"Mr Laffler! And friend! I am so pleased. So very, very pleased. No, do not stand; I will have a place made." Miraculously a seat appeared under the figure standing there at the table. "The lamb Amirstan will be an unqualified success, hurr? I myself have been stewing in the miserable kitchen all the day, prodding the foolish chef to do everything just so. The just so is the important part, hurr? But I see your friend does not know me. An introduction, perhaps?"

The words ran in a smooth, fluid eddy. They rippled, they purred, they hypnotized Costain so that he could do no more than stare. The mouth that uncoiled this sinuous monologue was alarmingly wide, with thin mobile lips that curled and twisted with every syllable. There was a flat nose with a straggling line of hair under it; wide-set eyes, almost oriental in appearance, that glittered in the unsteady flare of gaslight; and long, sleek hair that swept back from high on the unwrinkled forehead – hair so pale that it might have been bleached of all colour. An amazing face surely, and the sight of it tortured Costain with the conviction that it was somehow familiar. His brain twitched and prodded but could not stir up any solid recollection.

Laffler's voice jerked Costain out of his study. "Mr Sbirro. Mr Costain, a good friend and associate." Costain rose and shook the proffered hand. It was warm and dry, flint-hard against his palm.

"I am so very pleased, Mr Costain. So very, very pleased," purred the voice. "You like my little establishment, hurr? You have a great treat in store, I assure you."

Laffler chuckled. "Oh, Costain's been dining here regularly for two weeks," he said. "He's by way of becoming a great admirer of yours, Sbirro."

The eyes were turned on Costain. "A very great compliment. You compliment me with your presence and I return same with my food, hurr? But the lamb Amirstan is far superior to anything of your past experience, I assure you. All the trouble of obtaining it, all the difficulty of preparation, is truly merited."

Costain strove to put aside the exasperating problem of that face. "I have wondered," he said, "why with all these difficulties you mention, you even bother to present lamb Amirstan to the public. Surely your other dishes are excellent enough to uphold your reputation."

Sbirro smiled so broadly that his face became perfectly round. "Perhaps it is a matter of the psychology, hurr?

Someone discovers a wonder and must share it with others. He must fill his cup to the brim, perhaps, by observing the so evident pleasure of those who explore it with him. Or," he shrugged, "perhaps it is just a matter of good business."

"Then in the light of all this," Costain persisted, "and considering all the conventions you have imposed on your customers, why do you open the restaurant to the public instead of operating it as a private club?"

The eyes abruptly glinted into Costain's, then turned away. "So perspicacious, hurr? Then I will tell you. Because there is more privacy in a public eating place than in the most exclusive club in existence! Here no one inquires of your affairs; no one desires to know the intimacies of your life. Here the business is eating. We are not curious about names and addresses or the reasons for the coming and going of our guests. We welcome you when you are here; we have no regrets when you are here no longer. That is the answer, hurr?"

Costain was startled by his vehemence. "I had no intention of prying," he stammered.

Sbirro ran the tip of his tongue over his thin lips. "No, no," he reassured, "you are not prying. Do not let me give you that impression. On the contrary, I invite your questions."

"Oh, come, Costain," said Laffler. "Don't let Sbirro intimidate you. I've known him for years and I guarantee that his bark is worse than his bite. Before you know it, he'll be showing you all the privileges of the house – outside of inviting you to visit his precious kitchen, of course."

"Ah," smiled Sbirro, "for that, Mr Costain may have to wait a little while. For everything else I am at his beck and call."

Laffler slapped his hands jovially on the table. "What did I tell you?" he said. "Now let's have the truth, Sbirro. Has anyone, outside of your staff, ever stepped into the sanctum sanctorum?"

Sbirro looked up. "You see on the wall above you," he said earnestly, "the portrait of one to whom I did the honour. A very dear friend and a patron of most long standing, he is evidence that my kitchen is not inviolate."

Costain studied the picture and started with recognition. "Why," he said excitedly, "that's the famous writer – you know the one, Laffler – he used to do such wonderful short stories and cynical bits and then suddenly took himself off and disappeared in Mexico!"

"Of course!" cried Laffler. "And to think I've been sitting under his portrait for years without even realizing it!" He turned to Sbirro. "A dear friend, you say? His disappearance must have been a blow to you."

Sbirro's face lengthened. "It was, it was, I assure you. But think of it this way, gentlemen: he was probably greater in his death than in his life, hurr? A most tragic man, he often told me that his only happy hours were spent here at this very table. Pathetic, is it not? And to think the only favour I could ever show him was to let him witness the mysteries of my kitchen, which is, when all is said and done, no more than a plain, ordinary kitchen."

"You seem very certain of his death," commented Costain. "After all, no evidence has ever turned up to substantiate it."

Sbirro contemplated the picture. "None at all," he said softly. "Remarkable, hurr?"

With the arrival of the entrée Sbirro leaped to his feet and set about serving them himself. With his eyes alight he lifted the casserole from the tray and sniffed at the fragrance from within with sensual relish. Then, taking great care not to lose a single drop of gravy, he filled two platters with chunks of dripping meat. As if exhausted by this task, he sat back in his chair, breathing heavily. "Gentlemen," he said, "to your good appetite."

Costain chewed his first mouthful with great deliberation and swallowed it. Then he looked at the empty tines of his fork with glazed eyes.

"Good God!" he breathed.

"It is good, hurr? Better than you imagined?"

Costain shook his head dazedly. "It is as impossible," he said slowly, "for the uninitiated to conceive the delights of lamb Amirstan as for mortal man to look into his own soul."

"Perhaps" – Sbirro thrust his head so close that Costain could feel the warm, fetid breath tickle his nostrils – "perhaps you have just had a glimpse into your soul, hurr?"

Costain tried to draw back slightly without giving offence. "Perhaps." He laughed. "And a gratifying picture it made: all fang and claw. But without intending any disrespect, I should hardly like to build my church on lamb *en casserole*."

Sbirro rose and laid a hand gently on his shoulder.

"So perspicacious," he said. "Sometimes when you have nothing to do, nothing, perhaps, but sit for a very little while in a dark room and think of this world – what it is and what it is going to be – then you must turn your thoughts a little to the significance of the Lamb in religion. It will be so interesting. And now," he bowed deeply to both men, "I have held you long enough from your dinner. I was most happy," he said, nodding to Costain, "and I am sure we will meet again." The teeth gleamed, the eyes glittered, and Sbirro was gone down the aisle of tables.

Costain twisted around to stare after the retreating figure. "Have I offended him in some way?" he asked.

Laffler looked up from his plate. "Offended him? He loves that kind of talk. Lamb Amirstan is a ritual with him; get him started and he'll be back at you a dozen times worse than a priest making a conversion."

Costain turned to his meal with the face still hovering before him. "Interesting man," he reflected. "Very."

It took him a month to discover the tantalizing familiarity of that face, and when he did, he laughed aloud in his bed. Why, of course! Sbirro might have sat as the model for the Cheshire cat in *Alice*!

He passed his thought on to Laffler the very next evening as they pushed their way down the street to the restaurant against a chill, blustering wind. Laffler only looked blank.

"You may be right," he said, "but I'm not a fit judge.

It's a far cry back to the days when I read the book. A far cry, indeed."

As if taking up his words, a piercing howl came ringing down the street and stopped both men short in their tracks. "Someone's in trouble there," said Laffler. "Look!"

Not far from the entrance of Sbirro's two figures could be seen struggling in the near darkness. They swayed back and forth and suddenly tumbled into a writhing heap on the sidewalk. The piteous howl went up again, and Laffler, despite his girth, ran towards it at a fair speed with Costain tagging cautiously behind.

Stretched out full length on the pavement was a slender figure with the dusky complexion and white hair of one of Sbirro's servitors. His fingers were futilely plucking at the huge hands which encircled his throat, and his knees pushed weakly up at the gigantic bulk of a man who brutally bore down with his full weight.

Laffler came up panting. "Stop this!" he shouted. "What's going on here?"

The pleading eyes almost bulging from their sockets turned towards Laffler. "Help, sair. This man – drunk – "

"Drunk am I, ya dirty – " Costain saw now that the man was a sailor in a badly soiled uniform. The air around him reeked with the stench of liquor. "Pick me pocket and then call me drunk, will ya!" He dug his fingers in harder, and his victim groaned.

Laffler seized the sailor's shoulder. "Let go of him, do you hear! Let go of him at once!" he cried, and the next instant was sent careening into Costain, who staggered back under the force of the blow.

The attack on his own person sent Laffler into immediate and berserk action. Without a sound he leaped at the sailor, striking and kicking furiously at the unprotected face and flanks. Stunned at first, the man came to his feet with a rush and turned on Laffler. For a moment they stood locked together, and then as Costain joined the attack, all three went sprawling to the ground. Slowly Laffler and Costain got to their feet and looked down at the body before them.

"He's either out cold from liquor," said Costain, "or he

struck his head going down. In any case, it's a job for the police."

"No, no, sair!" The waiter crawled weakly to his feet, and stood swaying. "No police, sair. Mr Sbirro do not want such. You understand, sair." He caught hold of Costain with a pleading hand, and Costain looked at Laffler.

"Of course not," said Laffler. "We won't have to bother with the police. They'll pick him up soon enough, the murderous sot. But what in the world started all this?"

"That man, sair. He make most erratic way while walking, and with no meaning I push against him. Then he attack me, accusing me to rob him."

"As I thought." Laffler pushed the waiter gently along. "Now go on in and get yourself attended to."

The man seemed ready to burst into tears. "To you, sair, I owe my life. If there is anything I can do – "

Laffler turned into the areaway that led to Sbirro's door. "No, no, it was nothing. You go along, and if Sbirro has any questions send him to me. I'll straighten it out."

"My life, sair," were the last words they heard as the inner door closed behind them.

"There you are, Costain," said Laffler, as a few minutes later he drew his chair under the table, "civilized man in all his glory. Reeking with alcohol, strangling to death some miserable innocent who came too close."

Costain made an effort to gloss over the nerve-shattering memory of the episode. "It's the neurotic cat that takes to alcohol," he said. "Surely there's a reason for that sailor's condition."

"Reason? Of course there is. Plain atavistic savagery!" Laffler swept his arm in an all-embracing gesture. "Why do we all sit here at our meat? Not only to appease physical demands, but because our atavistic selves cry for release. Think back, Costain. Do you remember that I once described Sbirro as the epitome of civilization? Can you now see why? A brilliant man, he fully understands the nature of human beings. But unlike lesser men he bends all his efforts to the satisfaction of our innate natures without resultant harm to some innocent bystander."

"When I think back on the wonders of lamb Amirstan," said Costain, "I quite understand what you're driving at. And, by the way, isn't it nearly due to appear on the bill of fare? It must have been over a month ago that it was last served."

The waiter, filling the tumblers, hesitated. "I am so sorry, sair. No special this evening."

"There's your answer," Laffler grunted, "and probably just my luck to miss out on it altogether the next time."

Costain stared at him. "Oh, come, that's impossible."

"No, blast it." Laffler drank off half his water at a gulp and the waiter immediately refilled the glass. "I'm off to South America for a surprise tour of inspection. One month, two months, Lord knows how long."

"Are things that bad down there?"

"They could be better." Laffler suddenly grinned. "Mustn't forget it takes very mundane dollars and cents to pay the tariff at Sbirro's."

"I haven't heard a word of this around the office."

"Wouldn't be a surprise tour if you had. Nobody knows about this except myself – and now you. I want to walk in on them completely unsuspected. Find out what flim-flammery they're up to down there. As far as the office is concerned, I'm off on a jaunt somewhere. Maybe recuperating in some sanatorium from my hard work. Anyhow, the business will be in good hands. Yours, among them."

"Mine?" said Costain, surprised.

"When you go in tomorrow you'll find yourself in receipt of a promotion, even if I'm not there to hand it to you personally. Mind you, it has nothing to do with our friendship either; you've done fine work, and I'm immensely grateful for it."

Costain reddened under the praise. "You don't expect to be in tomorrow. Then you're leaving tonight?"

Laffler nodded. "I've been trying to wangle some reservations. If they come through, well, this will be in the nature of a farewell celebration."

"You know," said Costain slowly, "I devoutly hope that your reservations don't come through. I believe our dinners here have come to mean more to me than I ever dared imagine."

The waiter's voice broke in. "Do you wish to be served now, sair?" and they both started.

"Of course, of course," said Laffler sharply, "I didn't realize you were waiting."

"What bothers me," he told Costain as the waiter turned away, "is the thought of the lamb Amirstan I'm bound to miss. To tell you the truth, I've already put off my departure a week, hoping to hit a lucky night, and now I simply can't delay any more. I do hope that when you're sitting over your share of lamb Amirstan, you'll think of me with suitable regrets."

Costain laughed. "I will indeed," he said as he turned to his dinner.

Hardly had he cleared the plate when a waiter silently reached for it. It was not their usual waiter, he observed; it was none other than the victim of the assault.

"Well," Costain said, "how do you feel now? Still under the weather?"

The waiter paid no attention to him. Instead, with the air of a man under great strain, he turned to Laffler. "Sair," he whispered. "My life. I owe it to you. I can repay you!"

Laffler looked up in amazement, then shook his head firmly. "No," he said. "I want nothing from you, understand? You have repaid me sufficiently with your thanks. Now get on with your work and let's hear no more about it."

The waiter did not stir an inch, but his voice rose slightly. "By the body and blood of your God, sair, I will help you even if you do not want! *Do not go into the kitchen, sair*. I trade you my life for yours, sair, when I speak this. Tonight or any night of your life, do not go into the kitchen at Sbirro's!"

Laffler sat back, completely dumbfounded. "Not go into the kitchen? Why shouldn't I go into the kitchen if Mr Sbirro ever took it into his head to invite me there? What's all this about?"

A hard hand was laid on Costain's back, and another

gripped the waiter's arm. The waiter remained frozen to the spot, his lips compressed, his eyes downcast.

"What is all *what* about, gentlemen?" purred the voice. "So opportune an arrival. In time as ever, I see, to answer all the questions, hurr?"

Laffler breathed a sigh of relief. "Ah, Sbirro, thank heaven you're here. This man is saying something about my not going into your kitchen. Do you know what he means?"

The teeth showed in a broad grin. "But of course. This good man was giving you advice in all amiability. It so happens that my too emotional chef heard some rumour that I might have a guest into his precious kitchen, and he flew into a fearful rage. Such a rage, gentlemen! He even threatened to give notice on the spot, and you can understand what that would mean to Sbirro's, hurr? Fortunately, I succeeded in showing him what a signal honour it is to have an esteemed patron and true connoisseur observe him at his work firsthand, and now he is quite amenable. Quite, hurr?"

He released the waiter's arm. "You are at the wrong table," he said softly. "See that it does not happen again."

The waiter slipped off without daring to raise his eyes and Sbirro drew a chair to the table. He seated himself and brushed his hand lightly over his hair. "Now I am afraid that the cat is out of the bag, hurr? This invitation to you, Mr Laffler, was to be a surprise; but the surprise is gone, and all that is left is the invitation."

Laffler mopped beads of perspiration from his forehead. "Are you serious?" he said huskily. "Do you mean that we are really to witness the preparation of your food tonight?"

Sbirro drew a sharp fingernail along the tablecloth, leaving a thin, straight line printed in the linen. "Ah," he said, "I am faced with a dilemma of great proportions." He studied the line soberly. "You, Mr Laffler, have been my guest for ten long years. But our friend here – "

Costain raised his hand in protest. "I understand perfectly. This invitation is solely to Mr Laffler, and naturally my presence is embarrassing. As it happens, I have an early engagement for this evening and must be on my way anyhow. So you see there's no dilemma at all, really."

"No," said Laffler, "absolutely not. That wouldn't be fair at all. We've been sharing this until now, Costain, and I won't enjoy this experience half as much if you're not along. Surely Sbirro can make his conditions flexible, this one occasion."

They both looked at Sbirro who shrugged his shoulders regretfully.

Costain rose abruptly. "I'm not going to sit here, Laffler, and spoil your great adventure. And then too," he bantered, "think of that ferocious chef waiting to get his cleaver on you. I prefer not to be at the scene. I'll just say goodbye," he went on, to cover Laffler's guilty silence, "and leave you to Sbirro. I'm sure he'll take pains to give you a good show." He held out his hand and Laffler squeezed it painfully hard.

"You're being very decent, Costain," he said. "I hope you'll continue to dine here until we meet again. It shouldn't be too long."

Sbirro made way for Costain to pass. "I will expect you," he said. "*Au 'voir.*"

Costain stopped briefly in the dim foyer to adjust his scarf and fix his Homburg at the proper angle. When he turned away from the mirror, satisfied at last, he saw with a final glance that Laffler and Sbirro were already at the kitchen door, Sbirro holding the door invitingly wide with one hand, while the other rested, almost tenderly, on Laffler's meaty shoulders.

Camera Obscura
Introduction

*For all the controversy over the place of thud and blunder in
horror, and the impact of said style on the field, when it
comes to those writers who make indelible impressions, the
most personal terrors real, who produce the true shudders and
not the false shocks, it's the quiet ones you have to watch, the
ones who seem to know us better than we know ourselves.
They are the most dangerous. They are the ones who produce
not the contemporary phenomena, but the true classics. Like
'Camera Obscura': a precise, harrowing, and extremely
personal story of retribution, accumulating dread, and a
feeling that, though you may think you know what will come,
you don't really know the half of it.*

*This is Basil Copper's trademark; what you think you
believe is not only wrong, it's lethal. And while, in this piece,
Mr Sharsted is indeed a villain – not for what he's doing but
for his entirely human rationalization of it – there is such a
chilling dark side to Mr Gingold that one cannot help but
wonder. And that wondering, that ever-so-slight tilting of
what we understood the world to be, is what produces this
story's lasting, lingering, impact. Basil Copper is probably
the only one among us who could have achieved that with
such deceptively gentle power.*

*Gentle, on the other hand, cannot always be applied to all
the stories which have appeared in* The Pan Book of Horror
Stories *series. And this is one of its strengths. Diversity, a
sense of humour, and a knowledge of what's best in
contemporary horror is its hallmark. For thirty years it has
delighted, infuriated, and captivated its audiences. Say what
you will about this individual story or that one, you certainly
cannot say that these three decades have been dull. And if*

*there is any justice left in the publishing world, there will be
– my lips to God's ears – thirty years more.*

CHARLES L. GRANT
Author of The Pet, For Fear of the Night *and*
In A Dark Dream

Basil Copper

Camera Obscura

As Mr Sharsted pushed his way up the narrow, fussily conceived lanes that led to the older part of the town, he was increasingly aware that there was something about Mr Gingold he didn't like. It was not only the old-fashioned, outdated air of courtesy that irritated the moneylender but the gentle, absent-minded way in which he continually put off settlement. Almost as if money were of no importance.

The moneylender hesitated even to say this to himself; the thought was a blasphemy that rocked the very foundations of his world. He pursed his lips grimly and set himself to mount the ill-paved and flinty roadway that bisected the hilly terrain of this remote part of the town.

The moneylender's narrow, lopsided face was perspiring under his hard hat; lank hair started from beneath the brim, which lent him a curious aspect. This, combined with the green-tinted spectacles he wore, gave him a sinister, decayed look, like someone long dead. The thought may have occurred to the few, scattered passers-by he met in the course of his ascent, for almost to a person they gave one cautious glance and then hurried on as though eager to be rid of his presence.

He turned in at a small courtyard and stood in the shelter of a great old ruined church to catch his breath; his heart was thumping uncomfortably in the confines of his narrow chest and his breath rasped in his throat. Assuredly, he was out of condition, he told himself. Long hours of sedentary work huddled over his accounts were taking their toll; he really must get out more and take some exercise.

The moneylender's sallow face brightened momentarily as he thought of his increasing prosperity, but then he frowned again as he remembered the purpose of his errand. Gingold must be made to toe the line, he told himself, as he set out over the last half-mile of his journey.

If he couldn't raise the necessary cash, there must be many valuables in that rambling old house of his which he could sell and realize on. As Mr Sharsted forged his way deeper into this forgotten corner of the town, the sun, which was already low in the sky, seemed to have already set, the light was so constricted by the maze of small courts and alleys into which he had plunged. He was panting again when he came at last, abruptly, to a large green door, set crookedly at the top of a flight of time-worn steps.

He stood arrested for a moment or two, one hand grasping the old balustrade, even his mean soul uplifted momentarily by the sight of the smoky haze of the town below, tilted beneath the yellow sky. Everything seemed to be set awry upon this hill, so that the very horizon rushed slanting across the far distance, giving the spectator a feeling of vertigo. A bell pealed faintly as he seized an iron scrollwork pull set into a metal rose alongside the front door. The moneylender's thoughts were turned to irritation again; everything about Mr Gingold was peculiar, he felt. Even the fittings of his household were things one never saw elsewhere.

Though this might be an advantage if he ever gained control of Mr Gingold's assets and had need to sell the property; there must be a lot of valuable stuff in this old house he had never seen, he mused. Which was another reason he felt it strange that the old man was unable to pay his dues; he must have a great deal of money, if not in cash, in property, one way or another.

He found it difficult to realize why Mr Gingold kept hedging over a matter of three hundred pounds; he could easily sell the old place and go to live in a more attractive part of town in a modern, well-appointed villa and still keep his antiquarian interests. Mr Sharsted sighed. Still, it was none of his business. All he was concerned with was the matter of the money; he had been kept waiting long enough, and he wouldn't be fobbed off any longer. Gingold had got to settle by Monday, or he'd make things unpleasant for him.

Mr Sharsted's thin lips tightened in an ugly manner as he mused on, oblivious of the sunset staining the upper storeys of the old houses and dyeing the mean streets below the hill a rich carmine. He pulled the bell again impatiently, and this time the door was opened almost immediately.

Mr Gingold was a very tall, white-haired man with a gentle, almost apologetic manner. He stood slightly stooping in the doorway, blinking as though astonished at the sunlight, half afraid it would fade him if he allowed too much of it to absorb him.

His clothes, which were of good quality and cut, were untidy and sagged loosely on his big frame; they seemed washed out in the bright light of the sun and appeared to Mr Sharsted to be all of a part with the man himself; indeed, Mr Gingold was rinsed to a pale, insipid shade by the sunshine, so that his white hair and face and clothing ran into one another and, somehow, the different aspects of the picture became blurred and indeterminate.

To Mr Sharsted he bore the aspect of an old photograph which had never been properly fixed and had turned brown and faded with time. Mr Sharsted thought he might blow away with the breeze that had started up, but Mr Gingold merely smiled shyly and said, "Oh, there you are, Sharsted. Come on in," as though he had been expecting him all the time.

Surprisingly, Mr Gingold's eyes were of a marvellous shade of blue and they made his whole face come vividly alive, fighting and challenging the overall neutral tints of his clothing and features. He led the way into a cavernous hall. Mr Sharsted followed cautiously, his eyes adjusting with difficulty to the cool gloom of the interior. With courteous, old-world motions Mr Gingold beckoned him forward.

The two men ascended a finely carved staircase, whose balustrades, convoluted and serpentine, seemed to writhe sinuously upwards into the darkness.

"My business will only take a moment," protested Sharsted, anxious to present his ultimatum and depart. But Mr Gingold merely continued to ascend the staircase.

"Come along, come along," he said gently, as though he hadn't heard Mr Sharsted's expostulation. "You must take a glass of wine with me. I have so few visitors . . ."

Mr Sharsted looked about him curiously; he had never been in this part of the house. Usually, Mr Gingold received occasional callers in a big, cluttered room on the ground floor. This afternoon, for some reason known only to himself, he had chosen to show Mr Sharsted another part of his domain. Mr Sharsted thought that perhaps Mr Gingold intended to settle the matter of his repayments. This might be where he transacted business, perhaps kept his money. His thin fingers twitched with nervous excitement.

They continued to ascend what seemed to the money-lender to be enormous distances. The staircase still unwound in front of their measured progress. From the little light which filtered in through rounded windows, Sharsted caught occasional glimpses of objects that aroused his professional curiosity and acquisitive sense. Here a large oil painting swung into view round the bend of the stair; in the necessarily brief glance that Mr Sharsted caught, he could have sworn it was a Poussin.

A moment later, a large sideboard laden with porcelain slid by the corner of his eye. He stumbled on the stair as he glanced back over his shoulder and in so doing, almost missed a rare suit of Genoese armour which stood concealed in a niche set back from the staircase. The moneylender had reached a state of confused bewilderment when at length Mr Gingold flung aside a large mahogany door, high up in the house, and motioned him forward.

Mr Gingold must be a wealthy man and could easily realise enormous amounts on any one of the *objets d'art* Sharsted had seen; why then, thought the latter, did he find it necessary to borrow so frequently, and why was it so difficult to obtain repayment? With interest, the sum owed Sharsted had now risen to a considerable figure; Mr Gingold must be a compulsive buyer of rare items. Allied to the general shabbiness of the house as seen by the casual visitor, it must mean that his collector's instinct would refuse to allow him to part with anything once bought, which had made him run himself into debt. The moneylender's lips tightened again; well, he must be made to settle his debts, like anyone else.

If not, perhaps Sharsted could force him to part with something – porcelain, a picture – that could be made to realise a handsome profit on the deal. Business was business, and Gingold could not expect him to wait for ever. His musings were interrupted by a query from his host and Sharsted muttered an apology as he saw that Mr Gingold was waiting, one hand on the neck of a heavy silver and crystal decanter.

"Yes, yes, a sherry, thank you," he murmured in confusion, moving awkwardly. The light was so bad in this place that he felt it difficult to focus his eyes, and objects had a habit of shifting and billowing as though seen under water. Mr Sharsted was forced to wear tinted spectacles, as his eyes had been weak from childhood. They made these apartments seem twice as dark as they might be. But though Mr Sharsted squinted over the top of his lenses as Mr Gingold poured the sherry, he still could not make out objects clearly. He really would have to consult his oculist soon, if this trouble continued.

His voice sounded hollow to his own ears as he ventured a commonplace when Mr Gingold handed him the glass. He sat down gingerly on a ladderback chair indicated to him by Mr Gingold, and sipped at the amber liquid in a hesitant fashion. It tasted uncommonly good, but this unexpected hospitality was putting him on a wrong footing with Gingold. He must assert himself and broach the subject of his business. But he felt a curious reluctance and merely sat on in embarrassed silence, one hand round the stem of his goblet, listening to the soothing tick of an old clock, which was the only thing which broke the silence.

He saw now that he was in a large apartment, expensively furnished, which must be high up in the house, under the eaves. Hardly a sound from outside penetrated the windows, which were hung with thick blue-velvet curtains; the parquet floor was covered with exquisitely worked Chinese rugs and the room was apparently divided in half by heavy velvet curtaining to match those which masked the windows.

Mr Gingold said little, but sat at a large mahogany table, tapping his sherry glass with his long fingers; his bright blue eyes looked with mild interest at Mr Sharsted as they spoke of everyday matters. At last Mr Sharsted was moved to broach the object of his visit. He spoke of the long-outstanding sum which he had advanced to Mr Gingold, of the continued applications for settlement and of the necessity of securing early payment. Strangely, as Mr Sharsted progressed, his voice began to stammer and eventually he was at a loss for words; normally, as working-class people in the town had reason to know, he was brusque, business-like, and ruthless. He never hesitated to distrain on debtor's goods, or to evict if necessary and that he was the object of universal hatred in the outside world, bothered him not in the slightest.

In fact, he felt it to be an asset; his reputation in business affairs preceded him, as it were, and acted as an incentive to prompt repayment. If people were fool enough to be poor or to run into debt and couldn't meet their dues, well then, let them; it was all grist to his mill and he could not be expected to run his business on a lot of sentimental nonsense. He felt more irritated with Mr Gingold than he need have been, for his money was obviously safe; but what continued to baffle him was the man's gentle docility, his obvious wealth, and his reluctance to settle his debts.

Something of this must have eventually permeated his conversation, for Mr Gingold shifted in his seat, made no comment whatever on Mr Sharsted's pressing demands and only said, in another of his softly spoken sentences, "Do have another sherry, Mr Sharsted."

The moneylender felt all the strength going out of him as he weakly assented. He leaned back on his comfortable chair with a swimming head and allowed the second glass to be pressed into his hand, the thread of his discourse completely lost. He mentally cursed himself for a dithering fool and tried to concentrate, but Mr Gingold's benevolent smile, the curious way the objects in the room shifted and wavered in the heat haze; the general gloom and the discreet curtaining, came more and more to weigh on and oppress his spirits.

So it was with something like relief that Sharsted saw his host rise from the table. He had not changed the topic, but continued to speak as though Mr Sharsted had never mentioned money to him at all; he merely ignored the whole situation and with an enthusiasm Sharsted found difficult to share, murmured soothingly on about Chinese wall paintings, a subject of which Mr Sharsted knew nothing.

He found his eyes closing and with an effort opened them again. Mr Gingold was saying, "I think this will interest you, Mr Sharsted. Come along . . ."

His host had moved forward and the moneylender, following him down the room, saw that the large expanse of velvet curtaining was in motion. The two men walked through the parted curtains, which closed behind them, and Mr Sharsted then saw that they were in a semicircular chamber.

This room was, if anything, even dimmer than the one they had just left. But the moneylender's interest began to revive; his head felt clearer and he took in a large circular table, some brass wheels and levers which winked in the gloom, and a long shaft which went up to the ceiling.

"This has almost become an obsession with me," murmured Mr Gingold, as though apologizing to his guest. "You are aware of the principles of the camera obscura, Mr Sharsted?"

The moneylender pondered slowly, reaching back into memory. "Some sort of Victorian toy, isn't it?" he said at length. Mr Gingold looked pained, but the expression of his voice did not change.

"Hardly that, Mr Sharsted," he rejoined. "A most fascinating pursuit. Few people of my acquaintance have been here and seen what you are going to see."

He motioned to the shafting, which passed up through a louvre in the ceiling.

"These controls are coupled to the system of lenses and prisms on the roof. As you will see, the hidden camera, as the Victorian scientists came to call it, gathers a panorama of the town below and transmits it here on to the viewing table. An absorbing study, one's fellow man, don't you think? I spend many hours up here."

Mr Sharsted had never heard Mr Gingold in such a talkative mood and now that the wretchedness which had assailed him earlier had disappeared, he felt more suited to tackle him about his debts. First, he would humour him by feigning interest in his stupid toy. But Mr Sharsted had to admit, almost with a gasp of surprise, that Mr Gingold's obsession had a valid cause.

For suddenly, as Mr Gingold moved his hand upon the lever, the room was flooded with light of a blinding clarity and the moneylender saw why gloom was a necessity in this chamber. Presumably, a shutter over the camera obscura slid away upon the rooftop and almost at the same moment, a panel in the ceiling opened to admit a shaft of light directed upon the table before them.

In a second of God-like vision, Mr Sharsted saw a panorama of part of the old town spread out before him in superbly natural colour. Here were the quaint, cobbled streets dropping to the valley, with the blue hills beyond; factory chimneys smoked in the early evening air; people went about their business in half a hundred roads; distant traffic went noiselessly on its way; once, even, a great white bird soared across the field of vision, so apparently close that Mr Sharsted started back from the table.

Mr Gingold gave a dry chuckle and moved a brass wheel at his elbow. The viewpoint abruptly shifted and Mr Sharsted saw with another gasp, a sparkling vista of the estuary with a big coaling ship moving slowly out to sea. Gulls soared in the foreground and the sullen wash of the tide ringed the shore. Mr Sharsted, his errand quite forgotten, was fascinated. Half an hour must have passed, each view more enchanting than the last; from this height, the squalor of the town was quite transformed.

He was abruptly recalled to the present, however, by the latest of the views; Mr Gingold spun the control for the last time and a huddle of crumbling tenements wheeled into view. "The former home of Mrs Thwaites, I believe," said Mr Gingold mildly.

Mr Sharsted flushed and bit his lip in anger. The Thwaites business had aroused more notoriety than he had intended; the woman had borrowed a greater sum than she could afford, the interest mounted, she borrowed again; could he help it if she had a tubercular husband and three children? He had to make an example of her in order to keep his other clients in line; now there was a distraint on the furniture and the Thwaiteses were being turned on to the street. Could he help this? If only people would repay their debts all would be well; he wasn't a philanthropic institution, he told himself angrily.

And at this reference to what was rapidly becoming a scandal in the town, all his smouldering resentment against Mr Gingold broke out afresh; enough of all these views and childish playthings. Camera obscura, indeed; if Mr Gingold did not meet his obligations like a gentleman he could sell this pretty toy to meet his debt.

He controlled himself with an effort as he turned to meet Mr Gingold's gently ironic gaze.

"Ah, yes," said Mr Sharsted. "The Thwaites business is my affair, Mr Gingold. Will you please confine yourself to the matter in hand. I have had to come here again at great inconvenience; I must tell you that if the £300, representing the current instalment on our loan is not forthcoming by Monday, I shall be obliged to take legal action."

Mr Sharsted's cheeks were burning and his voice trembled as he pronounced these words; if he expected a violent reaction from Mr Gingold, he was disappointed. The latter merely gazed at him in mute reproach.

"This is your last word?" he said regretfully. "You will not reconsider?"

"Certainly not," snapped Mr Sharsted. "I must have the money by Monday."

"You misunderstand me, Mr Sharsted," said Mr Gingold, still in that irritatingly mild voice. "I was referring to Mrs Thwaites. Must you carry on with this unnecessary and somewhat inhuman action? I would . . ."

"Please mind your own business!" retorted Mr Sharsted, exasperated beyond measure. "Mind what I say . . ."

He looked wildly round for the door through which he had entered.

"That is your last word?" said Mr Gingold again. One look at the moneylender's set, white face was his mute answer.

"Very well, then," said Mr Gingold, with a heavy sigh. "So be it. I will see you on your way."

He moved forward again, pulling a heavy velvet cloth over the table of the camera obscura. The louvre in the ceiling closed with a barely audible rumble. To Mr Sharsted's surprise, he found himself following his host up yet another flight of stairs; these were of stone, fringed with an iron balustrade which was cold to the touch.

His anger was now subsiding as quickly as it had come; he was already regretting losing his temper over the Thwaites business and he hadn't intended to sound so crude and cold-blooded. What must Mr Gingold think of him? Strange how the story could have got to his ears; surprising how much information about the outside world a recluse could obtain just by sitting still.

Though, on this hill, he supposed Mr Gingold could be said to be at the centre of things. He shuddered suddenly, for the air seemed to have grown cold. Through a slit in the stone wall he could see the evening sky was already darkening. He really must be on his way; how did the old fool expect him to find his way out when they were still mounting to the very top of the house?

Mr Sharsted regretted, too, that in antagonizing Mr Gingold, he might have made it even more difficult to obtain his money; it was almost as though, in mentioning Mrs

Thwaites and trying to take her part, he had been trying a form of subtle blackmail.

He would not have expect it of Gingold; it was not like him to meddle in other people's affairs. If he was so fond of the poor and needy he could well afford to advance the family some money themselves to tide them over their difficulties.

His brain seething with these confused and angry thoughts, Mr Sharsted, panting and dishevelled, now found himself on a worn stone platform where Mr Gingold was putting the key into an ancient wooden lock.

"My workshop," he explained, with a shy smile to Mr Sharsted, who felt his tension eased away by this drop in the emotional atmosphere. Looking through an old, nearly triangular window in front of him, Mr Sharsted could see that they were in a small, turreted superstructure which towered a good twenty feet over the main roof of the house. There was a sprawl of unfamiliar alleys at the foot of the steep overhang of the building, as far as he could make out through the grimy panes.

"There is a staircase down the outside," explained Mr Gingold, opening the door. "It will lead you down the other side of the hill and cut over half a mile off your journey."

The moneylender felt a sudden rush of relief at this. He had come almost to fear this deceptively mild and quiet old man who, though he said little and threatened not at all, had begun to exude a faint air of menace to Mr Sharsted's now overheated imagination.

"But first," said Mr Gingold, taking the other man's arm in a surprisingly powerful grip, "I want to show you something else – and this really has been seen by very few people indeed."

Mr Sharsted looked at the other quickly, but could read nothing in Mr Gingold's enigmatic blue eyes.

He was surprised to find a similar, though smaller, chamber to the one they had just left. There was another table, another shaft ascending to a domed cupola in the ceiling, and a further arrangement of wheels and tubes.

"This camera obscura," said Mr Gingold, "is a very rare

model, to be sure. In fact, I believe there are only three in existence today, and one of those is in Northern Italy."

Mr Sharsted cleared his throat and made a non-committal reply.

"I felt sure you would like to see this before you leave," said Mr Gingold softly. "You are quite sure you won't change your mind?" he added, almost inaudibly, as he bent to the levers. "About Mrs Thwaites, I mean."

Sharsted felt another sudden spirt of anger, but kept his feelings under control.

"I'm sorry . . ." he began.

"No matter," said Mr Gingold, regretfully. "I only wanted to make sure, before we had a look at this."

He laid his hand with infinite tenderness on Mr Sharsted's shoulder as he drew him forward.

He pressed the lever and Mr Sharsted almost cried out with the suddenness of the vision. He was God; the world was spread out before him in a crazy pattern, or at least the segment of it representing the part of the town surrounding the house in which he stood.

He viewed it from a great height, as a man might from an aeroplane; though nothing was quite in perspective.

The picture was of enormous clarity; it was like looking into an old cheval-glass which had a faint distorting quality. There was something oblique and elliptical about the sprawl of alleys and roads that spread about the foot of the hill.

The shadows were mauve and violet, and the extremes of the picture were still tinged with the blood red of the dying sun.

It was an appalling, cataclysmic vision, and Mr Sharsted was shattered; he felt suspended in space, and almost cried out at the dizziness of the height.

When Mr Gingold twirled the wheel and the picture slowly began to revolve, Mr Sharsted did cry out and had to clutch at the back of a chair to prevent himself from falling.

He was perturbed, too, as he caught a glimpse of a big, white building in the foreground of the picture.

"I thought that was the old Corn Exchange," he said in

bewilderment. "Surely that burned down before the last war?"

"Eh," said Mr Gingold, as thought he hadn't heard.

"It doesn't matter," said Mr Sharsted, who now felt quite confused and ill. It must be the combination of the sherry and the enormous height at which he was viewing the vision in the camera obscura.

It was a demoniacal toy and he shrank away from the figure of Mr Gingold, which looked somewhat sinister in the blood-red and mauve light reflected from the image in the polished table surface.

"I thought you'd like to see this one," said Mr Gingold, in the same maddening, insipid voice. "It's really special, isn't it? Quite the best of the two . . . you can see all sorts of things that are normally hidden."

As he spoke there appeared on the screen two old buildings which Mr Sharsted was sure had been destroyed during the war; in fact, he was certain that a public garden and car park had now been erected on the site. His mouth suddenly became dry; he was not sure whether he had drunk too much sherry or the heat of the day had been too much for him.

He had been about to make a sharp remark that the sale of the camera obscura would liquidate Mr Gingold's current debt, but he felt this would not be a wise comment to make at this juncture. He felt faint, his brow went hot and cold and Mr Gingold was at his side in an instant.

Mr Sharsted became aware that the picture had faded from the table and that the day was rapidly turning to dusk outside the dusty windows.

"I really must be going," he said with feeble desperation, trying to free himself from Mr Gingold's quietly persistent grip.

"Certainly, Mr Sharsted," said his host. "This way." He led him without ceremony over to a small oval doorway in a corner of the far wall.

"Just go down the stairs. It will bring you on to the street. Please slam the bottom door – it will lock itself."
As he spoke, he opened the door and Mr Sharsted saw a

flight of clean, dry stone steps leading downwards. Light still flooded in from windows set in the circular walls.

Mr Gingold did not offer his hand and Mr Sharsted stood rather awkwardly, holding the door ajar.

"Until Monday, then," he said.

Mr Gingold flatly ignored this.

"Goodnight, Mr Gingold," said the moneylender with nervous haste, anxious to be gone.

"Goodbye, Mr Sharsted," said Mr Gingold with kind finality.

Mr Sharsted almost thrust himself through the door and nervously fled down the staircase, mentally cursing himself for all sorts of a fool. His feet beat a rapid tattoo that echoed eerily up and down the old tower. Fortunately, there was still plenty of light; this would be a nasty place in the dark. He slowed his pace after a few moments and thought bitterly of the way he had allowed old Gingold to gain the ascendancy over him; and what an impertinence of the man to interfere in the matter of the Thwaites woman.

He would see what sort of man Mr Sharsted was when Monday came and the eviction went according to plan. Monday would also be a day of reckoning for Mr Gingold – it was a day they would both remember and Mr Sharsted felt himself quite looking forward to it.

He quickened his pace again, and presently found himself confronted by a thick oak door.

It gave beneath his hand as he lifted the big, well-oiled catch and the next moment he was in a high-walled alley leading to the street. The door slammed hollowly behind him and he breathed in the cool evening air with a sigh of relief. He jammed his hard hat back on his head and strode out over the cobbles, as though to affirm the solidity of the outside world.

Once in the street, which seemed somewhat unfamiliar to him, he hesitated which way to go and then set off to the right. He remembered that Mr Gingold had told him that this way took him over the other side of the hill; he had never been in this part of the town and the walk would do him good.

The sun had quite gone and a thin sliver of moon was showing in the early evening sky. There seemed few people about and when, ten minutes later, Mr Sharsted came out into a large square which had five or six roads leading off it, he determined to ask the correct way back down to his part of the town. With luck he could catch a tram, for he had now had enough of walking for one day.

There was a large, smoke-grimed chapel on a corner of this square and as Mr Sharsted passed it, he caught a glimpse of a board with gold-painted letters.

NINIAN'S REVIVALIST BROTHERHOOD, it said. The date, in flaked gold paint, was 1925.

Mr Sharsted walked on and selected the most important of the roads which faced him. It was getting quite dark and the lamps had not yet been lit on this part of the hill. As he went farther down, the buildings closed in about his head, and the lights of the town below disappeared. Mr Sharsted felt lost and a little forlorn. Due, no doubt, to the faintly incredible atmosphere of Mr Gingold's big house.

He determined to ask the next passer-by for the right direction, but for the moment he couldn't see anyone about; the absence of street lights also bothered him. The municipal authorities must have overlooked this section when they switched on at dusk, unless it came under the jurisdiction of another body.

Mr Sharsted was musing in this manner when he turned the corner of a narrow street and came out opposite a large, white building that looked familiar. For years Mr Sharsted had a picture of it on the yearly calendar sent by a local tradesman, which used to hang in his office. He gazed at its façade with mounting bewilderment as he approached. The title, CORN EXCHANGE, winked back dully in the moonlight as he got near enough to make out the lettering.

Mr Sharsted's bewilderment changed to distinct unease as he thought frantically that he had already seen this building once before this evening, in the image captured by the lens of Mr Gingold's second camera obscura. And he knew with numbing certainty that the old Corn Exchange had burned down in the late thirties.

He swallowed heavily, and hurried on; there was something devilishly wrong, unless he were the victim of an optical illusion engendered by the violence of his thoughts, the unaccustomed walking he had done that day, and the two glasses of sherry.

He had the uncomfortable feeling that Mr Gingold might be watching him at that very moment, on the table of his camera obscura, and at the thought a cold sweat burst out on his forehead.

He sent himself forward at a smart trot and had soon left the Corn Exchange far behind. In the distance he heard the sharp clopping and the grating rattle of a horse and cart, but as he gained the entrance of an alley he was disappointed to see its shadow disappear round the corner into the next road. He still could not see any people about and again had difficulty in fixing his position in relation to the town.

He set off once more, with a show of determination he was far from feeling, and five minutes later arrived in the middle of a square which was already familiar to him.

There was a chapel on the corner and Mr Sharsted read for the second time that evening the legend: NINIAN'S REVIVALIST BROTHERHOOD.

He stamped his foot in anger. He had walked quite three miles and had been fool enough to describe a complete circle; here he was, not five minutes from Gingold's house, where he had set out, nearly an hour before.

He pulled out his watch at this and was surprised to find it was only a quarter past six, though he could have sworn this was the time he had left Gingold.

Though it could have been a quarter past five; he hardly knew what he was doing this afternoon. He shook it to make sure it was still going and then replaced it in his pocket.

His feet beat the pavement in his fury as he ran down the length of the square. This time he wouldn't make the same silly mistake. He unhesitatingly chose a large, well-kept metalled road that ran fair and square in the direction he knew must take him back to the centre of the town. He found himself humming a little tune under his breath. As he turned the next corner, his confidence increased.

Lights burned brightly on every hand; the authorities must have realized their mistake and finally switched on. But again he was mistaken; there was a little cart parked at the side of the road, with a horse in the shafts. An old man mounted a ladder set against a lamp-post and Mr Sharsted saw the thin blue flame in the gloom and then the mellow blossoming of the gas lamp.

Now he felt irritated again; what an incredibly archaic part of the town old Gingold lived in. It would just suit him. Gas lamps! And what a system for lighting them; Sharsted thought this method had gone out with the Ark.

Nevertheless, he was most polite.

"Good evening," he said, and the figure at the top of the lamp-post stirred uneasily. The face was in deep shadow.

"Good evening, sir," the lamplighter said in a muffled voice. He started climbing down.

"Could you direct me to the town centre?" said Mr Sharsted with simulated confidence. He took a couple of paces forward and was then arrested with a shock.

There was a strange, sickly stench which reminded him of something he was unable to place. Really, the drains in this place were terrible; he certainly would have to write to the town hall about this backward part of the locality.

The lamplighter had descended to the ground now and he put something down in the back of his cart; the horse shifted uneasily and again Mr Sharsted caught the charnel stench, sickly sweet on the summer air.

"This is the town centre as far as I know, sir," said the lamplighter. As he spoke he stepped forward and the pale lamplight fell on to his face, which had been in shadow before.

Mr Sharsted no longer waited to ask for any more directions but set off down the road at breakneck speed, not sure whether the green pallor of the man's face was due to a terrible suspicion or to the green-tinted glasses he wore.

What he was certain of was that something like a mass of writing worms projected below the man's cap, where his hair would normally have been. Mr Sharsted hadn't waited to find out if this Medusa-like supposition were correct; beneath his hideous fear burned a savage anger at Gingold, whom somehow he suspected to be at the back of all these troubles.

Mr Sharsted fervently hoped that he might soon wake to find himself at home in bed, ready to begin the day that had ended so ignominiously at Gingold's, but even as he formulated the thought, he knew this was reality. This cold moonlight, the hard pavement, his frantic flight, and the breath rasping and sobbing in his throat.

As the mist cleared from in front of his eyes, he slowed to a walk and then found himself in the middle of the square; he knew where he was and he had to force his nerves into a terrible, unnatural calm, just this side of despair. He walked with controlled casualness past the legend, NINIAN'S REVIVALIST BROTHERHOOD, and this time chose the most unlikely road of all, little more than a narrow alley that appeared to lead in the wrong direction.

Mr Sharsted was willing to try anything which would lead him off this terrifying, accursed hill. There were no lights here and his feet stumbled on the rough stones and flints of the unmade roadway, but at least he was going downhill and the track gradually spiralled until he was in the right direction.

For some little while Mr Sharsted had heard faint, elusive stirrings in the darkness about him and once he was startled to hear, some way ahead of him, a muffled cough. At least there were other people about, at last, he thought and he was comforted, too, to see, far ahead of him, the dim lights of the town.

As he grew nearer, Mr Sharsted recovered his spirits and was relieved to see that they did not recede from him, as he had half suspected they might. The shapes about him, too, were solid enough. Their feet rang hollow on the roadway; evidently they were on their way to a meeting.

As Mr Sharsted came under the light of the first lamp, his earlier panic fear had abated. He still couldn't recognize exactly where he was, but the trim villas they were passing were reminiscent of the town proper.

Mr Sharsted stepped up on to the pavement when they reached the well-lit area and in so doing, cannoned into a large, well-built man who had just emerged from a gateway to join the throng in the roadway.

Mr Sharsted staggered under the impact and once again his nostrils caught the sickly sweet perfume of decay. The man caught him by the front of the coat to prevent him from falling.

"Evening, Mordecai," he said in a thick voice. "I thought you'd be coming, sooner or later."

Mr Sharsted could not resist a cry of bubbling terror. It was not just the greenish pallor of the man's face or the rotted, leathery lips drawn back from the decayed teeth. He fell back against the fence as Abel Joyce passed on – Abel Joyce, a fellow moneylender and usurer who had died in the nineteen-twenties and whose funeral Mr Sharsted had attended.

Blackness was about him as he rushed away, a sobbing whistle in his throat. He was beginning to understand Mr Gingold and that devilish camera obscura; the lost and the damned. He began to babble to himself under his breath.

Now and again he cast a sidelong glimpse at his companions as he ran; there was old Mrs Sanderson who used to lay out corpses and rob her charges; there Grayson, the estate agent and undertaker; Amos, the war profiteer; Drucker, a swindler, all green of pallor and bearing with them the charnel stench.

All people Mr Sharsted had business with at one time or another and all of whom had one thing in common. Without exception all had been dead for quite a number of years. Mr Sharsted stuffed his handkerchief over his mouth to blot out that unbearable odour and heard the mocking laughter as his racing feet carried him past.

"Evening, Mordecai," they said. "We thought you'd be joining us." Mr Gingold equated him with these ghouls, he sobbed, as he ran on at headlong speed; if only he could make him understand. Sharsted didn't deserve such treatment. He was a businessman, not like these blood-suckers on society; the lost and the damned. Now he knew why the Corn Exchange still stood and why the town was unfamiliar. It existed only in the eye of the camera obscura. Now he knew that Mr Gingold had been trying to give him a last chance and why he had said goodbye, instead of goodnight.

There was just one hope; if he could find the door back to Mr Gingold's perhaps he could make him change his mind. Mr Sharsted's feet flew over the cobbles as he thought this, his hat fell down and he scraped his hands against the wall. He left the walking corpses far behind, but though he was now looking for the familiar square he seemed to be finding his way back to the Corn Exchange.

He stopped for a moment to regain his breath. He must work this out logically. How had it happened before? Why, of course, by walking away from the desired destination. Mr Sharsted turned back and set himself to walk steadily towards the lights. Though terrified, he did not despair, now that he knew what he was up against. He felt himself a match for Mr Gingold. If only he could find the door!

As he reached the warm circle cast by the glow of the street lamps, Mr Sharsted breathed a sigh of relief. For as he turned a corner there was the big square, with the soot-grimed chapel on the corner. He hurried on. He must remember exactly the turnings he had taken; he couldn't afford to make a mistake.

So much depended on it. If only he could have another chance – he would let the Thwaites family keep their house, he would even be willing to forget Gingold's debt. He couldn't face the possibility of walking these endless streets – for how long? And with the creatures he had seen . . .

Mr Sharsted groaned as he remembered the face of one old woman he had seen earlier that evening – or what was left of that face, after years of wind and weather. He suddenly recalled that she had died before the 1914 war. The sweat burst out on his forehead and he tried not to think of it.

Once off the square, he plunged into the alley he remembered. Ah! there it was. Now all he had to do was to go to the left and there was the door. His heart beat higher and he began to hope, with a sick longing, for the security of his well-appointed house and his rows of friendly ledgers. Only one more corner. He ran on and turned up the road towards Mr Gingold's door. Another thirty yards to the peace of the ordinary world.

The moonlight winked on a wide, well-paved square. Shone, too, on a legend painted in gold leaf on a large board: NINIAN'S REVIVALIST BROTHERHOOD. The date was 1925.

Mr Sharsted gave a hideous yell of fear and despair and fell to the pavement.

Mr Gingold sighed heavily and yawned. He glanced at the clock. It was time for bed. He went over once again and stared into the camera obscura. It had been a not altogether unsuccessful day. He put a black velvet cloth over the image in the lens and went off slowly to bed.

Under the cloth, in pitiless detail, was reflected the narrow tangle of streets round Mr Gingold's house, seen as through the eye of God; there went Mr Sharsted and his colleagues, the lost and the damned, trapped for eternity, stumbling, weeping, swearing, as they slipped and scrabbled along the alleys and squares of their own private hell, under the pale light of the stars.

No Flies on Frank
Introduction

*Yes, it all comes bark to meow. I was 18 and a loyal Beatle
fart with me own carpy of the brook* In His Own Write *by
John Lemon of the famous sisters. "No flies on Frank" wars
one of me flavoured stories, along perhaps with "Angry
Frank" to which it was maybe a sequin. Joycean Carrollean
pre-Pythonesque minimalism some might squeak. In realty,
"No Flies on Frank" is not very mulch a pleasured story,
what with the red gore and purple violents and without munch
of an end and no morals whatsoever. Almond lifelike you
might say if you were inclined to peek.*

F. PAUL WILSON
Author of The Keep, The Tomb *and* Black Wind

John Lennon
No Flies on Frank

There were no flies on Frank that morning – after all why not? He was a responsible citizen with a wife and child, wasn't he? It was a typical Frank morning and with an agility that defies description he leapt into the barthroom on to the scales. To his great harold he discovered he was twelve inches more tall heavy! He couldn't believe it and his blood raised to his head causing a mighty red colouring.

"I carn't not believe this incredible fact of truth about my very body which has not gained fat since mother begat me at childburn. Yea, though I wart through the valet of thy shadowy hut I will feed no norman. What grate qualmsy hath taken me thus into such a fatty hardbuckle."

Again Frank looked down at the awful vision which clouded his eyes with fearful weight. "Twelve inches more heavy, Lo!, but am I not more fatty than my brother Geoffrey whose father came from Alec came from Kenneth – through Leslies, who begat Arthur, son of Eric, by the house of Ronald and April – keepers of James of Newcastle who ran Madeline at 2–1 by Silver Flower, (10–2) past Wot-ro-Wot at 4s.3d. a pound?"

He journeyed downstairs crestfalled and defective – a great wait on his boulders – not even his wife's battered face could raise a smile on poor Frank's head – who as you know had no flies on him. His wife, a former beauty queer, regarded him with a strange but burly look.

"What ails thee, Frank?" she asked stretching her prune. "You look dejected if not informal," she addled.

"'Tis nothing but wart I have gained but twelve inches more tall heavy than at the very clock of yesterday at this time – am I not the most miserable of men? Suffer ye not

to spake to me or I might thrust you a mortal injury; I
must traddle this trial alone."

"Lo! Frank – thou has smote me harshly with such grave
talk – am I to blame for this vast burton?"

Frank looked sadly at his wife – forgetting for a moment
the cause of his misery. Walking slowly but slowly towards
her, he took his head in his hands and with a few swift
blows had clubbed her mercifully to the ground dead.

"She shouldn't see me like this," he mubbled, "not all
fat and on her thirty-second birthday."

Frank had to get his own breakfast that morning and
also on the following mornings.

Two (or was it three?) weeks later Frank awake again to
find that there were *still* no flies on him.

"No flies on this Frank boy," he thought; but to his
amazement there seemed to be a lot of flies on his wife –
who was still lying about the kitchen floor.

"I carn't not partake of bread and that with her lying
about the place," he thought allowed, writing as he spoke.
"I must deliver her to her home where she will be made
welcome."

He gathered her in a small sack (for she was only four foot
three) and headed for her rightful home. Frank knocked on
the door of his wife's mother's house. She opened the door.

"I've brought Marian home, Mrs Sutherskill," (he could
never call her Mum). He opened the sack and placed
Marian on the doorstep.

"I'm not having all those flies in my home," shouted Mrs
Sutherskill (who was very house-proud), shutting the door.
"She could have at least offered me a cup of tea," thought
Frank lifting the problem back on his boulders.

The Streets of Ashkelon
Introduction

I remember this story of Harry Harrison's very well. I was there at the christening, as it were.

In the early sixties, I started up the Penguin Books science fiction list, and produced three anthologies for them. Harry sent me this story, complaining in his usual genial way.

The complaints centred round the fact that his story had been previously rejected on the grounds that it might offend someone's religious feelings. I always liked a story that might offend someone; it generally denotes writing with a little life and feeling in it. That's certainly the case with 'The Streets of Ashkelon'.

My suggestion that he alter the title to 'Nudes of Ashkelon' was brusquely rejected. I took the story anyway. So its first acceptance was for a distinguished (?) anthology. Its first appearance, however, was in New Worlds, then edited in those dim days by Ted "No Nudes" Carnell. He was willing to publish anything that had been accepted by Penguin Books, who were then to literature rather what the Virgin Mary is to Christ, or vice versa.

Harry suggested to Ted that he change the title to "Nudes of Ashkelon". The suggestion was brusquely rejected, but Ted published the story anyway. It has since made the name of Harrison famous throughout the uncivilized world. It's horrible. It could make a good movie.

Well, there's no justice. It should be out there somewhere on our screens, making millions of dollars. Instead, here it is, kicking about in the pages of The Best from the Pan Book of Naked Horror Stories. *I still like it, for all that.*

BRIAN W. ALDISS
Author of the Helliconia *trilogy,* Frankenstein Unbound *and* Trillion Year Spree

Harry Harrison

The Streets of Ashkelon

Somewhere above, hidden by the eternal clouds of Wesker's World, a thunder rumbled and grew. Trader John Garth stopped when he heard it, his boots sinking slowly into the muck, and cupped his good ear to catch the sound. It swelled and waned in the thick atmosphere, growing louder.

"That noise is the same as the noise of your sky-ship," Itin said, with stolid Wesker logicality, slowly pulverizing the idea in his mind and turning over the bits one by one for closer examination. "But your ship is still sitting where you landed it. It must be, even though we cannot see it, because you are the only one who can operate it. And even if anyone else could operate it we would have heard it rising into the sky. Since we did not, and if this sound is a sky-ship sound, then it must mean . . ."

"Yes, another ship," Garth said, too absorbed in his own thoughts to wait for the laborious Weskerian chains of logic to clank their way through to the end. Of course it was another spacer, it had been only a matter of time before one appeared, and undoubtedly this one was homing on the SS radar reflector as he had done. His own ship would show up clearly on the newcomer's screen and they would probably set down as close to it as they could.

"You better go ahead, Itin," he said. "Use the water so you can get to the village quickly. Tell everyone to get back into the swamps, well clear of the hard ground. That ship is landing on instruments and anyone underneath at touch-down is going to be cooked."

This immediate threat was clear enough to the little Wesker amphibian. Before Garth finished speaking Itin's ribbed ears had folded like a bat's wing and he slipped silently into the nearby canal. Garth squelched on through the mud, making as good time as he could over the clinging surface. He had just reached the fringes of the village clearing when the rumbling grew to a head-splitting roar and the spacer broke through the low-hanging layer of clouds above. Garth shielded his eyes from the down-reaching tongue of flame and examined the growing form of the grey-black ship with mixed feelings.

After almost a standard year on Wesker's World he had to fight down a longing for human companionship of any kind. While this buried fragment of herd-spirit chattered for the rest of the monkey tribe, his trader's mind was busily drawing a line under a column of figures and adding up the total. This could very well be another trader's ship, and if it were his monopoly of the Wesker trade was at an end. Then again, this might not be a trader at all, which was the reason he stayed in the shelter of the giant fern and loosened his gun in its holster.

The ship baked dry a hundred square metres of mud, the roaring blast died, and the landing feet crunched down through the crackling crust. Metal creaked and settled into place while the cloud of smoke and steam slowly drifted lower in the humid air.

'Garth – you native-cheating extortionist – where are you?' the ship's speaker boomed. The lines of the spacer had looked only slightly familiar, but there was no mistaking the rasping tones of that voice. Garth wore a smile when he stepped out into the open and whistled shrilly through two fingers. A directional microphone ground out of its casing on the ship's fin and turned in his direction.

"What are you doing here, Singh?" he shouted towards the mike. "Too crooked to find a planet of your own and have to come here to steal an honest trader's profits?"

"Honest!" the amplified voice roared. "This from the man who has been in more jails than cathouses – and that a goodly number in itself, I do declare. Sorry, friend of my youth, but I cannot join you in exploiting this aboriginal pesthole. I am on course to a more fairly atmosphered world where a fortune is waiting to be made. I only stopped here since an opportunity presented to turn an honest credit by running a taxi service. I bring you friendship, the perfect companionship, a man in a different line of business who might help you in yours. I'd come out and say hello myself, except I would have to decon for biologicals. I'm cycling the passenger through the lock so I hope you won't mind helping with his luggage."

At least there would be no other trader on the planet now, that worry was gone. But Garth still wondered what sort of passenger would be taking one-way passage to an uninhabited world. And what was behind that concealed hint of merriment in Singh's voice? He walked around to the far side of the spacer where the ramp had dropped, and looked up at the man in the cargo lock who was wrestling ineffectually with a large crate. The man turned towards him and Garth saw the clerical dog-collar and knew just what it was Singh had been chuckling about.

"What are you doing here?" Garth asked; in spite of his attempt at self control he snapped the words. If the man noticed this he ignored it, because he was still smiling and putting out his hand as he came down the ramp.

"Father Mark," he said. "Of the Missionary Society of Brothers. I'm very pleased to – "

"I said what are you doing here." Garth's voice was under control now, quiet and cold. He knew what had to be done, and it must be done quickly or not at all.

"That should be obvious," Father Mark said, his good nature still unruffled. "Our missionary society has raised funds to send spiritual emissaries to alien worlds for the first time. I was lucky enough – "

"Take your luggage and get back into the ship. You're not wanted here and have no permission to land. You'll be a liability and there is no one on Wesker to take care of you. Get back into the ship."

"I don't know who you are sir, or why you are lying to me," the priest said. He was still calm but the smile was gone. "But I have studied galactic law and the history of this planet very well. There are no diseases or beasts here that I should have any particular fear of. It is also an open planet, and until the Space Survey changes that status I have as much right to be here as you do."

The man was of course right, but Garth couldn't let him know that. He had been bluffing, hoping the priest didn't know his rights. But he did. There was only one distasteful course left for him, and he had better do it while there was still time.

"Get back in that ship," he shouted, not hiding his anger now. With a smooth motion his gun was out of the holster and the pitted black muzzle only inches from the priest's stomach. The man's face turned white, but he did not move.

"What the hell are you doing, Garth!" Singh's shocked voice grated from the speaker. "The guy paid his fare and you have no rights at all to throw him off the planet."

"I have this right," Garth said raising his gun and sighting between the priest's eyes. "I give him thirty seconds to get back aboard the ship or I pull the trigger."

"Well I think you are either off your head or playing a joke," Singh's exasperated voice rasped down at them. "If a joke, it is in bad taste, and either way you're not getting away with it. Two can play at that game, only I can play it better."

There was the rumble of heavy bearings and the remote-controlled four-gun turret on the ship's side rotated and pointed at Garth. "Now – down gun and give Father Mark a hand with the luggage," the speaker commanded, a trace of humour back in the voice now. "As much as I would like to help, Old Friend, I cannot. I feel it is time you had a chance to talk to the father; after all, I have had the opportunity of speaking with him all the way from Earth."

Garth jammed the gun back into the holster with an acute feeling of loss. Father Mark stepped forward, the winning smile back now and a bible taken from a pocket of his robe, in his raised hand. "My son," he said.

"I'm not your son," was all Garth could choke out as defeat welled up in him. His fist drew back as the anger rose, and the best he could do was open the fist so he struck only with the flat of his hand. Still the blow sent the priest crashing to the ground and fluttered the pages of the book splattering into the thick mud.

Itin and the other Weskers had watched everything with seemingly emotionless interest, and Garth made no attempt to answer their unspoken questions. He started towards his house, but turned back when he saw they were still unmoving.

"A new man has come," he told them. "He will need help with the things he has brought. If he doesn't have any place for them, you can put them in the big warehouse until he has a place of his own."

He watched them waddle across the clearing towards the ship, then went inside and gained a certain satisfaction from slamming the door hard enough to crack one of the panes. There was an equal amount of painful pleasure in breaking out one of the remaining bottles of Irish whiskey that he had been saving for a special occasion. Well this was special enough, though not really what he had had in mind. The whiskey was good and burned away some of the bad taste in his mouth, but not all of it. If his tactics had worked, success would have justified everything. But he had failed and in addition to the pain of failure there was the acute feeling that he had made a horse's ass out of himself. Singh had blasted off without any goodbyes. There was no telling what sense he had made of the whole matter, though he would surely carry some strange stories back to the traders' lodge. Well, that could be worried about the next time Garth signed in. Right now he had to go about setting things right with the missionary. Squinting out through the rain he saw the man struggling to erect a collapsible tent while the entire population of the village stood in ordered ranks and watched. Naturally none of them offered to help.

By the time the tent was up and the crates and boxes stowed inside it the rain had stopped. The level of fluid in the bottle was a good bit lower and Garth felt more like facing up to the unavoidable meeting. In truth, he was looking forward to talking to the man. The whole nasty business aside, after an entire solitary year any human companionship looked good. *Will you join me now for dinner. John Garth*, he wrote on the back of an old invoice. But maybe the guy was too frightened to come? Which was no way to start any kind of relationship. Rummaging under the bunk, he found a box that was big enough and put his pistol inside. Itin was of course waiting outside the door when he opened it, since this was his tour as Knowledge Collector. He handed him the note and box.

"Would you take these to the new man," he said.

"Is the new man's name New Man?" Itin asked.

"No, it's not!" Garth snapped. "His name is Mark. But I'm only asking you to deliver this, not get involved in conversation."

As always when he lost his temper, the literal minded Weskers won the round. "You are not asking for conversation," Itin said slowly, "but Mark may ask for conversation. And others will ask me his name, if I do not know his na – " The voice cut off as Garth slammed the door. This didn't work in the long run either because next time he saw Itin – a day, a week, or even a month later – the monologue would be picked up on the very word it had ended and the thought rambled out to its last frayed end. Garth cursed under his breath and poured water over a pair of the tastier concentrates that he had left.

"Come in," he said when there was a quiet knock on the door. The priest entered and held out the box with the gun.

"Thank you for the loan, Mr Garth, I appreciate the spirit that made you send it. I have no idea of what caused the unhappy affair when I landed, but I think it would be best forgotten if we are going to be on this planet together for any length of time."

"Drink?" Garth asked, taking the box and pointing to the bottle on the table. He poured two glasses full and handed one to the priest. "That's about what I had in mind, but I still owe you an explanation of what happened out there." He scowled into his glass for a second, then raised it to the other man. "It's a big universe and I guess we have to make out as best we can. Here's to Sanity."

"God be with you," Father Mark said, and raised his glass as well.

"Not with me or with this planet," Garth said firmly. "And that's the crux of the matter." He half-drained the glass and sighed.

"Do you say that to shock me?" the priest asked with a smile. "I assure you it doesn't."

"Not intended to shock. I meant it quite literally. I suppose I'm what you would call an atheist, so revealed religion is no concern of mine. While these natives, simple and unlettered stone-age types that they are, have managed to come this far with no superstitions or traces of deism whatsoever. I had hoped that they might continue that way."

"What are you saying?" the priest frowned. "Do you mean they have no gods, no belief in the hereafter? They must die . . . ?"

"Die they do, and to dust returneth like the rest of the animals. They have thunder, trees and water without having thunder-gods, tree sprites, or water nymphs. They have no ugly little gods, taboos, or spells to hag-ride and limit their lives. They are the only primitive people I have ever encountered that are completely free of superstition and appear to be much happier and saner because of it. I just wanted to keep them that way."

"You wanted to keep them from God – from salvation?" the priest's eyes widened and he recoiled slightly.

"No," Garth said. "I wanted to keep them from superstition until they knew more and could think about it realistically without being absorbed and perhaps destroyed by it."

"You're being insulting to the Church, sir, to equate it with superstition . . ."

"Please," Garth said, raising his hand. "No theological arguments. I don't think your society footed the bill for this trip just to attempt a conversion on me. Just accept the fact that my beliefs have been arrived at through careful thought over a period of years, and no amount of under-

graduate metaphysics will change them. I'll promise not to
try and convert you – if you will do the same for me."

"Agreed, Mr Garth. As you have reminded me, my mis-
sion here is to save these souls, and that is what I must do.
But why should my work disturb you so much that you try
and keep me from landing? Even threaten me with your
gun, and – " the priest broke off and looked into his glass.

"And even slug you?" Garth asked, suddenly frowning.
"There was no excuse for that, and I would like to say that
I'm sorry. Plain bad manners and an even worse temper.
Live alone long enough and you find yourself doing that
kind of thing." He brooded down at his big hands where
they lay on the table, reading memories into the scars and
callouses patterned there. "Let's just call it frustration, for
lack of a better word. In your business you must have had
a lot of chance to peep into the darker places in men's minds
and you should know a bit about motives and happiness. I
have had too busy a life to ever consider settling down and
raising a family, and right up to recently I never missed it.
Maybe leak radiation is softening up my brain, but I had
begun to think of these furry and fishy Weskers as being a
little like my own children, that I was somehow responsible
to them."

"We are all His children," Father Mark said quietly.

"Well, here are some of His children that can't even
imagine His existence," Garth said, suddenly angry at himself for allowing gentler emotions to show through. Yet he
forgot himself at once, leaning forward with the intensity
of his feelings. "Can't you realize the importance of this?
Live with these Weskers awhile and you will discover a
simple and happy life that matches the state of grace you
people are always talking about. They get *pleasure* from
their lives – and cause no one pain. By circumstances they
have evolved on an almost barren world, so have never had
a chance to grow out of a physical stone age culture. But
mentally they are our match – or perhaps better. They have
all learned my language so I can easily explain the many
things they want to know. Knowledge and the gaining of
knowledge gives them real satisfaction. They tend to be

exasperating at times because every new fact must be related to the structure of all other things, but the more they learn the faster this process becomes. Some day they are going to be man's equal in every way, perhaps surpass us. If — would you do me a favour?"

"Whatever I can."

"Leave them alone. Or teach them if you must — history and science, philosophy, law, anything that will help them face the realities of the greater universe they never even knew existed before. But don't confuse them with your hatreds and pain, guilt, sin, and punishment. Who knows the harm . . ."

"You are being insulting, sir!" the priest said, jumping to his feet. The top of his grey head barely came to the massive spaceman's chin, yet he showed no fear in defending what he believed. Garth, standing now himself, was no longer the penitent. They faced each other in anger, as men have always stood, unbending in the defence of that which they think right.

"Yours is the insult," Garth shouted. "The incredible egotism to feel that your derivative little mythology, differing only slightly from the thousands of others that still burden men, can do anything but confuse their still fresh minds! Don't you realize that they believe in truth — and have never heard of such a thing as a lie. They have not been trained yet to understand that other kinds of minds can think differently from theirs. Will you spare them this . . . ?"

"I will do my duty which is His will, Mr Garth. These are God's creatures here, and they have souls. I cannot shirk my duty, which is to bring them His word, so that they may be saved and enter into the kingdom of heaven."

When the priest opened the door the wind caught it and blew it wide. He vanished into the stormswept darkness and the door swung back and forth and a splatter of raindrops blew in. Garth's boots left muddy footprints when he closed the door, shutting out the sight of Itin sitting patiently and uncomplaining in the storm, hoping only that

Garth might stop for a moment and leave with him some of the wonderful knowledge of which he had so much.

By unspoken consent that first night was never mentioned again. After a few days of loneliness, made worse because each knew of the other's proximity, they found themselves talking on carefully neutral grounds. Garth slowly packed and stowed away his stock and never admitted that his work was finished and he could leave at any time. He had a fair amount of interesting drugs and botanicals that would fetch a good price. And the Wesker Artefacts were sure to create a sensation in the sophisticated galactic market. Crafts on the planet here had been limited before his arrival, mostly pieces of carving painfully chipped into the hard wood with fragments of stone. He had supplied tools and a stock of raw metal from his own supplies, nothing more than that. In a few months the Weskers had not only learned to work with the new materials, but had translated their own designs and forms into the most alien – but most beautiful – artefacts that he had ever seen. All he had to do was release these on the market to create a primary demand, then return for a new supply. The Weskers wanted only books and tools and knowledge in return, and through their own efforts he knew they would pull themselves into the galactic union.

This is what Garth had hoped. But a wind of change was blowing through the settlement that had grown up around his ship. No longer was he the centre of attention and focal point of the village life. He had to grin when he thought of his fall from power; yet there was very little humour in the smile. Serious and attentive Weskers still took turns of duty as Knowledge Collectors, but their recording of dry facts was in sharp contrast to the intellectual hurricane that surrounded the priest.

Where Garth had made them work for each book and machine, the priest gave freely. Garth had tried to be progressive in his supply of knowledge, treating them as bright but unlettered children. He had wanted them to walk before they could run, to master one step before going on to the next.

Father Mark simply brought them the benefits of Christianity. The only physical work he required was the construction of a church, a place of worship and learning. More Weskers had appeared out of the limitless planetary swamps and within days the roof was up, supported on a framework of poles. Each morning the congregation worked a little while on the walls, then hurried inside to learn the all-promising, all-encompassing, all-important facts about the universe.

Garth never told the Weskers what he thought about their new interest, and this was mainly because they had never asked him. Pride or honour stood in the way of his grabbing a willing listener and pouring out his grievances. Perhaps it would have been different if Itin was on Collecting duty; he was the brightest of the lot; but Itin had been rotated the day after the priest had arrived and Garth had not talked to him since.

It was a surprise then when after seventeen of the trebly-long Wesker days, he found a delegation at his doorstep when he emerged after breakfast. Itin was their spokesman, and his mouth was open slightly. Many of the other Weskers had their mouths open as well, one even appearing to be yawning, clearly revealing the double row of sharp teeth and the purple-black throat. The mouths impressed Garth as to the seriousness of the meeting; this was the one Wesker expression he had learned to recognize. An open mouth indicated some strong emotion; happiness, sadness, anger, he could never be really sure which. The Weskers were normally placid and he had never seen enough open mouths to tell what was causing them. But he was surrounded by them now.

"Will you help us, John Garth," Itin said. "We have a question."

"I'll answer any question you ask," Garth said, with more than a hint of misgiving. "What is it?"

"Is there a God?"

"What do you mean by 'God'?" Garth asked in turn. What should he tell them?

"God is our Father in Heaven, who made us all and protects us. Whom we pray to for aid, and if we are Saved will find a place . . ."

"That's enough," Garth said. "There is no God."

All of them had their mouths open now, even Itin, as they looked at Garth and thought about his answer. The rows of pink teeth would have been frightening if he hadn't known these creatures so well. For one instant he wondered if perhaps they had been already indoctrinated and looked upon him as a heretic, but he brushed the thought away.

"Thank you," Itin said, and they turned and left.

Though the morning was still cool, Garth noticed that he was sweating and wondered why.

The reaction was not long in coming. Itin returned that same afternoon. "Will you come to the church?" he asked. "Many of the things that we study are difficult to learn, but none as difficult as this. We need your help because we must hear you and Father Mark talk together. This is because he says one thing is true and you say another is true and both cannot be true at the same time. We must find out what is true."

"I'll come, of course," Garth said, trying to hide the sudden feeling of elation. He had done nothing, but the Weskers had come to him anyway. There could still be grounds for hope that they might yet be free.

It was hot inside the church, and Garth was surprised at the number of Weskers who were there, more than he had seen gathered at any one time before. There were many open mouths. Father Mark sat at a table covered with books. He looked unhappy but didn't say anything when Garth came in. Garth spoke first.

"I hope you realize this is their idea – that they came to me of their own free will and asked me to come here?"

"I know that," the priest said resignedly. "At times they can be very difficult. But they are learning and want to believe, and that is what is important."

"Father Mark, Trader Garth, we need your help," Itin

said. "You both know many things that we do not know. You must help us come to religion which is not an easy thing to do." Garth started to say something, then changed his mind. Itin went on. "We have read the bibles and all the books that Father Mark gave us, and one thing is clear. We have discussed this and we are all agreed. These books are very different from the ones that Trader Garth gave us. In Trader Garth's books there is the universe which we have not seen, and it goes on without God, for he is mentioned nowhere; we have searched very carefully. In Father Mark's books He is everywhere and nothing can go without Him. One of these must be right and the other wrong. We do not know how this can be, but after we find out which is right then perhaps we will know. If God does not exist . . ."

"Of course He exists, my children," Father Mark said in a voice of heartfelt intensity. "He is our Father in Heaven who has created us all . . ."

"Who created God?" Itin asked and the murmur ceased and everyone of the Weskers watched Father Mark intensely. He recoiled a bit under the impact of their eyes, then smiled.

"Nothing created God, since He is the Creator. He always was . . ."

"If He always was in existence – why cannot the universe have always been in existence? Without having had a creator?" Itin broke in with a rush of words. The importance of the question was obvious. The priest answered slowly, with infinite patience.

"Would that the answers were that simple, my children. But even the scientists do not agree about the creation of the universe. While they doubt – we who have seen the light *know*. We can see the miracle of creation all about us. And how can there be creation without a Creator? That is He, our Father, our God in Heaven. I know you have doubts; that is because you have souls and free will. Still, the answer is so simple. Have faith, that is all you need. Just believe."

"How can we believe without proof?"

"If you cannot see that this world itself is proof of His

existence, then I say to you that belief needs no proof – if you have faith!"

A babble of voices arose in the room and more of the Wesker mouths were open now as they tried to force their thoughts through the tangled skein of words and separate the thread of truth.

"Can you tell us, Garth?" Itin asked, and the sound of his voice quieted the hubbub.

"I can tell you to use the scientific method which can examine all things – including itself – and give you answers that can prove the truth or falsity of any statement."

"That is what we must do," Itin said, "we had reached the same conclusion." He held a thick book before him and a ripple of nods ran across the watchers. "We have been studying the bible as Father Mark told us to do, and we have found the answer. God will make a miracle for us, thereby proving that He is watching us. And by this sign we will know Him and go to Him."

"That is the sin of false pride," Father Mark said. "God needs no miracles to prove His existence."

"But *we* need a miracle!" Itin shouted, and though he wasn't human there was need in his voice. "We have read here of many smaller miracles, loaves, fishes, wine, snakes – many of them, for much smaller reasons. Now all He need do is make a miracle and He will bring us all to Him – the wonder of an entire new world worshipping at His throne, as you have told us, Father Mark. And you have told us how important this is. We have discussed this and find that there is only one miracle that is best for this kind of thing."

His boredom at the theological wrangling drained from Garth in an instant. He had not been really thinking or he would have realized where all this was leading. He could see the illustration in the bible where Itin held it open, and knew in advance what picture it was. He rose slowly from his chair, as if stretching, and turned to the priest behind him.

"Get ready!" he whispered. "Get out the back and get

to the ship; I'll keep them busy here. I don't think they'll harm me."

"What do you mean?" Father Mark asked, blinking in surprise.

"Get out, you fool!" Garth hissed. "What miracle do you think they mean? What miracle is supposed to have converted the world to Christianity?"

"No!" Father Mark said. "It cannot be. It just cannot be . . . !"

"GET MOVING!" Garth shouted, dragging the priest from the chair and hurling him towards the rear wall. Father Mark stumbled to a halt, turned back. Garth leaped for him, but it was already too late. The amphibians were small, but there were so many of them. Garth lashed out and his fist struck Itin, hurling him back into the crowd. The others came on as he fought his way towards the priest. He beat at them but it was like struggling against waves. The furry, musky bodies washed over and engulfed him. He fought until they tied him, and he still struggled until they beat on his head until he stopped. Then they pulled him outside where he could only lie in the rain and curse and watch.

Of course the Weskers were marvellous craftsmen, and everything had been constructed down to the last detail, following the illustration in the bible. There was the cross, planted firmly on the top of a small hill, the gleaming metal spikes, the hammer. Father Mark was stripped and draped in a carefully pleated loincloth. They led him out of the church.

At the sight of the cross he almost fainted. After that he held his head high and determined to die as he had lived, with faith.

Yet this was hard. It was unbearable even for Garth, who only watched. It is one thing to talk of crucifixion and look at the gentle carved bodies in the dim light of prayer. It is another to see a man naked, ropes cutting into his skin where he hangs from a bar of wood. And to see the needle-tipped spike raised and placed against the soft flesh of his palm, to see the hammer come back with the calm deliberation of an artisan's measured stroke. To hear the thick sound of metal penetrating flesh.

Then to hear the screams.

Few are born to be martyrs; Father Mark was not one of them. With the first blows, the blood ran from his lips where his clenched teeth met. Then his mouth was wide and his head strained back and the guttural horror of his screams sliced through the susurration of the falling rain. It resounded as a silent echo from the masses of watching Weskers, for whatever emotion opened their mouths was now tearing at their bodies with all its force, and row after row of gaping jaws reflected the crucified priest's agony.

Mercifully he fainted as the last nail was driven home. Blood ran from the raw wounds, mixing with the rain to drop faintly pink from his feet as the life ran out of him. At this time, somewhere at this time, sobbing and tearing at his own bonds, numbed from the blows on the head, Garth lost consciousness.

He awoke in his own warehouse and it was dark. Someone was cutting away the woven ropes they had bound him with. The rain still dripped and splashed outside.

"Itin," he said. It could be no one else.

"Yes," the alien voice whispered back. "The others are all talking in the church. Lin died after you struck his head, and Inon is very sick. There are some that say you should be crucified too, and I think that is what will happen. Or perhaps killed by stoning on the head. They have found in the bible where it says . . ."

"I know." With infinite weariness. "An eye for an eye. You'll find lots of things like that once you start looking. It's a wonderful book." His head ached terribly.

"You must go, you can get to your ship without anyone seeing you. There has been enough killing." Itin as well, spoke with a new-found weariness.

Garth experimented, pulling himself to his feet. He pressed his head to the rough wood of the wall until the nausea stopped. "He's dead." He said it as a statement, not a question.

"Yes, some time ago. Or I could not have come away to see you."

"And buried of course, or they wouldn't be thinking about starting on me next."

"And buried!" There was almost a ring of emotion in the alien's voice, an echo of the dead priest's. "He is buried and he will rise on high. It is written and that is the way it will happen. Father Mark will be so happy that it has happened like this." The voice ended in a sound like a human sob.

Garth painfully worked his way towards the door, leaning against the wall so he wouldn't fall.

"We did the right thing, didn't we?" Itin asked. There was no answer. "He will rise up, Garth, won't he rise?"

Garth was at the door and enough light came from the brightly lit church to show his torn and bloody hands clutching at the frame. Itin's face swam into sight close to his, and Garth felt the delicate, many fingered hands with the sharp nails catch at his clothes.

"He will rise, won't he, Garth?"

"No," Garth said, "he is going to stay buried right where you put him. Nothing is going to happen because he is dead and he is going to stay dead."

The rain runnelled through Itin's fur and his mouth was opened so wide that he seemed to be screaming into the night. Only with effort could he talk, squeezing out the alien thoughts in an alien language.

"Then we will not be saved? We will not become pure?"

"You were pure," Garth said, in a voice somewhere between a sob and a laugh. "That's the horrible ugly dirty part of it. You were pure. Now you are . . ."

"Murderers," Itin said, and the water ran down from his lowered head and streamed away into the darkness.

Lucy Comes to Stay
Introduction

I used to read The Pan Book of Horror Stories *under my desk during maths lessons at school, and while I grew up to be monstrously bad at maths, there is no question how widely the series opened my eyes to the wonderful world of dark cellars and dripping things and less-than-genial psychopaths.*

Robert Bloch, the creator of that classic shocker Psycho *is the undisputed master of the psychopathic tale. Although he is best known for the nutty knife-wielding Norman, however, he hasn't been resting on his shower-curtains. Recently he published a supernatural thriller,* Lori, *and he has added* Psycho House *to the Bates Motel saga. He is also reworking* Dr Jekyll and Mr Hyde *with Andre Norton.*

Robert Bloch is a resident of Los Angeles, California, which is fertile territory for any writer with a special interest in fruitcakes. "Lucy Comes to Stay" *shows him on top schizophrenic form.*

GRAHAM MASTERTON
Author of The Manitou, Mirror *and* Walkers

Robert Bloch

Lucy Comes to Stay

"You can't go on this way."

Lucy kept her voice down low, because she knew the nurse had her room just down the hall from mine, and I wasn't supposed to see any visitors.

"But George is doing everything he can – poor dear, I hate to think of what all those doctors and specialists are costing him, and the sanatorium bill too. And now that nurse, that Miss Higgins, staying here every day."

"It won't do any good. You know it won't." Lucy didn't sound like she was arguing with me. She *knew*. That's because Lucy is smarter than I am. Lucy wouldn't have started the drinking and gotten into such a mess in the first place. So it was about time I listened to what she said.

"Look, Vi," she murmured. "I hate to tell you this. You aren't well, you know. But you're going to find out one of these days anyway, and you might as well hear it from me."

"What is it, Lucy?"

"About George, and the doctors. They don't think you're going to get well." She paused. "They don't want you to."

"Oh, Lucy!"

"Listen to me, you little fool. Why do you suppose they sent you to that sanatorium in the first place? They said it was to take the cure. So you took it. All right, you're cured, then. But you'll notice that you still have the doctor coming every day, and George makes you stay here in your room, and that Miss Higgins who's supposed to be a special nurse – you know what she is, don't you? She's a guard."

I couldn't say anything. I just sat there and blinked. I wanted to cry, but I couldn't, because deep down inside I knew that Lucy was right.

"Just try to get out of here," Lucy said. "You'll see how fast she locks the door on you. All that talk about special diets and rest doesn't fool me. Look at yourself – you're as well as I am! You ought to be getting out, seeing people, visiting your friends."

"But I have no friends," I reminded her. "Not after that party, not after what I did – "

"That's a lie," Lucy nodded. "That's what George wants you to think. Why, you have hundreds of friends, Vi. They still love you. They tried to see you at the hospital and George wouldn't let them in. They sent flowers to the sanatorium and George told the nurses to burn them."

"He did? He told the nurses to burn the flowers?"

"Of course. Look, Vi, it's about time you faced the truth. George wants them to think you're sick. George wants you to think you're sick. Why? Because, then he can put you away for good. Not in a private sanatorium, but in the – "

"No!" I began to shake. I couldn't stop shaking. It was ghastly. But it proved something. They told me at the sanatorium, the doctors told me, that if I took the cure I wouldn't get the shakes any more. Or the dreams, or any of the other things. Yet here it was – I was shaking again.

"Shall I tell you some more?" Lucy whispered. "Shall I tell you what they're putting in your food? Shall I tell you about George and Miss Higgins?"

"But she's older than he is, and besides he'd never – "

Lucy laughed.

"Stop it!" I yelled.

"All right. But don't yell, you little fool. Do you want Miss Higgins to come in?"

"She thinks I'm taking a nap. She gave me a sedative."

"Lucky I dumped it out." Lucy frowned. "Vi, I've got to get you away from here. And there isn't much time."

She was right. There wasn't much time. Seconds, minutes, hours, days, weeks – how long had it been since I'd had a drink?

"We'll sneak off," Lucy said. "We could take a room together where they wouldn't find us. I'll nurse you until you're well."

"But rooms cost money."

"You have that fifty dollars George gave you for a party dress – the one you didn't buy."

"Why Lucy," I said. "How did you know that?"

"You told me ages ago, dear. Poor thing, you don't remember things very well, do you? All the more reason for trusting me."

I nodded. I could trust Lucy. Even though she was responsible, in a way, for me starting to drink. She just had thought it would cheer me up when George brought all his high-class friends to the house and we went out to impress his clients. Lucy had tried to help. I could trust her. I must trust her –

"We can leave as soon as Miss Higgins goes tonight," Lucy was saying. "We'll wait until George is asleep, eh? Why not get dressed now, and I'll come back for you."

I got dressed. It ain't easy to dress when you have the shakes, because your hair keeps falling down and you can't find all the snaps on your dress.

But I did it. I even put on some makeup and trimmed my hair a little with the big scissors. Then I looked at myself in the mirror and said out loud, "Why, you can't tell, can you?"

"Of course not," said Lucy. "You look radiant. Positively radiant."

I stood there smiling, and the sun was going down, just shining through the window on the scissors in a way that hurt my eyes, and all at once I was so sleepy.

"George will be here soon, and Miss Higgins will leave," Lucy said. "I'd better go now. Why don't you rest until I come for you?"

"Yes," I said. "You'll be very careful?"

"Very careful," Lucy whispered, and tiptoed out quietly.

I lay down on the bed and then I was sleeping, really sleeping for the first time in weeks, sleeping so the scissors wouldn't hurt my eyes, the way George hurt me inside when he wanted to shut me up in the asylum so he and Miss Higgins could make love on my bed and laugh at me the way they all laughed except Lucy and she would take care of me she knew what to do now I could trust her when George came and I must sleep and sleep and nobody can blame you for what you think in your sleep or do in your sleep . . .

It was all right until I had the dreams, and even then I didn't really worry about them because a dream is only a dream and when I was drunk I had a lot of dreams and that's how I got into trouble because people didn't understand but I knew I was all right.

When I woke up I had the shakes again, but it was Lucy shaking me, standing there in the dark shaking me. I looked around and saw that the door to my room was open, but Lucy didn't bother to whisper.

She stood there with the scissors in her hand and called to me.

"Come on, let's hurry."

What are you doing with the scissors?" I asked.

"Cutting the telephone wires, silly! I got into the kitchen after Miss Higgins left and dumped some of that sedative into George's coffee. Remember, I told you the plan."

I couldn't remember now, but I knew it was all right. Lucy and I went out through the hall, past George's room, and he never stirred. Then we went downstairs and out the front door and the street lights hurt my eyes. Lucy made me hurry right along, though.

We took a streetcar around the corner. It was crowded, but I managed to find a seat next to a fat man. Lucy just stood there, and when I wanted to talk she put her hand up to her lips, quickly, and I kept silent.

This was the difficult part, getting away. Once we were out of the neighbourhood, there'd be no worry. The wires were cut.

The lady at the rooming house on the South Side didn't know about the wires being cut. She didn't know about me, either, because Lucy got the room.

Lucy marched in bold as brass and laid my fifty dollars down on the desk. The rent was $12.50 a week in advance, and Lucy didn't even ask to see the room. I guess that's why the landlady wasn't worried about baggage.

We got upstairs and locked the door, and then I had the shakes again.

Lucy said, "Vi – cut it out!"

"But I can't help it. What'll I do now, Lucy? Oh, what'll I do? Why did I ever let myself – "

"Shut up!" Lucy opened my purse and pulled something out. I had been wondering why my purse felt so heavy but I never dreamed about the secret.

She held the secret up. It glittered under the light, like the scissors, only this was a nice glittering. A golden glittering.

"A whole pint!" I gasped. "Where did you get it?"

"From the cupboard downstairs, naturally. You knew George still keeps the stuff around. I slipped it into your purse, just in case."

I had the shakes, but I got that bottle open in ten seconds. One of my fingernails broke, and then the stuff was burning and warming and softening –

"Pig!" said Lucy.

"You know I had to have it," I whispered. "That's why you brought it."

"I don't like to see you drink," Lucy answered. "I never drink and I don't like to see you hang one on, either."

"Please, Lucy. Just this once."

"Why can't you take a shot and then leave it alone? That's all I ask."

"Just this once, Lucy, I have to."

"I won't sit here and watch you make a spectacle of yourself. You know what always happens – another mess."

I took another gulp. The bottle was half empty.

"I did all I could for you, Vi. But if you don't stop now, I'm going."

That made me pause. "You couldn't do that to me. I need you, Lucy. Until I'm straightened out, anyway."

Lucy laughed, the way I didn't like. "Straightened out! That's a hot one! Talking about straightening out with a bottle in your hand. It's no use, Vi. Here I do everything I can for you, I stop at nothing to get you away, and you're off on another bender."

"Please. You know I can't help it."

"Oh yes you can help it, Vi. But you don't want to. You've always had to make a choice, you know. George or the bottle. Me or the bottle. And the bottle always wins. I think deep down inside you hate George. You hate me."

"You're my best friend."

"Nuts!" Lucy talked vulgar sometimes, when she got really mad. And she was mad, now. It made me so nervous I had another drink.

"Oh, I'm good enough for you when you're in trouble, or have nobody else around to talk to. I'm good enough to lie for you, pull you out of your messes. But I've never been good enough for your friends, for George. And I can't even win out over a bottle of rotgut whisky. It's no use, Vi. What I've done for you today you'll never know. And it isn't enough. Keep your lousy whisky. I'm going."

I know I started to cry. I tried to get up, but the room was turning round and round. Then Lucy was walking out the door and I dropped the bottle and the light kept shining the way it did on the scissors and I closed my eyes and dropped after the bottle to the floor . . .

When I woke up they were all pestering me, the landlady and the doctor and Miss Higgins and the man who said he was a policeman.

I wondered if Lucy had gone to them and betrayed me, but when I asked the doctor said no, they just discovered me through a routine checkup on hotels and rooming-houses after they found George's body in his bed with my scissors in his throat.

All at once I knew what Lucy had done, and why she ran out on me that way. She knew they'd find me and call it murder.

So I told them about her and how it must have happened. I even figured out how Lucy managed to get my fingerprints on the scissors.

But Miss Higgins said she'd never seen Lucy in my house, and the landlady told a lie and said I had registered for the room alone, and the man from the police just laughed when I kept begging him to find Lucy and make her tell the truth.

Only the doctor seemed to understand, and when we were alone together in the little room he asked me all about her and what she looked like, and I told him.

Then he brought over the mirror and held it up and asked me if I could see her. And sure enough –

She was standing right behind me, laughing. I could see her in the mirror and I told the doctor so, and he said yes, he thought he understood now.

So it was all right after all. Even when I got the shakes just then and dropped the mirror, so that the little jagged pieces hurt my eyes to look at, it was all right.

Lucy was back with me now, and she wouldn't ever go away any more. She'd stay with me for ever. I knew that. I knew it, because even though the light hurt my eyes, Lucy began to laugh.

After a minute, I began to laugh, too. And then the two of us were laughing together, we couldn't stop even when the doctor went away. We just stood there against the bars, Lucy and I, laughing like crazy.

The Fly
Introduction

Jeff Goldblum handed me this story while we were on a plane together sometime during the pre-production of my own movie version of The Fly. *I had heard of it, of course, and knew that it was the basis of the original 1958 version of the movie, whose screenplay was written by the novelist James Clavell. Somehow I had never gotten around to reading it.*

I was immediately struck by how polite and Victorian – and yes, stodgy – in tone the writing was. Though dealing with madness, murder, suicide and mutilation, Langelaan is never out of control, and neither are his characters; logic is the ruling principle – a strange approach to what is truly a very grotesque and provocative premise.

The Hollywood film was also genteel, probably the most polite horror film of substance ever made; yet despite the film's unwillingness to go quite all the way with the heroine's fate, the film remains a more passionate experience, possibly because certain key incidents are depicted with an immediacy and elaboration of detail that the story steps back from, preferring to present them as anecdotes recounted in safety rather than moments of intense involvement for the reader.

It's interesting to note that almost all the wonderful stuff in the movie is also in the story in one way or another: even the strange name of the cat (not "Fluffy", but "Dandelo"), even the much-remembered (though entomologically laughable) fly's POV shot of Madame Delambre, which is suggested by a comment of Monsieur Delambre concerning newly-developed problems with his eyesight (I can say no more).

"Help me, please help me!" is not in the story, and this is the key to its odd character. Because the reader is in effect shielded from the worst – and most cathartic moment – by the

writer, the story hums along like a perfectly functioning, inexorable little machine whose most telling moments come later, in the middle of the night, when it buzzes around your ears, wakes you up, and refuses to be swatted so that you can go back to sleep.

DAVID CRONENBERG
Writer/director of Videodrome, The Fly *and* Dead Ringers

George Langelaan

The Fly

Telephones and telephone bells have always made me uneasy. Years ago, when they were mostly wall fixtures, I disliked them, but nowadays, when they are planted in every nook and corner, they are a downright intrusion. We have a saying in France that a coalman is master in his own house; with the telephone that is no longer true, and I suspect that even the Englishman is no longer king in his own castle.

At the office, the sudden ringing of the telephone annoys me. It means that, no matter what I am doing, in spite of the switchboard operator, in spite of my secretary, in spite of doors and walls, some unknown person is coming into the room and on to my desk to talk right into my very ear, confidentially – and that whether I like it or not. At home, the feeling is still more disagreeable, but the worst is when the telephone rings in the dead of night. If anyone could see me turn on the light and get up blinking to answer it, I suppose I would look like any other sleepy man annoyed at being disturbed. The truth in such a case, however, is that I am struggling against panic, fighting down a feeling that a stranger has broken into the house and is in my bedroom. By the time I manage to grab the receiver and say, "*Ici Monsieur Delambre. Je vous écoute,*" I am outwardly calm, but I only get back to a more normal state when I recognize the voice at the other end and when I know what is wanted of me.

This effort at dominating a purely animal reaction and fear had become so effective that when my sister-in-law called me at two in the morning, asking me to come over, but first to warn the police that she had just killed my brother, I quietly asked her how and why she had killed André.

"But, François! . . . I can't explain all that over the telephone. Please call the police and come quickly."

"Maybe I had better see your first, Hélène?"

"No, you'd better call the police first; otherwise they will start asking you all sorts of awkward questions. They'll have enough trouble as it is to believe that I did it alone. . . . And, by the way, I suppose you ought to tell them that André . . . André's body, is down at the factory. They may want to go there first."

"Did you say that André is at the factory?"

"Yes . . . under the steam-hammer."

"Under the what?"

"The steam-hammer! But don't ask so many questions. Please come quickly François! Please understand that I'm afraid . . . that my nerves won't stand it much longer!"

Have you ever tried to explain to a sleepy police officer that your sister-in-law has just phoned to say that she has killed your brother with a steam-hammer? I repeated my explanation, but he would not let me.

"*Oui, Monsieur, oui*, I hear . . . but who are you? What is your name? Where do you live? I said, where do you live!"

It was then that Commissaire Charas took over the line and the whole business. He at least seemed to understand everything. Would I wait for him? Yes, he would pick me up and take me over to my brother's house. When? In five or ten minutes.

I had just managed to pull on my trousers, wriggle into a sweater and grab a hat and coat, when a black Citroën, headlights blazing, pulled up at the door.

"I assume you have a night watchman at your factory, Monsieur Delambre. Has he called you?" asked Commissaire Charas, letting in the clutch as I sat down beside him and slammed the door of the car.

"No, he hasn't. Though of course my brother could have entered the factory through his laboratory where he often works late at night . . . all night sometimes."

"Is Professor Delambre's work connected with your business?"

"No, my brother is, or was, doing research work for the *Ministère de l'Air*. As he wanted to be away from Paris and yet within reach of where skilled workmen could fix up or make gadgets big and small for his experiments, I offered him one of the old workshops of the factory and he came to live in the first house built by our grandfather on the top of the hill at the back of the factory."

"Yes, I see. Did he talk about his work? What sort of research work?"

"He rarely talked about it, you know; I suppose the Air Ministry could tell you. I only know that he was about to carry out a number of experiments he had been preparing for some months, something to do with the disintegration of matter, he told me."

Barely slowing down, the commissaire swung the car off the road, slid it through the open factory gate and pulled up sharp by a policeman apparently expecting him.

I did not need to hear the policeman's confirmation. I knew now that my brother was dead, it seemed that I had been told years ago. Shaking like a leaf, I scrambled out after the commissaire.

Another policeman stepped out of a doorway and led us towards one of the shops where all the lights had been turned on. More policemen were standing by the hammer, watching two men setting up a camera. It was tilted downward, and I made an effort to look.

It was far less horrid than I had expected. Though I had never seen my brother drunk, he looked just as if he were sleeping off a terrific binge, flat on his stomach across the narrow line on which the white-hot slabs of metal were rolled up to the hammer. I saw at a glance that his head and arm could only be a flattened mess, but that seemed quite impossible; it looked as if he had somehow pushed his head and arm right into the metallic mass of the hammer.

Having talked to his colleagues, the commissaire turned towards me.

"How can we raise the hammer, Monsieur Delambre?"

"I'll raise it for you."

"Would you like us to get one of your men over?"

"No, I'll be all right. Look, here is the switchboard. It was originally a steam-hammer, but everything is worked electrically here now. Look, Commissaire, the hammer has been set at fifty tons and its impact at zero."

"At zero . . . ?"

"Yes, level with the ground if you prefer. It is also set for single strokes, which means that it has to be raised after each blow. I don't know what Hélène, my sister-in-law, will have to say about all this, but one thing I am sure of: she certainly did not know how to set and operate the hammer."

"Perhaps it was set that way last night when work stopped?"

"Certainly not. The drop is never set at zero, Monsieur le Commissaire."

"I see. Can it be raised gently?"

"No. The speed of the upstroke cannot be regulated. But in any case it is not very fast when the hammer is set for single strokes."

"Right. Will you show me what to do? It won't be very nice to watch, you know."

"No, no, Monsieur le Commissaire. I'll be all right."

"All set?" asked the Commissaire of the others. "All right then, Monsieur Delambre. Whenever you like."

Watching my brother's back, I slowly but firmly pushed the upstroke button.

The unusual silence of the factory was broken by the sigh of compressed air rushing into the cylinders, a sigh that always makes me think of a giant taking a deep breath before solemnly socking another giant, and the steel mass of the hammer shuddered and then rose swiftly. I also heard the sucking sound as it left the metal base and thought I was going to panic when I saw André's body heave forward as a sickly gush of blood poured all over the ghastly mess bared by the hammer.

"No danger of it coming down again, Monsieur Delambre?"

"No, none whatever," I mumbled as I threw the safety switch and, turning around, I was violently sick in front of a young green-faced policeman.

For weeks after, Commissaire Charas worked on the case, listening, questioning, running all over the place, making out reports, telegraphing and telephoning right and left. Later, we became quite friendly and he owned that he had for a long time considered me as suspect number one, but had finally given up that idea because, not only was there no clue of any sort, but not even a motive.

Hélène, my sister-in-law, was so calm throughout the whole business that the doctors finally confirmed what I had long considered the only possible solution: that she was mad. That being the case, there was of course no trial.

My brother's wife never tried to defend herself in any way and even got quite annoyed when she realized that people thought her mad, and this of course was considered proof that she was indeed mad. She owned up to the murder of her husband and proved easily that she knew how to handle the hammer; but she would never say why, exactly how, or under what circumstances she had killed my brother. The great mystery was how and why had my brother so obligingly stuck his head under the hammer, the only possible explanation for his part in the drama.

The night watchman had heard the hammer all right; he had even heard it twice, he claimed. This was very strange, and the stroke-counter which was always set back to naught after a job, seemed to prove him right, since it marked the figure two. Also, the foreman in charge of the hammer confirmed that after cleaning up the day before the murder, he had as usual turned the stroke-counter back to naught. In spite of this, Hélène maintained that she had only used the hammer once, and this seemed just another proof of her insanity.

Commissaire Charas who had been put in charge of the case at first wondered if the victim were really my brother. But of that there was no possible doubt, if only because of the great scar running from his knee to his thigh, the result of a shell that had landed within a few feet of him during the retreat in 1940; and there were also the fingerprints of his left hand which corresponded to those found all over his laboratory and his personal belongings up at the house.

A guard had been put on his laboratory and the next day half a dozen officials came down from the Air Ministry. They went through all his papers and took away some of his instruments, but before leaving they told the commissaire that the most interesting documents and instruments had been destroyed.

The Lyons police laboratory, one of the most famous in the world, reported that André's head had been wrapped up in a piece of velvet when it was crushed by the hammer, and one day Commissaire Charas showed me a tattered drapery which I immediately recognized as the brown velvet cloth I had seen on a table in my brother's laboratory, the one on which his meals were served when he could not leave his work.

After only a very few days in prison, Hélène had been transferred to a nearby asylum, one of the three in France where insane criminals are taken care of. My nephew Henri, a boy of six, the very image of his father, was entrusted to me, and eventually all legal arrangements were made for me to become his guardian and tutor.

Hélène, one of the quietest patients of the asylum, was allowed visitors and I went to see her on Sundays. Once or twice the commissaire had accompanied me and, later, I learned that he had also visited Hélène alone. But we were never able to obtain any information from my sister-in-law who seemed to have become utterly indifferent. She rarely answered my questions and hardly ever those of the commissaire. She spent a lot of her time sewing, but her favourite pastime seemed to be catching flies which she invariably released unharmed after having examined them carefully.

Hélène only had one fit of raving – more like a nervous breakdown than a fit said the doctor who had administered morphia to quieten her – the day she saw a nurse swatting flies.

The day after Hélène's one and only fit, Commissaire Charas came to see me.

"I have a strange feeling that there lies the key to the whole business, Monsieur Delambre," he said.

I did not ask him how it was that he already knew all about Hélène's fit.

"I do not follow you, Commissaire. Poor Madame Delambre could have shown an exceptional interest for anything else, really. Don't you think that flies just happen to be the border-subject of her tendency to raving?"

"Do you believe she is really mad?" he asked.

"My dear Commissaire, I don't see how there can be any doubt. Do you doubt it?"

"I don't know. In spite of all the doctors say, I have the impression that Madame Delambre has a very clear brain . . . even when catching flies."

"Supposing you were right, how would you explain her attitude with regard to her little boy? She never seems to consider him as her own child."

"You know, Monsieur Delambre, I have thought about that also. She may be trying to protect him. Perhaps she fears the boy or, for all we know, hates him?"

"I'm afraid I don't understand, my dear Commissaire."

"Have you noticed, for instance, that she never catches flies when the boy is there?"

"No. But come to think of it, you are quite right. Yes, that is strange . . . Still, I fail to understand."

"So do I, Monsieur Delambre. And I'm very much afraid that we shall never understand, unless perhaps your sister-in-law should *get better*."

"The doctors seem to think that there is no hope of any sort, you know."

"Yes. Do you know if your brother ever experimented with flies?"

"I really don't know, but I shouldn't think so. Have you asked the Air Ministry people? They knew all about the work."

"Yes, and they laughed at me."

"I can understand that."

"You are very fortunate to understand anything. Monsieur Delambre. I do not . . . but I hope to some day."

"Tell me, Uncle, do flies live a long time?"

We were just finishing our lunch and, following an established tradition between us, I was just pouring some wine into Henri's glass for him to dip a biscuit in.

Had Henri not been staring at his glass gradually being filled to the brim, something in my look might have frightened him.

This was the first time that he had ever mentioned flies, and I shuddered at the thought that Commissaire Charas might quite easily have been present. I could imagine the glint in his eye as he would have answered my nephew's question with another question. I could almost hear him saying,

"I don't know, Henri. Why do you ask?"

"Because I have again seen the fly that *Maman* was looking for."

And it was only after drinking off Henri's own glass of wine that I realized that he had answered my spoken thought.

"I did not know that your mother was looking for a fly."

"Yes, she was. It has grown quite a lot, but I recognized it all right."

"Where did you see this fly, Henri, and . . . how did you recognize it?"

"This morning on your desk, Uncle François. Its head is white instead of black, and it has a funny sort of leg."

Feeling more and more like Commissaire Charas, but trying to look unconcerned, I went on:

"And when did you see this fly for the first time?"

"The day that Papa went away. I had caught it, but *Maman* made me let it go. And then after, she wanted me to find it again. She'd changed her mind." And shrugging his shoulders just as my brother used to, he added, "You know what women are."

"I think that fly must have died long ago, and you must

be mistaken, Henri," I said, getting up and walking to the door.

But as soon as I was out of the dining room, I ran up the stairs to my study. There was no fly anywhere to be seen.

I was bothered, far more than I cared to even think about. Henri had just proved that Charas was really closer to a clue than had seemed when he told me about his thoughts concerning Hélène's pastime.

For the first time I wondered if Charas did not really know much more than he let on. For the first time also, I wondered about Hélène. Was she really insane? A strange, horrid feeling was growing on me, and the more I thought about it, the more I felt that, somehow, Charas was right: Hélène was *getting away with it*!

What could possibly have been the reason for such a monstrous crime? What had led up to it? Just what had happened?

I thought of all the hundreds of questions that Charas had put to Hélène, sometimes gently like a nurse trying to soothe, sometimes stern and cold, sometimes barking them furiously. Hélène had answered very few, always in a calm quiet voice and never seeming to pay any attention to the way in which the question had been put. Though dazed, she had seemed perfectly sane then.

Refined, well-bred and well-read, Charas was more than just an intelligent police official. He was a keen psychologist and had an amazing way of smelling out a fib or an erroneous statement even before it was uttered. I knew that he had accepted as true the few answers she had given him. But then there had been all those questions which she had never answered: the most direct and important ones. From the very beginning, Hélène had adopted a very simple system. "I cannot answer that question," she would say in her low quiet voice. And that was that! The repetition of the same question never seemed to annoy her. In all the hours of questioning that she underwent, Hélène did not once point out to the commissaire that he had already asked her this or that. She would simply say, "I cannot answer that question," as though it were the very first time that that particular question had been asked and the very first time she had made that answer.

This cliché had become the formidable barrier beyond which Commissaire Charas could not even get a glimpse, an idea of what Hélène might be thinking. She had very willingly answered all questions about her life with my brother – which seemed a happy and uneventful one – up to the time of his end. About his death, however, all that she would say was that she had killed him with the steam-hammer, but she refused to say why, what had led up to the drama and how she got my brother to put his head under it. She never actually refused outright; she would just go blank and, with no apparent emotion, would switch over to, "I cannot answer that question."

Hélène, as I have said, had shown the commissaire that she knew how to set and operate the steam-hammer.

Charas could only find one single fact which did not coincide with Hélène's declarations, the fact that the hammer had been used twice. Charas was no longer willing to attribute this to insanity. That evident flaw in Hélène's stonewall defence seemed a crack which the commissaire might possibly enlarge. But my sister-in-law finally cemented it by acknowledging:

"All right, I lied to you. I did use the hammer twice. But do not ask me why, because I cannot tell you."

"Is that your only . . . mis-statement, Madame Delambre?" had asked the commissaire, trying to follow up what looked at last like an advantage.

"It is . . . and you know it, *Monsieur le Commissaire*."

And, annoyed, Charas had seen that Hélène could read him like an open book.

I had thought of calling on the commissaire, but the knowledge that he would inevitably start questioning Henri made me hesitate. Another reason also made me hesitate, a vague sort of fear that he would look for and find the fly Henri had talked of. And that annoyed me a good deal because I could find no satisfactory explanation for that particular fear.

André was definitely not the absent-minded sort of professor who walks about in pouring rain with a rolled umbrella under his arm. He was human, had a keen sense of humour, loved children and animals and could not bear to see anyone suffer. I had often seen him drop his work to watch a parade of the local fire brigade, or see the *Tour de France* cyclists go by, or even follow a circus parade all around the village. He liked games of logic and precision, such as billiards and tennis, bridge and chess.

How was it then possible to explain his death? What could have made him put his head under that hammer? It could hardly have been the result of some stupid bet or a test of his courage. He hated betting and had no patience with those who indulged in it. Whenever he heard a bet proposed, he would invariably remind all present that, after all, a bet was but a contract between a fool and a swindler, even if it turned out to be a toss-up as to which was which.

It seemed there were only two possible explanations to Anndré's death. Either he had gone mad, or else he had a reason for letting his wife kill him in such a strange and terrible way. And just what could have been his wife's role in all this? They surely could not have been both insane?

Having finally decided not to tell Charas about my nephew's innocent revelations, I thought I myself would try to question Hélène.

She seemed to have been expecting my visit for she came into the parlour almost as soon as I had made myself known to the matron and been allowed inside.

"I wanted to show you my garden," explained Hélène as I looked at the coat slung over her shoulders.

As one of the "reasonable" inmates, she was allowed to go into the garden during certain hours of the day. She had asked for and obtained the right to a little patch of ground where she could grow flowers, and I had sent her seeds and some rosebushes out of my garden.

She took me straight to a rustic wooden bench which had been made in the men's workshop and only just set up under a tree close to her little patch of ground.

Searching for the right way to broach the subject of

André's death, I sat for a while tracing vague designs on the ground with the end of my umbrella.

"François, I want to ask you something," said Hélène after a while.

"Anything I can do for you, Hélène?"

"No, just something I want to know. Do flies live very long?"

Staring at her, I was about to say that her boy had asked the very same question a few hours earlier when I suddenly realized that here was the opening I had been searching for and perhaps even the possibility of striking a great blow, a blow perhaps powerful enough to shatter her stonewall defence, be it sane or insane.

Watching her carefully, I replied:

"I don't really know, Hélène; but the fly you were looking for was in my study this morning."

No doubt about it I had struck a shattering blow. She swung her head round with such force that I heard the bones crack in her neck. She opened her mouth, but said not a word; only her eyes seemed to be screaming with fear.

Yes, it was evident that I had crashed through something, but what? Undoubtedly, the commissaire would have known what to do with such an advantage; I did not. All I knew was that he would never have given her time to think, to recuperate, but all I could do, and even that was a strain, was to maintain my best poker-face, hoping against hope that Hélène's defences would go on crumbling.

She must have been quite a while without breathing, because she suddenly gasped and put both her hands over her still open mouth.

"François . . . Did you kill it?" she whispered, her eyes no longer fixed, but searching every inch of my face.

"No."

"You have it then . . . You have it on you! Give it to me!" she almost shouted touching me with both her hands, and I knew that had she felt strong enough, she would have tried to search me.

"No, Hélène, I haven't got it."

"But you know now . . . You have guessed, haven't you?"

"No, Hélène. I only know one thing, and that is that you are not insane. But I mean to know all, Hélène, and, somehow, I am going to find out. You can choose: either you tell me everything and I'll see what is to be done, or . . ."

"Or what? Say it!"

"I was going to say it, Hélène . . . or I assure you that your friend the commissaire will have that fly first thing tomorrow morning."

She remained quite still, looking down at the palms of her hands on her lap and, although it was getting chilly, her forehead and hands were moist.

Without even brushing aside a wisp of long brown hair blown across her mouth by the breeze, she murmured,

"If I tell you . . . will you promise to destroy that fly before doing anything else?"

"No, Hélène. I can make no such promise before knowing."

"But François, you must understand. I promised André that fly would be destroyed. That promise must be kept and I can say nothing until it is."

I could sense the deadlock ahead. I was not yet losing ground, but I was losing the initiative. I tried a shot in the dark.

"Hélène, of course you understand that as soon as the police examine that fly, they will know that you are not insane, and then . . ."

"François, no! For Henri's sake! Don't you see? I was expecting that fly; I was hoping it would find me here but it couldn't know what had become of me. What else could it do but go to others it loves, to Henri, to you . . . you who might know and understand what was to be done!"

Was she really mad, or was she simulating again? But mad or not, she was cornered. Wondering how to follow up and how to land the knockout blow without running the risk of seeing her slip away out of reach, I said very quietly,

"Tell me all, Hélène. I can then protect your boy."

"Protect my boy from what? Don't you understand that if I am here, it is merely so that Henri won't be the son of a woman who was guillotined for having murdered his father? Don't you understand that I would by far prefer the guillotine to the living death of this lunatic asylum?"

"I understand, Hélène, and I'll do my best for the boy whether you tell me or not. If you refuse to tell me, I'll still do the best I can to protect Henri, but you must understand that the game will be out of my hands, because Commissaire Charas will have the fly."

"But why must you know?" said, rather than asked, my sister-in-law, struggling to control her temper.

"Because I must and will know how and why my brother died, Hélène."

"All right. Take me back to the . . . house. I'll give you what your commissaire would call my 'Confession'."

"Do you mean to say that you have written it!"

"Yes. It was not really meant for you, but more likely for *your friend*, the commissaire. I had foreseen that, sooner or later, he would get too close to the truth."

"You then have no objection to his reading it?"

"You will act as you think fit, François. Wait for me a minute."

Leaving me at the door of the parlour, Hélène ran upstairs to her room. In less than a minute she was back with a large brown envelope.

"Listen, François; you are not nearly as bright as was your poor brother, but you are not unintelligent. All I ask is that you read this alone. After that, you may do as you wish."

"That I promise you, Hélène," I said taking the precious envelope. "I'll read it tonight and although tomorrow is not a visiting day, I'll come down to see you."

"Just as you like," said my sister-in-law without even saying goodbye as she went back upstairs.

It was only on reaching home, as I walked from the garage to the house, that I read the inscription on the envelope:

TO WHOM IT MAY CONCERN
(Probably Commissaire Charas)

Having told the servants that I would have only a light supper to be served immediately in my study and that I was not to be disturbed after, I ran upstairs, threw Hélène's envelope on my desk and made another careful search of the room before closing the shutters and drawing the curtains. All I could find was a long since dead mosquito stuck to the wall near the ceiling.

Having motioned to the servant to put her tray down on a table by the fireplace, I poured myself a glass of wine and locked the door behind her. I then disconnected the telephone – I always did this now at night – and turned out all the lights but the lamp on my desk.

Slitting open Hélène's fat envelope, I extracted a thick wad of closely written pages. I read the following lines neatly centred in the middle of the top page:

This is not a confession because, although I killed my husband, I am not a murderess. I simply and very faithfully carried out his last wish by crushing his head and right arm under the steam-hammer of his brother's factory.

Without even touching the glass of wine by my elbow, I turned the page and started reading.

For very nearly a year before his death (*the manuscript began*), my husband had told me of some of his experiments. He knew full well that his colleagues of the Air Ministry would have forbidden some of them as too dangerous, but he was keen on obtaining positive results before reporting his discovery.

Whereas only sound and pictures had been, so far, transmitted through space by radio and television, André claimed to have discovered a way of transmitting matter. Matter, any solid object, placed in his "transmitter" was instantly disintegrated and reintegrated in a special receiving set.

André considered his discovery as perhaps the most important since that of the wheel sawn off the end of a tree trunk. He reckoned that the transmission of matter by instantaneous "disintegration-reintegration" would completely change life as we had known it so far. It would mean the end of all means of transport, not only of goods including food, but also of human beings. André, the practical scientist who never allowed theories or daydreams to get the better of him, already foresaw the time when there would no longer be any aeroplanes, ships, trains, or cars and, therefore, no longer any roads or railway lines, ports, airports, or stations. All that would be replaced by matter-transmitting and receiving stations throughout the world. Travellers and goods would be placed in special cabins and, at a given signal, would simply disappear and reappear almost immediately at the chosen receiving station.

André's receiving set was only a few feet away from his transmitter, in an adjoining room of his laboratory, and he at first ran into all sorts of snags. His first successful experiment was carried out with an ash tray taken from his desk, a souvenir we had brought back from a trip to London.

That was the first time he told me about his experiments and I had no idea of what he was talking about the day he came dashing into the house and threw the ash tray in my lap.

"Hélène, look! For a fraction of a second, a bare ten-millionth of a second, that ash tray has been completely disintegrated. For one little moment it no longer existed! Gone! Nothing left, absolutely nothing. Only atoms travelling through space at the speed of light! And the moment after, the atoms were once more gathered together in the shape of an ash tray!"

"André, please . . . please! What on earth are you raving about?"

He started sketching all over a letter I had been writing. He laughed at my wry face, swept all my letters off the table and said,

"You don't understand? Right. Let's start all over again. Hélène, do you remember I once read you an article about the mysterious flying stones that seem to come from nowhere in particular, and which are said to occasionally fall in certain houses in India? They come flying in as though thrown from outside and that, in spite of closed doors and windows."

"Yes, I remember. I also remember that Professor Augier, your friend of the *Collège de France*, who had come down for a few days, remarked that if there was no trickery about it, the only possible explanation was that the stones had been disintegrated after having been thrown from outside, come through the walls, and then been reintegrated before hitting the floor or the opposite walls."

"That's right. And I added that there was, of course, one other possibility, namely the momentary and partial disintegration of the walls as the stone or stones came through."

"Yes, André. I remember all that, and I suppose you also remember that I failed to understand, and that you got quite annoyed. Well, I still do not understand why and how, even disintegrated, stones should be able to come through a wall or a closed door."

"But it is possible, Hélène, because the atoms that go to make up matter are not close together like the bricks of a wall. They are separated by relative immensities of space."

"Do you mean to say that you have disintegrated that ash tray, and then put it together again after pushing it through something?"

"Precisely, Hélène. I projected it through the wall that separates my transmitter from my receiving set."

"And would it be foolish to ask how humanity is to benefit from ash trays that can go through walls?"

André seemed quite offended, but he soon saw that I was only teasing and again waxing enthusiastic, he told me of some of the possibilities of his discovery.

"Isn't it wonderful, Hélène?" he finally gasped, out of breath.

"Yes, André. But I hope you won't ever transmit me; I'd be too much afraid of coming out at the other end like your ash tray."

"What do you mean?"

"Do you remember what was written under that ash tray?"

"Yes, of course: Made in Japan. That was the great joke of our typically British souvenir."

"The words are still there, André; but . . . look!"

He took the ash tray out of my hands, frowned, and walked over to the window. Then he went quite pale, and I knew that he had seen what had proved to me that he had indeed carried out a strange experiment.

The three words were still there, but reversed and reading:

Made in Japan

Without a word, having completely forgotten me, André rushed off to his laboratory. I only saw him the next morning, tired and unshaven after a whole night's work.

A few days later André had a new reverse which put him out of sorts and made him fussy and grumpy for several weeks. I stood it patiently enough for a while, but being myself bad tempered one evening, we had a silly row over some futile thing, and I reproached him for his moroseness.

"I'm sorry, *chérie*. I've been working my way through a maze of problems and have given you all a very rough time. You see, my very first experiment with a live animal proved a complete fiasco."

"André! You tried that experiment with Dandelo, didn't you?"

"Yes. How did you know?" he answered sheepishly. "He disintegrated perfectly, but he never reappeared in the receiving set."

"Oh, André! What became of him then?"

"Nothing . . . there is just no more Dandelo; only the dispersed atoms of a cat wandering, God knows where, in the universe."

Dandelo was a small white cat the cook had found one morning in the garden and which we had promptly adopted. Now I knew how it had disappeared and was quite angry about the whole thing, but my husband was so miserable over it all that I said nothing.

I saw little of my husband during the next few weeks. He had most of his meals sent down to the laboratory. I would often wake up in the morning and find his bed unslept in. Sometimes, if he had come in very late, I would find that storm-swept appearance which only a man can give a bedroom by getting up very early and fumbling around in the dark.

One evening he came home to dinner all smiles, and I knew that his troubles were over. His face dropped, however, when he saw I was dressed for going out.

"Oh. Were you going out, Hélène?"

"Yes, the Drillons invited me for a game of bridge, but I can easily phone them and put it off."

"No, it's all right."

"It isn't all right. Out with it, dear!"

"Well, I've at last got everything perfect and I wanted you to be the first to see the miracle."

"*Magnifique*, André! Of course I'll be delighted."

Having telephoned our neighbours to say how sorry I was and so forth, I ran down to the kitchen and told the cook that she had exactly ten minutes in which to prepare a "celebration dinner".

"An excellent idea, Hélène," said my husband when the maid appeared with the champagne after our candlelight dinner. "We'll celebrate with reintegrated champagne!" and taking the tray from the maid's hands, he led the way down to the laboratory.

"Do you think it will be as good as before its disintegration?" I asked, holding the tray while he opened the door and switched on the lights.

"Have no fear. You'll see! Just bring it here, will you," he said, opening the door of a telephone call-box he had bought and which had been transformed into what he called a transmitter. "Put it down on that now," he added, putting a stool inside the box.

Having carefully closed the door, he took me to the other end of the room and handed me a pair of very dark sun glasses. He put on another pair and walked back to a switchboard by the transmitter.

"Ready, Hélène?" said my husband, turning out all the lights. "Don't remove your glasses till I give the word."

"I won't budge, André. Go on," I told him, my eyes
fixed on the tray which I could just see in a greenish shimmering light through the glass panelled door of the telephone booth.

"Right, said André throwing a switch.

The whole room was brilliantly illuminated by an orange
flash. Inside the booth I had seen a crackling ball of fire
and felt its heat on my face, neck, and hands. The whole
thing lasted but the fraction of a second, and I found myself
blinking at green-edged black holes like those one sees after
having stared at the sun.

"*Et voilà!* You can take off your glasses, Hélène."

A little theatrically perhaps, my husband opened the door
of the booth. Though André had told me what to expect,
I was astonished to find that the champagne, glasses, tray,
and stool were no longer there.

André ceremoniously led me by the hand into the next
room in a corner of which stood a second telephone booth.
Opening the door wide, he triumphantly lifted the champagne tray off the stool.

Feeling somewhat like the good-natured kind-member-
of-the-audience who has been dragged on to the music hall
stage by the magician, I refrained from saying "All done
with mirrors", which I knew would have annoyed my
husband.

"Sure it's not dangerous to drink?" I asked as the cork
popped.

"Absolutely sure, Hélène," he said handing me a glass.
"But that was nothing. Drink this off and I'll show you
something much more astounding."

We went back into the other room.

"Oh, André! Remember poor Dandelo!"

"This is only a guinea pig, Hélène. But I'm positive it
will go through all right."

He set the furry little beast down on the green enamelled
floor of the booth and quickly closed the door. I again put
on my dark glasses and saw and felt the vivid crackling
flash.

Without waiting for André to open the door, I rushed

into the next room where the lights were still on and looked into the receiving booth.

"Oh, André! *Chéri!* He's there all right!" I shouted excitedly, watching the little animal trotting round and round. "It's wonderful, André. It works! You've succeeded!"

"I hope so, but I must be patient. I'll know for sure in a few weeks' time."

"What do you mean? Look! He's as full of life as when you put him in the other booth."

"Yes, so he seems. But we'll have to see if all his organs are intact, and that will take some time. If that little beast is still full of life in a month's time, we then consider the experiment a success."

I begged André to let me take care of the guinea pig.

"All right, but don't kill it by overfeeding," he agreed with a grin for my enthusiasm.

Though not allowed to take Hop-la – the name I had given the guinea pig – out of its box in the laboratory, I tied a pink ribbon round its neck and was allowed to feed it twice a day.

Hop-la soon got used to its pink ribbon and became quite a tame little pet, but that month of waiting seemed a year.

And then one day, André put Miquette, our cocker spaniel, into his "transmitter". He had not told me beforehand, knowing full well that I would never have agreed to such an experiment with our dog. But when he did tell me, Miquette had been successfully transmitted half a dozen times and seemed to be enjoying the operation thoroughly; no sooner was she let out of the "reintegrator" than she dashed madly into the next room, scratching at the "transmitter" door to have "another go", as André called it.

I now expected that my husband would invite some of his colleagues and Air Ministry specialists to come down. He usually did this when he had finished a research job and, before handing them long detailed reports which he always typed himself, he would carry out an experiment or two before them. But this time, he just went on working. One morning I finally asked him when he intended throwing his usual "surprise party", as we called it.

"No, Hélène; not for a long while yet. This discovery is much too important. I have an awful lot of work to do on it still. Do you realize that there are some parts of the transmission proper which I do not yet myself fully understand? It works all right, but you see, I can't just say to all these eminent professors that I do this and that and, poof, it works! I must be able to explain how and why it works. And what is even more important, I must be ready and able to refute every destructive argument they will not fail to trot out, as they usually do when faced with anything really good."

I was occasionally invited down to the laboratory to witness some new experiment, but I never went unless André invited me, and only talked about his work if he broached the subject first. Of course it never occurred to me that he would, at that stage at least, have tried an experiment with a human being; though, had I thought about it – knowing André – it would have been obvious that he would never have allowed anyone into the "transmitter" before he had been through to test it first. It was only after the accident that I discovered he had duplicated all his switches inside the disintegration booth, so that he could try it out by himself.

The morning André tried this terrible experiment, he did not show up for lunch. I sent the maid down with a tray, but she brought it back with a note she had found pinned outside the laboratory door: DO NOT DISTURB ME, I AM WORKING.

He did occasionally pin such notes on his door and, though I noticed it, I paid no particular attention to the unusually large handwriting of his note.

It was just after that, as I was drinking my coffee, that Henri came bouncing into the room to say that he had caught a funny fly, and would I like to see it. Refusing even to look at his closed fist, I ordered him to release it immediately.

"But, *Maman*, it has such a funny white head!"

Marching the boy over to the open window, I told him to release the fly immediately, which he did. I knew that

Henri had caught the fly merely because he thought it looked curious or different from other flies, but I also knew that his father would never stand for any form of cruelty to animals, and that there would be a fuss should he discover that our son had put a fly in a box or a bottle.

At dinner time that evening, André had still not shown up and, a little worried, I ran down to the laboratory and knocked at the door.

He did not answer my knock, but I heard him moving around and a moment later he slipped a note under the door. It was typewritten:

Hélène, I am having trouble. Put the boy to bed and come back in an hour's time. A.

Frightened, I knocked and called, but André did not seem to pay any attention and, vaguely reassured by the familiar noise of his typewriter, I went back to the house.

Having put Henri to bed, I returned to the laboratory where I found another note slipped under the door. My hand shook as I picked it up because I knew by then that something must be radically wrong. I read:

Hélène, first of all I count on you not to lose your nerve or do anything rash because you alone can help me. I have had a serious accident. I am not in any particular danger for the time being though it is a matter of life or death. It is useless calling to me or saying anything. I cannot answer, I cannot speak. I want you to do exactly and very carefully all that I ask. After having knocked three times to show that you understand and agree, fetch me a bowl of milk laced with rum. I have had nothing all day and can do with it.

Shaking with fear, not knowing what to think and repressing a furious desire to call André and bang away until he opened, I knocked three times as requested and ran all the way home to fetch what he wanted.

In less than five minutes I was back. Another note had been slipped under the door:

Hélène, follow these instructions carefully. When you knock I'll open the door. You are to walk over to my desk and put down the bowl of milk. You will then go into the other room where the receiver is. Look carefully and try to find a fly which ought to be there but which I am unable to find. Unfortunately I cannot see small things very easily.

Before you come in you must promise to obey me implicitly. Do not look at me and remember that talking is quite useless. I cannot answer. Knock again three times and that will mean I have your promise. My life depends entirely on the help you can give me.

I had to wait a while to pull myself together, and then I knocked slowly three times.

I heard André shuffling behind the door, then his hand fumbling with the lock, and the door opened.

Out of the corner of my eye, I saw that he was standing behind the door, but without looking round, I carried the bowl of milk to his desk. He was evidently watching me and I must at all costs appear calm and collected.

"*Chéri*, you can count on me," I said gently, and putting the bowl down under his desk lamp, the only one alight, I walked into the next room where all the lights were blazing.

My first impression was that some sort of hurricane must have blown out of the receiving booth. Papers were scattered in every direction, a whole row of test tubes lay smashed in a corner, chairs and stools were upset and one of the window curtains hung half torn from its bent rod. In a large enamel basin on the floor a heap of burned documents was still smouldering.

I knew that I would not find the fly André wanted me to look for. Women know things that men only suppose by reasoning and deduction; it is a form of knowledge very rarely accessible to them and which they disparagingly call intuition. I already knew that the fly André wanted was the one which Henri had caught and which I had made him release.

I heard André shuffling around in the next room, and then a strange gurgling and sucking as though he had trouble in drinking his milk.

"André, there is no fly here. Can you give me any sort of indication that might help? If you can't speak, rap or something . . . you know: once for yes, twice for no."

I had tried to control my voice and speak as though perfectly calm, but I had to choke down a sob of desperation when he rapped twice for "no".

"May I come to you, André? I don't know what can have happened, but whatever it is, I'll be courageous, dear."

After a moment of silent hesitation, he tapped once on his desk.

At the door I stopped aghast at the sight of André standing with his head and shoulders covered by the brown velvet cloth he had taken from the table by his desk, the table on which he usually ate when he did not want to leave his work. Suppressing a laugh that might easily have turned to sobbing, I said:

"André, we'll search thoroughly tomorrow, by daylight. Why don't you go to bed? I'll lead you to the guest room if you like, and won't let anyone else see you."

His left hand tapped the desk twice.

"Do you need a doctor, André?"

"No," he rapped.

"Would you like me to call up Professor Augier? He might be of more help . . ."

Twice he rapped "no" sharply. I did not know what to do or say. And then I told him:

"Henri caught a fly this morning which he wanted to show me, but I made him release it. Could it have been the one you are looking for? I didn't see it, but the boy said its head was white."

André emitted a strange metallic sigh, and I just had time to bite my fingers fiercely in order not to scream. He had let his right arm drop, and instead of his long-fingered muscular hand, a grey stick with little buds on it like the branch of a tree, hung out of his sleeve almost down to his knee.

"André, *mon chéri*, tell me what happened. I might be of more help to you if I knew. André . . . oh, it's terrible!" I sobbed, unable to control myself.

Having rapped once for yes, he pointed to the door with his left hand.

I stepped out and sank down crying as he locked the

door behind me. He was typing again and I waited. At last
he shuffled to the door and slid a sheet of paper under it.

Hélène, come back in the morning. I must think and will have
typed out an explanation for you. Take one of my sleeping tablets
and go straight to bed. I need you fresh and strong tomorrow, *ma
pauvre chérie.*

"Do you want anything for the night, André?" I shouted
through the door.

He knocked twice for no, and a little later I heard the
typewriter again.

The sun full on my face woke me up with a start. I had
set the alarm clock for five but had not heard it, probably
because of the sleeping tablets. I had indeed slept like a
log, without a dream. Now I was back in my living nightmare and crying like a child I sprang out of bed. It was
just on seven!

Rushing into the kitchen, without a word for the startled
servants, I rapidly prepared a trayload of coffee, bread, and
butter with which I ran down to the laboratory.

André opened the door as soon as I knocked and closed
it again as I carried the tray to his desk. His head was still
covered, but I saw from his crumpled suit and his open
camp bed that he must have at least tried to rest.

On his desk lay a typewritten sheet for me which I picked
up. André opened the other door, and taking this to mean
that he wanted to be left alone, I walked into the next
room. He pushed the door to and I heard him pouring out
the coffee as I read:

Do you remember the ash tray experiment? I have had a similar
accident. I "transmitted" myself successfully the night before last.
During a second experiment yesterday a fly which I did not see
must have got into the "disintegrator". My only hope is to find
that fly and go through again with it. Please search for it carefully
since, if it is not found, I shall have to find a way of putting an
end to all this.

If only André had been more explicit! I shuddered at the
thought that he must be terribly disfigured and then cried
softly as I imagined his face inside-out, or perhaps his eyes

in place of his ears, or his mouth at the back of his neck, or worse!

André must be saved! For that, the fly must be found!

Pulling myself together, I said, "André, may I come in?" He opened the door.

"André, don't despair; I am going to find that fly. It is no longer in the laboratory, but it cannot be very far. I suppose you're disfigured, perhaps terribly so, but there can be no question of putting an end to all this, as you say in your note; that I will never stand for. If necessary, if you do not wish to be seen, I'll make you a mask or a cowl so that you can go on with your work until you get well again. If you cannot work, I'll call Professor Augier, and he and all your other friends will save you, André."

Again I heard that curious metallic sigh as he rapped violently on his desk.

"André, don't be annoyed; please be calm. I won't do anything without first consulting you, but you must rely on me, have faith in me and let me help you as best I can. Are you terribly disfigured, dear? Can't you let me see your face? I won't be afraid . . . I am your wife, you know."

But my husband again rapped a decisive "no" and pointed to the door.

"All right. I am going to search for the fly now, but promise me you won't do anything foolish; promise you won't do anything rash or dangerous without first letting me know all about it!"

He extended his left hand, and I knew I had his promise.

I will never forget that ceaseless day-long hunt for a fly. Back home, I turned the house inside-out and made all the servants join in the search. I told them that a fly had escaped from the Professor's laboratory and that it must be captured alive, but it was evident they already thought me crazy. They said so to the police later, and that day's hunt for a fly most probably saved me from the guillotine later.

I questioned Henri and as he failed to understand right away what I was talking about, I shook him and slapped him, and made him cry in front of the round-eyed maids. Realising that I must not let myself go, I kissed and petted

the poor boy and at last made him understand what I
wanted of him. Yes, he remembered, he had found the
fly just by the kitchen window; yes, he had released it
immediately as told to.

Even in summer time we had very few flies because our
house is on the top of a hill and the slightest breeze coming
across the valley blows round it. In spite of that, I managed
to catch dozens of flies that day. On all the window sills
and all over the garden I had put saucers of milk, sugar,
jam, meat — all the things likely to attract flies. Of all those
we caught, and many others which we failed to catch but
which I saw, none resembled the one Henri had caught the
day before. One by one, with a magnifying glass, I examined every unusual fly, but none had anything like a white
head.

At lunch time, I ran down to André with some milk and
mashed potatoes. I also took some of the flies we had
caught, but he gave me to understand that they could be
of no possible use to him.

"If that fly has not been found tonight, André, we'll have
to see what is to be done. And this is what I propose: I'll
sit in the next room. When you can't answer by the yes-no
method of rapping, you'll type out whatever you want to
say and then slip it under the door. Agreed?"

"Yes," rapped André.

By nightfall we had still not found the fly. At dinner
time, as I prepared André's tray, I broke down and sobbed
in the kitchen in front of the silent servants. My maid
thought that I had had a row with my husband, probably
about the mislaid fly, but I learned later that the cook was
already quite sure that I was out of my mind.

Without a word, I picked up the tray and then put it
down again as I stopped by the telephone. That this was
really a matter of life and death for André, I had no doubt.
Neither did I doubt that he fully intended committing
suicide, unless I could make him change his mind, or at
least put off such a drastic decision. Would I be strong
enough? He would never forgive me for not keeping a
promise, but under the circumstances, did that really

matter? To the devil with promises and honour! At all costs André must be saved! And having thus made up my mind, I looked up and dialled Professor Augier's number.

"The Professor is away and will not be back before the end of the week," said a polite neutral voice at the other end of the line.

That was that! I would have to fight alone and fight I would. I would save André come what may.

All my nervousness had disappeared as André let me in and, after putting the tray of food down on his desk, I went into the other room, as agreed.

"The first thing I want to know," I said as he closed the door behind me, "is what happened exactly. Can you please tell me, André?"

I waited patiently while he typed an answer which he pushed under the door a little later.

Hélène, I would rather not tell you. Since go I must, I would rather you remember me as I was before. I must destroy myself in such a way that none can possibly know what has happened to me. I have of course thought of simply disintegrating myself in my transmitter, but I had better not because, sooner or later, I might find myself reintegrated. Some day, somewhere, some scientist is sure to make the same discovery. I have therefore thought of a way which is neither simple nor easy, but you can and will help me.

For several minutes I wondered if André had not simply gone stark raving mad.

"André," I said at last, "whatever you may have chosen or thought of, I cannot and will never accept such a cowardly solution. No matter how awful the result of your experiment or accident, you are alive, you are a man, a brain . . . and you have a soul. You have no right to destroy yourself! You know that!"

The answer was soon typed and pushed under the door.

I am alive all right, but I am already no longer a man. As to my brain or intelligence, it may disappear at any moment. As it is, it is no longer intact, and there can be no soul without intelligence . . . and you know that!

"Then you must tell the other scientists about your discovery. They will help you and save you, André!"

I staggered back frightened as he angrily thumped the door twice.

"André . . . why? Why do you refuse the aid you know they would give you with all their hearts?"

A dozen furious knocks shook the door and made me understand that my husband would never accept such a solution. I had to find other arguments.

For hours, it seemed, I talked to him about our boy, about me, about his family, about his duty to us and to the rest of humanity. He made no reply of any sort. At last I cried:

"André . . . do you hear me?"

"Yes," he knocked very gently.

"Well, listen then. I have another idea. You remember your first experiment with the ash tray? . . . Well, do you think that if you had put it through again a second time, it might possibly have come out with the letters turned back the right way?"

Before I had finished speaking, André was busily typing and a moment later I read his answer:

I have already thought of that. And that was why I needed the fly. It has got to go through with me. There is no hope otherwise.

"Try all the same, André. You never know!"

"I have tried seven times already," was the typewritten reply I got to that.

"André! Try again, please!"

The answer this time gave me a flutter of hope, because no woman has ever understood, or will ever understand, how a man about to die can possibly consider anything funny.

I deeply admire your delicious feminine logic. We could go on doing this experiment until Doomsday. However, just to give you that pleasure, probably the very last I shall ever be able to give you, I will try once more. If you cannot find the dark glasses, turn your back to the machine and press your hands over your eyes. Let me know when you are ready.

"Ready, André!" I shouted, without even looking for the glasses and following his instructions.

I heard him move around and then open and close the door of his "disintegrator". After what seemed a very long wait, but probably was not more than a minute or so, I heard a violent crackling noise and perceived a bright flash through my eyelids and fingers.

I turned around as the booth door opened.

His head and shoulders still covered with the brown velvet cloth, André was gingerly stepping out of it.

"How do you feel, André? Any difference?" I asked, touching his arm.

He tried to step away from me and caught his foot in one of the stools which I had not troubled to pick up. He made a violent effort to regain his balance, and the velvet cloth slowly slid off his shoulders and head as he fell heavily backwards.

The horror was too much for me, too unexpected. As a matter of fact, I am sure that, even had I known, the horror-impact could hardly have been less powerful. Trying to push both hands into my mouth to stifle my screams and although my fingers were bleeding, I screamed again and again. I could not take my eyes off him, I could not even close them, and yet I knew that if I looked at the horror much longer, I would go on screaming for the rest of my life.

Slowly, the monster, the thing that had been my husband, covered its head, got up and groped its way to the door and passed it. Though still screaming, I was able to close my eyes.

I who had ever been a true Catholic, who believed in God and another, better life hereafter, have today but one hope: that when I die, I really die, and that there may be no after-life of any sort because, if there is, then I shall never forget! Day and night, awake or asleep, I see it, and I know that I am condemned to see it forever, even perhaps into oblivion!

Until I am totally extinct, nothing can, nothing will ever made me forget that dreadful white hairy head with its low flat skull and its two pointed ears. Pink and moist, the nose was also that of a cat, a huge cat. But the eyes! Or rather, where the eyes should have been were two brown bumps the size of saucers. Instead of a mouth, animal or human, was a long hairy vertical slit from which hung a black quivering trunk that widened at the end, trumpet-like, and from which saliva kept dripping.

I must have fainted, because I found myself flat on my stomach on the cold cement floor of the laboratory, staring at the closed door behind which I could hear the noise of André's typewriter.

Numb, numb and empty, I must have looked as people do immediately after a terrible accident, before they fully understand what has happened. I could only think of a man I had once seen on the platform of a railway station, quite conscious, and looking stupidly at his leg still on the line where the train had just passed.

My throat was aching terribly, and that made me wonder if my vocal cords had not perhaps been torn, and whether I would ever be able to speak again.

The noise of the typewriter suddenly stopped and I felt I was going to scream again as something touched the door and a sheet of paper slid from under it.

Shivering with fear and disgust, I crawled over to where I could read it without touching it:

Now you understand. That last experiment was a new disaster, my poor Hélène. I suppose you recognized part of Dandelo's head. When I went into the disintegrator just now, my head was only that of a fly. I now only have eyes and mouth left. The rest has been replaced by parts of the cat's head. Poor Dandelo whose atoms had never come together. You see now that there can only be one possible solution, don't you? I must disappear. Knock on the door when you are ready and I shall explain what you have to do.

Of course he was right, and it had been wrong and cruel of me to insist on a new experiment. And I knew that there was now no possible hope, that any further experiments could only bring about worse results.

Getting up dazed, I went to the door and tried to speak, but no sound came out of my throat . . . so I knocked once!

You can of course guess the rest. He explained his plan in short typewritten notes, and I agreed, I agreed to everything!

My head on fire, but shivering with cold, like an automaton, I followed him into the silent factory. In my hand was a full page of explanations: what I had to know about the steam-hammer.

Without stopping or looking back, he pointed to the switchboard that controlled the steam-hammer as he passed it. I went no farther and watched him come to a halt before the terrible instrument.

He knelt down, carefully wrapped the cloth round his head, and then stretched out flat on the ground.

It was not difficult. I was not killing my husband. André, poor André, had gone long ago, years ago it seemed. I was merely carrying out his last wish . . . and mine.

Without hesitating, my eyes on the long still body, I firmly pushed the "stroke" button right in. The great metallic mass seemed to drop slowly. It was not so much the resounding clang of the hammer that made me jump as the sharp cracking which I had distinctly heard at the same time. My hus..the thing's body shook a second and then lay still.

It was then I noticed that he had forgotten to put his right arm, his fly leg, under the hammer. The police would never understand but the scientists would, and they must not! That had been André's last wish, also!

I had to do it and quickly, too; the night watchman must have heard the hammer and would be round any moment. I pushed the other button and the hammer slowly rose. Seeing but trying not to look, I ran up, leaned down, lifted and moved forward the right arm which seemed terribly light. Back at the switchboard, again I pushed the red button, and down came the hammer a second time. Then I ran all the way home.

You know the rest and can now do whatever you think right.

So ended Hélène's manuscript.

The following day I telephoned Commissaire Charas to invite him to dinner.

"With pleasure, Monsieur Delambre. Allow me, however, to ask: is it the commissaire you are inviting, or just Monsieur Charas?"

"Have you any preference?"

"No, not at the present moment."

"Well then, make it whichever you like. Will eight o'clock suit you?"

Although it was raining, the commissaire arrived on foot that evening.

"Since you did not come tearing up to the door in your black Citroën, I take it you have opted for Monsieur Charas, off duty?"

"I left the car up a side-street," mumbled the commissaire with a grin as the maid staggered under the weight of his raincoat.

"*Merci*," he said a minute later as I handed him a glass of Pernod into which he tipped a few drops of water, watching it turn the golden amber liquid to pale blue milk.

"You heard about my poor sister-in-law?"

"Yes, shortly after you telephoned me this morning. I am sorry, but perhaps it was all for the best. Being already in charge of your brother's case, the inquiry automatically comes to me."

"I suppose it was suicide."

"Without a doubt. Cyanide the doctors say quite rightly; I found a second tablet in the unstitched hem of her dress."

"*Monsieur est servi*," announced the maid.

"I would like to show you a very curious document afterwards, Charas."

"Ah, yes. I heard that Madame Delambre had been writing a lot, but we could find nothing beyond the short note informing us that she was committing suicide."

During our tête-à-tête dinner, we talked politics, books,

and films, and the local football club of which the commissaire was a keen supporter.

After dinner, I took him up to my study where a bright fire – a habit I had picked up in England during the war – was burning.

Without even asking him, I handed him his brandy and mixed myself what he called "crushed-bug juice in soda water" – his appreciation of whisky.

"I would like you to read this, Charas; first because it was partly intended for you and, secondly, because it will interest you. If you think Commissaire Charas has no objection, I would like to burn it after."

Without a word, he took the wad of sheets Hélène had given me the day before and settled down to read them.

"What do you think of it all?" I asked some twenty minutes later as he carefully folded Hélène's manuscript, slipped it into the brown envelope, and put it into the fire.

Charas watched the flames licking the envelope from which wisps of grey smoke were escaping, and it was only when it burst into flames that he said slowly raising his eyes to mine:

"I think it proves very definitely that Madame Delambre was quite insane."

For a long time we watched the fire eating up Hélène's "confession".

"A funny thing happened to me this morning, Charas. I went to the cemetery where my brother is buried. It was quite empty and I was alone."

"Not quite, Monsieur Delambre. I was there, but I did not want to disturb you."

"Then you saw me . . ."

"Yes. I saw you bury a matchbox."

"Do you know what was in it?"

"A fly, I suppose."

"Yes. I had found it early this morning, caught in a spider's web in the garden."

"Was it dead?"

"No, not quite. I . . . crushed it . . . between two stones. Its head was . . . white . . . all white."

The Emissary
Introduction

*I am delighted at this opportunity to introduce "The
Emissary", one of my favourite stories by the man who made
all the difference in my life. Believe me when I tell you that
without Ray Bradbury I would never have become a writer.
As Bradbury has observed, there comes in every life a moment
of awakening – as if from a dream, to know that one is alive
in the universe. This is the dawning of self-consciousness, and
it comes simultaneously with the awareness of death. It
usually happens somewhere between childhood and
adolescence; after it has happened one can never be a child
again. It is the single most important moment in any life, the
one that shapes everything that comes after.*

*For me it occurred one summer's day when I was ten. I
will never forget the electricity in the air that afternoon, or
the quivering intensity of my awakened senses, or the new
emotions that pulsed through my veins: happy and sad,
exultant and unspeakably melancholy at the same time, as if
my body chemistry and my consciousness had been altered for
all time. After that point there was no going back, no turning
away from life; I was on a trip that had no end, a high that
informed every waking and sleeping breath. I was wrenched
out of childhood and reborn on the terrifying and exhilarating
path of self-knowledge. I would never cease trying to
understand what had happened to me, no more than Terence
and Dennis McKenna have been able to forget their
transcendent experience in La Chorrera and the jungles of
the Amazon.*

*Ray Bradbury has spent his adult life writing about such
epiphanies. It happens that the town where I grew up had
much in common with his Waukegan, though the two were*

separated by a continent. I discovered The Golden Apples of the Sun *and* The October Country *and* The Martian Chronicles, *coming to him as naturally as a pilgrim to another soul on the same road. In his writing I found the expression of a kindred spirit, and that brought comfort, for his stories taught me that the joy and pain were not mine alone. He articulated it for me, with words that had the colour and smell and taste and texture of life in a way that I had not guessed possible. He showed me that written words could be used to transmit some of the intensity, that they were a way to receive and share in turn some meaningful measure of subjective experience as art.*

I began reading as much of his work as I could lay my hands on, and to write down as much of my experience as I dared. Through him I discovered others in the worldwide community of writers, took heart and was able to go on with less fear and trepidation. I have not yet stopped. His voice is no longer mine, but it continues to exist as a living skeleton embedded at the deepest level in the body of my work, and in my life.

"The Emissary" is as pure a statement about The Moment as Bradbury has ever produced, and it easily transcends "The Monkey's Paw", upon which it was modelled, in the same way that the poetry of the human heart's song transcends the dead bones of a classroom chalk-talk. It lives. It is alive. *As we are, because one day we will die.*

DENNIS ETCHISON
Author of The Dark Country, The Blood Kiss *and* Darkside

Ray Bradbury
The Emissary

He knew it was autumn again, because Torry came romping into the house bringing the windy crisp cold smell of autumn with him. In every black curl of his dog hair he carried autumn. Leaf flakes tangled in his dark ears and muzzle, dropping from his white vest, and off his flourished tail. The dog smelled just like autumn.

Martin Christie sat up in bed and reached down with one pale small hand. Torry barked and displayed a generous length of pink, rippling tongue, which he passed over and along the back of Martin's hand. Torry licked him like a lollipop. "Because of the salt," declared Martin, as Torry leaped upon the bed.

"Get down," warned Martin. "Mom doesn't like you up here." Torry flattened his ears. "Well . . ." Martin relented. "Just for a while, then."

Torry warmed Martin's thin body with his dog warmness. Martin relished the clean dog smell and the litter of fallen leaves on the quilt. He didn't care if Mom scolded. After all, Torry was new born. Right out of the stomach of autumn Torry came, reborn in the firm sharp cold.

"What's it like outside, Torry? Tell me."

Lying there, Torry would tell him. Lying there, Martin would know what autumn was like; like in the old days before sickness had put him to bed. His only contact with autumn now was this brief chill, this leaf-flaked fur; the compact canine representation of summer gone – this autumn-by-proxy.

"Where'd you go today, Torry?"

But Torry didn't have to tell him. He knew. Over a fall-burdened hill, leaving a pad-pattern in the brilliantly piled leaves, down to where the kids ran shouting on bikes and roller skates and wagons at Barstow's Park, that's where Torry ran, barking out his canine delight. And down into the town where rain had fallen dark, earlier; and mud furrowed under car wheels, down between the feet of weekend shoppers. That's where Torry went.

And wherever Torry went, then Martin could go; because Torry would always tell him by the touch, feel, consistency, the wet, dry, or crispness of his coat. And, lying there holding Torry, Martin would send his mind out to retrace each step of Torry's way through fields, over the shallow glitter of the ravine creek, darting across the marbled spread of the graveyard, into the wood, over the meadow; where all the wild, laughing autumn sports went on, Martin could go now through his emissary.

Mother's voice sounded downstairs, angrily.

Her short angry walking came up the hall steps.

Martin pushed. "Down, Torry!"

Torry vanished under the bed just before the bedroom door opened and Mom looked in, blue eyes snapping. She carried a tray of salad and fruit juices, firmly.

"Is Torry here?" she demanded.

Torry gave himself away with a few bumps of his tail against the floor.

Mom set the tray down impatiently. "That dog is more trouble. Always upsetting things and digging places. He was in Miss Tarkins's garden this morning, and dug a big hole. Miss Tarkins is mad."

"Oh." Martin held his breath. There was silence under the bed. Torry knew when to keep quiet.

"And it's not the only time," said Mom. "This is the third hole he's dug this week!"

"Maybe he's looking for something."

"Something fiddlesticks! He's just a curious nuisance. He can't keep that black nose out of anything. *Always* curious!"

There was a hairy pizzicato of tail under the bed. Mom couldn't help smiling.

"Well," she ended, "if he doesn't stop digging in yards, I'll have to keep him in and not let him run."

Martin opened his mouth wide. "Oh, no, Mom! Don't do that! Then I wouldn't know – anything. He *tells* me."

Mom's voice softened. "Does he, son?"

"Sure. He goes around and comes back and tells what happens, tells everything!"

Mom's hand was spun glass touching his head. "I'm glad he tells you. I'm glad you've got him."

They both sat a moment, considering how worthless the last year would've been without Torry. Only two more months, thought Martin, of being in bed, like the doctor said, and he'd be up and around.

"Here, Torry!"

Jangling, Martin locked the special collar attachment around Torry's neck. It was a note, painted on a tin square:

MY NAME IS TORRY. WILL YOU VISIT MY MASTER, WHO IS SICK? FOLLOW ME!

It worked. Torry carried it out into the world every day.

"Will you let him out, Mom?"

"Yes, if he's good and stops his digging!"

"He'll stop; won't you, Torry?"

The dog barked.

You could hear the dog yipping far down the street and away, going to fetch visitors. Martin was feverish and his eyes stood out in his head as he sat, propped up, listening, sending his mind rushing along with the dog, faster, faster. Yesterday Torry had brought Mrs Holloway from Elm Avenue, with a story book for a present; the day before Torry had sat up, begged at Mr Jacobs, the jeweller. Mr Jacobs had bent and near-sightedly deciphered the tag message and, sure enough, had come shuffling and waddling to pay Martin a little how-do-you-do.

Now, Martin heard the dog returning through the smoky afternoon, barking, running, barking again.

Footsteps came lightly after the dog. Somebody rang the downstairs bell, softly. Mom answered the door. Voices talked.

Torry raced upstairs, leaped on the bed. Martin leaned forward excitedly, his face shining, to see who'd come upstairs this time. Maybe Miss Palmborg or Mr Ellis or Miss Jendriss, or–

The visitor walked upstairs, talking to Mom. It was a young woman's voice, talking with a laugh in it.

The door opened.

Martin had company.

Four days passed in which Torry did his job, reported morning, afternoon and evening temperatures, soil consistencies, leaf colours, rain levels, and, most important of all, brought visitors.

Miss Haight again, on Saturday. She was the young, laughing, handsome woman with the gleaming brown hair and the soft way of talking. She lived in the big house on Park Street. It was her third visit in a month.

On Sunday it was Reverend Vollmar, on Monday Miss Clark and Mr Henricks.

And to each of them Martin explained his dog. How in spring he was odorous of wild flowers and fresh earth; in summer he was baked, warm, sun-crisp; in autumn, now, a treasure trove of gold leaves hidden in his pelt for Martin to explore out. Torry demonstrated this process for the visitors, lying over on his back waiting to be explored.

Then, one morning, Mom told Martin about Miss Haight, the one who was so handsome and young and laughed.

She was dead.

Killed in a motoring accident in Glen Falls.

Martin held on to his dog, remembering Miss Haight, thinking of the way she smiled, thinking of her bright eyes, her closely cropped chestnut hair, her slim body, her quick walk, her nice stories about seasons and people.

So now she was dead. She wasn't going to laugh or tell stories any more. That's all there was to it. She was dead.

"What do they do in the graveyard, Mom, under the ground?"

"Nothing."

"You mean they just lay there?"

"Lie there," corrected Mom.

"*Lie* there . . . ?"

"Yes," said Mom, "that's all they do."

"It doesn't sound like much fun."

"It's not supposed to be."

"Why don't they get up and walk around once in a while if they get tired of lying there?"

"I think you've said enough, now," said Mom.

"I just wanted to know."

"Well, now you know."

"Sometimes I think God's pretty silly."

"Martin!"

Martin scowled. "You'd think He'd treat people better than throw dirt in their faces and tell them to lay still for keeps. You'd think He'd find a better way. What if I told Torry to play dead-dog? He does it awhile, but then he gets sick of it and wags his tail or blinks his eyes, or pants, or jumps off the bed, and walks around. I bet those graveyard people do the same, huh, Torry?"

Torry barked.

"That will *do*!" said Mom, firmly. "I don't like such talk!"

The autumn continued. Torry ran across forests, over the creek, prowling through the graveyard as was his custom, and into town and around and back, missing nothing.

In mid-October, Torry began to act strangely. He couldn't seem to find anybody to come to visit Martin. Nobody seemed to pay attention to his begging. He came home seven days in a row without bringing a visitor. Martin was deeply despondent over it.

Mom explained it. "Everybody's busy. The war, and all. People have lots to worry over beside little begging dogs."

"Yeah," said Martin, "I guess so."

But there was more than that to it. Torry had a funny gleam in his eyes. As if he wasn't really trying, or didn't care, or – something. Something Martin couldn't figure

out. Maybe Torry was sick. Well, to heck with visitors. As
long as he had Torry, everything was fine.

And then one day Torry ran out and didn't come back
at all.

Martin waited quietly at first. Then – nervously. Then –
anxiously.

At supper time he heard Mom and Dad call Torry.
Nothing happened. It was no use. There was no sound of
paws along the path outside the house. No sharp barking
in the cold night air. Nothing. Torry was gone. Torry
wasn't coming home – ever.

Leaves fell past the window. Martin sank on his pillow,
slowly, a pain deep and hard in his chest.

The world was dead. There was no autumn because there
was no fur to bring it into the house. There would be no
winter because there would be no paws to dampen the
quilt with snow. No more seasons. No more time. The go-
between, the emissary, had been lost in the wild thronging
of civilization, probably hit by a car, or poisoned, or stolen,
and there was no time.

Sobbing, Martin turned his face to his pillow. There was
no contact with the world. The world was dead.

Martin twisted in bed and in three days the Hallowe'en
pumpkins were rotting in trash cans, masks were burnt in
incinerators, the bogeys were stacked away on shelves until
next year. Hallowe'en was withdrawn, impersonal,
untouchable. It had simply been one evening when he had
heard horns blowing off in the cold autumn stars, people
yelling and thumping windows and porches with soap and
cabbages. That was all.

Martin stared at the ceiling for the first three days of
November, watching alternate light and dark shift across
it. Days got shorter, darker, he could tell by the window.
The trees were naked. The autumn wind changed its tempo
and temperature. But it was just a pageant outside his
window, nothing more. He couldn't get at it.

Martin read books about the seasons and the people in

that world that was now non-existent. He listened each day, but didn't hear the sounds he wanted to hear.

Friday night came. His parents were going to the theatre. They'd be back at eleven. Miss Tarkins, from next door, would come over for a while until Martin got sleepy, and then she would go home.

Mom and Dad kissed him good night and walked out of the house into the autumn. He heard their footsteps go down the street.

Miss Tarkins came over, stayed a while, and then when Martin confessed to being tired, she turned out all the lights and went back home.

Silence, then. Martin just lay there and watched the stars moving slowly across the sky. It was a clear, moonlit evening. The kind when he and Torry had once run together across the town, across the sleeping graveyard, across the ravine, through the meadows, down the shadowed streets, chasing phantasmal childish dreams.

Only the wind was friendly. Stars don't bark. Trees don't sit up and beg. The wind, of course, did wag its tail against the house a number of times, startling Martin.

Now it was after nine o'clock.

If only Torry would come home, bringing some of the world with him. A burr or a rimed thistle, or the wind in his ears. If only Torry would come home.

And then, way off somewhere, there was a sound.

Martin arose in his covers, trembling. Starlight was reflected in his small eyes. He threw back the covers and tensed, listening. There, again, was the sound.

It was so small it was like a needle-point moving through the air miles and miles away.

It was the dreamy echo of a dog – barking.

It was the sound of a dog coming across meadows and fields, down dark streets, the sound of a dog running and letting his breath out to the night. The sound of a dog circling and running. It came and went, it lifted and faded, it came forward and went back, as if it was being led by someone on a chain. As if the dog was running and some-

body whistled under the chestnut tree and the dog ran
back, circled, and darted again for home.

Martin felt the room revolve under him, and the bed
tremble with his body. The spring complained with metal,
tining voices.

The faint barking continued for five minutes, growing
louder and louder.

*Torry, come home! Torry, come home! Torry, boy, oh Torry,
where've you been? Oh, Torry, Torry!*

Another five minutes. Nearer and nearer, and Martin
kept saying the dog's name over and over again. Bad dog,
good dog, to go off and leave him for all these days. Bad
dog, good dog, come home, oh, Torry, hurry home and
tell me about the world! Tears fell and dissolved into the
quilt.

Nearer now. Very near. Just up the street, barking.
Torry!

Martin held his breath. The sound of dog feet in the
piled dry leaves, down the path. And now – right outside
the house, barking, barking, barking! Torry!

Barking to the door.

Martin shivered. Did he dare run down and let the dog
in, or should he wait for Mom and Dad to come home!
Wait. Yes, he must wait. But it would be unbearable if,
while he waited, the dog ran away again. No, he would go
down and release the lock and his own special dog would
leap into his arms again. Good Torry!

He started to move from bed when he heard the other
sound. The door opened downstairs. Somebody was kind
enough to have opened the door for Torry.

Torry had brought a visitor, of course. Mr Buchanan, or
Mr Jacobs, or perhaps Miss Tarkins.

The door opened and closed and Torry came racing
upstairs and flung himself, yipping, on the bed.

"Torry, where've you been, what've you done all this
week?"

Martin laughed and cried all in one. He grabbed the
dog and held him. Then he stopped laughing and crying,
suddenly. He just stared at Torry with wide, strange eyes.

The odour arising from Torry was – different.

It was a smell of earth. Dead earth. Earth that had lain cheek by jowl with unhealthy decaying things six feet under. Stinking, stinking, rancid earth. Clods of decaying soil fell off Torry's paws. And – something else – a small withered fragment of – *skin*?

Was it? Was it! WAS IT!

What kind of message was this from Torry? What did such a message mean? The stench – the ripe and awful cemetery earth.

Torry was a bad dog. Always digging where he shouldn't dig.

Torry was a *good* dog. Always making friends so easily. Torry took to liking everybody. He brought them home with him.

And now this latest visitor was coming up the stairs. Slowly. Dragging one foot after the other, painfully, slowly, slowly, slowly.

"Torry, Torry – where've you *been*!' screamed Martin.

A clod of rank crawling soil dropped from the dog's chest.

The door to the bedroom moved inwards.

Martin had company.

Pornography
Introduction

They were the first horror stories I ever read. They were the first horror stories that ever frightened me. For turning me into a squeamish, easily frightened, timid individual I extend my heartiest thanks to The Pan Book of Horror Stories. *At the tender age of nine I read them all one summer (well, all you could get then – I think there were about ten volumes at the time). I still have the yellowed volumes on my shelves now, the pages may be fading but the memories of the pleasure I got from the stories are still as strong.*

To keep up such a high standard over thirty years is quite some achievement and, from one who now terrorizes for a living I thank the Pan Books of Horror Stories for, in their time (and sometimes even now, when the house is a bit too quiet) terrorizing me.

'Pornography' is a classic example of how the stories or their selection has brought the books up to date. It contains all the elements which good horror should have. The undercurrent of unease, shock and a dark sense of humour. It is realistic and gritty, sometimes as sordid as the magazines which its clap-ridden central character is so fond of thumbing through. The character is unlikeable, unfeeling. A nasty piece of work. It's McEwan's ambivalent attitude to the man which makes the story so good. It's the kind of story which makes you feel like washing your hands after you've read it. I loved it for that. And for the twist in the tale which is what I can only politely term "a leg-crosser". I was sweating at the thought.

But don't take my word, read it yourself. There's a line in it which sums up perfectly the appeal of horror stories: You're scared of what you like. *We like the unknown, we like to find out what is hiding behind that door or under the bed, but we're afraid to. If you turn that sentence around you get the* real *truth:* You like to be scared. *Damn right. That's why we read horror. We like to be scared. So go on, look behind the door . . . peer under the bed. You never know what you'll find waiting for you . . .*

SHAUN HUTSON
Author of Slugs, Victims *and* Nemesis

Ian McEwan

Pornography

O'Byrne walked through Soho market to his brother's shop in Brewer Street. A handful of customers leafing through the magazines and Harold watching them through pebble-thick lenses from his raised platform in the corner. Harold was barely five foot and wore built-up shoes. Before becoming his employee O'Byrne used to call him Little Runt. At Harold's elbow a miniature radio rasped details of race meetings for the afternoon. "So," said Harold with thin contempt, "the prodigal brother . . ." His magnified eyes fluttered at every consonant. He looked past O'Byrne's shoulder. "All the magazines are for sale, gentlemen." The readers stirred uneasily like troubled dreamers. One replaced a magazine and walked quickly from the shop. "Where d'you get to?" Harold said in a quieter voice. He stepped from the dais, put on his coat and glared up at O'Byrne, waiting for an answer. Little Runt. O'Byrne was ten years younger than his brother, detested him and his success but now, strangely, wanted his approbation. "I had an appointment, didn't I," he said quietly. "I got the clap." Harold was pleased. He reached up and punched O'Byrne's shoulder playfully. "Serves you," he said and cackled theatrically. Another customer edged out of the shop. From the doorway Harold called, "I'll be back at five." O'Byrne smiled as his brother left. He hooked his thumbs into his jeans and sauntered towards the tight knot of customers. "Can I help you gentlemen, the magazines are all for sale." They scattered before him like frightened fowl, and suddenly he was alone in the shop.

A plump woman of fifty or more stood in front of a plastic shower curtain, naked but for panties and gasmask.

Her hands hung limply at her sides and in one of them a
cigarette smouldered. Wife of the Month. Since gasmasks
and a thick rubber sheet on the bed, wrote J.N. of Andover,
we've never looked back. O'Byrne played with the radio
for a while then switched it off. Rhythmically he turned
the pages of the magazine, and stopped to read the letters.
An uncircumcised male virgin, without hygiene, forty-two
next May, dared not peel back his foreskin now for fear of
what he might see. I get these nightmares of worms.
O'Byrne laughed and crossed his legs. He replaced the
magazine, returned to the radio, switched it on and off
rapidly and caught the unintelligible middle of a word. He
walked about the shop straightening the magazines in the
racks. He stood by the door and stared at the wet street
intersected by the coloured strips of the plastic walk-thro.
He whistled over and over a tune whose end immediately
suggested its beginning. Then he returned to Harold's
raised platform and made two telephone calls, both to the
hospital, the first to Lucy. But Sister Drew was busy in the
ward and could not come to the phone. O'Byrne left a
message that he would not be able to see her that evening
after all and would phone again tomorrow. He dialled the
hospital switchboard and this time asked for trainee Nurse
Shepherd in the children's ward. "Hi," O'Byrne said when
Pauline picked up the phone. "It's me." And he stretched
and leaned against the wall. Pauline was a silent girl who
once wept in a film about the effects of pesticides on butter-
flies, who wanted to redeem O'Byrne with her love. Now
she laughed, "I've been phoning you all morning," she
said. "Didn't your brother tell you?"

"Listen," said O'Byrne, "I'll be at your place about
eight," and replaced the receiver.

Harold did not return till after six, and O'Byrne was almost
asleep, his head pillowed on his forearm. There were no
customers. O'Byrne's only sale was *American Bitch*. "Those
American mags," said Harold as he emptied the till of £15
and a handful of silver, "are *good*." Harold's new leather
jacket. O'Byrne fingered it appreciatively. "Seventy-eight

quid," said Harold and braced himself in front of the fish-eye mirror. His glasses flashed. "It's all right," said O'Byrne. "Fucking right it is," said Harold, and began to close up shop. "Never take much on Wednesdays," he said wistfully as he reached up and switched on the burglar alarm. "Wednesday's a cunt of a day." Now O'Byrne was in front of the mirror, examining a small trail of acne that led from the corner of his mouth. "You're not fucking kidding," he agreed.

Harold's house lay at the foot of the Post Office Tower and O'Byrne rented a room from him. They walked along together without speaking. From time to time Harold glanced sideways into a dark shop window to catch the reflection of himself and his new leather jacket. Little Runt. O'Byrne said, "Cold, innit?" and Harold said nothing. Minutes later, when they were passing a pub, Harold steered O'Byrne into the dank, deserted public saying, "Since you got the clap I'll buy you a drink." The publican heard the remark and regarded O'Byrne with interest. They drank three Scotches apiece, and as O'Byrne was paying for the fourth round Harold said, "Oh yeah, one of those two nurses you've been knocking around with phoned." O'Byrne nodded and wiped his lips. After a pause Harold said, "You're well in there . . ." O'Byrne nodded again. "Yep." Harold's jacket shone. When he reached for his drink it creaked. O'Byrne was not going to tell him anything. He banged his hands together. "Yep," he said once more, and stared over his brother's head at the empty bar. Harold tried again. "She wanted to know where you'd been . . ." "I bet she did," O'Byrne muttered, and then smiled.

Pauline, short and untalkative, her face bloodlessly pale, intersected by a heavy black fringe, her eyes large, green and watchful, her flat small, damp and shared with a secretary who was never there. O'Byrne arrived after ten, a little drunk and in need of a bath to purge the faint purulent scent that lately had hung about his fingers. She sat on a small wooden stool to watch him luxuriate. Once she leaned

forwards and touched his body where it broke the surface.
O'Byrne's eyes were closed, his hands floating at his side,
the only sound the diminishing hiss of the cistern. Pauline
rose quietly to bring a clean white towel from her bedroom,
and O'Byrne did not hear her leave or return. She sat down
again and ruffled, as far as it was possible, O'Byrne's damp,
matted hair. "The food is ruined," she said without accu-
sation. Beads of perspiration collected in the corners of
O'Byrne's eyes and rolled down the line of his nose like
tears. Pauline rested her hand on O'Byrne's knee where it
jutted through the grey water. Steam turned to water on
the cold walls, senseless minutes passed. "Never mind,
love," said O'Byrne, and stood up.

Pauline went out to buy beer and pizzas, and O'Byrne
lay down in her tiny bedroom to wait. Ten minutes passed.
He dressed after cursory examination of his clean but swelling meatus, and wandered listlessly about the sitting room.
Nothing interested him in Pauline's small collection of
books. There were no magazines. He entered the kitchen
in search of a drink. There was nothing but an overcooked
meat pie. He picked round the burnt bits and as he ate
turned the pages of a picture calendar. When he finished
he remembered again he was waiting for Pauline. He looked
at his watch. She had been gone now almost half an hour.
He stood up quickly, tipping the kitchen chair behind him
to the floor. He paused in the sitting room and then walked
decisively out of the flat and slammed the front door on his
way. He hurried down the stairs, anxious not to meet her
now he had decided to get out. But she was there. Halfway
up the second flight, a little out of breath, her arms full of
bottles and tinfoil parcels. "Where d'you get to?" said
O'Byrne. Pauline stopped several steps down from him,
her face tilted up awkwardly over her goods, the white of
her eyes and the tinfoil vivid in the dark. "The usual place
was closed. I had to walk miles . . . sorry." They stood.
O'Byrne was not hungry. He wanted to go. He hitched his
thumbs into the waist of his jeans and cocked his head
towards the invisible ceiling, then he looked down at Pauline who waited. "Well," he said at last, "I was thinking

of going." Pauline came up, and as she pushed past whispered, "Silly." O'Byrne turned and followed her, obscurely cheated.

He leaned in the doorway, she righted the chair. With a movement of his head O'Byrne indicated that he wanted none of the food Pauline was setting out on plates. She poured him a beer and knelt to gather a few black pastry droppings from the floor. They sat in the sitting room. O'Byrne drank, Pauline ate slowly, neither spoke. O'Byrne finished all the beer and placed his hand on Pauline's knee. She did not turn. He said cheerily, "What's wrong with you?" and she said, "Nothing." Alive with irritation O'Byrne moved closer and placed his arm protectively across her shoulders. "Tell you what," he half whispered. "Let's go to bed." Suddenly Pauline rose and went into the bedroom. O'Byrne sat with his hands clasped behind his head. He listened to Pauline undress, and he heard the creak of the bed. He got to his feet and, still without desire, entered the bedroom.

Pauline lay on her back and O'Byrne, having undressed quickly, lay beside her. She did not acknowledge him in her usual way, she did not move. O'Byrne raised his arm to stroke her shoulder, but instead let his hand fall back heavily against the sheet. They both lay on their backs in mounting silence, until O'Byrne decided to give her one last chance and with naked grunts hauled himself on to his elbow and arranged his face over hers. Her eyes, thick with tears, stared past him. "What's the matter?" he said in resignatory sing-song. The eyes budged a fraction and fixed on his own. "You," she said simply. O'Byrne returned to his side of the bed, and after a moment said threateningly, "I see." Then he was up, and on top of her, and then past her and on the far side of the room. "All right then . . ." he said. He wrenched his laces into a knot, and searched for his shirt. Pauline's back was to him. But as he crossed the sitting room her rising, accelerating wail of denial made him stop and turn. All white, in a cotton nightdress, she was there in the bedroom doorway and in the air, simultaneously at every point of arc in the intervening space,

like the trick photographer's diver, she was on the far side
of the room and she was at his lapels, knuckles in her
mouth and shaking her head. O'Byrne smiled, and put his
arms around her shoulders. Forgiveness swept through
him. Clinging to each other they returned to the bedroom.
O'Byrne undressed and they lay down again, O'Byrne on
his back, Pauline with her head pillowed on his shoulder.

O'Byrne said. "I never know what's going on in your
mind," and deeply comforted by this thought, he fell
asleep. Half an hour later he woke. Pauline, exhausted by
a week of twelve-hour shifts, slept deeply on his arm. He
shook her gently. "Hey," he said. He shook her firmly,
and as the rhythm of her breathing broke and she began
to stir, he said in a laconic parody of some unremembered
film, "Hey, there's something we ain't done yet . . ."

Harold was excited. When O'Byrne walked into the shop
towards noon the following day Harold took hold of his
arms and waved in the air a sheet of paper. He was almost
shouting. "I've worked it all out. I know what I want to
do with the shop." "Oh yeah," said O'Byrne dully, and
put his finger in his eyes and scratched till the intolerable
itch there became a bearable pain. Harold rubbed his small
pink hands together and explained rapidly. "I'm going All
American. I spoke to their rep on the phone this morning
and he'll be here in half an hour. I'm getting rid of all the
quid a time piss-in-her-cunt letters. I'm gonna carry the
whole of the House of Florence range at £4.50 a time."

O'Byrne walked across the shop to where Harold's jacket
was spread across a chair. He tried it on. It was, of course,
too small. "And I'm going to call it Transatlantic Books,"
Harold was saying. O'Byrne tossed the jacket on to the
chair. It slid to the floor and deflated there like some rep-
tilian air sac. Harold picked it up, and did not cease talking.
"If I carry Florence exclusive I get a special discount *and*,"
he giggled, "they pay for the fucking neon sign."

O'Byrne sat down and interrupted his brother. "How
many of those soddin' inflatable women did you unload?
There's still twenty-five of the fuckers in the cellar." But

Harold was pouring out Scotch into two glasses. "He'll be here in half an hour," he repeated, and offered one glass to O'Byrne. "Big deal," said O'Byrne, and sipped. "I want you to take the van over to Norbury and collect the order this afternoon. I want to get into this straight away."

O'Byrne sat moodily with his drink while his brother whistled and was busy about the shop. A man came in and bought a magazine. "See," said O'Byrne sourly while the customer was still lingering over the tentacled condoms, "he bought English, didn't he?" The man turned guiltily and left. Harold came and crouched by O'Byrne's chair and spoke as one who explains copulation to an infant. "And what do I make? Forty per cent of 75p. Thirty p. Thirty fucking p. On House of Florence I'll make fifty per cent of £4.50. And that," he rested his hand briefly on O'Byrne's knee, "is what I call business."

O'Byrne wriggled his empty glass in front of Harold's face, and waited patiently for his brother to fill it . . . Little Runt.

The House of Florence warehouse was a disused church in a narrow terraced street on the Brixton side of Norbury. O'Byrne entered by the main porch. A crude plasterboard office and waiting room had been set up in the west end. The font was a large ash-tray in the waiting room. An elderly woman with a blue rinse sat alone in the office typing. When O'Byrne tapped on the sliding window she ignored him, then she rose and slid aside the glass panel. She took the order form he pushed towards her, glancing at him with unconcealed distaste. She spoke primly. "You better wait there." O'Byrne tap-danced abstractly about the font, and combed his hair, and whistled the tune that went in a circle. Suddenly a shrivelled man with a brown coat and clipboard was at his side. "Transatlantic Books?" he said. O'Byrne shrugged and followed him. They moved together slowly down long aisles of bolted steel shelves, the old man pushing a large trolley and O'Byrne walking a little in front with his hands clasped behind his back. Every few yards the warehouseman stopped, and with bad-tempered gasps lifted a thick pile of magazines from the shelves. The load on the trolley grew. The old man's breath echoed hoarsely around the church. At the end of the first aisle he sat down on the trolley, between his neat piles, and coughed and hawked for a minute or so into a paper handkerchief. Then, carefully folding the tissue and its ponderous green contents back into his pocket, he said to O'Byrne, "Here, you're young. You push the thing." And O'Byrne said, "Push the fucker yourself. It's your job," and offered the man a cigarette and lit it for him.

O'Byrne nodded at the shelves. "You get some reading done here." The old man exhaled irritably. "It's all rubbish. It ought to be banned." They moved on. At the end, he was signing the invoice. O'Byrne said, "Who you got lined up for tonight? Madam in the office there?" The warehouseman was pleased. His cackles rang out like bells, then tailed into another coughing fit. He leaned feebly against the wall, and when he had recovered sufficiently he raised his head and meaningfully winked his watery eye. But O'Byrne had turned and was wheeling the magazines out to the van.

Lucy was ten years older than Pauline, and a little plump. But her flat was large and comfortable. She was a sister and Pauline no more than a trainee nurse. They knew nothing of each other. At the underground station O'Byrne bought flowers for Lucy, and when she opened the door to him he presented them with a mock bow and the clicking of heels. "A peace offering?" she said contemptuously and took the daffodils away. She had led him into the bedroom. They sat down side by side on the bed. O'Byrne ran his hand up her leg in a perfunctory kind of way. She pushed away his arm and said, "Come on then. Where have you been the past three days?" O'Byrne could barely remember. Two nights with Pauline, one night in the pub with friends of his brother.

He stretched back luxuriously on the pink candlewick. "You know . . . working late for Harold. Changing the shop around. That kind of thing."

"Those dirty books," said Lucy with a little high-pitched laugh.

O'Byrne stood up and kicked off his shoes. "Don't start that," he said, glad to be off the defensive. Lucy leaned forwards and gathered up his shoes. 'You're going to ruin the backs of these,' she said busily, "kicking them off like that."

They both undressed. Lucy hung her clothes neatly in the wardrobe. When O'Byrne stood almost naked before her she wrinkled her nose in disgust. "Is that you smelling?" O'Byrne was hurt. "I'll have a bath," he offered curtly.

Lucy stirred the bathwater with her hand, and spoke loudly over the thunder of the taps. "You should have brought me some clothes to wash." She hooked her fingers into the elastic of his pants. "Give me these now and they'll be dry by the morning." O'Byrne laced his fingers into hers in a decoy of affection. "No, no," he shouted rapidly. "They were clean on this morning, they were." Playfully Lucy tried to get them off. They wrestled across the bathroom floor, Lucy shrieking with laughter, O'Byrne excited but determined.

Finally Lucy put on her dressing gown and went away. O'Byrne heard her in the kitchen. He sat in the bath and washed away the bright green stains. When Lucy returned his pants were drying on the radiator. "Women's Lib, innit?" said O'Byrne from the bath. Lucy said, "I'm getting in too," and took off her dressing gown. O'Byrne made room for her. "Please yourself," he said with a smile as she settled herself in the grey water.

O'Byrne lay on his back on the clean white sheets, and Lucy eased herself on to his belly like a vast nesting bird. She would have it no other way, from the beginning she had said, "I'm in charge." O'Byrne had replied, "We'll see about that." He was horrified, sickened, that he could enjoy being overwhelmed, like one of those cripples in his brother's magazines. Lucy had spoken briskly, the kind of voice she used for difficult patients. "If you don't like it then don't come back." Imperceptibly O'Byrne was initiated into Lucy's wants. It was not simply that she wished to squat on him. She did not want him to move. "If you move again," she warned him once, "you've had it." From mere habit O'Byrne thrust upwards and deeper, and quick as the tongue of a snake she lashed his face several times with her open palm. On the instant she came, and afterwards lay across the bed, half sobbing, half laughing. O'Byrne one side of his face swollen and pink, departed sulking. "You're a bloody pervert," he had shouted from the door.

Next day he was back, and Lucy agreed not to hit him again. Instead she abused him. "You pathetic helpless little shit," she would scream at the peak of her excitement. And she seemed to intuit O'Byrne's guilty thrill of pleasure, and wish to push it further. One time she had suddenly lifted herself clear of him and, with a far-away smile, urinated on his head and chest. O'Byrne had struggled to get clear, but Lucy held him down and seemed deeply satisfied by his unsought orgasm. This time O'Byrne left the flat enraged. Lucy's strong, chemical smell was with him for days, and it was during this time that he met Pauline. But within the week he was back at Lucy's to collect, so he insisted, his razor, and Lucy was persuading him to try on her underwear. O'Byrne resisted with horror and excitement. "The trouble with you," said Lucy, "is that you're scared of what you like."

Now Lucy gripped his throat in one hand. "You dare move," she hissed, and closed her eyes. O'Byrne lay still. Above him Lucy swayed like a giant tree. Her lips were forming a word, but there was no sound. Many minutes later she opened her eyes and stared down, frowning a little as though struggling to place him. And all the while she eased backwards and forwards. Finally she spoke, more to herself than to him. "Worm . . ." O'Byrne moaned. Lucy's legs and thighs tightened and trembled. "Worm . . . worm . . . you little worm. I'm going to tread on you . . . dirty little worm." Once more her hand was closed about his throat. His eyes were sunk deep, and his word travelled a long way before it left his lips. "Yes," he whispered.

The following day O'Byrne attended the clinic. The doctor
and his male assistant were matter-of-fact, unimpressed.
The assistant filled out a form and wanted details of
O'Byrne's recent sexual history. O'Byrne invented a whore
at Ipswich bus station. For many days after that he kept
to himself. Attending the clinic mornings and evenings, for
injections, he was sapped of desire. When Pauline or Lucy
phoned, Harold told them he did not know where O'Byrne
was. "Probably taken off for somewhere," he said, winking
across the shop at his brother. Both women phoned each
day for three or four days, and then suddenly there were
no calls from either.

O'Byrne paid no attention. The shop was taking good
money now. In the evenings he drank with his brother and
his brother's friends. He felt himself to be both busy and
ill. Ten days passed. With the extra cash Harold was giving
him, he bought a leather jacket, like Harold's, but somewhat better, sharper, lined with red imitation silk. It both
shone and creaked. He spent many minutes in front of the
fish-eye mirror, standing sideways on, admiring the manner
in which his shoulders and biceps pulled the leather to a
tight sheen. He wore his jacket between the shop and the
clinic and sensed the glances of women in the street. He
thought of Pauline and Lucy. He passed a day considering
which to phone first. He chose Pauline, and phoned her
from the shop.

Trainee Nurse Shepherd was not available, O'Byrne was
told after many minutes of waiting. She was sitting an
examination. O'Byrne had his call transferred to the other
side of the hospital. "Hi," he said when Lucy picked up
the phone. "It's me." Lucy was delighted. "When did you
get back? Where have you been? When are you coming
round?" He sat down. "How about tonight?" he said. Lucy
whispered in sex-kitten French, "I can 'ardly wait . . ."
O'Byrne laughed and pressed his thumb and forefinger
against his forehead and heard other distant voices on the
line. He heard Lucy giving instructions. Then she spoke
rapidly to him. "I've got to go. They've just brought a case
in. About eight tonight then . . ." and she was gone.

O'Byrne prepared his story, but Lucy did not ask him where he had been. She was too happy. She laughed when she opened the door to him, she hugged him and laughed again. She looked different. O'Byrne could not remember her so beautiful. Her hair was shorter and a deeper brown, her nails were pale orange, she wore a short black dress with orange dots. There were candles and wine glasses on the dining table, music on the record player. She stood back, her eyes bright, almost wild, and admired his leather jacket. She ran her hands up the red lining. She pressed herself against it. "Very smooth," she said. "Reduced to sixty quid," O'Byrne said proudly, and tried to kiss her. But she laughed again and pushed him into a chair. "You wait there and I'll get something to drink."

O'Byrne lay back. From the record player a man sang of love in a restaurant with clean white tablecloths. Lucy brought an icy bottle of white wine. She sat on the arm of his chair and they drank and talked. Lucy told him recent stories of the ward, of nurses who fell in and out of love, patients who recovered or died. As she spoke she undid the top buttons of his shirt and pushed her hand down to his belly. And when O'Byrne turned in his chair and reached up for her she pushed him away, leaned down and kissed him on the nose. "Now, now," she said primly. O'Byrne exerted himself. He recounted anecdotes he had heard in the pub. Lucy laughed crazily at the end of each, and as he was beginning the third she let her hand drop lightly between his legs and rest there. O'Byrne closed his eyes. The hand was gone and Lucy was nudging him. "Go on," she said. "It was getting interesting." He caught her wrist and wanted to pull her on to his lap. With a little sigh she slipped away and returned with a second bottle. "We should have wine more often," she said, "if it makes you tell such funny stories."

Encouraged, O'Byrne told his story, something about a car and what a garage mechanic said to a vicar. Once again Lucy was fishing round his fly and laughing, laughing. It was a funnier story than he thought. The floor rose and fell beneath his feet. And Lucy so beautiful, scented, warm . . .

her eyes glowed. He was paralysed by her teasing. He loved her, and she laughed and robbed him of his will. Now he saw, he had come to live with her, and each night she teased him to the edge of madness. He pressed his face into her breasts. "I love you," he mumbled, and again Lucy was laughing, shaking, wiping the tears from her eyes. "Do you . . . do you . . ." she kept trying to say. She emptied the bottle into his glass. "Here's a toast . . ." "Yeah," said O'Byrne, "To us." Lucy was holding down her laughter. "No, no," she squealed. "To *you*." "All right," he said, and downed his wine in one. Then Lucy was standing in front of him pulling his arm. "C'mon," she said. "C'mon." O'Byrne struggled out of the chair. "What about dinner then?" he said. "You're the dinner," she said, and they giggled as they tottered towards the bedroom.

As they undressed Lucy said, "I've got a special little surprise for you so . . . no fuss." O'Byrne sat on the edge of Lucy's large bed and shivered. "I'm ready for anything," he said. "Good . . . good," and for the first time she kissed him deeply, and pushed him gently backwards on to the bed. She climbed forward and sat astride his chest. O'Byrne closed his eyes. Months ago he would have resisted furiously. Lucy lifted his left hand to her mouth and kissed each finger. "Hmmm . . . the first course." O'Byrne laughed. The bed and the room undulated softly about him. Lucy was pushing his hand towards the top corner of the bed. O'Byrne heard a distant jingle, like bells. Lucy knelt by his shoulder, holding down his wrist, buckling it to a leather strap. She had always said she would tie him up one day and fuck him. She bent low over his face and they kissed again. She was licking his eyes and whispering, "You're not going anywhere." O'Byrne gasped for air. He could not move his face to smile. Now she was tugging at his right arm, pulling it, stretching it to the far corner of the bed. With a dread thrill of compliance O'Byrne felt his arm die. Now that was secure and Lucy was running her hands along the inside of his thigh, and on down to his feet. . . . he lay stretched almost to breaking, splitting, fixed to each corner, spread out against the white sheet.

Lucy knelt at the apex of his legs. She stared down at him
with a faint, objective smile and fingered herself delicately.
O'Byrne lay waiting for her to settle on him like a vast
white nesting bird. She was tracing with the top of one
finger the curve of his excitement, and then with the thumb
and forefinger making a tight ring about its base. A sigh
fled between his teeth. Lucy leaned forwards. Her eyes
were wild. She whispered, "We're going to get you, me
and Pauline are . . ."

Pauline. For an instant, syllables hollow of meaning.
"What?" said O'Byrne, and as he spoke the word he
remembered, and understood a threat. "Untie me," he said
quickly. But Lucy's finger curled under her crotch and her
eyes half closed. Her breathing was slow and deep. "Untie
me," he shouted, and struggled hopelessly with his straps.
Lucy's breath came now in light little gasps. As he struggled, so they accelerated. She was saying something . . .
moaning something. What was she saying? He could not
hear. "Lucy," he said, "please untie me." Suddenly she
was silent, her eyes wide open and clear. She climbed off
the bed. "Your friend Pauline will be here, soon," she said,
and began to get dressed. She was different, her movements
brisk and efficient, she no longer looked at him. O'Byrne
tried to sound casual. His voice was a little high. "What's
going on?" Lucy stood at the foot of the bed buttoning her
dress. Her lip curled. "You're a bastard," she said. The
doorbell rang and she smiled. "Now that's good timing,
isn't it?"

"Yes, he went down very quietly," Lucy was saying as she
showed Pauline into the bedroom. Pauline said nothing.
She avoided looking at either O'Byrne or Lucy. And
O'Byrne's eyes were fixed on the object she carried in her
arms. It was large and silver, like an outsized electric toas-
ter. "It can plug in just here," said Lucy. Pauline set it
down on the bedside table. Lucy sat down at her dressing
table and began to comb her hair. "I'll get some water for
it in a minute," she said.

Pauline went and stood by the window. There was

silence. Then O'Byrne said hoarsely. "What's that thing?"
Lucy turned in her seat. "It's a sterilizer," she said breezily.
"Sterilizer?" "You know, for sterilizing surgical instruments." The next question O'Byrne did not dare to ask. He
felt sick and dizzy. Lucy left the room. Pauline continued to
stare out the window into the dark. O'Byrne felt the need
to whisper. "Hey, Pauline, what's going on?" She turned
to face him, and said nothing. O'Byrne discovered that the
strap round his right wrist was slackening a little, the
leather was stretching. His hand was concealed by pillows.
He worked it backwards and forwards, and spoke urgently.
"Look, let's get out of here. Undo these things."

For a moment she hesitated, then she walked round the
side of the bed and stared down at him. She shook her
head. "We're going to get you." The repetition terrified
him. He thrashed from side to side. "It's not my idea of a
fucking joke," he shouted. Pauline turned away. "I hate
you," he heard her say. The right-hand strap gave a little
more. "I hate you. I hate you." He pulled till he thought
his arm would break. His hand was too large still for the
noose around his wrist. He gave up.

Now Lucy was at the bedside pouring water into the
sterilizer. "This is a sick joke," said O'Byrne. Lucy lifted
a flat, black case on to the table. She snapped it open and
began to take out long-handled scissors, scalpel and other
bright, tapering, silver objects. She lowered them carefully
into the water. O'Byrne started to work his right hand
again. Lucy removed the black case and set on the table
two white kidney bowls with blue rims. In one lay two
hypodermic needles, one large, one small. In the other was
cotton wool. O'Byrne's voice shook. "What is all this?"
Lucy rested her cool hand on his forehead. She enunciated
with precision. "This is what they should have done for
you at the clinic." "The clinic . . . ?" he echoed. He could
see now that Pauline was leaning against the wall drinking
from a bottle of Scotch. "Yes," said Lucy, reaching down
to take his pulse. "Stop you spreading round your secret
little diseases." "And telling lies," said Pauline, her voice
strained with indignation.

O'Byrne laughed uncontrollably. "Telling lies . . . telling lies," he spluttered. Lucy took the Scotch from Pauline and raised it to her lips. O'Byrne recovered. His legs were shaking. "You're both out of your minds." Lucy tapped the sterilizer and said to Pauline, "This will take a few minutes yet. We'll scrub down in the kitchen." O'Byrne tried to raise his head. "Where are you going?" he called after them. "Pauline . . . Pauline."

But Pauline had nothing more to say. Lucy stopped in the bedroom doorway and smiled at him. "We'll leave you a pretty little stump to remember us by," and she closed the door.

On the bedside table the sterilizer began to hiss. Shortly after it gave out the low rumble of boiling water, and inside the instruments clinked together gently. In terror he pumped his hand. The leather was flaying the skin off his wrist. The noose was riding now round the base of his thumb. Timeless minutes passed. He whimpered and pulled and the edge of the leather cut deep into his hand. He was almost free.

The door opened, and Lucy and Pauline carried in a small low table. Through his fear O'Byrne felt excitement once more, horrified excitement. They arranged the table close to the bed. Lucy bent low over his erection. "Oh dear . . . oh dear," she murmured. With tongs Pauline lifted the instruments from the boiling water and laid them out in neat silver rows on the starched white tablecloth she had spread across the table. The leather noose slipped forwards fractionally. Lucy sat on the edge of the bed and took the large hypodermic from the bowl. "This will make you a little sleepy," she promised. She held it upright and expelled a small jet of liquid. And as she reached for the cotton wool O'Byrne's arm pulled clear. Lucy smiled. She set aside the hypodermic. She leaned forwards once more . . . warm, scented . . . she was fixing him with wild red eyes . . . her fingers played over his tip . . . she held him still between her fingers. "Lie back, Michael, my sweet." She nodded briskly at Pauline. "If you'll secure that strap, Nurse Shepherd, then I think we can begin."

Ringing the Changes
Introduction

My relationship with horror literature began to get serious around 1975, after I had published Julia, *my first supernatural novel. My old friend Thom Tessier, a real devotee of the* outré *and outrageous, pointed me toward the kind of people I ought to be reading if I wanted to know what had been done in the field – people like Lovecraft, Frank Belknap Long, Richard Matheson, Robert Bloch, Le Fanu, Machen, Blackwood. That we both lived in London meant that I could find books by all these people in 1975, that many of them were represented in* The Pan Book of Horror Stories, *and that the world around us did not immediately condemn these writers as inept weirdos. Horror writing was accepted as writing in England, where people had longer memories than in America.*

One of the writers Tessier was always going on about was Robert Aickman, and I eventually tracked down some of his stories. From the first I understood that he was a deeply original artist. This in no way implies that I understood Aickman immediately, because I didn't. Sometimes I would look up at the end of a story, feeling that the whole thing had just twisted itself inside out and turned into smoke – I had blinked, and missed it all. It took me a little while to learn to accept this experience as valuable in itself, and to begin to see how the real oddness of most of Aickman's work is directly related to its psychological, even psychoanalytic, acuity. Unconscious forces move the stories itself, as well as the characters, and what initially looks like a distressing randomness of detail and event is its opposite – everything is necessary, everything is logical, but not at all in a linear way. To pull off this kind of dream-like associativeness, to pack

*it with the menace that results from a narrative deconstruction
of the notion of "ordinary reality", to demonstrate again and
again in excellent prose (no dumb experimentation or
affectation here) that our lives are literally shaped by what
we do not understand about ourselves, requires a talent that
yokes together an uncommon literary sensitivity with a lush,
almost tropical inventiveness.*

*Along with "The Inner Room", "Into the Wood", and
several others, "Ringing the Changes" is one of Aickman's
greatest stories. It's a simple as a fable – a perverse fable
about sex and death – and its deep emotional charge comes
right out of Aickman's powerful feelings about the unknowable
other gender.* "At heart women are creatures of darkness
all the time," *says the disgraced, ambiguous commandant;
Aickman must have felt like this from time to time, but the
story distributes blame and grandeur more wisely. A marriage
has been illuminated, as if by lightning-bolt; and the hints
of misunderstanding in the story's first pages are resolved in a
wife's mysterious ecstasy forever out of the reach of her
timorous husband.*

PETER STRAUB
Author of Ghost Story,
Floating Dragon *and* Koko

Robert Aickman
Ringing the Changes

He had never been among those many who deeply dislike church bells, but the ringing that evening at Holihaven changed his view. Bells could certainly get on one's nerves, he felt, although he had only just arrived in the town.

He had been too well aware of the perils attendant upon marrying a girl twenty-four years younger than himself to add to them by a conventional honeymoon. The strange force of Phrynne's love had borne both of them away from their previous selves: in him a formerly haphazard and easy-going approach to life had been replaced by much deep planning to wall in happiness; and she, though once thought cold and choosy, would now agree to anything as long as she was with him. He had said that if they were to marry in June, it would be at the cost of not being able to honey-moon until October. Had they been courting longer, he had explained, gravely smiling, special arrangements could have been made; but, as it was, business claimed him. This, indeed, was true; because his business position was less influential than he had led Phrynne to believe. Finally, it would have been impossible for them to have courted longer, because they had courted from the day they met, which was less than six weeks before the day they married.

" 'A village,' " he had quoted as they entered the branch-line train at the junction (itself sufficiently remote), " 'from which (it was said) persons of sufficient longevity might hope to reach Liverpool Street.' " By now he was able to make jokes about age, although perhaps he did so rather too often.

"Who said that?"

"Bertrand Russell."

She had looked at him with her big eyes in her tiny face.

"Really." He had smiled confirmation.

"I'm not arguing." She had still been looking at him. The romantic gas light in the charming period compartment had left him uncertain whether she was smiling back or not. He had given himself the benefit of the doubt, and kissed her.

The guard had blown his whistle and they had rumbled into the darkness. The branch line swung so sharply away from the main line that Phrynne had been almost toppled from her seat.

"Why do we go so slowly when it's so flat?"

"Because the engineer laid the line up and down the hills and valleys such as they are, instead of cutting through and embanking over them." He liked being able to inform her.

"How do you know? Gerald! You said you hadn't been to Holihaven before."

"It applies to most of the railways in East Anglia."

"So that even though it's flatter, it's slower?"

"Time matters less."

"I should have hated going to a place where time mattered or that you'd been to before. You'd have had nothing to remember me by."

He hadn't been quite sure that her words exactly expressed her thought, but the thought had lightened his heart.

Holihaven station could hardly have been built in the days of the town's magnificence, for they were in the Middle Ages; but it still implied grander functions than came its way now. The platforms were long enough for visiting London expresses, which had since gone elsewhere; and the architecture of the waiting-rooms would have been not insufficient for occasional use by Foreign Royalty. Oil lamps on perches like those occupied by macaws lighted the uniformed staff, who numbered two, and, together with every other native of Holihaven, looked like storm-habituated mariners.

The stationmaster and porter, as Gerald took them to be, watched him approach down the platform, with a heavy suitcase in each hand and Phrynne walking deliciously by his side. He saw one of them address a remark to the other, but neither offered to help. Gerald had to put down the cases in order to give up their tickets. The other passengers had already disappeared.

"Where's the Bell?"

Gerald had found the hotel in a reference book. It was the only one the book allotted to Holihaven. But as Gerald spoke, and before the ticket collector could answer, the sudden deep note of an actual bell rang through the darkness. Phrynne caught hold of Gerald's sleeve.

Ignoring Gerald, the stationmaster, if such he was, turned to his colleague. "They're starting early."

"Every reason to be in good time," said the other man.

The stationmaster nodded, and put Gerald's tickets indifferently in his jacket pocket.

"Can you please tell me how I get to the Bell Hotel?"

The stationmaster's attention returned to him. "Have you a room booked?"

"Certainly."

"Tonight?" The stationmaster looked inappropriately suspicious.

"Of course."

Again the stationmaster looked at the other man.

"It's them Pascoes."

"Yes," said Gerald. "That's the name, Pascoe."

"We don't use the Bell," explained the stationmaster. "But you'll find it in Wrack Street." He gesticulated vaguely and unhelpfully. "Straight ahead. Down Station Road. Then down Wrack Street. You can't miss it."

"Thank you."

As soon as they entered the town, the big bell began to boom regularly.

"What narrow streets!" said Phrynne.

"They follow the lines of the medieval city. Before the river silted up, Holihaven was one of the most important seaports in Great Britain."

"Where's everybody got to?"

Although it was only six o'clock, the place certainly seemed deserted.

"Where's the hotel got to?" rejoined Gerald.

"Poor Gerald! Let me help." She laid her hand beside his on the handle of the suitcase nearest to her, but as she was about fifteen inches shorter than he, she could be of little assistance. They must already have gone more than a quarter of a mile. "Do you think we're in the right street?"

"Most unlikely, I should say. But there's no one to ask."

"Must be early closing day."

The single deep notes of the bell were now coming more frequently.

"Why are they ringing that bell? Is it a funeral?"

"Bit late for a funeral."

She looked at him a little anxiously.

"Anyway it's not cold."

"Considering we're on the east coast it's quite astonishingly warm."

"Not that I care."

"I hope that bell isn't going to ring all night."

She pulled on the suitcase. His arms were in any case almost parting from his body. "Look! We've passed it."

They stopped, and he looked back. "How could we have done that?"

"Well, we have."

She was right. He could see a big ornamental bell hanging from a bracket attached to a house about a hundred yards behind them.

They retraced their steps and entered the hotel. A woman dressed in a navy blue coat and skirt, with a good figure but dyed red hair and a face ridged with make-up, advanced upon them.

"Mr and Mrs Bantead? I'm Hilda Pascoe. Don, my husband, isn't very well."

Gerald felt full of doubts. His arrangements were not going as they should. Never rely on guide-book recommendations. The trouble lay partly in Phrynne's insistence that they go somewhere he did not know. "I'm sorry to hear that," he said.

"You know what men are like when they're ill?" Mrs Pascoe spoke understandingly to Phrynne.

"Impossible," said Phrynne. "Or very difficult."

"Talk about Woman in our hours of ease."

"Yes," said Phrynne. "What's the trouble?"

"It's always the same trouble with Don," said Mrs Pascoe, then checked herself. "It's his stomach," she said. "Ever since he was a kid, Don's had trouble with the lining of his stomach."

Gerald interrupted, "I wonder if we could see our room?"

"So sorry," said Mrs Pascoe. "Will you register first?" She produced a battered volume bound in peeling imitation leather. "Just the name and address." She spoke as if Gerald might contribute a résumé of his life.

It was the first time he and Phrynne had ever registered in a hotel; but his confidence in the place was not increased by the long period which had passed since the registration above.

"We're always quiet in October," remarked Mrs Pascoe, her eyes upon him. Gerald noticed that her eyes were slightly bloodshot. "Except sometimes for the bars, of course."

"We wanted to come out of the season," said Phrynne soothingly.

"Quite," said Mrs Pascoe.

"Are we alone in the house?" inquired Gerald. After all the woman was probably doing her best.

"Except for Commandant Shotcroft. You won't mind him, will you? He's a regular."

"I'm sure we shan't," said Phrynne.

"People say the house wouldn't be the same without Commandant Shotcroft."

"I see."

"What's that bell?" asked Gerald. Apart from anything else, it really was much too near.

Mrs Pascoe looked away. He thought she looked shifty

under her entrenched make up. But she only said, "Practice."

"Do you mean there will be more of them later?"

She nodded. "But never mind," she said encouragingly. "Let me show you to your room. Sorry there's no porter."

Before they had reached the bedroom, the whole peal had commenced.

"Is this the quietest room you have?" inquired Gerald. "What about the other side of the house?"

"This *is* the other side of the house. Saint Guthlac's is over there." She pointed out through the bedroom door.

"Darling," said Phrynne, her hand on Gerald's arm, "they"ll soon stop. They're only practising."

Mrs Pascoe said nothing. Her expression indicated that she was one of those people whose friendliness has a precise and seldom exceeded limit.

"If *you* don't mind," said Gerald to Phrynne, hesitating.

"They have ways of their own in Holihaven," said Mrs Pascoe. Her undertone of militancy implied, among other things, that if Gerald and Phrynne chose to leave, they were at liberty to do so. Gerald did not care for that either: her attitude would have been different, he felt, had there been anywhere else for them to go. The bells were making him touchy and irritable.

"It's a very pretty room," said Phrynne. "I adore four-posters."

"Thank you," said Gerald to Mrs Pascoe. "What time's dinner?"

"Seven-thirty. You've time for a drink in the bar first." She went.

"We certainly have," said Gerald when the door was shut. "It's only just six."

"Actually," said Phrynne, who was standing by the window looking down into the street, "I *like* church bells."

"All very well," said Gerald, "but on one's honeymoon they distract the attention."

"Not mine," said Phrynne simply. Then she added, "There's still no one about."

"I expect they're all in the bar."

"I don't want a drink. I want to explore the town."

"As you wish. But hadn't you better unpack?"

"I ought to, but I'm not going to. Not until after I've seen the sea." Such small shows of independence in her enchanted Gerald.

Mrs Pascoe was not about when they passed through the lounge, nor was there any sound of activity in the establishment.

Outside, the bells seemed to be booming and bounding immediately over their heads.

"It's like warriors fighting in the sky," shouted Phrynne. "Do you think the sea's down there?" She indicated the direction from which they had previously retraced their steps.

"I imagine so. The street seems to end in nothing. That would be the sea."

"Come on. Let's run." She was off, before he could even think about it. Then there was nothing to do but run after her. He hoped there were not eyes behind blinds.

She stopped, and held wide her arms to catch him. The top of her head hardly came up to his chin. He knew she was silently indicating that his failure to keep up with her was not a matter for self-consciousness.

"Isn't it beautiful?"

"The sea?" There was no moon; and little was discernible beyond the end of the street.

"Not only."

"Everything but the sea. The sea's invisible."

"You can smell it."

"I certainly can't hear it."

She slackened her embrace and cocked her head away from him. "The bells echo so much, it's as if there were two churches."

"I'm sure there are more than that. There always are in old towns like this." Suddenly he was struck by the significance of his words in relation to what she had said. He shrank into himself, tautly listening.

"Yes," cried Phrynne delightedly. "It *is* another church."

"Impossible," said Gerald. "Two churches wouldn't have practice ringing on the same night."

"I'm quite sure. I can hear one lot of bells with my left ear, and another lot with my right."

They had still seen no one. The sparse gas lights fell on the furnishings of a stone quay, small but plainly in regular use.

"The whole population must be ringing the bells." His own remark discomfited Gerald.

"Good for them." She took his hand. "Let's go down on the beach and look for the sea."

They descended a flight of stone steps at which the sea had sucked and bitten. The beach was as stony as the steps, but lumpier.

"We'll just go straight on," said Phrynne. "Until we find it."

Left to himself, Gerald would have been less keen. The stones were very large and very slippery, and his eyes did not seem to be becoming accustomed to the dark.

"You're right, Phrynne, about the smell."

"Honest sea smell."

"Just as you say." He took it rather to be the smell of dense rotting weed; across which he supposed they must be slithering. It was not a smell he had previously encountered in such strength.

Energy could hardly be spared for talking, and advancing hand in hand was impossible.

After various random remarks on both sides and the lapse of what seemed a very long time, Phrynne spoke again. "Gerald, where is it? What sort of seaport is it that has no sea?"

She continued onwards, but Gerald stopped and looked back. He had thought the distance they had gone overlong, but was startled to see how great it was. The darkness was doubtless deceitful, but the few lights on the quay appeared as on a distant horizon.

The far glimmering specks still in his eyes, he turned and looked after Phrynne. He could barely see her. Perhaps she was progressing faster without him.

"Phrynne! Darling!"

Unexpectedly she gave a sharp cry.

"Phrynne!"

She did not answer.

"Phrynne!"

Then she spoke more or less calmly. "Panic over. Sorry, darling. I stood on something."

He realized that a panic it had indeed been; at least in him.

"You're all right?"

"Think so."

He struggled up to her. "The smell's worse than ever." It was overpowering.

"I think it's coming from what I stepped on. My foot went right in, and then there was the smell."

"I've never known anything like it."

"Sorry, darling,' she said gently mocking him. "Let's go away."

"Let's go back. Don't you think?"

"Yes," said Phrynne. "But I must warn you I'm very disappointed. I think that seaside attractions should include the sea."

He noticed that as they retreated, she was scraping the sides of one shoe against the stones, as if trying to clean it.

"I think the whole place is a disappointment,' he said. "I really must apologize. We'll go somewhere else."

"I like the bells," she replied, making a careful reservation.

Gerald said nothing.

"I don't want to go somewhere where you've been before."

The bells rang out over the desolate, unattractive beach. Now the sound seemed to be coming from every point along the shore.

"I suppose all the churches practice on the same night in order to get it over with," said Gerald.

"They do it in order to see which can ring the loudest," said Phrynne.

"Take care you don't twist your ankle."

The din as they reached the rough little quay was such as to suggest that Phrynne's idea was literally true.

The Coffee Room was so low that Gerald had to dip beneath a sequence of thick beams.

"Why 'Coffee Room'?" asked Phrynne, looking at the words on the door. "I saw a notice that coffee will only be served in the lounge."

"It's the *lucus a non lucendo* principle."

"That explains everything. I wonder where we sit." A single electric lantern, mass produced in an antique pattern, had been turned on. The bulb was of that limited wattage which is peculiar to hotels. It did little to penetrate the shadows.

"The *lucus a non lucendo* principle is the principle of calling white black."

"Not at all," said a voice from the darkness. "On the contrary. The word black comes from an ancient root which means 'to bleach'."

They had thought themselves alone, but now saw a small man seated by himself at an unlighted corner table. In the darkness he looked like a monkey.

"I stand corrected," said Gerald.

They sat at the table under the lantern.

The man in the corner spoke again. 'Why are you here at all?"

Phrynne looked frightened, but Gerald replied quietly.

"We're on holiday. We prefer it out of the season. I presume you are Commandant Shotcroft?'

"No need to presume." Unexpectedly the commandant switched on the antique lantern which was nearest to him. His table was littered with a finished meal. It struck Gerald that he must have switched off the light when he heard them approach the Coffee Room. "I'm going anyway."

"Are we late?" asked Phrynne, always the assuager of situations.

"No, you're not late," said the commandant in a deep, moody voice. 'My meals are prepared half an hour before the time the rest come in. I don't like eating in company." He had risen to his feet. "So perhaps you'll excuse me."

Without troubling about an answer, he stepped quickly out of the Coffee Room. He had cropped white hair; tragic, heavy-lidded eyes; and a round face which was yellow and lined.

A second later his head reappeared round the door.

"Ring," he said; and again withdrew.

"Too many other people ringing," said Gerald. "But I don't see what else we can do."

The Coffee Room bell, however, made a noise like a fire alarm.

Mrs Pascoe appeared. She looked considerably the worse for drink.

"Didn't see you in the bar."

"Must have missed us in the crowd," said Gerald amiably.

"Crowd?" inquired Mrs Pascoe drunkenly. Then, after a difficult pause, she offered them a hand-written menu.

They ordered; and Mrs Pascoe served them throughout. Gerald was apprehensive lest her indisposition increase during the course of the meal; but her insobriety, like her affability, seemed to have an exact and definite limit.

"All things considered, the food might be worse," remarked Gerald, towards the end. It was a relief that something was going reasonably well. "Not much of it, but at least the dishes are hot."

When Phrynne translated this into a compliment to the cook, Mrs Pascoe said, "I cooked it all myself, although I shouldn't be the one to say so."

Gerald felt really surprised that she was in a condition to have accomplished this. Possibly, he reflected with alarm, she had had much practice under similar conditions.

"Coffee is served in the lounge," said Mrs Pascoe.

They withdrew. In a corner of the lounge was a screen decorated with winning Elizabethan ladies in ruffs and hoops. From behind it projected a pair of small black boots. Phrynne nudged Gerald and pointed to them. Gerald nodded. They felt themselves constrained to talk about things which bored them.

The hotel was old and its walls thick. In the empty

lounge the noise of the bells could not prevent conversation being overheard, but still came from all around, as if the hotel were a fortress beleaguered by surrounding artillery.

After their second cups of coffee, Gerald suddenly said he couldn't stand it.

"Darling, it's not doing us any harm. I think it's rather cosy." Phrynne subsided in the wooden chair with its sloping back and long mud-coloured mock-velvet cushions; and opened her pretty legs to the fire.

"Every church in the town must be ringing its bells. It's been going on for two and a half hours and they never seem to take the usual breathers."

"We wouldn't hear. Because of all the other bells ringing. I think it's nice of them to ring the bells for us."

Nothing further was said for several minutes. Gerald was beginning to realize that they had yet to evolve a holiday routine.

"I'll get you a drink. What shall it be?"

"Anything you like. Whatever *you* have." Phrynne was immersed in female enjoyment of the fire's radiance on her body.

Gerald missed this, and said, "I don't quite see why they have to keep the place like a hothouse. When I come back, we'll sit somewhere else."

"Men wear too many clothes, darling," said Phrynne drowsily.

Contrary to his assumption, Gerald found the lounge bar as empty as everywhere else in the hotel and the town. There was not even a person to dispense.

Somewhat irritably, Gerald struck a brass bell which stood on the counter. It rang out sharply as a pistol shot.

Mrs Pascoe appeared at a door among the shelves. She had taken off her jacket, and her make-up had begun to run.

"A cognac, please. Double. And a Kümmel."

Mrs Pascoe's hands were shaking so much that she could not get the cork out of the brandy bottle.

"Allow me." Gerald stretched his arm across the bar.

Mrs Pascoe stared at him blearily. "OK. But I must pour it."

Gerald extracted the cork and returned the bottle. Mrs Pascoe slopped a far from precise dose into a balloon.

Catastrophe followed. Unable to return the bottle to the high shelf where it resided, Mrs Pascoe placed it on a waist-level ledge. Reaching for the alembic of Kümmel, she swept the three-quarters full brandy bottle on to the tiled floor. The stuffy air became fogged with the fumes of brandy from behind the bar.

At the door from which Mrs Pascoe had emerged appeared a man from the inner room. Though still young-ish, he was puce and puffy, and in his braces, with no collar. Streaks of sandy hair laced his vast red scalp. Liquor oozed all over him, as if from a perished gourd. Gerald took it that this was Don.

The man was too drunk to articulate. He stood in the doorway clinging with each red hand to the ledge, and savagely struggling to flay his wife with imprecations.

"How much?" said Gerald to Mrs Pascoe. It seemed useless to try for the Kümmel. The hotel must have another bar.

"Three and six," said Mrs Pascoe, quite lucidly; but Gerald saw that she was about to weep.

He had the exact sum. She turned her back on him and flicked the cash register. As she returned from it, he heard the fragmentation of glass as she stepped on a piece of the broken bottle. Gerald looked at her husband out of the corner of his eye. The sagging, loose-mouthed figure made him shudder. Something moved him.

"I'm sorry about the accident," he said to Mrs Pascoe. He held the balloon in one hand, and was just going.

Mrs Pascoe looked at him. The slow tears of desperation were edging down her face, but she now seemed quite sober. "Mr Banstead," she said in a flat, hurried voice. "May I come and sit with you and your wife in the lounge? Just for a few minutes."

"Of course." It was certainly not what he wanted, and he wondered what would become of the bar, but he felt

unexpectedly sorry for her, and it was impossible to say
no.

To reach the flap of the bar she had to pass her husband.
Gerald saw her hesitate for a second; then she advanced
resolutely and steadily and looking straight before her. If
the man had let go with his hands, he would have fallen;
but as she passed him, he released a great gob of spit. He
was far too incapable to aim, and it fell on the side of his
own trousers. Gerald lifted the flap for Mrs Pascoe and
stood back to let her precede him from the bar. As he
followed her, he heard her husband maundering off into
unintelligible inward searchings.

"The Kümmel!" said Mrs Pascoe, remembering in the
doorway.

"Never mind," said Gerald. "Perhaps I could try one of
the other bars?"

"Not tonight. They're shut. I'd better go back."

"No. We'll think of something else." It was not yet nine
o'clock, and Gerald wondered about the Licensing Justices.

But in the lounge was another unexpected scene. Mrs
Pascoe stopped as soon as they entered, and Gerald, caught
between two imitation-leather armchairs, looked over her
shoulder.

Phrynne had fallen asleep. Her head was slightly on one
side, but her mouth was shut, and her body no more than
gracefully relaxed, so that she looked most beautiful, and,
Gerald thought, a trifle unearthly, like a dead girl in an
early picture by Millais.

The quality of her beauty seemed also to have impressed
Commandant Shotcroft; for he was standing silently behind
her and looking down at her, his sad face transfigured.
Gerald noticed that a leaf of the pseudo-Elizabethan screen
had been folded back, revealing a small cretonne-covered
chair, with an open tome face downward in its seat.

"Won't you join us?" said Gerald boldly. There was that
in the commandant's face which boded no hurt. "Can I get
you a drink?"

The commandant did not turn his head, and seemed

unable to speak. Then in a low voice he said, "For a moment only."

"Good," said Gerald. "Sit down. And you, Mrs Pascoe." Mrs Pascoe was dabbing at her face. Gerald addressed the commandant. "What shall it be?"

"Nothing to drink," said the Commandant in the same low mutter. It occurred to Gerald that if Phrynne awoke, the commandant would go.

"What about you?" Gerald looked at Mrs Pascoe, earnestly hoping she would decline.

"No, thanks." She was glancing at the commandant. Clearly she had not expected him to be there.

Phrynne being asleep, Gerald sat down too. He sipped his brandy. It was impossible to romanticize the action with a toast.

The events in the bar had made him forget about the bells. Now, as they sat silently round the sleeping Phrynne, the tide of sound swept over him once more.

"You mustn't think," said Mrs Pascoe, "that he's always like that." They all spoke in hushed voices. All of them seemed to have reason to do so. The commandant was again gazing sombrely at Phrynne's beauty.

"Of course not." But it was hard to believe.

"The licensed business puts temptations in a man's way."

"It must be very difficult."

"We ought never to have come here. We were happy in South Norwood."

"You must do good business during the season."

"Two months," said Mrs Pascoe bitterly, but still softly. "Two and a half at the very most. The people who come during the season have no idea what goes on out of it."

"What made you leave South Norwood?"

"Don's stomach. The doctor said the sea air would do him good."

"Speaking of that, doesn't the sea go too far out? We went down on the beach before dinner, but couldn't see it anywhere."

On the other side of the fire, the commandant turned his eyes from Phrynne and looked at Gerald.

"I wouldn't know," said Mrs Pascoe. "I never have time to look from one year's end to the other." It was a customary enough answer, but Gerald felt that it did not disclose the whole truth. He noticed that Mrs Pascoe glanced uneasily at the commandant, who by now was staring neither at Phrynne nor at Gerald but at the toppling citadels in the fire.

"And now I must get on with my work," continued Mrs Pascoe, "I only came in for a minute." She looked Gerald in the face. "Thank you," she said, and rose.

"Please stay a little longer," said Gerald. "Wait till my wife wakes up." As he spoke, Phrynne slightly shifted.

"Can't be done," said Mrs Pascoe, her lips smiling. Gerald noticed that all the time she was watching the commandant from under her lids, and knew that were he not there, she would have stayed.

As it was, she went. "I'll probably see you later to say good night. Sorry the water's not very hot. It's having no porter."

The bells showed no sign of flagging.

When Mrs Pascoe had closed the door, the commandant spoke.

"He was a fine man once. Don't think otherwise."

"You mean Pascoe?"

The Commandant nodded seriously.

"Not my type," said Gerald.

"DSO and bar. DFC and bar."

"And now bar only. Why?"

"You heard what she said. It was a lie. They didn't leave South Norwood for the sea air."

"So I supposed."

"He got into trouble. He was fixed. He wasn't the kind of man to know about human nature and all its rottenness."

"A pity," said Gerald. "But perhaps, even so, this isn't the best place for him?"

"It's the worst," said the commandant, a dark flame in his eyes. "For him or anyone else."

Again Phrynne shifted in her sleep: this time more convulsively, so that she nearly awoke. For some reason the two men remained speechless and motionless until she was again breathing steadily. Against the silence within, the bells sounded louder than ever. It was as if the tumult were tearing holes in the roof.

"It's certainly a very noisy place," said Gerald, still in an undertone.

"Why did you have to come tonight of all nights?" The commandant spoke in the same undertone, but his vehemence was extreme.

"This doesn't happen often?"

"Once every year."

"They should have told us."

"They don't usually accept bookings. They've no right to accept them. When Pascoe was in charge they never did."

"I expect that Mrs Pascoe felt they were in no position to turn away business."

"It's not a matter that should be left to a woman."

"Not much alternative surely?"

"At heart women are creatures of darkness all the time."

The commandant's seriousness and bitterness left Gerald without a reply.

"My wife doesn't mind the bells," he said after a moment. "In fact she rather likes them." The commandant really was converting a nuisance, though an acute one, into a melodrama.

The commandant turned and gazed at him. It struck Gerald that what he had just said in some way, for the commandant, placed Phrynne also in a category of the lost.

"Take her away, man," said the commandant, with scornful ferocity.

"In a day or two perhaps," said Gerald, patiently polite. "I admit that we are disappointed with Holihaven."

"Now. While there's still time. This *instant*."

There was an intensity of conviction about the commandant which was alarming.

Gerald considered. Even the empty lounge, with its dreary decorations and commonplace furniture, seemed inimical. "They can hardly go on practising all night," he said. But now it was fear that hushed his voice.

"Practising!" The commandant's scorn flickered coldly through the overheated room.

"What else?"

"They're ringing to wake the dead."

A tremor of wind in the flue momentarily drew on the already roaring fire. Gerald had turned very pale.

"That's a figure of speech," he said, hardly to be heard.

"Not in Holihaven." The commandant's gaze had returned to the fire.

Gerald looked at Phrynne. She was breathing less heavily. His voice dropped to a whisper. "What happens?"

The commandant also was nearly whispering. "No one can tell how long they have to go on ringing. It varies from year to year. I don't know why. You should be all right up to midnight. Probably for some while after. In the end the dead awake. First one or two; then all of them. Tonight even the sea draws back. You have seen that for yourself. In a place like this there are always several drowned each year. This year there've been more than several. But even so that's only a few. Most of them come not from the water but from the earth. It is not a pretty sight."

"Where do they go?"

"I've never followed them to see. I'm not stark staring mad." The red of the fire reflected in the commandant's eyes. There was a long pause.

"I don't believe in the resurrection of the body," said Gerald. As the hour grew later, the bells grew louder. "Not of the body."

"What other kind of resurrection is possible? Everything else is only theory. You can't even imagine it. No one can."

Gerald had not argued such a thing for twenty years. "So," he said, "you advise me to go. Where?"

"Where doesn't matter."

"I have no car."

"Then you'd better walk."

"With her?" He indicated Phrynne only with his eyes.

"She's young and strong." A forlorn tenderness lay

within the Commandant's words. "She's twenty years younger than you and therefore twenty years more important."

"Yes," said Gerald. "I agree . . . What about you? What will you do?"

"I've lived here some time now. I know what to do."

"And the Pascoes?"

"He's drunk. There is nothing in the world to fear if you're thoroughly drunk. DSO and bar. DFC and bar."

"But you are not drinking yourself?"

"Not since I came to Holihaven. I lost the knack."

Suddenly Phrynne sat up. "Hullo," she said to the commandant; not yet fully awake. Then she said, "What fun! The bells are still ringing."

The Commandant rose, his eyes averted. "I don't think there's anything more to say," he remarked, addressing Gerald. "You've still got time." He nodded slightly to Phrynne, and walked out of the lounge.

"What have you still got time for?" asked Phrynne, stretching. "Was he trying to convert you? I'm sure he's an Anabaptist."

"Something like that," said Gerald, trying to think.

"Shall we go to bed? Sorry, I'm so sleepy."

"Nothing to be sorry about."

"Or shall we go for another walk? That would wake me up. Besides the tide might have come in."

Gerald, although he half-despised himself for it, found it impossible to explain to her that they should leave at once; without transport or a destination; walk all night if necessary. He said to himself that probably he would not go even were he alone.

"If you're sleepy, it's probably a *good* thing."

"Darling!"

"I mean with these bells. God knows when they will stop." Instantly he felt a new pang of fear at what he had said.

Mrs Pascoe had appeared at the door leading to the bar, and opposite to that from which the commandant had departed. She bore two steaming glasses on a tray. She looked about, possibly to confirm that the commandant had really gone.

"I thought you might both like a nightcap. Ovaltine, with something in it."

"Thank you," said Phrynne. "I can't think of anything nicer."

Gerald set the glass on a wicker table, and quickly finished his cognac.

Mrs Pascoe began to move chairs and slap cushions. She looked very haggard.

"Is the commandant an Anabaptist?" asked Phrynne over her shoulder. She was proud of her ability to outdistance Gerald in beginning to consume a hot drink.

Mrs Pascoe stopped slapping for a moment. "I don't know what that is," she said.

"He's left his book," said Phrynne, on a new tack.

Mrs Pascoe looked at it indifferently across the lounge.

"I wonder what he's reading," continued Phrynne. "Fox's *Lives of the Martyrs*, I expect." A small unusual devil seemed to have entered into her.

But Mrs Pascoe knew the answer. "It's always the same," she said, contemptuously. "He only reads one. It's called *Fifteen Decisive Battles of the World*. He's been reading it ever since he came here. When he gets to the end, he starts again."

"Should I take it up to him?" asked Gerald. It was neither courtesy nor inclination, but rather a fear lest the commandant return to the lounge: a desire, after those few minutes of reflection, to cross-examine.

"Thanks very much," said Mrs Pascoe, as if relieved of a similar apprehension. "Room One. Next to the suit of Japanese armour." She went on tipping and banging. To Gerald's inflamed nerves, her behaviour seemed too consciously normal.

He collected the book and made his way upstairs. The volume was bound in real leather, and the tops of its pages were gilded: apparently a presentation copy. Outside the lounge, Gerald looked at the flyleaf: in a very large hand was written: "To my dear Son, Raglan, on his being honoured by the Queen. From his proud Father, B. Shotcroft, Major-General." Beneath the inscription a very ugly military crest had been appended by a stamper of primitive type.

The suit of Japanese armour lurked in a dark corner as the commandant himself had done when Gerald had first encountered him. The wide brim of the helmet concealed the black eyeholes in the headpiece; the moustache bristled realistically. It was exactly as if the figure stood guard over the door behind it. On this door was no number, but, there being no other in sight, Gerald took it to be the door of Number One. A short way down the dim empty passage was a window, the ancient sashes of which shook in the din and blast of the bells. Gerald knocked sharply.

If there was a reply, the bells drowned it; and he knocked again. When to the third knock there was still no answer, he gently opened the door. He really had to know whether all would, or could, be well if Phrynne, and doubtless he also, were at all costs to remain in their room until it was dawn. He looked into the room and caught his breath.

There was no artificial light, but the curtains, if there were any, had been drawn back from the single window, and the bottom sash forced up as far as it would go. On the floor by the dusky void, a maelstrom of sound, knelt the commandant, his cropped white hair faintly catching the moonless glimmer, as his head lay on the sill, like that of a man about to be guillotined. His face was in his hands, but slightly sideways, so that Gerald received a shadowy distorted idea of his expression. Some might have called it ecstatic, but Gerald found it agonized. It frightened him more than anything which had yet happened. Inside the room the bells were like plunging roaring lions.

He stood for some considerable time quite unable to move. He could not determine whether or not the commandant knew he was there. The commandant gave no direct sign of it, but more than once he writhed and shuddered in Gerald's direction, like an unquiet sleeper made more unquiet by an interloper. It was a matter of doubt whether Gerald should leave the book; and he decided to do so mainly because the thought of further contact with it displeased him. He crept into the room and softly laid it on a hardly visible wooden trunk at the foot of the plain metal bedstead. There seemed no other furniture in the room. Outside the door, the hanging mailed fingers of the Japanese figure touched his wrist.

He had not been away from the lounge for long, but it was long enough for Mrs Pascoe to have begun again to drink. She had left the tidying up half-completed, or rather the room half-disarranged; and was leaning against the overmantel, drawing heavily on a dark tumbler of whisky. Phrynne had not yet finished her Ovaltine.

"How long before the bells stop?" asked Gerald as soon as he opened the lounge door. Now he was resolved that, come what might, they must go. The impossibility of sleep should serve as excuse.

"I don't expect Mrs Pascoe can know any more than we can," said Phrynne.

"You should have told us about this – this annual event – before accepting our booking."

Mrs Pascoe drank some more whisky. Gerald suspected that it was neat. "It's not always the same night," she said throatily, looking at the floor.

"We're not staying," said Gerald wildly.

"Darling!" Phrynne caught him by the arm.

"Leave this to me, Phrynne." He addressed Mrs Pascoe. "We'll pay for the room, of course. Please order me a car."

Mrs Pascoe was now regarding him stonily. When he asked for a car, she gave a very short laugh. Then her face changed. She made an effort, and said, "You mustn't take the commandant so seriously, you know."

Phrynne glanced quickly at her husband.

The whisky was finished. Mrs Pascoe placed the empty glass on the plastic overmantel with too much of a thud. "No one takes Commandant Shotcroft seriously," she said. "Not even his nearest and dearest."

"Has he any?" asked Phrynne. "He seemed so lonely and pathetic."

"He's Don and I's mascot," she said, the drink interfering with her grammar. But not even the drink could leave any doubt about her rancour.

"I thought he had personality," said Phrynne.

"That and a lot more, no doubt," said Mrs Pascoe. "But they pushed him out, all the same."

"Out of what?"

"Cashiered, court-martialled, badges of rank stripped off, sword broken in half, muffled drums, the works."

"Poor old man. I'm sure it was a miscarriage of justice."

"That's because you don't know him."

Mrs Pascoe looked as if she were waiting for Gerald to offer her another whisky.

"It's a thing he could never live down," said Phrynne, brooding to herself, and tucking her legs beneath her. "No wonder he's so queer if all the time it was a mistake."

"I just told you it was not a mistake," said Mrs Pascoe insolently.

"How can we possibly know?"

"*You* can't. *I* can. No one better." She was at once aggressive and tearful.

"If you want to be paid," cried Gerald, forcing himself in, "make out your bill. Phrynne, come upstairs and pack." If only he hadn't made her unpack between their walk and dinner.

Slowly Phrynne uncoiled and rose to her feet. She had no intention of either packing or departing, nor was she going to argue. "I shall need your help," she said. "If I'm going to pack."

In Mrs Pascoe there was another change. Now she looked terrified. "Don't go. Please don't go. Not now. It's too late."

Gerald confronted her. "Too late for what?" he asked harshly.

Mrs Pascoe looked paler than ever. "You said you wanted a car," she faltered. "You're too late." Her voice trailed away.

Gerald took Phrynne by the arm. "Come on up."

Before they reached the door, Mrs Pascoe made a further attempt. "You'll be all right if you stay. Really you will."

Her voice, normally somewhat strident, was so feeble that the bells obliterated it. Gerald observed that from somewhere she had produced the whisky bottle and was refilling her tumbler.

With Phrynne on his arm he went first to the stout front door. To his surprise it was neither locked nor bolted, but opened at a half-turn of the handle. Outside the building the whole sky was full of bells, the air an inferno of ringing.

He thought that for the first time Phrynne's face also seemed strained and crestfallen. "They've been ringing too long," she said, drawing close to him. "I wish they'd stop."

"We're packing and going. I needed to know whether we could get out this way. We must shut the door quietly."

It creaked a bit on its hinges, and he hesitated with it half-shut, uncertain whether to rush the creak or to ease it. Suddenly, something dark and shapeless, with its arm seeming to hold a black vesture over its head, flitted, all sharp angles, like a bat, down the narrow ill-lighted street, the sound of its passage audible to none. It was the first being that either of them had seen in the streets of Holihaven; and Gerald was acutely relieved that he alone had set eyes upon it. With his hand trembling, he shut the door much too sharply.

But no one could possibly have heard, although he stopped for a second outside the lounge. He could hear Mrs Pascoe now weeping hysterically; and again was glad that Phrynne was a step or two ahead of him. Upstairs the commandant's door lay straight before them: they had to pass close beside the Japanese figure, in order to take the passage to the left of it.

But soon they were in their room, with the key turned in the big rim lock.

"Oh, God," cried Gerald, sinking on the double bed. "It's pandemonium." Not for the first time that evening he was instantly more frightened than ever by the unintended appositeness of his own words.

"It's pandemonium all right," said Phrynne, almost calmly. "And we're not going out in it."

He was at a loss to divine how much she knew, guessed,

or imagined; and any word of enlightenment from him might be inconceivably dangerous. But he was conscious of the strength of her resistance, and lacked the reserves to battle with it.

She was looking out of the window into the main street. "We might *will* them to stop," she suggested wearily.

Gerald was now far less frightened of the bells continuing than of their ceasing. But that they should go on ringing until day broke seemed hopelessly impossible.

Then one peal stopped. There could be no other explanation for the obvious diminution in sound.

"You see!" said Phrynne.

Gerald sat up straight on the side of the bed.

Almost at once further sections of sound subsided, quickly one after the other, until only a single peal was left, that which had begun the ringing. Then the single peal tapered off into a single bell. The single bell tolled on its own, disjointedly, five or six or seven times. Then it stopped, and there was nothing.

Gerald's head was a cave of echoes, mountingly muffled by the noisy current of his blood.

"Oh goodness," said Phrynne, turning from the window and stretching her arms above her head. "Let's go somewhere else tomorrow." She began to take off her dress.

Sooner than usual they were in bed, and in one another's arms. Gerald had carefully not looked out of the window, and neither of them suggested that it should be opened, as they usually did.

"As it's a four-poster, shouldn't we draw the curtains?' asked Phrynne. "And be really snug? After those damned bells?"

"We should suffocate."

"Did they suffocate when everyone had four-posters?"

"They only drew the curtains when people were likely to pass through the room."

"Darling, you're shivering. I think we *should* draw them."

"Lie still instead and love me."

But all his nerves were straining out into the silence.

There was no sound of any kind, beyond the hotel or within it; not a creaking floorboard nor a prowling cat nor a distant owl. He had been afraid to look at his watch when the bells stopped, or since; the number of the dark hours before they could leave Holihaven weighed on him. The vision of the commandant kneeling in the dark window was clear before his eyes; as if the intervening panelled walls were made of stage gauze; and the thing he had seen in the street darted on its angular way back and forth through memory.

Then passion began to open its petals within him, layer upon slow layer; like an illusionist's red flower which, without soil or sun or sap, grows as it is watched. The languor of tenderness began to fill the musty room with its texture and perfume. The transparent walls became again opaque, the old man's vaticinations mere obsession. The street must have been empty, as it was now; the eye deceived.

But perhaps rather it was the boundless sequacity of love that deceived, and most of all in the matter of the time which had passed since the bells stopped ringing; for suddenly Phrynne drew very close to him, and he heard steps in the thoroughfare outside, and a voice calling. These were loud steps, audible from afar even through the shut window; and the voice had the possessed stridency of the street evangelist.

"The dead are awake!"

Not even the thick bucolic accent, the guttural vibrato of emotion, could twist or mask the meaning. At first Gerald lay listening with all his body, and concentrating the more as the noise grew; then he sprang from the bed and ran to the window.

A burly, long-limbed man in a seaman's jersey was running down the street, coming clearly into a view for a second at each lamp, and between them lapsing into a swaying lumpy wraith. As he shouted his joyous message, he crossed from side to side and waved his arms like a negro. By flashes, Gerald could see that this weatherworn face was transfigured.

"The dead are awake!"

Already, behind him, people were coming out of their

houses, and descending from the rooms above shops. There were men, women, and children. Most of them were fully dressed, and must have been waiting in silence and darkness for the call; but a few were dishevelled in night attire or the first garments which had come to hand. Some formed themselves into groups, and advanced arm in arm, as if towards the conclusion of a Blackpool beano. More came singly, ecstatic and waving their arms above their heads, as the first man had done. All cried out, again and again, with no cohesion or harmony. "The dead are awake! The dead are awake!"

Gerald become aware the Phrynne was standing behind him.

"The commandant warned me," he said brokenly. "We should have gone."

Phrynne shook her head and took his arm. "Nowhere to go," she said. But her voice was soft with fear, and her eyes blank. "I don't expect they'll trouble *us*."

Swiftly Gerald drew the thick plush curtains, leaving them in complete darkness. "We'll sit it out," he said, slightly histrionic in his fear. "No matter what happens."

He scrambled across to the switch. But when he pressed it, light did not come. "The current's gone. We must get back into bed."

"Gerald! Come and help me." He remembered that she was curiously vulnerable in the dark. He found his way to her, and guided her to the bed.

"No more love," she said ruefully and affectionately, her teeth chattering.

He kissed her lips with what gentleness the total night made possible.

"They were going towards the sea," she said timidly.

"We must think of something else."

But the noise was still growing. The whole community seemed to be passing down the street, yelling the same dreadful words again and again.

"Do you think we can?"

"Yes," said Gerald. "It's only until tomorrow."

"They can't be actually dangerous," said Phrynne. "Or it would be stopped."

"Yes, of course."

By now, as always happens, the crowd had amalgamated their utterances and were beginning to shout in unison. They were like agitators bawling a slogan, or massed trouble-makers at a football match. But at the same time the noise was beginning to draw away. Gerald suspected that the entire population of the place was on the march.

Soon it was apparent that a processional route was being followed. The tumult could be heard winding about from quarter to quarter; sometimes drawing near, so that Gerald and Phrynne were once more seized by the first chill of panic, then again almost fading away. It was possibly this great variability in the volume of the sound which led Gerald to believe that there were distinct pauses in the massed shouting; periods when it was superseded by far, disorderly cheering. Certainly it began also to seem that the thing shouted had changed; but he could not make out the new cry, although unwillingly he strained to do so.

"It's extraordinary how frightened one can be," said Phrynne, "even when one is not directly menaced. It must prove that we all belong to one another, or whatever it is, after all."

In many similar remarks they discussed the thing at one remove. Experience showed that this was better than not discussing it at all.

In the end there could be no doubt that the shouting had stopped, and that now the crowd was singing. It was no song that Gerald had ever heard, but something about the way it was sung convinced him that it was a hymn or psalm set to an out-of-date popular tune. Once more the crowd was approaching; this time steadily, but with strange, interminable slowness.

"What the *hell* are they doing now?" asked Gerald of the blackness, his nerves wound so tight that the foolish question was forced out of them.

Palpably the crowd had completed its peregrination, and was returning up the main street from the sea. The singers seemed to gasp and fluctuate, as if worn out with gay exercise, like children at a party. There was a steady undertow of scraping and scuffling. Time passed and more time.

Phrynne spoke. "I believe they're *dancing*."

She moved slightly, as if she thought of going to see.

"No, no," said Gerald and clutched her fiercely.

There was a tremendous concussion on the ground floor below them. The front door had been violently thrown back. They could hear the hotel filling with a stamping, singing mob.

Doors banged everywhere, and furniture was overturned, as the beatific throng surged and stumbled through the involved darkness of the old building. Glasses went and china and Birmingham brass warming pans. In a moment, Gerald heard the Japanese armour crash to the boards. Phrynne screamed. Then a mighty shoulder, made strong by the sea's assault, rammed at the panelling and their door was down.

The living and the dead dance together.
Now's the time. Now's the place. Now's the weather.

At last Gerald could make out the words.

The stresses in the song were heavily beaten down by much repetition.

Hand in hand, through the dim grey gap of the doorway, the dancers lumbered and shambled in, singing frenziedly but brokenly; ecstatic but exhausted. Through the stuffy blackness they swayed and shambled, more and more of them, until the room must have been packed tight with them.

Phrynne screamed again. "The smell. Oh God, the smell."

It was the smell they had encountered on the beach; in the congested room, no longer merely offensive, but obscene, unspeakable.

Phrynne was hysterical. All self-control gone, she was scratching and tearing, and screaming again and again. Gerald tried to hold her, but one of the dancers in the darkness struck him so hard that she was jolted out of his arms. Instantly it seemed that she was no longer there at all.

The dancers were thronging everywhere, their limbs whirling, their lungs bursting with the rhythm of the song. It was difficult for Gerald even to call out. He tried to struggle after Phrynne, but immediately a blow from a massive elbow knocked him to the floor, an abyss of invisible trampling feet.

But soon the dancers were going again; not only from the room, but, it seemed, from the building also. Crushed and tormented though he was, Gerald could hear the song being resumed in the street, as the various frenzied groups debouched and reunited. Within, before long there was nothing but the chaos, the darkness, and the putrescent odour. Gerald felt so sick that he had to battle with unconsciousness. He could not think or move, despite the desperate need.

Then he struggled into a sitting position, and sank his head on the torn sheets of the bed. For an uncertain period he was insensible to everything; but in the end he heard steps approaching down the dark passage. His door was pushed back, and the commandant entered gripping a lighted candle. He seemed to disregard the flow of hot wax which had already congealed on much of his knotted hand.

"She's safe. Small thanks to you."

The commandant stared icily at Gerald's undignified figure. Gerald tried to stand. He was terribly bruised, and so giddy that he wondered if this could be concussion. But relief rallied him.

"Is it thanks to *you*?"

"She was caught up in it. Dancing with the rest." The commandant's eyes glowed in the candle-light. The singing and dancing had almost died away.

Still Gerald could do no more than sit up on the bed. His voice was low and indistinct, as if coming from outside his body. "Were they . . . were some of them . . ."

The commandant replied more scornful then ever of his weakness. "She was between two of them. Each had one of her hands."

Gerald could not look at him. "What did you do?" he asked in the same remote voice.

"I did what had to be done. I hope I was in time." After the slightest possible pause he continued. "You'll find her downstairs."

"I'm grateful. Such a silly thing to say, but what else is there?"

"Can you walk?"

"I think so."

"I'll light you down." The commandant's tone was as uncompromising as always.

There were two more candles in the lounge, and Phrynne, wearing a woman's belted overcoat which was not hers, sat between them drinking. Mrs Pascoe, fully dressed but with eyes averted, pottered about the wreckage. It seemed hardly more than as if she were completing the task which earlier she had left behind.

"Darling, look at you!" Phrynne's words were still hysterical, but her voice was as gentle as it usually was.

Gerald, bruises and thoughts of concussion forgotten, dragged her into his arms. They embraced silently for a long time; then he looked into her eyes.

"Here I am," she said, and looked away. "Not to worry."

Silently and unnoticed, the commandant had already retreated.

Without returning his gaze, Phrynne finished her drink as she stood there. Gerald supposed that it was one of Mrs Pascoe's concoctions.

It was so dark where Mrs Pascoe was working that her labours could have been achieving little; but she said nothing to her visitors, nor they to her. At the door Phrynne unexpectedly stripped off the overcoat and threw it on a chair. Her nightdress was so torn that she stood almost naked. Dark though it was, Gerald saw Mrs Pascoe regarding Phrynne's pretty body with a stare of animosity.

"May we take one of the candles?" he asked, normal standards reasserting themselves in him.

But Mrs Pascoe continued to stand silently staring; and they lighted themselves through the wilderness of broken

furniture to the ruins of their bedroom. The Japanese figure
was still prostrate, and the commandant's door shut. And
the smell had almost gone.

Even by seven o'clock the next morning surprisingly much
had been done to restore order. But no one seemed to be
about, and Gerald and Phrynne departed without a word.

In Wrack Street a milkman was delivering, but Gerald
noticed that his cart bore the name of another town. A
minute boy whom they encountered later on an obscure
purposeful errand might, however, have been indigenous;
and when they reached Station Road, they saw a small plot
of land on which already men were silently at work with
spades in their hands. They were as thick as flies on a
wound, and as black. In the darkness of the previous evening, Gerald and Phrynne had missed the place. A board
named it the New Municipal Cemetery.

In the mild light of an autumn morning the sight of the
black and silent toilers was horrible; but Phrynne did not
seem to find it so. On the contrary, her cheeks reddened
and her soft mouth became fleetingly more voluptuous still.

She seemed to have forgotten Gerald, so that he was able
to examine her closely for a moment. It was the first time
he had done so since the night before. Then, once more,
she became herself. In those previous seconds Gerald had
become aware of something dividing them which neither
of them would ever mention or ever forget.

The Quiet Girl
Introduction

In the peaceful, quiet village of Methwick, the houses are silent and the members of the Conservative Club play their polite card games. A peaceful town means peaceful minds. Or does it? Because in one of these silent houses on Methwick's cobbled streets, an old and terrible secret is about to burst forth like ooze from an untidy wound.

Its form is a quiet girl who does not eat and does not drink, who stares at nothing but a fire in the grate, who seems to have no past and whose future is uncertain.

Behind this door, in a house in peaceful Methwick, the quiet girl is waiting . . .

ROBERT R. McCAMMON
Author of Bethany's Sin, Swan Song *and* Stinger!

Robert Holdstock
The Quiet Girl

These were peaceful times in Methwick, although by Aberdeen standards the tiny village had never known more than a murmur of excitement. Cobbled streets and rows of silent houses made the town seem dead, which it certainly wasn't. The life, on any night, was concentrated by the river wharf (where the Piper's Arms was still a place to get moonshine at ten pence a shot) or at the other end of the high street, where the Conservative Club attracted the card-players and the heavy smokers. The noise of voices would guide tourists to these high-spots of community life, but there were never tourists in Methwick. Few people came to live here, either, although the occasional new arrival added blood to the town. James Gray, for example, who had moved into the old Malbraith house just seven weeks before, and who had already settled nicely into the community.

In the silent street, beneath one of the few electric lamps, John Taggard felt the stillness of Methwick, and loved it. A peaceful town meant peaceful minds, and peaceful minds meant peaceful bodies; as the doctor in the town he appreciated a healthy community. Peaceful minds also meant peaceful souls, although that was the Reverend Crocker's department, and though Taggard himself was a man of the cloth, he had had no parish in his life, and merely contributed to the local religious community when Crocker was ill, or away, or when it was a time of special feasting.

Walking down the hill, across the painfully obtrusive cobbles, Taggard listened to the droning of a distant car; he stopped and waited for the vehicle to charge past. So still was the atmosphere that the noise of an engine could be heard over two or three miles.

It was a truck, when it came, and it wobbled and bumped through Methwick with the solemn-faced driver fighting the wheel to keep his vehicle steady. Taggard smiled as the truck braked at the bottom of the hill, and then vanished, but after a moment he realized that it had vanished into the old Malbraith house . . . Had that ashen-faced man in the driver's seat been James Gray? And since when had he owned a truck?

Puzzled, Taggard increased his pace down the hill. Gray had asked him to call just this evening; he had known the doctor would have been on his way, so wouldn't it have been a simple courtesy to have stopped as he passed? He had surely *seen* Taggard.

Although Gray had not indicated the problem when he had called, Taggard – professional to a fault – had brought his small medical bag in case. He was glad, now, that he had. Gray looked ill, very ill, and the call had certainly not been a social invitation, as Taggard had half expected.

He pushed through the gate, noticing as he entered the house's small grounds that the truck was parked, half visible, around the side of the building. Knocking at the door he waited, but took the opportunity of the pause to peer through the window of the dining room, which Gray, for some reason, had converted into a study. Gray was leaving the room to answer the door, and Taggard glanced quickly around the well-lit premises; a large desk had been pushed into one corner, with various book-cases leaning precariously forward all about. There was a suite in the middle of the room. A girl sat in an arm-chair, her eyes fixed on the glowing fire in the hearth. She looked very young, very pale; she hardly moved.

Taggard understood now. A relative, a niece, perhaps, who had taken ill.

Gray opened the door.

"Glad to see you, doctor," he said, taking Taggard's arm and ushering him into the hallway.

Gray was small in stature, and of middle age, perhaps forty-five, perhaps a little more. He was smartly dressed in tweed (who wasn't these days?) but the tweed was muddy, and Gray wiped his hands as if compulsively, glancing down at the palms occasionally. His normal complacency of expression had been replaced by a haunted look, his eyes rimmed with dark (a sign of sleepless nights), his mouth open and tense.

Taggard hung up his coat. "You look terrible, James."

"I'm sure I do. I sleep very badly. You might like to prescribe something."

Taggard paused. "You called me here for sleeping pills?"

Gray laughed. "No, no. I have a guest, a young girl – "

"I saw her. Through the window," in answer to Gray's querying expression. "She looks very quiet."

"Painfully quiet, John. She hasn't spoken a word, doesn't move, doesn't eat . . . Look, come and see her, and I'll tell you about her. I'm worried, though. Since Jeanette died . . ." he glanced at Taggard. "Well, you know . . ."

Taggard didn't know, though he thought he could guess. He followed Gray through into the study, glancing as he went at the colour portrait of Gray's wife, Elspeth, that hung in the hallway. She had been a beautiful woman, well worth the modern expense of having her portrait painted. But the picture that Gray held closest to his heart was of Jeanette, his only daughter, who had died in the same accident (a car crash) that had taken the life of his wife. No doubt Gray felt the need for company and had sent for one of his relations' daughters to come and visit.

"This is Elizabeth," said Gray, walking round in front of the seated girl.

"Hello, Elizabeth," Taggard smiled and stared down at the child. Elizabeth didn't move, or flinch, but remained staring into the fire. Taggard watched her, repeated her name, then glanced at Gray. Gray was shaking his head. "This is why I called you, John. She seems completely withdrawn, and, what's worse, she doesn't eat, or drink."

"For how long?"

"Three days now. Elizabeth isn't her real name, that's just the name I gave her. I've asked her many times, tried to get her to speak, but she just stares at me, then gradually looks off to the left, gazing at anything or nothing, but usually the fire."

Taggard sat in the arm-chair facing the girl. He studied her closely, and as he watched her so her head turned and her eyes fixed upon him. He felt a cold chill run down his spine as her gaze rested on him, seeming to look right through him.

"She's very pale, James. Was she like this when you brought her here?"

Gray nodded. "She is no relation of mine. Perhaps I shouldn't have bothered, but I couldn't just let her sit there, by the roadside."

"You found her on the road? A waif?"

"That's about the size of it. Wouldn't go down too well round here, I know, so I want to keep it quiet. But now I've taken the responsibility, John, I want to get her better and give her . . . I don't know . . . something, anything. A direction, money, a foster family? What *can* one give a parentless child who doesn't say a bloody word to you?"

Taggard watched the girl. After a while he rose and knelt before her; her green eyes followed his at all times. He took her pulse, which was weak and slow, and her skin felt cold, almost clammy. He rubbed her left hand to try and get some circulation into it, but it remained cool.

"Have you washed her since you found her?"

Gray shook his head. "Haven't liked to. The smell, you mean . . . it's very strong, I know, but I didn't realize how helpless she would be. It seems strange, but she doesn't . . . you know . . . pass things from her."

"She needs a good wash, a good meal, and two or three days' observation in a hospital; but you know, James, she isn't *obviously* ill at all. She has the expression and bearing of a catatonic . . . but she isn't anything like that – she looks around, she's taking things in. The way she's looking at me is creepy. But kids *are* creepy." He laughed, took the girl's hand again. "Elizabeth . . . Elizabeth, you're in good hands . . . can you say something? Anything? Is Elizabeth your real name?"

Her stare withdrew and her head turned back to the left, regarding the flickering wood fire in silence.

Taggard sighed and leaned back on his haunches; he noticed her clothes for the first time. Shredded, torn, dirty, the skirt she wore was a hand-woven woollen garment, styleless, designless, a functional body covering, not particularly warm. It was all she wore.

He and Gray picked her up and carried her upstairs to the bath, where Taggard, alone, stripped her and scrubbed her. She lay passive in the water, unafraid, regarding Taggard with an emotionless stare. He guessed her to be perhaps sixteen or seventeen years old; she was built very small; her body was almost encrusted with filth, and beneath the filth were scars and sores that he treated and covered. As she stood on the bath mat and he dried her he noticed the pattern of moles on her back, a square of black skin markings, two of them with hideous wounds in them. He dried her hair and the brown tresses seemed more alive than they had before; as he combed it back, slowly and carefully, he noticed the bruising on her neck; had someone tried to kill her, he wondered?

He dressed her in one of Gray's pyjama tops that came down to her knees.

"I'll bring you proper clothes in the morning."

She walked with him down the stairs and into the study. She curled up in the chair again and watched the fire.

"Where did you find her?" asked Taggard after a while. "And how did you get into that filthy state?" He sipped brandy from a glass that shook because his hands were shaking. Gray, without a drink, obviously still very anxious, looked down at the mud on his trousers.

"I don't know, to be honest. I've been doing a lot of strange things lately, but I guess that's just my insomnia. I black out quite a lot. Where did I find her? Tarston; quite a long way from here. I use the truck to take metal fencing to customers scattered about; I've only borrowed it for a few days. I was driving back at dusk a couple of days ago and she was just outside Tarston, walking along the road and waving me down. I offered her a lift and she just

climbed into the truck without a word; she didn't offer to
get down anywhere, but followed me into the house when
I parked outside. That's how it's been . . . and that's how
she's been."

"Tarston," murmured Taggard thoughtfully.
"Tarston . . ." He shook his head after a moment. "I read
about Tarston a few weeks ago. Can't think where or why;
it's a small town, isn't it?"

"Bigger than Methwick, but just as quiet. You think she
might belong to someone there? A runaway?"

"It's possible. Anything's possible. If it would be of any
help I can contact the police for you at Tarston . . . you
don't have a phone yet, do you?"

Gray shook his head. "Still using the call box. Very
inconvenient."

"Well, look after her, James, and I'll call back tomorrow.
We'll try and feed her something, otherwise I think she'd
best go straight into hospital."

"Yes. Okay, John. Many thanks for coming round."

If Taggard had felt uneasy in the house, then as he walked
up the hill, away from the strange girl, he became almost
obsessed with suspicion. There was no denying that these
were superstitious parts of the world, that there was an
ingrained fear of ghosts and evil in the local people, but it
was a fear held by the young and by the old, and not by
the sensible middle-aged. People joked about the Beyond,
and made mocking assertions as to the inherent supernatural forces in the countryside, but it was not a serious
fear . . . not serious enough, he hoped, he *believed*, to lead
to the torture of a young girl, the defiling of her body
because she was quiet, withdrawn . . . and had strange
marks on her body!

The wounds on those two moles on her back were frightening Taggard. The more he thought of them the more
they assumed significance. Like a knife being pushed a
quarter of an inch into her flesh, probing the devil's stigma
to see if she squealed – testing for a witch! Had it happened

to her in Tarston? Had she been abused in the name of some ancient and irrational fear by a small group of "believers"?

It had often happened before, and it would happen again. But Taggard hoped with all his heart that it wouldn't happen in *his* district. He was a man of peace, and the fear of darkness was something that led people to unexpected heights of violence.

The good were always to be feared more than the wicked. It had been that way through the ages of man.

He stopped and looked back at the Malbraith house, at the light in the window. As he watched so he saw Gray leave the house and begin to unload the truck; there was a clang as of metal on concrete, and Gray cursed in loud undertones. Taggard smiled.

He slept fitfully, uneasily, the girl's pale face haunting him in his quietest moments. Some time early in the morning the sound of the truck outside roused him into wakefulness. He listened to its engine straining on the hill, and finally fading away as it passed the church and moved out of earshot. Later he slept.

He woke at seven in the morning, abruptly, alertly. Jumping out of bed, he splashed his face with cold water and dressed without concern for appearance. At the bottom of the stairs he realized what he was doing, and paused; something was motivating him, an inner anxiety, a nagging tension; he was going to Tarston. He sat down for a moment and collected his wits. Yes, Tarston might yield *some* clue as to the girl's identity, and the local police might have information on any local practices that did not exactly conform to Christian thinking (though they might to Christian tradition).

What an effect the girl had had upon him! To cause him to move from sleep to wake with a single objective: to find out about her.

He chuckled, crept back upstairs and found his wife still sleeping despite his energetic departure from the bed. He left a note, and placed a cancellation notice on his surgery door. Rolling his car out of the drive as quietly as he could, he drove up the hill and over.

It was a dull day, heavily overcast, and with a promise of rain. That might keep the good souls of Methwick at home, and not knocking on his surgery door, he thought. He drove past the church on the hill and noticed, with amusement, that three cows had again broken into the grounds and were happily cropping the grass of the lawn that bordered the gravel pathway.

Something white was flapping in the early morning breeze, out in the cemetery. Puzzled, Taggard slowed the car and stopped. A piece of cloth, like a gown . . .

He went cold, turned off the engine and climbed out. He could recognize what he saw from this distance, but he kept his eyes to the ground as he walked across the cemetery until he stood a few feet away, and stopped.

It was the body of an old woman who had died just five days before, and had been buried the day before yesterday. Her body was sprawled across the pile of earth that had been excavated from the grave, one leg dangling naked into the pit, her shroud blown up across her body to obscure her face, but not her wrinkled, grey breast. There were gaping knife cuts in her chest, above her heart, and when Taggard pulled the shroud down from the corpse's head he saw hideous excavations across her neck, deep cuts that exposed the bone and teeth on one side of the dead woman's face.

Taggard stood slowly and looked around him. He saw no sign of a living soul, and he left the cemetery at a run, sat in his car for a long while, watching the fluttering white robe and thinking of what he had observed.

He would have to tell the police; he would have to tell Crocker, if Crocker, who was an early service man himself, had not already seen the horrifying spectacle. Somewhere in the vicinity would be a clue as to who had done the defiling of the grave, and Taggard was very much afraid that he knew to whom that evidence would point. If *he* had heard Gray's truck, then so would many other people in the street; and somewhere there would be tyre-prints, and in Gray's house there would be dirt, a fragment of the shroud perhaps . . .

There could be no hiding the deed if Gray were responsible; but why should a man like Gray do such a thing? Taggard had known him a mere seven weeks, but he had come to know him well in that time, and if he was still a man distraught and depressed at the loss of his wife and daughter, some months before, he was not, so Taggard believed, a man made irrational and insane by his loss.

No, it was not Gray as Gray had been! Taggard, unconscious of passing time, found himself obsessed with the idea that Gray was no longer his own man, that something *recent* had upset him, unbalanced him, and made him act in a truly despicable way. And the more he thought about it, the more he came to believe that the upsetting force was the girl, Elizabeth.

If that *was* the case, he wondered, who was she? What was she? What was her hold over Gray, an adult and mature man. How could a child of sixteen dominate him?

Thirty minutes of jumping to conclusions passed, and Taggard made a decision. He would go straight to Tarston, and not back into town. He started up the car and drove on, slowly at first, but picking up speed as he distanced himself from the church and from Methwick.

Inspector William Kurland was a warm and friendly man, red-haired, clean-shaven, and he seemed glad of the visit. They sat on opposite sides of Kurland's paper-littered desk and sipped coffee.

"Crime on paper," said Kurland with a smile, tapping the sheets before him. "There's not much on the streets, it all happens in tight little lines of print. What a way to keep order." Taggard smiled. Kurland, more seriously, said, "Now, Dr Taggard. What may I do for you?"

Taggard placed his cup on the table and composed his thoughts. "I have a patient, Inspector . . . an amnesiac. I think, in fact I'm sure, that the key to her memory lies in Tarston."

"Oh, well, that should be easy enough. We have few missing persons filed here . . ."

"Inspector . . . before you do anything, I'd like to ask you something."

"Ask away . . ."

"Where . . . or rather *why* . . . why have I read of Tarston recently?"

"In the newspapers, you mean?"

"The nationals, yes."

Kurland seemed surprised. "The nationals, eh? I don't read the papers myself; I'm surprised the stories reached them. I know we had good coverage in the local papers, and the Aberdeen papers."

"What was the problem?"

Kurland leaned back, became pensive. "We had a series of grave-robberies; mostly ancient graves, scattered bones and a lot of trouble for the keepers; but there were two genuine cases of body-snatching that weren't so pleasant . . ."

Now Taggard remembered; he should have remembered when he had seen the woman's corpse earlier in the morning. He said, "Yes, that's right. The Burkers return to Tarston . . . that was how most papers ran the story. I remember."

Kurland laughed. "The Burkers. Yes. They're a widespread superstition, well, you know that. But here in Tarston they're just a little more important than most other places. The Burkers are our local bogey men . . . send the kids scuttling to bed with tales of the body-snatchers. Very good medicine. The end of last century, though, the Burkers were much more in the news than now. Tarston suffered an appalling raid by Burkers . . . probably students, or a mixture of students and locals, earning themselves some blood money. They came in the night and carried off twenty women and children, cut their throats in the coach they used, and the next morning the streets were just running with blood. Some said it was tinkers, taking revenge for locals of Tarston having raided tinker camps for the same grisly purpose. It was all the same to the medical schools. They say you can still hear the hearse rattling down the street on that night of every year, and if you touch the ground you can feel the warmth of blood running across the cobbles." He paused, savouring the imagery he was invoking.

Taggard said, "That was a hundred years ago. What about these more recent cases?"

"A young lad," said Kurland, straightening up. "Very strange case. Just a lad, perhaps eighteen, nineteen – a local boy, from a farm a few miles away. He robbed one grave and was hauling the fresh body out of a second a few nights later when we surprised him."

"And he died, right?"

Kurland nodded, looked slightly crestfallen. "He fell into the open grave and split his skull on the metal edge of the casket. Died about a week ago."

Taggard thought hard. It was difficult to tell if things were falling into place or not. "Did the lad have a sister?"

The police inspector thought about the question, and finally said, no. "He had a brother, though. Older than himself. And he had a girl friend, strange little thing, very miserable, very cold. Not a local girl, probably a gypsy's girl left behind for whatever reason gypsies leave their extra children scattered across the country."

Taggard described Elizabeth. The description matched. Now things *were* falling into place; but he was still confused as to the reason for body-snatching.

That would take some very careful thought.

"The girl vanished, said Kurland. "Probably because your man . . . Gray you said? Probably because he picked her up."

"And you have no idea where she might have come from?"

"Out of nowhere, out of the dead. That's what the local people say when a stranger turns up. A very superstitious lot." Kurland chuckled. "We have more ghosts in Tarston than you've ever dreamed of. I've seen one myself, too, so it's not *all* fairy story."

Taggard smiled. An unbeliever himself, he was surprised

that the local police chief should take the supernatural so matter-of-factly for granted.

Kurland expanded, seeing Taggard's interest. "A Burker called William Lyon, who lived locally and would drop the nod to the diggers when someone was buried fresh. He might have got away with it for many years, but one night they dug in the wrong grave and dug up a witch who had been buried two hundred years before."

"A witch? On Holy Ground?"

"The story goes that she was really no witch at all, and after being hanged her parents fought for years to get the body interred in the churchyard; they finally succeeded. The Burker, Lyon – so the story goes – found her body intact and she killed him on the spot, cutting his throat open with her nails and covering herself with his blood. His ghost walks the southern road between the churchyard and the signal point he would use. I've seen him. A miserable-looking fellow."

Taggard laughed. "Yes, well, thanks very much for your help, but my problem deals more with the living."

It was the girl; that much was obvious. Possessed or diseased, she was in some way able to affect the minds of men, and drive them to do her wishes; why grave-robbing, it was difficult to understand, but it led to another frightening thought: when did the stealing of the dead, for whatever reason, lead to the stealing of the living?

At the door of Kurland's office Taggard stopped, looked back. "The body that your youth *did* steal . . . was it ever recovered?"

"It was found back in the grave, yes."

"Was it mutilated?"

"Why, yes. The heart and throat had been stabbed. Don't ask me why. Some sort of ritual sadism was the official verdict."

Yes, thought Taggard. And no. Not ritual sadism. The heart and the throat. Where blood would flow the fastest, and the easiest . . . if there was blood to flow!

Walking back to the car he thought over what Kurland

had told him, thought of the girl, of her hidden power. Children had a way with adults, and they had strong minds, and often frightening minds. It was not beyond belief that Elizabeth, whatever her real name, was exerting her will in the way of, say, a hypnotist, making her sympathetic companions do what she wanted, sending them on her insane missions of defilement . . .

A witch indeed!

And a thought struck him, an unpleasant thought, and one which he might have pushed from his mind at any other time. He was a man who did not believe in things supernatural, despite his being a man of God; religious manifestation, yes, but ghosts and ghouls, no. He believed that there were perfectly reasonable explanations for many things that had been thought unnatural, and frightening.

But the thought welled up in his mind now, and he could not deny it, could not push it aside. It would answer the strange behaviour of the body-snatchers, it would explain much . . .

Uncomfortably, but with resolve, he sought out the church, and the historical records of the town.

Taggard ran through the gate of the Milbraith house, hammered on the door and shouted for Gray.

He ran to the window, peered into the darkness. The fire was burning low, throwing a dull red light through the darkened room. He saw the girl sitting in her arm-chair. She was watching him.

Glancing at his watch (ten o'clock) Taggard wondered where Gray would be so late at night. Not at the cemetery; he had already checked there.

He banged on the door again.

"James – for God's sake let me in!"

James Gray opened the door. In the dim light from the street lamp at the bottom of his short driveway, his face was ashen grey, his eyes deep pools of blackness. He blocked the entrance.

"You can't help me, John. Go away. Don't risk yourself . . ."

"Let me in, James. You don't know what you've got in there . . . !"

"I *know* what I've got, John. Go away. Don't interfere! I know what I've done, and what I will do again until I die. I'm helpless, John. I'm helpless. No one can help me." He closed the door. Taggard leapt forward and flung it open, slamming it shut behind him.

"Get out, you fool!" screamed Gray. "She's realized how to get what she wants . . . !"

Recklessly, terribly afraid, Taggard led the way into the study. He turned on the lights; the girl made a slight moaning sound, but otherwise didn't move.

Glancing at Gray, Taggard confirmed what he had suspected. The man was in a shocking condition, gaunt, dishevelled, and covered with dirt from a second excavation, perhaps. He watched Taggard through black-rimmed eyes, and there was something in his expression . . . a mixture of hopelessness and cunning. It frightened Taggard, but after a moment Gray's features relaxed and he looked at the motionless girl, still wearing his pyjama top, still deathly white and silent.

"I found out who she is," said Taggard. As he spoke her head moved and her eyes fixed him with their stare.

"I don't care who she is," said Gray. "It no longer matters . . ."

"Her name is Matilda Reid . . ." The girl tensed, began to shake. "Yes, Matilda, you know your name. Matilda Reid, born Tarston in 1623, and hanged as a witch in the same town in 1639 . . ." A thin stream of saliva began to run from each corner of her mouth; her skin remained white, but a new life seemed to pump into her frail body. A whining sound escaped her lips.

Gray looked aghast. "What are you saying?"

Taggard smiled. "I went to Tarston today. Something that the police there told me made me doubt my common-sense viewpoint for a moment and I went through the early records that are kept in the church. It had a listing, like most churches do, of the witch trials from before 1500. Matilda Reid was a silent child, never spoke, and when examined by a suspicious parish council was found to have a square of devil's marks on her back. Two were probed and though they emitted blood they did not cause her to scream. She was hanged, despite her parents' protesting, but after some years her body, which had been kept on the parents' own land, was allowed to be buried on consecrated ground in the light of evidence suggesting she had not been a witch at all. The grave was kept, and the story forgotten in substance, until an unfortunate body-snatcher released the girl by accident . . ."

"And you're saying that this . . . this is the living body of Matilda Reid?"

"The living-dead body, yes . . ."

Standing firm, Taggard watched the wild distortions on the girl's face, the eyes bulging, the lips drawn back into a hideous snarl, listened to the animal sounds she emitted. Her hands clasped and unclasped the arms of the chair, her body strained, slowly moving upright. Taggard stood his ground, reaching into his pocket for what he had brought with him.

"And since her release," gasped Gray, backing away from the slowly rising figure, "she has been like . . . like a vampire, using people to bring her bodies to feed upon . . ."

"Sometimes hiding, perhaps; at other times using sympathetic people to help her with her desperate quest – "

"My God, she is truly the work of the devil!"

"NO!" cried Taggard, losing his concentration for just a moment. "Not the devil! She was buried on holy ground, James. Don't you understand? They believed, after her death, that she had *not* been a witch, and she was buried there, on God's ground. But she *was* a witch! She had been baptised with the blood of a witch, during a devil's mass. And when she was buried there, in holy ground, it was defilement! It was defilement until such a time as she was baptized in the HOLY way . . . She has been seeking such a baptism since . . . She is GOD's work, James, not Satan's. She is a force of evil, acting for GOOD."

A scream, and Taggard could not react as the body of

the girl flung towards him. He had noticed the way her hand had scrabbled in the cushion of the chair, and now he saw the dulled blade descending towards him . . .

He threw up his arm to protect himself, but the girl's body hit him, the insane face shrieking just inches from his own, the knife burying deeply into his body, above the heart.

"I have holy water . . ." screamed Taggard as he fell, the girl on top of him. "James . . . James, help me . . . James, I have water to baptize her . . . JAMES . . ."

"It has to be blood," cried Gray, backing further from the room. "I'm sorry . . . I tried to warn you . . . it has to be the blood of a man of God . . . she only just realized the fact . . ."

"HELP ME!"

But Gray just stood and watched.

As Matilda Reid soaked her face and her hair in the pumping blood from Taggard's fatal wound . . .

Christian blood, the blood of a man of the cloth. The blood of God, that relinquished her from her terrible predicament.

She rolled quietly from Taggard's body, and the life went out of them both together.

The Hunter
Introduction

The Christmas present I most prized when I was thirteen years old was the first Pan Book of Horror Stories. *It came at a time when anthologies of horror and ghost stories were few, and most of those few seemed to recycle their predecessors, with a lack of imagination and a trust in the appeal of the predictably familiar which we find today in the makers of the* Friday the 13th *films and other such regurgitations. In those days I suffered from an odd compulsion to read everything in each publication I bought, or even borrowed from the library, and I found myself rereading 'Lost Hearts' until I knew it by one, 'The Fall of the House of Usher' so often that I began to feel like an usher myself, and if I'd had a wish for every time I read 'The Monkey's Paw' . . . (Ironically, and perhaps because of those years of recycling, it is now often difficult to find the classics of the field). But Herbert van Thal's name on the front of an anthology had guaranteed surprises in the past, and that proved to be the case with this new three-and-sixpenny anthology, even though the cover seemed to threaten the reader with nothing more daunting than an irritable old mog.*

Indeed, the series had a good many surprises in store: fine unreprinted tales by writers as varied as H. E. Ewers and William Sansom, and new tales by some real discoveries (for instance, the outrageous humour and horrors of M. S. Waddell, an inimitable talent now producing children's fiction). One of its most important achievements was to keep in print almost the entire contents of two collections (The Cell and Fengriffen) by David Case. Perhaps then, as the sixties came to an end, Case's problem as a writer was that he was ahead of his time: the gruesome violence of his tale 'Among the Wolves' can hold its own against the most extreme of today's horror fiction, partly because rather than encouraging the reader to gawk at the spectacle, the gruesomeness of Case's tale seeks to make one feel what the victim feels. That story and 'The Hunter' both prefigure the early novels of David Morrell in their examination of the psychology of the hunter and the hunted, and it's time Case gained comparable recognition. Those readers who are familiar only with the films based on his work, the stolidly Gothic - And Now the Screaming Starts! (based on 'Fengriffen') and the intermittently effective Scream of the Wolf (based on the story that follows) are in for a discovery. Let us hear more of David Case, and not only reprints! The field needs more from the author of 'The Hunter', a modern classic worthy to stand beside 'The Most Dangerous Game'.

RAMSEY CAMPBELL
Author of The Hungry Moon,
The Influence *and* Ancient Images

David Case
The Hunter

It was a fine bright morning.

Ralph Conrad came out of the Bridge Hotel and shrugged his knapsack into a more comfortable position across his shoulders; smiled at the low sun and mopped his florid brow with a red polka-dot handkerchief. There were several motor-cars in the parking lot, but no traffic on the road at this early hour, and Ralph was very much at peace with himself. He felt especially peaceful because the hotel clerk, befuddled and sleepy, had made a ten-shilling error in Ralph's favour, and Ralph was of a thrifty nature. That was why he was on a walking tour of Dartmoor. When he had first retired several years before, he had contemplated taking up golf for exercise, but the expense of that game had troubled him more than his inability to predict the direction the ball would travel, and since the exercise gained by walking through open country was certainly equal to that gained by pursuing an elusive little white ball through various frustrating hazards and roughs, Ralph had forsaken golf in favour of leisurely walking tours. He had walked through the Lake District and Northern Wales and this was the third day of his tour of Dartmoor. He planned, vaguely, to walk on the Continent some day, but that wasn't definite or immediate; it was a thing to think about rather than do, because Ralph liked the English life he was accustomed to, liked to have a destination where he would find a hot meal and a comfortable bed, familiar food and conversation in a familiar language beside an open fire when he relaxed after a long day's tramp. He had also heard that the Continent was frightfully expensive.

Ralph walked up to the highway and along the shoulder

for several hundred yards, anxious to progress some distance before the clerk discovered his error. He wore stout shoes and carried a walking stick with an electric torch built into the handle; he had an Ordnance Survey map and knew how to cross rough country without getting lost, impressing the landscape upon his mind and using his wristwatch and the sun to estimate the points of the compass. This ability pleased him, since it had saved him the expense of purchasing a compass. He carried a light lunch and a Thermos of coffee and had planned to arrive comfortably at his next stop around dinnertime. His route had been meticulously laid out on the map, and presently he turned from the road and set out across the moors.

The sun was hot. Ralph thought that perhaps it would be unpleasantly warm later in the day, and he walked rather more quickly than usual so that he could slow down later, if the heat made it necessary. His route took him along the crest of a hill. A narrow stream wound through the marshy land below on the left, and a higher ridge of land studded with rocky tors bordered his path on the right. The tors were individually marked on his excellent map and he judged his progress by them, admiring the formations as he studied the terrain. This was some of the loveliest and most desolate country in England, and Ralph appreciated it greatly. He was all alone. There was no noise of motorcar or factory to disturb his tranquillity, no scent of petrol or fumes of industry to overwhelm the dry perfume of the heather, no black smoke twisted against the fluffy white clouds. The stream twinkled through the mossy ground and his heavy shoes crunched on the coarse tufts of grass, squelching occasionally when he moved too low on the slope. Ralph drew deep breaths of clean air into his lungs. He had stopped smoking years before, when the rising tax on tobacco had made the expense greater than the satisfaction, but this pure air was even better than nicotine and he complimented himself on the willpower it had taken to forsake cigarettes, not even considering the economies of the sacrifice.

When he had been walking for nearly an hour, Ralph

came to a low, flat rock and sat down to rest. He scraped some mud from his shoes with the tip of his stick and unscrewed the cap from his Thermos jug, poured some coffee into the cap and was about to drink when he noticed something in the reeds near the stream. He lowered the cup and looked harder. He couldn't quite make out what it was. He wished that he had sunglasses, but didn't think the frequency of sunlight justified buying them; he thought that he really should have a pair of field-glasses and wondered what they might cost in a pawn shop.

Ralph didn't want to move down the hill because the land was damp and marshy there and he hated to get his feet wet, but he was basically a curious man, and who knew but what the object might be something valuable? He knew he would never forgive himself if he walked on without investigating.

He climbed up on the rock to get a higher angle, but still couldn't make out what it was. It looked almost like a man, he thought, but that could hardly be possible. A man wouldn't be lying in that swampy ground, surely. Not with the exorbitant prices that dry cleaners charged these days.

He climbed down again and finished his coffee, still undecided whether he should risk the dampness, replaced the Thermos jug in his pack, looked ahead, then shrugged and started cautiously down the incline.

The lower he went, the softer the ground became. His feet squished as the mud sucked at them, his stick sank deeply and gave little support. Reeds replaced the coarse grass, and he found it more difficult to keep the object in sight since, although he was closer to it, he no longer had the advantage of elevation. He was just about to deny his curiosity and return to the high ground when he came upon a shoe.

His eyes narrowed as he looked at it. It was quite definitely a shoe, sunk well down in the muck. He crouched and pried it up with his stick; lifted it between thumb and forefinger. It had apparently been sucked off as its owner walked or ran through the mud and abandoned there. Ralph turned it about and saw that it was in fairly good condition, a bit run down at the heel but with a great deal of wear left in it; measured it beside his own shoe and decided it would be too small for him. He couldn't understand this. Someone had recently passed this way in a hurry – such a great hurry that he had not paused to retrieve his shoe. Such reckless abandoning of a useful article was beyond Ralph's comprehension. He looked around, hoping perhaps to find the other shoe. They might fit him, after all. There was no other shoe, but he noticed an indentation in the ground and moved to it. It looked like a footprint. Water had seeped into it and the edge had crumbled. There was another similar indentation beyond, and Ralph moved in that direction, the shoe still gripped gingerly in his fingers. He was very curious indeed now. After all, one shoe was useless to its owner, and there seemed a reasonably good chance that the mate had also been abandoned.

Then he saw the object that had first caught his attention. The footprints led in that direction, and it looked like a bundle of rags glimpsed through the reeds. Perhaps, he thought, a complete outfit of clothing cast off in some moment of insanity.

Ralph approached warily; halted abruptly.

It was certainly a pile of clothing, and from one end protruded a human foot. Ralph stared at the foot. It wore a sock but no shoe. Ralph looked at the shoe he held and then back at the foot. He felt confused and dazed. He had never come upon a situation like this before in all his rambles; he felt that he should do something but had no precedent to help him decide what steps were called for. After a few moments he took a firmer grip on his stick and advanced with resolution and determination, until he was standing beside the body. One arm was outflung, the other hidden in the shredded rags. The rags were darkly stained with blood and the coat had been pulled above the shoulders so that it covered the man's head.

"I say there," Ralph said.

There was no reply.

"I say, my man. Are you all right?"

The rags were silent.

Ralph took a deep breath. He hated to get involved in difficulties that didn't concern him, but saw that he had no choice. He crouched and drew the coat down so he could see the man's face.

And then the peaceful countryside was shattered by his scream.

The man had no head.

And Ralph had never encountered such a thing before . . .

John Wetherby was in the habit of dining several times a week at his club in St James's. He invariably ate the same well-balanced meal, drank the same full-bodied burgundy, and then went into the bar for the same excellent brandy and Havana cigar. But Wetherby was not a creature of thoughtless habit. He simply found this a comfortable and satisfying routine, and saw no reason to alter it, any more than he would have changed his tailor or the rather outdated cut of his suits.

Wetherby's club was The Venturers. He had been a member for many years, and, not being plagued by a compulsion to join and belong, he subscribed to no other club. The Venturers had, however, changed considerably over the years. It had become fashionable rather than purposeful and the requirements for membership were based more on social standing than accomplishment. It was no longer the sort of club that Wetherby would have selected for himself, but he didn't contemplate a change; he doubted if any new club would prove more suitable and thought, if he thought of it at all, that it was more likely the tempo of the world rather than the tone of his club which had changed. Or perhaps, he sighed at the idea that he himself had changed with age, and failed to keep up with life.

There were times when he regretted this, such as when he walked into the bar and saw the younger members lounging about in well-cut suits and seldom-cut hair, with pretence and affectation. Wetherby was a tolerant man. He could regret without resenting. But he felt a definite longing for

former days, when there had been mutual interest among
the members – adventures to be recalled over the brandy,
or better still, further adventures to be planned and antici-
pated. But this was in the past. It had been a long time
since Wetherby had had an adventure, and even if some of
the old members had been present, the conversation would
of necessity have dwelt on the past; it would have been a
sad pleasure, recalling things that could no longer be.

Wetherby glanced around the dining-room. There was
no one there he knew. There seldom was now. Of all the
friends and companions he could recall from better days,
only Byron had not succumbed to the advance of age; only
Byron, timelessly pursuing his curious theories of life and
death, might have had some new tale to tell. But Byron
never came to London now. He still lived a life of adventure, and had no need to reminisce about the past.
Wetherby admired Byron without envying him, approved
of the man without approving of his methods. It had been
nearly ten years since he had last seen Byron and Wetherby
vividly recalled that evening.

They had been drinking brandy at the bar. Byron had
just returned from Africa and Wetherby had just decided
it was time for him to give up big-game hunting. They had
talked for a while about the last expedition they'd been on
together, in north-west Canada, and then Wetherby had
mentioned his decision to retire. Byron had been annoyed,
almost angry, about it. Wetherby himself was rather sad,
but the decision was unalterable. He was no longer young,
his eyes and his reflexes had lost the sharpness required.
He had spent his youth practising a passion for hunting;
but now his youth was over, and Wetherby did not care to
pursue danger when he might not enjoy it, might prove a
liability rather than an asset to his companions.

But hunting, to Byron, was far more than a pleasure or
a pastime; it was more than a passion, it was a philosophy
of life. Byron had become excited, trying to convince
Wetherby he was making a grave mistake in deciding to
live a life of comfort in London. Byron's voice was resonant

and deep, and with the fervour of his words, he began speaking loudly, gesturing widely.

Several of the younger members had been standing beside them at the bar, and they looked on with interest, obviously amused by the intensity of Byron's speech, undoubtedly considering him an anachronism in their modern world. One of them, a large young man with an insolent face, drew closer. A leader of the liberal new aristocracy. He winked at his companions and hovered beside Byron. He was so close that Byron, despite his impassioned monologue, could not fail to notice him.

Byron paused in the middle of a sentence and turned towards the young man; stared at him. Byron's eyes were piercing, he did not stare the way a man stares in a city, he stared as one does, with full concentration and awareness, in the jungle. He said nothing. The young man tried to return the gaze but his civilized eyes faltered, and he sought refuge in words.

"I couldn't help but overhear you, sir," he said. He had a cultured voice and emphasized the "sir".

Byron didn't seem to hear.

"You are, I understand, a big-game hunter?"

Byron said nothing. Wetherby said, "That is correct, young man. We both are."

But the man wasn't interested in Wetherby. His face had become flushed under Byron's eyes.

"Perhaps you can tell me – something I've always wondered – what on earth is the pleasure that full-grown and presumably intelligent men get out of murdering defenceless animals?"

It was not the thing to say to Byron.

Wetherby was angry himself. Tolerance has limits. The young man's cohorts moved closer, grinning behind their champion. But Byron still said nothing. He continued to stare, but, slowly, his expression shifted until he was regarding the man in precisely the same manner as one might some foul object upon which one has inadvertently trod.

The young man became intensely uncomfortable. His

friends were expecting him to make some brilliant comment which would terminate the encounter, and yet he could not force himself to look at Byron's eyes.

"I don't mean to intrude, of course," he said. "But tell me – " Encouraged by the sound of his own educated voice, he smiled again. "Tell me, is it a sense of power? Of accomplishment? Some regression to the past, when killing was an honourable and necessary thing?"

"I cannot tell you," Byron said.

"I thought not," the man said. He started to turn away, his lips smirking. His friends grinned at their clever comrade.

"However, I could show you," Byron said.

The young man turned back, surprised. Byron had moved out from the bar. He was smiling, too. They say a tiger smiles and a hyena laughs, but perhaps they are mistaken.

"I beg your pardon?" the young man said.

"The pleasure I get from killing," Byron said. "I could show you just what it is. I think it could be a very great pleasure, showing you, although I doubt you would die with the nobility of an animal."

Everyone was very quiet. The young man's lips parted, but he said nothing. His friends no longer smiled. They had seen something very dark in Byron's eyes, something they would never comprehend. After a moment the young man turned away; Byron shrugged and leaned on the bar again. Wetherby let his breath out slowly. He had seen Byron kill, and he knew the face very well. It was not a face one could forget. The young man left very soon.

"I thought, for a moment – " Wetherby said.

Byron nodded.

"It would have been so easy," he said.

Wetherby didn't doubt it.

That was Byron . . .

The waiter brought the bill, knowing from experience that Wetherby would not take brandy at the table. Wetherby signed it and stood up; headed for the bar, through the solid, oak-panelled rooms. He was a tall man with steel-grey hair and angular features, wearing a new suit which was tailored so well that it looked old. Middle age may have dulled his vision and blunted his reflexes, but a life of civilized comfort had not harmed him noticeably. He was lean and hard and straight, and weighed exactly the same as he had on his last hunting trip, with Byron in Canada. Wetherby was thinking about Byron as he entered the bar.

It was a strange coincidence.

Detective Superintendent Justin Bell was drinking a pint of beer at the bar. He had a brick-red face and a nondescript grey suit and looked very much like a policeman. He raised his glass and Wetherby joined him. He was pleased to see him; Bell was one of the older members, and Wetherby had seconded his application, following a tongue-in-cheek discussion over whether police work qualified as adventurous endeavour and, therefore, met the requirements of membership. That was before the rules had been changed, when The Venturers had a purpose. Bell was well liked and had the proper outlook and temperament for the club, and so he had been admitted to the rolls, even though his occupation was suspect.

"Hello, John," Bell said.

"How are you, Justin?"

"Tired."

"You haven't been here for quite a while."

"No time. I envy your life of ease. Always have. It's a fortunate man who can retire from a life of pleasure to a life of relaxation without a period of work in between."

Wetherby laughed. He had always felt the same way; had, without the slightest taint of snobbery, considered himself very lucky to have been born wealthy.

"Drink?" he asked.

Bell finished his beer and slid the glass across the bar. The barman wore a wine-coloured jacket and was very efficient and polite; although young, he was able to distinguish between the old-established Venturers and the fashionable new members; knew the difference between dignity and familiarity. Wetherby had a brandy and Bell had another pint of beer. His preference for beer had begun to extend to his waistline slightly, but that merely made him look more like an efficient lawman.

"It's good to see you," Wetherby said.

"As a matter of fact, I came here to see you. Thought you'd be here."

"Good Lord. Not about that parking ticket?"

They laughed at the private reference to a slight bending of a minor law.

After a moment, Bell said, "I need your advice, John."

"Whatever for?"

"Possibly a murder."

Wetherby blinked. Bell drank.

"At least, we're treating it as murder. I don't really know that it is."

"Surely there's no advice I can give you on that?"

"Perhaps not. Not if it actually is murder."

"This sounds very mysterious," Wetherby said. He began to fill his pipe very carefully. He hadn't tasted the brandy yet.

"Well, it is, in a way. I expect you've read something about it. The headless body on Dartmoor. I believe that was how the newspapers billed it."

"Oh yes. Yes, I did see something about that. A bit out of your territory, isn't it?"

"Well, there are curious aspects. It baffled the chief constable down there and he asked for assistance. Good judge, I'd say. It baffles me, too. Anyway, the commissioner assigned Thurlow and me to the case. I've just come back from there. Came back to see you specifically."

Wetherby had the briar filled; he lighted it, tamped it down and touched the flame again. He smoked Afrikander and, like most good tobaccos, it didn't smell as good as it tasted. Bell lit a cigarette.

"Well?" Wetherby asked.

"There's a very distinct possibility that this killing was the work of some animal. Everything, bar one curious fact, points to that. And I can't think of anyone who would be more qualified to advise me on that. One way or the other."

"I see," Wetherby said. He tasted the brandy. "What sort of animal did you have in mind?"

"None. I don't know a damn thing about animals and Thurlow knows less. My wife had a cat once, but it ran away. And I think there's a mole in my garden. That's the lot."

Wetherby smiled.

"I thought maybe you could tell me by examining the marks on the body and the plaster casts of the tracks."

Wetherby nodded. "Yes, I should think I could," he said. "Were the tracks plain?"

"Not very."

"Well, I can certainly get an idea what sort of animal it was, if nothing else. A carnivore, I assume?"

"I don't know. The body wasn't devoured, if that's anything to go on. But it was savaged. Mangled. The police doctor swears that only a wild and savage animal could have done it. In fact, we would have been definite on that, except for the one curious fact – the one the papers all stressed, of course – the remarkable incident of the decapitation, as Doyle might have said. That was what confused the local police. The chief is a doddery old sort anyhow, all vintage port and confusion." Bell gestured with his pint.

"We never did find the head," he added.

Wetherby thought for a few moments, drawing on his pipe. It was rather like old times, pondering a problem at this bar, although the conversation on all sides dealt more with fashion and art than life and death.

"So this animal – if it was an animal – was something powerful enough to tear a man's head off, eh?"

Bell shrugged.

"In England? It seems doubtful. Possibly a pack of wild dogs, but I shouldn't think so. You've checked with all the zoos and circuses about an escaped carnivore, of course?"

Bell looked pained.

Wetherby said, "Of course. Sorry Justin."

"It's a bit more confusing than that, actually," Bell said. "The head wasn't torn off. Not the way an animal would tear a body. The body was ripped and clawed, almost shredded, but the head was severed quite neatly."

Wetherby frowned through the tobacco haze.

"That would mean enormous strength. Some animal powerful enough to take the skull in its jaws and yank it off with one explosive jerk. And hold the body down at the same time."

"As clean as a knife or a guillotine," Bell said. His face was clouded as he recalled the corpse. "What animal could have done that?"

"I don't know. Perhaps if I saw the tracks. A buffalo, for instance, might be able to hook a man's head off with one stroke of its horns. But if the body was clawed – I don't know, Justin. Perhaps some madman with a weapon that inflicted wounds like talons?"

"No. They were claw marks, all right. Fangs, too. No man could have done that."

"Well, I'll be glad to help you in any way I can."

"Could you come down to Dartmoor with me. On expenses, of course. The ground was soft and we've got some fair casts of the prints. You might recognize them."

Bell remembered that he, too, was on expenses. He signalled for another round.

"It's been a long time since I've done any tracking. Still, I suppose that knowledge doesn't leave entirely. I could give it a try."

Bell was unfolding a map. He spread it out on the bar, holding one corner down with his beer glass. Several of the young members looked over in interest. It had been a long time since a map had been studied at that bar. Wetherby leaned over and Bell pointed with a thick finger.

"The body was found – " The finger described a circle, then jabbed on to the map. "Here. Beside this stream."

Wetherby nodded, automatically forming an image of the terrain as he studied the contour map. Then, as his area of interest widened, he looked surprised; he took the pipe from his mouth, frowning.

"You knew Byron, didn't you?"

"Oh yes."

"Why, he lives there." Wetherby looked at the map again. It was remarkably detailed. "His house can't be more than a mile from where the body was discovered."

"Yes, I know."

"You could have saved yourself a trip by asking his advice. Or isn't he in the country?"

Bell looked uncomfortable.

"Actually, I did go to Byron," he said. "He wasn't interested in helping me. Always was a strange sort. The whole damn thing seemed to amuse him and he said something about it being just as well to kill people off, to counterbalance the population explosion. Said there were too damn many people in the world as it was."

"Yes, that's Byron. But surely he would have been interested in a challenge of this nature?"

"He was interested in the plaster casts, all right. Looked at them for quite a while, and I thought he had an idea what might have made them. But then he just shrugged and wouldn't venture an opinion. In fact, he suggested that I see you. Said you'd be more interested and concerned about what happened to humanity." Bell paused. "Of course, I intended to see you anyway. I only went to Byron's first because it was closer."

Wetherby grinned.

"Rather like hunting tigers in Africa," he said. "Are you sure you checked the zoo?"

They laughed and Wetherby bought a round of drinks.

"It certainly isn't like Byron to pass up an opportunity like this," Wetherby said. "Not that he ever had much regard for life, human or otherwise – he was more concerned with death – but if he thought this was a dangerous animal he'd be out with his gun. The more dangerous, the faster he'd be out. Last time I saw him he cursed me for giving up danger and living in town. Either he doesn't think it's an animal or, perhaps, he didn't want to help the authorities. That seems more likely. He might be out looking for the killer on his own. And, knowing Byron, he'll find it. Still, as you say, he's a strange fellow and I don't pretend to understand him."

"Will you come down with me, John?"

"You could have brought the casts with you."

"Yes, I considered it. But I'd like you down there. This is one of those killings without apparent motive which may never be solved. And the worst thing about them is they are so often repeated. Whether it was a man or a beast, there seems a good chance it will kill again."

"And you'd like me there if it does."

"Exactly. If anyone could track the killer, it would be you. And if, God forbid, it kills again, it would be better if you had a fresh trail. If we ever solve this, I think it more likely to be by physical means, rather than deduction. As Doyle surely never said."

Wetherby nodded. There was nothing to keep him in London, and the thought of getting into the open again was pleasant. He thought it might be nice to see Byron again, too. Byron and he had shared danger many times, and if that was the sole bond between them, it was a strong bond.

"All right, Justin. I'll come."

Bell folded the map and stuffed it in his pocket. His suit bulged with the encumbrance of such stuffings, and Wetherby wondered, smiling, if there was a magnifying glass somewhere in those drooping pockets. They sat at a table in the corner and had a last drink, making their plans to go down to Dartmoor in the morning. More through habits of conversation, than because Wetherby needed the information, Bell filled in the details of the killing. There was a great deal and yet there wasn't enough. The man who discovered the body was certainly not connected in any way other than circumstances. The body, with some difficulty, had been identified. It was an old fellow named Randal who had lived a hermitic life in the area, and who had been arrested for poaching several times. It seemed likely that he'd been doing just that when his death found him. The tracks made it obvious that Randal had been walking along the firm ground higher up the hill, and had fled towards the stream when he had seen his killer. He had almost reached the water when it overtook him, and he had died at the same spot where his body had been found. There was no sign that he had been injured as he ran, as might have been the case had an animal worried him, snapping at his heels until he was brought down. As soon as his killer caught him, it killed him. There were some signs of short but violent struggle, Randal had rolled over several times and his fingernails were splintered. His clothing had been torn to shreds, but his pockets hadn't been emptied, and contained four shillings and half an ounce of rolling tobacco. Randal had been an amusing local character, an eccentric with no known enemies, and the killing seemed entirely pointless.

Bell stopped talking; shook his head.

"It was a particularly ugly death," he said. "I don't suppose it was any worse for poor old Randal than any number of deaths might have been, but I'll tell you, John – I don't relish the thought of seeing another corpse like this."

Bell shook his head again.

He was going to.

Damn me, thought Brian Hammond. Damn me for a fool.

He leaned forward, both hands clamped on the steering wheel, and peered out through the rain-washed windscreen. It was hard to see the road. The wipers left curved blurs across the glass and the headlights shot pale beams futilely against the trees. Hammond's dark-jowled face, illuminated in the green glow of the dashlights, was angry and worried. He was a salesman but he looked like a merchant seaman. He had, in fact, been a merchant seaman when he was younger, but then he had looked more like a salesman. It was the type of face destined to foil enterprise. Brian sat rigidly in the seat, a cigar clamped in his teeth, as he steered along the dark and winding country lane.

How did I manage to miss that turning? he wondered. And why don't they put signposts on these blasted roads. How do they expect a man to find his way without any signs? All the taxes I pay, and I can't even find a road sign. Not to mention a petrol station.

His eyes turned down to the fuel gauge. The needle was hovering on the empty mark.

Damn this God-forsaken area, he thought. All the local country bumpkins are asleep, no one to ask directions, haven't even seen a house. Can't see anything anyway in this damn rain. Don't think I've got petrol for more than another mile or so. Damn car drinks petrol. Ought to get a smaller car, except then I wouldn't have any room for all these damn samples. Not that it would matter much. Haven't sold a damn thing all day. The boss will squawk like a stuck pig, too, damn him. How does he expect me to sell electronic equipment in this bloody area? Nothing here but sheep. These yokels probably never even heard of of electricity and I'm supposed to sell them equipment. Ought to give Cornwall independence, and then give them Dartmoor. Get rid of the damn place.

He turned a sharp corner and the lane rose ahead, dark and deserted.

That damn Ed Davis is working in London, too, he thought. Probably made plenty of sales today and now he's celebrating in the West End. Lucky bastard. Probably drinking champagne. Damn him, anyway. Why should he get all the choice territory just because he's been with the company longer? It isn't fair.

The car banged against the high shoulder of the road and Hammond snarled as he turned the wheel. He felt very sorry for himself. If there was any justice in the world he would be home by his fireside watching television while his wife made him a nice cup of tea. I wonder what my wife is doing now? he thought. She hates it when I have to travel. Course she knows I can't get into any trouble down here. I guess she just hates to have me be away. Real passionate, that wife of mine. I wonder if she went up to the pub tonight? He bit hard on the cigar. Ah, she wouldn't go to the pub alone. She's not like that. Faithful, my wife. But that damn Humphries is always trying to flirt with her in the pub. Caught her smiling back at him once, too. I'l bet she's gone up to the pub to flirt with Humphries.

Hammond looked at his watch. It was past closing time

No, she isn't in the pub, he thought. Must be home. I'd phone her if this damn place had any phone boxes. All the taxes I pay and I can't even find a phone box when I want one. But if I phoned and she wasn't home – ah, she'd be home. I wonder if that damn Humphries is home with her? If I thought for one minute that she –

Hammond shook his head and squinted into the black night. The wipers skimmed ineffectively over a film of water and the car veered from side to side. The samples slid around on the back seat, the tyres hummed, the foul cigar smoke hung heavy in the air. He had to drive slowly and it seemed he'd been driving for a very long time. And then the motor coughed and sputtered.

Oh no, Hammond thought.

The motor gulped the last ounce of petrol and the car glided to a silent stop. Brian sat scowling behind the wheel, thinking of the futility of joining the AA when he couldn't phone for aid. His mood was black. He felt sure that his wife was with that rogue Humphries and that he was going to lose his job because he'd sold nothing. He relighted his cigar and puffed away, wondering what to do. He had no idea where he was, and saw little sense in trying to walk somewhere in the dark. The rain was falling heavily. Hammond sighed and resigned himself to a cramped night in the car. The battery wasn't new, and he turned the lights off. But the road was narrow and dark, and it was dangerous without lights in the remote possibility that another car might come along. He opened the glove box and took out the flasher, pulled his collar up and opened the door. The rain singled him out, finding chinks in the armour of his clothing, and he swore to himself as he walked back a few hundred yards and placed the flasher on its tripod behind the car. He snapped it on and the red light began to blink. It lighted the trees with an eerie effect. It was very unreal. He stood there for a moment, watching the trees appear red and black, red and black. His cigar had gone out again and a loose leaf curled down. He was looking at the trees and then he was looking at something else that came out from the trees. For a moment he merely looked surprised, then his eyes widened and the cigar dropped as his mouth opened to scream. But only a whimper of fear came out.

Hammond turned and ran, without thinking where he was heading. He ran past his car, blind and dumb with terror. He ran for perhaps fifty yards before it caught him . . .

John Wetherby sat by the dying embers of his fire, drinking a last brandy and considering the things that Bell had told him. It was a comfortable room. The grandfather clock ticked with soothing regularity in the corner, the pendulum catching flashes of reflection through the arc. The walls were lined with beautifully bound books, the carpet was deep and soft, heavy tapestries were drawn across the wide windows. But Wetherby, in his thoughts, was dissociated from this room; he was back in a former way of life, with a different pattern of reason. He was trying to anticipate what he would learn in Dartmoor, to predict before seeing them what the tracks might be, what animal could be responsible for the unusual aspects of the case. And, not the least remarkable aspect, to one who knew Byron, was the man's failure to rise to a challenge of this nature, even for purely selfish reasons. That was a mystery in itself, quite apart from the killing. Byron was a man who had always gone out of his way to find a challenge; he invariably did things in the most risky and dangerous fashion simply to create a challenge against his life itself. And, the older he got, the greater this need became. As Wetherby began to feel himself slowing down and relied on his experience to do things the safest and easiest way, Byron had seemed compelled to increase the difficulties of the tasks he took in hand. Wetherby had hunted with Byron many times, in India and Africa and once, the last time, in the wilderness of northern Canada. He vividly recalled that Canada expedition. Never had Byron taken a risk that seemed more pointless – danger for the pure sake of danger. Byron wanted a Kodiak bear, and he wanted it alone, insisted that Wetherby wait at a distance too great to be of any possible

aid. And, although he had splendid guns, he had borrowed
a .30–06 from their guide, a good gun but much too light
for the job; a gun he had not even fired before. Wetherby
had protested in vain. Byron was not a man to listen to
reason, much less argument, and so Wetherby had waited.
He could still recall the tenseness he had felt on that memorable day. He had been waiting on a hill, surrounded by
evergreens. It was autumn. The forest was burning with
colour, trees ablaze in reds and yellows. The ground was
crisp with early frost and a chill wind stirred from the
north. Wetherby had watched Byron's figure diminish as
he strode away moving towards where they knew the bear
was waiting. Byron looked very casual, but that was deceptive. His red and black plaid shooting coat blended against
the background of the leaves. He looked very small, drawing farther away, towards the dense thicket where his
quarry waited. He was already out of effective range,
Wetherby would be helpless from where he stood. He
gripped his rifle, but knew it was useless. Byron was completely on his own. Byron was almost at the thicket when
the bear reared up. Even at that distance, Wetherby was
astounded at the monster's size. He saw Byron raise the
rifle, a tiny manikin only a few yards from those fourteen
hundred pounds of power and fury. The bear's head seemed
larger than Byron, towering three feet above him as the
beast rose on its hind legs. And then the bear was off
balance, twisting around and down, thrashing in death, and
it seemed a long time later that the sharp crack of the rifle
reached Wetherby's ears. Byron had turned and raised the
gun, motioning for Wetherby to advance. Wetherby had
advanced.

Byron was smiling, looking down at the bear. It was a
smile of pure pleasure. He had fired once, as the bear roared
in warning, and the slug had gone up through the roof of
that terrible mouth and into the brain. It had not emerged.
There was no mark on the trophy.

"A fine shot," Wetherby said.

"I couldn't very well have missed at that range. Couldn't
afford to, either."

"Not with that," Wetherby said, looking at the rifle.

"Oh, a .30–06 will kill a bear if the shot is placed right."

"Obviously."

Byron was amused. "Why should I use a heavier weapon than I need? That just makes a man sloppy. That .402 you carry, for instance. You could have dropped it even with a bad shot, broken its shoulder or shattered its leg and then finished it at your leisure. That isn't hunting, John. That isn't living. That's not the way to keep life and give death. You're a fine hunter and a splendid shot, but your values are wrong."

"Perhaps," Wetherby said with a mixture of admiration and annoyance, half understanding what Byron meant, and resenting an understanding he did not follow.

"Not perhaps. A categorical fact. An objective truth."

"But if you hadn't made a perfect shot – if something had happened, if the bear had shifted just a few inches as you fired – you couldn't have stopped a wounded charge with a rifle that light. Even if your second shot had been perfect, it would have killed you through sheer impetus and reflex."

Byron smiled again. This was a different smile.

"No," he said. "But that's a moot point."

Wetherby raised his eyebrows.

Byron tossed the rifle to him. Wetherby caught it. He knew, absolutely, what Byron meant then. He worked the lever. The empty shell ejected. There had been only one bullet in the rifle.

"You're mad," Wetherby said.

And Byron laughed in mad delight . . .

Later, by the campfire, Byron had been in a thoughtful, philosphical mood. His immediate pleasure had faded, and he seemed possessed with a need to share his attitudes with Wetherby. They were alone. Their guide was skinning the bear where it had fallen; it was too huge to move. Wetherby was still greatly disturbed by the enormous risk Byron had taken; a risk that seemed to border on the unbalance of madness.

"Can't you understand, John?" Byron said. He was almost pleading for understanding.

"I don't know. I see the emotion of it – even the accomplishment. But it's suicidal, Byron. Some day – "

Byron silenced him with a gesture. His eyes were bright in the firelight.

"Danger, John. Only in danger are we alive. Only by risking our lives can we appreciate them. How much fuller our existence is than that of a city man, castrated by civilization, emasculated by society and safety. There is no life there, no danger and no joy, no risk and, therefore, nothing to risk. And we give life as we take it, John. That bear was never more alive than the instant before the bullet entered his brain. If we, the hunters, are more alive and aware, then it must work even more so for the hunted. I love the things I kill, John. The things that would kill me if I was too slow, if I failed to observe, if my shot failed. I love them, I say. I could have been the world's greatest animal tamer, you know. I have a rapport with wild creatures. I can sense their thoughts, their feelings, and meet them on their own level. There is no animal I could not manage, no bestial level upon which I couldn't meet them. If I chose to befriend a beast, instead of killing it – " His voice softened, he looked off into the distance, across the darkening hills of an endless wilderness. He did not look at Wetherby when he spoke again. Perhaps he was not speaking to Wetherby.

"But I like to kill," he said. "I think, perhaps, I might even like to be killed – in the proper fashion . . ."

Their guide returned, dragging the skin behind him on a travois, and they talked no more of such things. That was the last time they hunted together.

Wetherby felt a vague uneasiness, recalling these strange words from that faraway place. Byron had often made him uneasy, in some indefinite way, in much the same way that he felt uneasy about an animal that was acting peculiar – when he couldn't tell if it intended to charge or to flee. There were many traits of the animal in Byron, at that. A strange man. Wetherby wondered if he had changed at all with the years, and looked forward to seeing him again. And that reminded him that it was late, and that he must rise early. He had arranged to meet Bell at eight o'clock in the morning, and didn't want to oversleep. Wetherby refused to have a telephone or an alarm clock, and depended on a method he had developed of setting his mind to awake at a given hour, but it had been some time since he had been forced to use this ability. He wasn't sure if it would still be effective; he decided that he had better go to bed.

Wetherby stood and finished his nightcap, regarding the glowing embers. The door knocker clanked disturbingly through the quiet rooms.

Wetherby frowned, looking at the clock. It was a strange hour for visitors, and he didn't welcome unexpected visits at any hour. Then he shrugged, went into the hall and walked down to the door.

Bell stood on the threshold, looking flustered.

"Sorry to disturb you," he said.

"Quite all right. Come in."

Bell entered, holding his hat in both hands. He seemed uncertain, preoccupied, no longer the same man who had recently been with Wetherby at the club.

"Was there something you forgot to tell me?"

Bell shook his head.

"Come on into the study. There's a fire there. Will you have a drink?"

"I haven't time, John. I'll have to go down to Dartmoor immediately. I'd like you to come with me."

"Tonight?" Wetherby said. He didn't relish the idea. "Can't it wait until morning? I can take a train down and meet you there."

"I want you to have a look at the tracks while they're still fresh."

Wetherby blinked.

"What?" he asked.

Bell seemed to snap out of the mood that blanketed his thoughts then. He looked sheepish.

"Sorry, John. I guess I'm not thinking. I didn't tell you."

"Tell me what?" Wetherby asked.

"The killer, whatever it is, has killed again."

The police driver was expert, the motor-car was fast, and the roads were empty. Wetherby and Bell rode in the back seat. Wetherby had brought one of his sporting rifles and wore an old bush jacket. He felt a touch of the familiar old thrill at the start of the hunt, although it was greatly modified by circumstance. It was more like going after a man-eating tiger than a trophy. It was very much like going after a man-eater, in fact. They didn't talk much. Bell looked weary, his hard red face drawn and tense, chain-smoking cigarettes. It was a black night. The lights of London were behind, and on Salisbury Plain they ran into the storm that was sweeping the West Country. The slippery road didn't seem to trouble the driver and they shot on through the rain without reducing the speed. Dawn had just begun to pale the sky behind them when they pulled into the parking lot at The Bridge Hotel.

The driver consulted a map with the quick efficiency of long practice, pulled out of the parking lot and turned on to a secondary road leading north. He had to go slower now. They ran through hedgerows and trees, flickering shadows in the headlights, and then they cornered into a blinding glare of white light.

The area was cordoned off and arc lamps had been rigged. The narrow lane was starkly flooded in the powerful crossbeams and uniformed policemen moved in the shadows of the trees on either side. Several police cars were drawn up along the shoulder of the road and Hammond's warning flasher was still blinking weakly against the greater light.

Detective Sergeant Thurlow came over and opened the door. His face was grim. He carried an electric torch and his shoes were thick with mud.

"I've left the body where it was," he said.

"Identity?" Bell asked. He got out of the car. Wetherby got out the other side.

"Yes," Thurlow said. "Driver's licence and credit cards in the glove box. Man named Hammond. A salesman from London. Apparently he'd run out of petrol and went behind the car to set up a flasher." He glanced at the winking light. It was a sad little effort, overwhelmed in the glare.

"Turn it off, for God's sake," Bell said, irritably.

Someone snapped the flasher off.

"The killer came out from the trees there, and Hammond ran some fifty yards up the road before it got him," Thurlow said. Bell looked up the road.

"He ran past his car, eh?"

Thurlow nodded.

"You'd think he would have tried to get back in the car and lock the door, wouldn't you?" Bell said, more to himself than anything else.

Thurlow nodded. "The locks worked on all doors," he said. "I considered that. I suppose he didn't have time to open the door, or was too frightened to think of it."

Wetherby had come around the front of the police car. He was carrying his rifle. Thurlow raised an eyebrow and Bell introduced them. They shook hands and Thurlow's palm was damp.

"Anything else?" Bell asked.

"The same things. Plenty of tracks. They look like the same ones. The same thing that got Randal."

"Who found the body?"

"Young fellow bicycling home from his girl's house. He's waiting in my car. Must have come along just a few minutes after it happened. The body was still warm when I got here. Gave him one hell of a jolt."

"He's lucky he didn't come a bit sooner," Bell said. "I'll speak to him later. Let's have a look at the body."

They walked on past Hammond's car. Wetherby still carried the rifle. The body had been covered with a rubber sheet, and blood had seeped out at the sides in thick coils along the road. A young constable with a very white face stood to attention.

"Pull it down," Bell said.

The constable squatted and pulled the sheet down. Wetherby winced. The body was horribly mangled, the belly was torn open and the intestines trailed out in twisted loops. Wetherby had seen death like this before, and his first thought was that it looked like the mauling of a leopard. The young constable stood up quickly and walked to the side of the road; he leaned over and made noises.

"Did you find the head?" Bell asked.

"No. It's gone," Thurlow said.

No leopard did that, Wetherby thought.

"Well, John?" Bell asked.

Wetherby was kneeling on the wet earth, looking at the tracks. Farther into the trees a detective was taking plaster casts and another was photographing them. Behind them a group was fingerprinting the car inside and out and measuring distances and positions. They all worked with quick skill, and would miss nothing, if anything was there. Wetherby looked up, frowning. Bell's face was suddenly etched in the flash of the photographer's camera.

"I don't know. I have an idea I've seen tracks like these before. But damned if I can place them. They're almost like a gigantic weasel at this point, but notice how deep the claw marks are. And farther back they're different."

"Different?" Bell asked sharply.

Wetherby nodded.

"You mean there may have been two animals? Different animals?"

"Perhaps. More likely, the tracks changed when the creature began to run. The different stride, you see."

Bell nodded. Wetherby stood up, brushing at his knees.

"It was walking up to this point," Wetherby said. He glanced back at the road. "It walked to here, and then it ran after its prey. That's when the tracks change. But Justin – when it walked – it walked on two legs."

And they were silent for some time.

"Can you trail it?" Bell asked.

They were standing back at his car. The rain was still slashing through the light and black clouds had become visible as the sky paled above them. Thurlow stood beside them, nervously looking from side to side.

"Maybe. In the morning, perhaps. I'll need daylight."

Bell nodded.

"There's nothing more we can do here now, then. We may as well go back to The Bridge Hotel and wait for daylight. We can get an early start from there."

"If only we knew what the hell we were looking for," Thurlow said. "A man or an animal?"

"Something that walks on two legs and runs on four," Bell added. "A man or an animal?"

"Or some combination of the two?" Thurlow said.

Bell looked at him and Thurlow shrugged sheepishly.

"You don't believe in such things?" Bell asked.

"No. Of course not."

But he looked very strange.

It foreshadowed the dark fear to come.

Wetherby and Bell returned to The Bridge Hotel in the morning. The rain had stopped but the day was grim with fog. They went into the lounge and sat by the window, their shoes caked with mud and their faces dark with the stubble of beards. They were both tired. It had been a night long with futility. Wetherby had attempted to follow the killer's tracks in the early light, had followed the spoor easily enough for several hundred feet beyond the road, and then lost the trail. The trail has simply vanished abruptly, as though deliberately obliterated, with no period of transition. There was a spoor, and then there was no spoor. Bell had followed, silent and dependent in this aspect of the hunt, while Wetherby sought a continuation of the tracks farther on. They had walked in a wide circle around the point where the tracks ended, but had found nothing; repeated the circle farther back, thinking that the killer might have back-tracked and left the original trail on a tangent; followed a long arc on the opposite side of the lane from the visible trail, in case it had back-tracked all the

way with the instinct of a cunning beast knowing it will be
pursued. But there was no further trace. It walked like a
man, and ran like a beast, and Wetherby's tired mind
wondered if it also flew like a bird.

They had returned to the lane after that. A police car was
waiting for them, the driver leaning on the wing smoking a
cigarette. Hammond's body had been removed but the dark
stain of his blood still marked the spot where he had died.
Bell stopped by the car but Wetherby had one more check
to make. He squatted in the muddy lane and, using his
fountain pen as a makeshift ruler, measured the depth of
the animal's tracks; he also measured Hammond's tracks
and then his own. Bell stood scratching his head. Wetherby
had moved from the lane and taken a fourth measurement
at the point where the killer had been walking. His forehead
had corrugated as he looked at the fountain pen and struggled with his conclusions, and then he had walked slowly
back to the car and they had been driven to the hotel.

"Sorry, Justin." Wetherby sat, looking out of the window.
The fog was drifting in long streams across the moors, a
few motor-cars passed on the road.

"You did your best, John. If any man could have followed the trail, it would have been you."

Wetherby shrugged; he didn't deny it.

"What now?" he asked.

"I don't know. I'm worried, John. I'm having some dogs
brought down, but I wouldn't count on them. You still
have no opinion on what it might be?"

"Less than before. None of the facts fit together. The
marks on the body, for instance. I should say they were
the work of a cat. Particularly the disembowelment. Not
something as powerful as a lion or tiger. A powerful beast,
mauling the body that way, would have crushed the bones,
whereas these wounds were comparatively superficial . . .
the ribs weren't broken, even though the stomach was
ripped out. More like the work of a leopard. Something
fairly light and completely ferocious, tearing with sharp
talons rather than crushing. But that doesn't tie in with the

strength necessary to sever the neck cleanly. That would take unbelievable force."

Bell nodded, crossing his legs. A shard of mud dropped on to the carpet and he regarded it thoughtfully.

"And the tracks?" he asked.

"They're vaguely familiar to me, but damned if I can remember where I saw them before."

"There can't be many animals that walk on their hind legs and run on all fours," Bell said.

"Possibly an ape of some sort . . . a bear for a short distance, although it's not likely. But there's another thing about the prints that I find even more confusing. The way they change when this animal begins to run. They become more shallow. Naturally, with the animal's weight distributed on four feet, the tracks wouldn't be as deep, but the difference was much greater than it should have been. I measured the depth of the prints, using my own footprints to test the resistance of the soil, and using Hammond's prints to make sure the rain hadn't affected the quality of the ground to any great degree. The conclusion was rather startling."

Bell waited, leaning on his elbow. A waiter looked in the door, then withdrew. They could hear voices at the desk as someone registered.

"When the creature was walking," Wetherby said, "it weighed somewhat more than I do. Presumably it was balanced on its hind legs, and the print it left was roughly the same in area as my own print, but it was deeper. I should say it weighed somewhere around fourteen stone . . . the weight of a leopard, possibly, nothing larger. But when it ran, the prints were much more shallow than the double distribution of that weight can account for. They were no deeper than a smallish animal would have made. Something around forty pounds."

Bell considered this without expression and said, "What would account for that?"

"It seems as though this creature just skimmed over the ground . . . as if it were a large bird, an ostrich perhaps, not actually flying but using its wings to take most of its weight from the ground. And if it also had the power of flight, this could account for the way the trail vanished."

"A gigantic man-eating bird?" Bell said, rather louder than he'd intended.

Wetherby's smile was weary.

"No, that isn't possible. I was just toying with some of the conflicting facts. No bird runs on four legs and has five distinctly clawed toes."

"Well then?"

"The only alternative seems to be that it was fairly bowling along . . . running so fast that it just skimmed the surface of the ground. Incredible speed from a standing start."

Bell's eyes flickered as he added another meagre grain to his knowledge of the killer.

"So we know it must be exceptionally fast," he said.

"But that raises another paradox."

"Oh?"

"The victim . . . Hammond . . . ran for some fifty yards . . ."

"Fifty-three and some inches," Bell said.

"Yes. And how could a man have run so far if his pursuer was so fast? It didn't overtake him immediately, it followed him at an apparently great speed, and yet it didn't catch him for some fifty yards. Probably six or seven seconds. And they must have been terrible seconds for Hammond."

"It must have allowed him a head start . . . toyed with him . . . that would be like a cat, wouldn't it?"

"Possibly. I don't know what to think. It almost seems as though there were two different animals. A large, two-legged one and a smaller four-legged one, but there weren't two sets of tracks, only one set that changed form."

There was a considerable silence, although Bell's mind was soaring with activity.

"An animal . . . a creature . . . a being that can change its form at will?" Bell asked the window. Or perhaps he asked the dark fog beyond. He was thinking of what Thurlow had hinted, and Wetherby knew what was in his mind.

But that was too monstrous for serious consideration. Too preposterous for belief. At this stage . . .

"There must be some explanation," Wetherby said. "Some fact eludes us or some simple point that we have failed to see, or to understand."

"Of course," Bell said.

He continued to stare at the fog.

The waiter looked in again. He was a nervous little man, overawed by the presence of a law enforcement officer, and suffering the guilt that all totally innocent men feel when confronted by an agent of the superstructure – fearing law far more than crime.

Bell signalled to him and the waiter came over slowly.

"Sir?"

"Coffee," Bell said.

"Right away, sir."

"And bring me some paper."

"Paper, sir?"

"Paper, for God's sake. Something to write on."

"Yes, sir."

The waiter retreated with squared shoulders.

"Obviously a man who has never broken a law," Bell said, showing remarkable insight considering his trade. He smiled slightly, perfunctorily, a man who would not hesitate to bend the law to achieve justice.

"We know so little," he said. "So many various facts without a pattern. The only way to get a killer like this is to wait until a pattern is established, and that is obviously not a satisfying method. How many deaths must occur before it links up? Do beasts conform to a pattern, too, John?"

"Definitely. More than men, I'd say. In their fashion."

"Will this killer conform?"

"Yes. If only in the territory and the time when it kills . . . the frequency of its kills. But it doesn't devour its victims, so we can't very well anticipate it by a hunger cycle. It will be strictly a bloodlust cycle, and to form a pattern from that we must know what the killer is . . . or wait, as you say, until it establishes its own pattern."

Bell winced. The waiter returned with a tray, coffee and a pad of writing paper, placed the objects carefully on the table and stood at attention. Bell waved and he departed. Bell tore a sheet of paper from the pad and squared it before him.

"Both deaths occurred within a mile or so of each other," he said. "Maybe that narrows the field, maybe not." He began marking the paper with a ball-point pen. "If it's an animal, it must have a lair somewhere in this area . . . a cave, a burrow, a tree . . . some place it regards as home. All animals have a well-developed sense of territorial possession, I believe." Wetherby nodded, but Bell was looking at the paper and talking to himself. His pen moved swiftly. He was sketching a crude map. Wetherby watched the lines take form and content, and saw that Bell had committed the terrain to memory. He made a dark cross against a vertical line and the top of the pen lingered over it for a moment, then moved on to inscribe a second cross. He regarded it for a moment, nodded, and printed a few words on the map, nodded again and turned it round. He tapped his pen against the paper as Wetherby looked at it and saw, with his trained eye, that Bell had incorporated all the significant points, and that the rough map nicely outlined the area and placed the territory he had seen in context.

The highway ran diagonally across the paper in a gradual south-westerly arc from top right to bottom left and this line was divided by a stream twisting horizontally across the centre of the sheet. The stream passed under the highway, and the hotel – named for the bridge over the water – was at the junction. The hotel was south of the highway, and opposite another line, representing a secondary road, made a right angle to the north. Beside the stream, west of the hotel, was the cross where Randal had died, and on the secondary road north of the hotel was Hammond's cross. The hotel and the two morbid crosses formed a triangle.

Bell's pen moved between the crosses.

"You can see that there isn't much distance between the kills, cross-country," he said.

"What is it, about two miles?"

"About that."

"Where is Byron's house?"

"Byron's?"

"I'd like to have a word with him."

Bell drew the paper back and added another line and a square. The line represented a narrow lane running west from the secondary road and Byron's house was at the end.

"The lane leaves the secondary road quite near where Hammond was killed," Bell said. "Runs through the hedge-rows for a mile or so and ends at Byron's. His place was the manor house at one time, but that was before motor-cars and the lane is quite narrow."

Wetherby was judging distances, thinking he might walk to Byron's. He realized that adding Byron's house to the three points of the triangle formed a rough square. But that meant nothing. Bell was marking the paper again, just doodling now; he added the ridge lined with tors that ran parallel between the stream and the lane. There are no great distances in England, and the confined area gave Wetherby an idea. He looked out of the window and raised his eyebrows.

"Any ideas?" Bell asked.

"Possibly. I think we might treat this the same way we'd treat a man-eating tiger. I've done that before. Instead of trying to track it or anticipate it, we might attract it."

"Set a trap for it?"

Wetherby nodded.

"How?" Bell asked.

"We could stake out a goat or something, I suppose. But obviously it prefers human prey . . ."

"And obviously we can't stake out a man."

"If we could leave the corpse where it was . . ."

"This isn't India, John. You know I can't do that. There'd be hell to pay."

"Of course. Suppose I were to wait myself. Not in one spot particularly, just wander around the moors and roads at night? It's a remote possibility, but not all that far-fetched. There can't be many people on the moors at night, and if the territory is limited, then the killer's opportunities are limited as well. If I made my presence obvious . . ."

Bell scowled.

"Make yourself a potential victim? I didn't bring you down here for that."

"It's been done before."

Bell shook his head, considering more than refusing. Wetherby, now that he had had the idea, was rather excited by the prospect. It had been a long time . . .

"I couldn't let you go alone," Bell said.

"It would have to be alone, Justin. This is work for a solitary hunter, not a posse. Too many people would simply give it warning. And, of course, it's not a question of you giving permission. I have every right to walk on the moors at night. Nothing official. Nor repercussions at all."

"Well, I can't stop you."

"It might work, Justin. I think it's well worth a try."

Bell was still scowling. He sipped his coffee.

"What can we lose?" Wetherby asked.

"Your head," Bell told him.

They finished the coffee in silence.

"I might be able to persuade Byron to join me," Wetherby said. He glanced at the map again. "We've worked together on man-eaters. I'll go out to his place this afternoon. But I'd like to try, with or without Byron."

"As I said, I can't stop you. Officially. You still have your gun permits?"

"Yes. It shouldn't be dangerous, really. We're letting the confusing aspects of this affect our thinking, Justin. It can certainly be no more dangerous than any big-game hunting. It's not a ghost, nothing uncanny, just a beast that has to be killed – something I've done often enough for pleasure. Just because this is England the facts have made greater impact on us, the contrast has fired our imagination. But if I keep away from the rocks and trees, keep well in the open where it can't surprise me, it should be safe enough. Both the victims were surprised and unarmed, and both

had a chance to run for a considerable distance before it
brought them down. But even if it is as fast as those tracks
imply, I'll be ready for it. I won't be running."

"You sound as if you like the idea."

"Ah, the old thrill, eh?"

"Any help you want . . . "

"Unofficial?"

"I never impose limits," Bell said.

Wetherby said, "I'll let you know."

"More coffee?" Bell asked.

He had seen the waiter's eye appear around the corner.
The eye disappeared again and they heard whispering in
the hallway. Bell scowled at the door.

"No, I think not. I'd like to get cleaned up now and
then go over to Byron's."

"I'll leave the car and driver at your disposal."

"Want to come along?"

Bell shook his head. He had no desire to see Byron again;
he had an irritating idea that Byron had been laughing at
him when he had requested an opinion on his former visit.
He wanted more coffee and looked fiercely towards the
door, willing the waiter to appear. Another man appeared.
Wetherby stood up and the man walked directly over to
the table. He was a small fellow, prematurely bald with
soft eyes and a disreputably rumpled jacket. He looked like
a rookie reporter and had a notebook and pens in his breast
pocket.

"Oh God, the Press," Bell said.

The reporter stuck his hand out at Wetherby.

"Detective Superintendent Bell?" he asked.

"Do I look like a detective?" Wetherby asked, in a tone
of horror, that was only half assumed.

"Aaron Rose," the reporter said, and mentioned the
name of his newspaper. It was a Sunday scandal sheet. He
moved past Wetherby and pointed his handshake across
the table. Bell looked up morosely.

"Detective Superintendent Bell?" Rose asked.

"Do I look like a detective?" Bell snarled.

Bell sounded like a detective. Wetherby moved smiling

towards the door and reporter Aaron Rose stood scratching
his scalp and considering the deception of appearances.

The driver knew where Byron's was. Wetherby sat beside
him, filling his pipe, as they drove from the hotel parking
lot and turned across the highway. It was the same way
they had gone before, when they first went to the scene of
the killing and later, in the daylight, when Wetherby had
attempted to follow the trail. This time they didn't travel
so far up the secondary road but turned off on a lane to
the left. Wetherby remembered noticing the turning before.
They ran along smoothly, following the winding lane
through hedgerows and sudden glimpses of open, rolling
land. It was still foggy. The fog hugged the open land and
Wetherby regarded it thoughtfully; he imagined how the
moors would be at night and thought that, despite what he
had told Bell, a night alone on the moors might well prove
more terrifying than any jungle. It was a question of the
unexpected, the startling contrast between danger and the
placid everyday reality of this mild country. But this realization only served to increase his eagerness, and he looked
forward to the hunt as he would have in the past.
   Half a mile down the lane they passed a public house, a
little thatched building which the driver eyed with a thirsty
eye. It was called, with a nice twist on the traditional, The
King's Torso. But in the light of recent events, it was an
ominous name.
   "You won't have to wait for me at Byron's," Wetherby
said.
   The driver looked delighted. They drove on and after
another half-mile came to Byron's. Wetherby got out and
the driver reversed into the drive and headed back down
the lane, where The King's Torso waited. Wetherby stood
for a moment, his pipe in his teeth, surveying the manor
house of former years. It was impressive. The building was
well back from the lane, a timeless structure of different
centuries and different architectural style, with gables and
turrets and stone chimneys, grey and grim against the wind-

swept moors. From the back came the steady thump of someone cutting wood. The sound stopped as Wetherby walked up the drive, and Byron came around the side of the house, an axe over his shoulder. He smiled and walked down to meet Wetherby.

"I thought you'd be around," Byron said.

His grip was as firm as ever. Byron hadn't changed at all, he was as timeless as his home. He was tall and lean, an immensely powerful man with the long muscles of endurance defined without bulk. His face was weathered leather and his eyes were bright with life; his hair was clipped short and his clothing was ancient. He rested the axe against the ground and leaned on the handle.

"So Bell has persuaded you to join the witch hunt, eh?" Wetherby smiled and shrugged.

"I rather thought you might. I'm pleased to see you haven't lost the urge to action."

Byron's eyes moved up and down, and Wetherby had the uncomfortable thought that he was being critically inspected. He puffed on his pipe and stared back. Then Byron laughed and clapped a big hand on Wetherby's shoulder and they walked back up to the house.

"I'm surprised you declined the offer," Wetherby said.

"Oh, I have other interests. I haven't stopped living yet, John. I'm planning a South American trip early next year, as a matter of fact. Interested?"

"No, I'm still retired."

Byron shook his head. They went into the house and down a cold and impersonal hallway with an atmosphere like a National Trust castle. They turned into a huge room hung with trophies. A wood fire was burning fiercely and the comfortable leather chairs drew the light deeply below the polished surface. They sat by the fire. Byron noticed the Kodiak bear he had watched Byron bring down with a single shot from a gun which was far too light for the job. It was mounted upright in the corner, its gigantic head snarling some nine feet above the floor, and Wetherby felt again that awe of a man facing that monster with one bullet in a .30–06.

"Drink?" Byron asked.

"I'd like some coffee."

"Grant!" Byron barked.

A man appeared at the doorway. His clothing was, if anything, more ancient than Byron's, his hands large and gnarled and his face etched with deep lines. He had a twisted leg.

"Bring some coffee," Byron said.

The man nodded sullenly and moved off, his leg wheeling after him.

"My servant," Byron said.

"I thought you disapproved of servants?"

Byron shook his head.

"No, I disapprove of servile men. Grant is a most inefficient servant, but he isn't servile. He used to be a Cornish tin miner, a man who has experienced life to the limits. Restricted within those limits, of course. I hired him because he almost beat me hand wrestling."

"What?"

"You remember the game, surely?"

Byron raised his forearm, hand open and fingers extended upwards, and made a pressing motion across his chest. Wetherby nodded.

"Oh, that. Yes, I remember."

"We had a contest once."

"You beat me."

"Yes. It's not a game I lose. But it took seven minutes by the stop watch before I put your arm down, and I gained a great respect for you, John. I put Grant down in five minutes, by the way. Can you still hold your own?"

Byron placed his elbow on the table; he looked expectant, almost hopeful. But Wetherby laughed and shook his head, and Byron sighed.

"You look fit enough."

"I'm all right," Wetherby said.

"A pity you've given up life."

"Just moved on to a different life."

"Oh, it's the same thing," Byron said.

"You can't expect everyone to agree with your ideas."

"Never mind. What of this man-killer? What do you think?"

"I don't really know. You've heard that it killed again last night?"

"Yes. I heard."

"I came down from London with Bell just afterwards."

"You saw the tracks?"

"Yes. They looked vaguely familiar."

Byron leaned back in his chair.

"Couldn't you identify them?" he asked.

"No. I believe I've seen similar tracks before, but I couldn't place them."

"You should have been able to, John. Ten years ago you would have."

Wetherby didn't like that.

"Bell told me you didn't recognize the casts," he said.

Byron smiled, started to speak and then shrugged.

"Well? Did you?"

"Oh, casts are a different thing," he said. "I dare say I would have recognized the tracks themselves."

"But you couldn't be bothered."

"Exactly."

Wetherby wanted to say more. Instead he refilled his pipe. It was hard to know just how much to say to Byron. Grant returned with the coffee on a silver tray, swaying from good leg to bad with a curiously rapid gait. He banged the tray down on the table. The coffee spilled into the saucers, hands accustomed to ravaging the earth were not suited to the more delicate tasks of a servant. He swivelled about and clumped out of the room without speaking.

"I'm sure you'll be able to track this animal, anyway, John," Byron said. "You won't have lost all your skill."

"I didn't this morning."

"Oh, you'll probably have another chance."

Wetherby stared at him.

"Well, if an animal kills twice, it's a good bet it will kill again, eh? I'm just being practical."

"You think it is an animal, then?"

"Undoubtedly."

"I suppose so. But what animal could have severed the heads that way?"

"It should prove interesting, finding out."

"Interesting? My God, Byron. Two men have been brutally killed. This isn't a pleasure trip."

Byron sipped his coffee placidly.

"Hunting should always be a pleasure, John. You know that. If it's necessary, that should merely add to the pleasure. And if it's dangerous, all the better."

"I am rather excited about it," Wetherby admitted.

"And it could be dangerous," Byron said.

"Well, it certainly has the ability to kill a man."

"What gun are you using?"

"I have the Winchester with me."

"Too much gun," Byron said. He sighed and sipped his coffee. "You've seen the tracks, it isn't a large animal. You always did tend to carry too much firepower. It makes a man careless about his shooting."

"But it will stop it," Wetherby said.

"Oh, it will do that. If efficiency is what you look for. And if you hit it, of course."

"I'll hit it. I haven't lost everything."

"That's good. How do you propose to find it?"

Byron sounded interested and Wetherby leaned forward, hoping to get his old companion enthused enough to join the hunt.

"I expect I'll apply the usual methods. Treat it as a hunt. Try to follow a fresh trail if it kills again. Or try to anticipate it . . . wait for it, let it find me."

"On the moors at night?" Byron's eyes gleamed. "That would be like the old days, John. Remember the man-eater of Sunda?"

Byron gestured at the wall. Wetherby turned. The tiger's head snarled viciously at them. Wetherby remembered, all right. They had left the half-devoured corpse of a Hindu villager and waited for the tiger to return to its kill. The man's widow had howled heart-rendingly at such a misuse of her late husband, but the headman had showed more sense, or less emotion, which amounted to the same thing.

"You waited in a tree, John," Byron said.

"And you waited on the ground by the body. Yes, I remember it. It was a near thing for you."

"You never did see the beauty of that . . . that the risk had to be positive to make it worthwhile, that the man-eater had to have his chance to live or die the same as I did."

Wetherby looked at the tiger's head again. He remembered the sudden blur of orange and black through the jungle night, that quick rush of death that had carried the cat's dead body past its executioner. Byron had fired from a crouch and hurled himself to one side as the tiger, already dead, stormed past to collapse at the base of the tree where Wetherby waited, where Wetherby had no time to fire.

"That fellow had already killed over two hundred human beings, Byron. It wasn't – it shouldn't have been – a question of the thrill. Killing it was a worthwhile end no matter how we'd managed it."

Byron was looking at the trophy, too.

"Do you really believe that the lives of two hundred primitive and ignorant savages are equal to the life of that magnificent killer? Yes, I expect you do. Don't you see that the life of the killer is invariably superior to the life of the victim?"

Wetherby stared, not quite sure how serious Byron was. Even in the old days, his curious attitudes had never extended this far.

"You had all the ability a man could need, John. If only you'd had the philosophy. You could have been as good as I was. You were as fast, you shot as well, your instincts were as fine. But you waited in a tree, John." The scorn was evident. It might not have been intentional, but Byron could not keep it from his tone. "I could no more have waited in safety than I could use a weapon so heavy that even a poor shot would bring the quarry down. That was where we differed, and where you failed."

Wetherby was stung. He sat rigidly on the end of his chair.

"Wasn't I as good as you?" he asked.

"Oh, perhaps. In your way. That's not what I'm talking about, John. Not ability, not achievement. Understanding. A way of life. Did I tell you I'm writing a book?" He stood up. Wetherby followed him across the room. A battered old typewriter was surrounded by disordered paper on a table in the corner. Byron picked up several sheets and looked at them; put them down again. "A book about my philosophy," he said. "I'd like you to read it some day. You might understand, then. But not until it's finished."

He turned and looked out of the window. The land rolled away behind the house, mist and cloud merging in the distance.

"Or perhaps out there at night," Byron said.

"What?"

"On the moors at night. Perhaps you might learn to understand then, John."

"But you won't come with me?"

"This – this is more to my taste, I will say. You are doing the proper thing when you make yourself the bait. It appeals to me. If I thought you were still the man I once knew I might join you – I might give you this beast. But you're soft now, John. We aren't compatible."

"I'm not soft," Wetherby said.

"Oh? Well, perhaps not. Perhaps I have misjudged you. But I'm seldom wrong about man or beast."

"I'll be going now," Wetherby said.

"You're quite welcome to stay here."

"I've already booked at the hotel."

They walked back across the room. The bear loomed up above them, the tiger grimaced in its eternal snarl. But these things were dead.

"You're angry, John," Byron said.

Wetherby shrugged.

"Perhaps I was wrong. If I was wrong, I'll join your hunt. Will you prove me wrong?"

"I can't prove anything," Wetherby said.

"You can, you know."

Byron sat. He placed his elbow on the table and smiled up at Wetherby.

"You lasted seven minutes once, John. Can you last seven now? Five? If you can hold me for one minute I'll join you?"

"This is childish."

"Childish? Basic, possibly. But how then are we to judge our fellow men? Come, John."

Stung to anger, Wetherby sat opposite Byron. He flexed his arm several times and placed his elbow on the table level with Byron's. They locked hands. Wetherby wanted very much to beat Byron at this game. It was no longer childish to him, he was taut with that need. Byron was still smiling. His hand felt rough and dry, and he was relaxed. They stared at each other across their hands.

"Are you ready, John?"

Wetherby nodded.

Byron placed his left hand on the table and looked at his wristwatch.

"Proceed," he said.

Wetherby drew a deep breath and snapped into sudden pressure, using all his strength in the first surge, trying to gain an initial advantage. It was like pressing against a concrete slab. Byron's hand did not move, it did not quiver. His long bicep seemed hardly to tense, but his forearm was a bar of steel that would not bend. His smile was unchanged.

"Ten seconds," he said. "I'm waiting, John."

Wetherby pressed with all the power he possessed. His arm leaped with the effort, his chest swelled as the pressure ran along his muscles. He knew his face was flushed and his hand began to falter. Byron hardly seemed aware of the energy summoned against him. He looked at his watch again, and then he applied his own strength. Wetherby's hand began to move back through a steady arc. He was powerless to resist. His forearm drew towards the level, his wrist bent back, he felt as though his bones were bending.

And then his arm was down.

"Fifty seconds," Byron said.

Wetherby shook his hand. It was limp and lifeless. All his energy had seeped away, even his anger had gone.

"Yes, I am seldom wrong about a man," Byron said. "But good luck in your quest, John."

Wetherby walked back along the narrow lane. His arm ached. The police car was parked outside The King's Torso, but he walked on past without taking much notice. He was preoccupied with a sense of failure, a self-doubt and a troubling idea that Byron had, after all, been right.

The wind billowed across the rolling moors, shredding the fog in its wake. Wetherby walked through ribbons of grey mist against a black night. He made no attempt at stealth. His pipe crackled as he drew on it and trailed smoke lighter than the fog, a warm companion on a cold night. He was wrapped in a heavy cloak and had a hip flask of brandy and an electric torch. The torch was unlighted, and his rifle was loaded, the safety catch under his thumb. He was following the course of the stream westward from the highway and south of the ridge. The tors were black against a dark sky and the water made a rippling background noise punctuated by the regular croaking of frogs along the bank. His rubber boots squelched in the soft mud and reeds bent beneath his stride. Wetherby was enjoying this solitary trek; he hadn't realised how much he had missed the tingle of danger and the sharp sense of readiness. In that much, at least, Byron had been right.

Wetherby had left the hotel as soon as it was dark. The lights were still on in the bar, traffic moved along the highway and cars pulled in and out of the parking lot. But as soon as he had left the road he was alone. It wasn't a case of distance, he hadn't come more than a mile along the bank of the stream, and yet the feeling of solitude was absolute. He could just as easily have been in the darkest heart of a forest. It was the feeling he wanted, the situation he had looked for. He planned to follow the stream to the point where Randal had been killed, and then cut back across country, over the ridge and the open land beyond, across the lane that led to Byron's and on to the secondary road somewhere near where Hammond had been killed.

From there he could follow the secondary road back to the highway and the hotel. It wasn't any great distance and he had all night. It was, he decided, the likeliest way to find his quarry. Since he was offering himself as the hunted as well as the hunter, there was little sense in waiting in a static blind. Concealing himself would have defeated his purpose, and there was little chance of seeing anything moving on the moors unless it came to him.

Wetherby walked on at a regular pace, carefully avoiding the large rocks and occasional trees which might have offered concealment, both to expose himself and to limit the danger of a sudden, unexpected attack. He moved in a zig-zag pattern, alternately heading upwards towards the ridge and then back down towards the stream. When his pipe had burned out he whistled tunelessly for a while, the innocent sound of a man who expects nothing, who is unaware of danger. Presently he filled the pipe again, and lighted it with the match cupped in one hand so that it did not dazzle his eyes.

He was very near the spot where Randal's body had been found when he stopped and took some brandy from his flask. It seemed a peaceful place, the stream bubbling along beside him and the moon attempting to get through the clouds. It was hard to imagine sudden death here. But Wetherby didn't allow himself to be lulled into false security. He remembered the mangled body in the road as he turned up towards the ridge. There were more rocks as he drew higher and he circled around the larger ones, knowing that whatever the thing was he hunted, it had to get at him to kill him, and as long as he could see it coming he would be all right. All he needed was a few yards in which to bring his gun on to it. He came to the crest and paused, outlined against the sky from all directions. He could see the headlights of a motor-car moving along the highway and the land was a black gulf between. Somewhere in that gulf, it might be waiting, and he hoped so. He walked on.

But he didn't find it.

Or, perhaps, it didn't find him.

The King's Torso was owned by a retired naval man named Bruce Newton. Bruce was a dapper fellow with a clipped moustache and brightly checked shirts who didn't much care if he had many customers. That was why he had retired to this little pub on the seldom-travelled lane between Byron's house and the secondary road. One of the few regulars at The King's Torso was a young man named Ronald Lake, who lived with his young and recent bride in a pleasant cottage on the moors, a brisk ten minutes' walk north from the lane. Lake always walked. He had no motor-car, and there was no road leading to his cottage anyway, so he had to walk even had he not wanted to. But Lake liked walking. He had renounced the conveniences of the modern world after a few years of hectic endeavour in London, and was fortunate enough to have a wife who agreed completely with his desire for simplicity, and was perfectly happy to lead an uncomplicated life. They were both very lazy in a fine fashion. Lake had a small private income which maintained them in an economic and sufficient manner and left their time free. Lake dabbled at painting. He wasn't a good painter and knew he wasn't and didn't really care. He might have preferred to be good, given the choice, but didn't think much about it; he simply enjoyed painting and had no aspirations to fame or art. His wife was content to spend her time reading *Wuthering Heights*. They were pleasant people without pretence. Bruce liked Lake. It was the sort of customer he had visualized when deciding to become a country publican, and Lake was in the habit of strolling down to the pub four or five nights a week for a pint or two of beer. He always bought Bruce a drink on the first round and Bruce always bought the second. If he stayed for a third they played darts for it. Quite frequently, Lake was the only customer in The King's Torso, and that suited them both very nicely.

Lake stood up and stretched.

He had been working on a still life with flowers and an aubergine, and his clothes were smudged with bright reds and yellows and purple. When he pushed a fallen lock of hair back from his forehead, he left a smear of colour on his brow. Lake didn't concern himself with such trifles. His wife was reading in an armchair by the fire, a pretty young woman who might be overweight in later years.

"Well, that's enough for tonight," Lake said.

"Ummm."

"I think maybe I'll toddle on down to Bruce's for half a hour, dear."

"Ummm."

"Want to come?"

"Oh, I think not. I'll just read for a while, darling. I'll wait up for you." She smiled and turned back to her book. Lake looked admiringly at the clean line of her neck. He loved her very much and considered himself a very fortunate man; often he wished he were able to express his love more intensely; but he knew it wasn't necessary. He bent over and kissed her neck and she smiled without looking up.

"I'll be back soon, dear," Lake said.

He pulled a corduroy jacket on and tied a woollen scarf around his neck as he went out. He closed the door behind him and heard the latch drop into place. There was no lock on the door – in keeping with a simple life. After all, they had no enemies and nothing of much value, and locks had no place in such a way of life.

Lake walked quite rapidly for one of such a lackadaisical nature, swinging his arms vigorously. He could see the lights of the pub ahead and, to his right and somewhat farther away, the lights of Byron's big house. He had never met Byron, and thought without envy that it might be pleasant to live in such a grand home. But it was only a fleeting idea. He came out on the lane and walked on down to the pub. There were no customers. Bruce was leaning on the bar chewing a toothpick and a cosy fire jumped in the grate.

"Didn't expect to see you tonight," Bruce said.

"Oh?"

Bruce was filling a pint mug without asking.

"I thought you wouldn't be walking around at night with this killer on the prowl."

"Killer?" Lake asked. He scratched his head.

"Haven't you seen the papers?"

"Well, I never take the papers. Since I renounced the hurly-burly of life I find no interest in the affairs of the world."

"Yeah. Well this happened right near here. Two men have been killed in the last few days. Did you know old Randal?"

"Randal? The odd old fellow? Sure, I've seen him around."

"Well, he was the first victim."

"Good Lord."

"Then there was some salesman fella last night. Got done right up the road."

"A maniac?"

Bruce shrugged.

"They say it's some kind of animal. Must have escaped from a zoo somewhere. I had a copper in here this afternoon, told me all about it. Said he was driving some big-game hunter around, someone they brought down from London. So I guess it's an animal, all right."

Lake glanced towards the window.

"So I wouldn't be all that keen on walking around after dark," Bruce said.

"Oh, I'll be all right."

They each took a drink.

"I don't suppose I should leave Hazel home alone, though. She doesn't know anything about this, if she heard something prowling about outside she might go out to have a look."

"That wouldn't do," Bruce said.

"What sort of animal do they figure it is?"

"Well, this copper that was here wouldn't say. Claimed he didn't know. But I figure they know all right, it's just that coppers never tell you anything. The way I see it, if they brought this geezer down from London, they must have a pretty fair idea what he's supposed to shoot. That figures, doesn't it?"

Lake nodded doubtfully. He was troubled, not so much

by death itself, but by the concept that death could intrude on his peaceful existence. He finished his pint.

"Have one with me," Bruce said.

"Well . . . maybe I'd better get back home. Just in case. I wouldn't want Hazel to be frightened."

"Yeah. You'd better be careful yourself. If I were you I'd move a bit lively across the moor. They say it tore old Randal to pieces." Bruce nodded then, as an afterthought of less importance, said, "The salesman bloke, too."

Lake looked a trifle uneasy.

"Well, thanks for warning me," he said. He moved to the door and hesitated. The night was dark and the idea of another pint attractive. But he couldn't very well leave Hazel alone. He waved to Bruce and went out. He walked down the lane more rapidly than usual, his shoulders hunched. The cold was very noticeable and he shivered, wishing that he had worn a warmer coat. He left the lane through a gap in the hedgerow and started across the familiar route to his cottage, following the contour of the land rather than a definite footpath. He noticed that the lights were out at the manor house and glanced at his wristwatch, squinting in the dark; he had only been gone twenty-five minutes. He told himself there was nothing to worry about and smiled at himself as he looked nervously over his shoulder. He wondered if Bruce had been pulling his leg. The idea of some man-killing animal stalking these civilized lands was absurd . . . as absurd as the eerie feeling he had of being watched or followed. But he walked even faster so that he was breathing quite heavily by the time he could see the lights from his cottage. Some of this tenseness left him then, and he slowed down for a moment, then frowned. He saw the little square of illumination from the window but he saw another pillar of light beside it, a narrow ledge cast out on the ground which could only have come from the doorway. The door was ajar. He looked around quickly and stumbled as his pace increased once more.

The door was open a few inches and Lake was shivering as he walked into the geometric rectangle of light that dropped from the opening. He pushed the door before him and went in, then smiled. His fear had been ridiculous, the dark night had seized his imagination. Everything was as it had been when he left. He could see his wife's arm on the chair.

"I'm home, dear," he said.

'There was no reply.

Lake wandered towards his easel. The bright reds and yellows flooded his vision. There seemed to be too much red. Lake noticed that he had been more careless than usual with his paint, there were heavy red smears on the carpet and red paint was dripping from the bookcase. His face clouded. It looked as if he had absent-mindedly squirted the oil from the tube in all directions. There was even a long red smear across the back of Hazel's chair. That must have happened when he'd bent over to kiss her neck, Lake thought. He remembered standing in this same spot, looking at the line of his wife's neck and thinking how fortunate he was. He looked now, but he could not see her neck. Only the red smear. He hoped she had not leaned back and got the paint in her hair.

"Are you awake, dear?"

There was no reply.

"Bruce was telling me a rather disturbing thing . . ."

His wife was silent.

She must have fallen asleep, Lake thought. He moved towards her chair. He thought he'd better wipe that paint away before she straightened up and rubbed her head across it. It didn't seem the right colour, somehow. It was a darker red than he had been using on the canvas. He looked back towards the painting, wondering about that, and reached down to touch his wife on the shoulder. His hand was on her left shoulder and he was looking back at the canvas. The red seemed to be lighter there. He let his hand slide over to stroke Hazel's hair. It slid on to her right shoulder. There seemed to be a great deal of slippery oil paint all over her shoulders.

Lake turned, very slowly, and looked down into the chair . . .

Wetherby had the reflexes of the hunter.

He was crouched, the rifle levelled, before the sound registered in his conscious brain. His finger caressed the trigger and his nerves vibrated with the jangling surge of adrenalin, the heart-stopping song of action. And then the magic of readiness was gone, and he cursed silently.

"Wetherby!" Thurlow called.

Thurlow's torch turned in an arc across the heather.

Wetherby pushed the safety catch back on and came out of his crouch. Thurlow jumped, startled, and Wetherby saw that the detective carried a shotgun in nervous hands.

"It's all right," he called.

He advanced. Thurlow stood waiting. Wetherby had just descended from the line of tors and Thurlow had come from the lane.

"Here you are," Thurlow said. He pointed the shotgun away.

"Damn! If the killer was around, you've certainly given him warning," Wetherby said. "I told Bell I didn't want any interference."

"Bell sent me to find you, sir."

"Did you have to be so obvious?"

"Sorry if I startled you," Thurlow said. He didn't sound apologetic.

"Apart from the fact I might have shot you, you've ruined any chance of finding this beast."

"It's too late for stealth tonight."

Wetherby started to reply, then paused. He looked at Thurlow's eyes and saw the truth adumbrated there.

"It's killed again," he said. It wasn't a question, and Thurlow nodded, pointing back towards the lane.

"Just on the other side of the lane," he said.

They headed back together.

The bright flash of bulbs whitened the little room; whitened the pale faces of the detectives who were dusting for prints and blackened the streams of blood. Lake sat in the corner staring at his red hands with the wide eyes of shock and horror. The full reality had not yet pierced the defences of his sanity. Bell said nothing. He pointed toward the chair and Wetherby crossed the room and looked into it. He winced. He hadn't expected it to be a woman. *Wuthering Heights* was in her lap, one page half torn out, her lifeless hand drooped over the arm of the chair and her legs were extended towards the dying fire. Her shoulders met in a dark mass of gore. The chair was torn with the marks of bloody claws.

"Well?" Bell asked.

Wetherby felt his vocal cords rebel as he started to speak. He closed his eyes against the surge of nausea.

"An animal?" Bell asked.

"It has to be. An animal or some dark fiend from hell itself."

"But how did it get in?"

Lake moaned.

"I closed the door," he said.

"Get him out of here," Bell said.

Thurlow moved towards Lake. Lake would not move. His limbs were solid and would not bend.

"It was closed," he said.

Wetherby looked at Bell. Bell grimaced. They moved back behind the chair, but they could still see her hand hanging over the arm; saw a heavy drop of blood move sluggishly down her middle finger and dangle for a moment before it dropped to the carpet. It made a remarkably wet sound as it merged with the blood beneath. Thurlow and a constable were attempting to get Lake to his feet.

"Whatever it was, it opened the door," Bell said.

"Locked?"

"No. There isn't a lock. But it's on a latch, it has to be lifted from the outside." They moved to the door. A detective was dusting the latch and they waited until he had finished. A photographer flashed a photo of it. There was no blood on the door. Wetherby squatted, judging the distance from the ground to the latch.

"What creature that left those claw marks could have opened a door?" Bell asked. It was obviously rhetorical.

They stepped aside as Thurlow led Lake out. Lake was still looking at his hands.

"I thought it was paint," he said.

He laughed suddenly, an abrupt burst of laughter followed by a hysterical giggling which choked into a sob. Thurlow guided him towards a police van which had come bumping across the moors. He got in willingly enough, sitting rigidly in the seat. The constable got in beside him and Thurlow came back.

"There's something here we don't understand," he said.

"That's a goddamn brilliant statement," Bell snapped.

"No, I don't mean that." He looked at Bell, a searching glance, and Bell turned his eyes away. "Something we may never know," Thurlow said. "Something beyond the comprehension of man, perhaps . . . I think I believe that, sir. Something of ancient legend and derided superstition is stalking these moors at night. If it were . . . anything . . . it wouldn't surprise me."

"Shut up, Thurlow."

Thurlow shook his head.

"I can't help what I feel, sir," he said. "You can't alter that."

"You're tired. You aren't being rational."

Thurlow shrugged. He clamped his mouth closed, but he looked at the chair, and then he looked at the latch on the door.

The body had been removed, the police experts had made a thorough search which revealed nothing, and Wetherby and Bell remained in the cottage. Wetherby didn't expect to find anything that had escaped the keen and practised eye of the police, but he hoped he might possibly see something in a different light, place a new interpretation on something already noticed and passed over. But there was nothing. Not a single hair had the animal shed, which was surprising considering the ferocity of its attack. There were plenty of claw marks etched in blood, but only around and on the chair. No bloody trail led to the door. It seemed almost as if the killer had wiped his bloody talons clean on the carpet before slinking off.

"You don't recognize those marks?" Bell asked, without hope.

"No. This is more difficult than prints on the ground. They were long, sharp claws but it isn't possible to tell any more than that. There may be some prints outside, though. Although, as you've undoubtedly noticed, the blood trail doesn't return to the door. Unless this beast can leap a considerable distance from a standstill, or fly, it appears that it has quite deliberately covered its tracks."

"Shall we look outside?"

"We can try, although I think we'll have a better chance in the morning."

They moved to the door. The lights of a motor vehicle came bobbing towards them, rising and falling over the uncertain terrain. Wetherby crouched and inspected the ground beside the door in the beam of his torch. He found nothing. The ground was fairly firm, but some track should have been left. The vehicle drew nearer, the twin beams flashed on the cottage wall and stopped moving. A door closed and a confused, howling din arose. The headlights went out and a single torch beam moved towards the cottage, bringing the noise with it. Thurlow came over.

"The dogs are here, sir," he said.

"I have ears," Bell said.

"There's nothing here," Wetherby said, standing up. The dogs were straining and baying on their leads and the handler had difficulty in restraining them. Bell snapped quick instructions to the handler. He didn't like using dogs, they had no part in his way of detection . . . an element from the past, before scientific methods, and he had summoned them as a last resort when science was baffled. But he didn't like it. There was nothing about this case that he liked.

"You'd better wait," he said to Wetherby. "If these brutes can pick up the scent I'd like you to come."

"Of course."

"If there is a scent, they'll find it," the handler said, his loyalty stung by the reference to brutes.

"Well, get on with it then."

The handler took the dogs into the cottage. Wetherby and Bell waited outside. A cold wind was dipping across the land, singing a background mood below the excited cries of the dogs. Both men were struck by a feeling of displacement, as if this scene were occurring in the past, was somehow not real, as if they stood apart and observed but had no part in it. Thurlow's face reflected his own thoughts, and he said nothing. The dogs came crowding en masse through the door, tugging against their leads and digging at the ground.

"There's a scent in there, all right," the handler said. "I can smell it myself."

Wetherby nodded.

"You noticed it?" Bell asked.

"Vaguely. It must have been quite strong before the room was filled with cigarette smoke and sweating men. But it was still noticeable. Like the prints, it's somehow familiar to me but I just can't place it."

"An animal smell?"

"Certainly not a human smell."

"This killer must be some animal," Bell said. "Some frightfully clever animal that can open doors and cover its tracks behind it . . . so clever that it leads us to believe it must be human, even. But why in hell does it kill? The other two . . . it might have suddenly been disturbed by them, been frightened or attacked through instinct when they fled . . . but this . . . it came into this cottage. It opened the door and deliberately entered to kill. Purely for the love of killing, the desire to destroy. If it is an animal – and it seems it must be – we can forget about a pattern, of course. But there must be some motive; even animals act for some reason. But why? We can eliminate hunger, it doesn't eat its victims . . ." Bell paused. His face twisted in a terrible grimace.

"Unless," he said. "Unless it eats only the heads."

Somehow, for some reason which was strictly emotional and strictly human, it was a terrible concept.

The dogs set out in a determined fashion, as if they knew their job and were proceeding to do it well. Ten minutes later they were as baffled as their masters. They didn't seem to know what was expected of them, what trail to follow. They tried to branch off in various directions, snapping at each other in their frustration. Wetherby took careful note of their actions. He had worked with dogs before, and he understood them. He knew that they were defeated before the dogs themselves knew it. He remembered how the tracks had changed as they left the road on the previous trail, and wondered if this was what was throwing them off the scent somehow. It seemed unlikely, far more unlikely than the changing tracks themselves. It was not inconceivable that a beast would run on four feet and walk on two, but the idea that it could also change its scent was a different matter. And yet the fact remained that the dogs could not follow it over open ground. There was no water to hide the trail, no tree into which it could have climbed, but the scent abruptly halted a few hundred feet from the cottage door. The handler was leading the dogs in a circle around the cottage in an attempt to pick up a second trail, in case the killer had back-tracked, and Wetherby looked up at the sky. It was preposterous to imagine a creature with those other characteristics flying, and he didn't believe it possible, but he looked upwards. He didn't know what he expected to see moving across that dark sky, but all he saw were clouds.

"Apparently it has obliterated its scent, somehow," the handler said. He looked annoyed. "The dogs can't seem to follow it beyond this point."

"Then get those howling fiends away from here," Bell snapped. And they were indeed howling, not in the excitement they had showed upon arrival, but in a tone that showed their absolute frustration, their tails lowered and their eyes baleful. They followed their handler back to the van willingly, whining now. The door slammed after them.

"Want to try in the morning?" Bell asked.

"I'll try. But I wouldn't hope for much, Justin. If it can lose a pack of trained dogs so easily – "

"Dogs!" he snorted.

"Don't underestimate the dogs," Wetherby said. "I would have thought they could follow it. Not very far, perhaps, but certainly until it had reached water or trees, some means of breaking the scent."

"I honestly don't know what else to do," Bell said. He gestured with open palms upwards. "Maybe this isn't a police matter at all, I don't know. Maybe I should put you in charge. Our methods don't seem very effective. How do you apply modern detection against something that kills without motive? Without a common denominator among the victims? Even with a madman, some pattern emerges. We could catch Jack the Ripper if he were still around, his murders had a pattern. His victims were prostitutes. But this thing . . . it doesn't kill whores, or poachers or salesmen or housewives. It merely kills. It seems to leave an abundance of evidence at the scene, but no way to follow it or deduce where it has gone. What in hell do I do, John?"

Wetherby didn't know.

They returned in the morning, dull with the anticipation of futility. The driver pulled over to the edge of the lane just beyond The King's Torso. They couldn't quite see the cottage from there because the land rolled up between. Bell told the driver to stay with the car and they got out. The driver lighted a cigarette and settled for the wait. A man came down the lane, wearing a belted trenchcoat and a felt hat and walking with a bouncy step. He had been standing outside The King's Torso, waiting for them. Bell scowled. It was Aaron Rose, the reporter, looking exceptionally eager as he approached. Another man followed behind him with a camera slung over his shoulder.

"Any comments for the Press?" he asked.

"None."

"Can you predict when you'll be making an arrest?"

He had his notebook out.

"How in hell can I? I don't even know what we're going to arrest, let alone when."

"May I quote that?"

"For Christ's sake no."

"You didn't make any comments to the reporters back at the hotel, did you?" Rose asked, suddenly afraid that he'd blundered by anticipation, by arriving here ahead of the police.

Bell didn't answer. He moved towards the break in the hedgerow and Wetherby followed.

"Mind if I tag along?" Rose asked.

"Yes," Bell said, with neither sarcasm nor anger.

"Oh. Well, is it all right to take some pictures at the cottage? The constable there wouldn't let us in earlier."

"Yes, I do mind. Especially for that rag you work for."

Rose winced at such reference to the Press.

"Listen, you wait here. Perhaps I'll have a statement when I get back. All right?"

"Yeah. Sure."

Rose watched the two men walk away. The photographer fingered his camera eagerly. All he had photographed so far was the exterior of the cottage, and he was feeling slighted. But Rose suddenly blinked; his expression changed. He had just realized what line his story should take. Murders were one a hundred, man-killing beasts a novelty but not unheard of. What he needed was a completely different approach, a means of capitalizing on the shock and horror of human torment in the greatest possible manner. This was Rose's first big assignment and he desperately wanted to make it a success for sensational journalism.

"I think I've got it," he said.

"Huh?"

"The angle. I think I have an idea."

The photographer grunted. He resented ideas. They could not be captured on film. Rose began to walk slowly back towards the pub, his mind leaping violently. He didn't for a moment believe what he intended to write, but that was of no importance whatsoever. Few of the readers would

believe it, either. But they would see the startling headline,
and they would buy the paper, and Aaron Rose would be
a success. He was impatient to begin his story, and annoyed
that he knew so little background material; he wished he
were in London so he could go to the library and gather
knowledge of lycanthropy, to add a touch of learning as a
sober background for the sensational headline. He visualized how that headline would look in print . . . how it
would scream from the front page.

Does a werewolf stalk the moors?

Surprisingly, there were tracks.

The ground was firm, and Wetherby had not expected
to find tracks, but they were there and they were obvious,
deep and plain. They came from the house, but did not
begin at the house. The ground hadn't changed, it was as
firm as it was by the door, but the tracks began some
distance away and continued in a straight line heading
roughly north, and then they stopped. They went in the
same direction that the dogs had attempted to follow the
scent, and they began just about where the dogs had lost
the scent. It was as if the trail had been deliberately left at
this point, or deliberately erased on both sides, and the
inconsistency was baffling. A creature able to move without
trace wouldn't have blundered at random points, unless it
was a deliberate attempt to lead its pursuers in a false
direction. But then it seemed that the trail would have been
left from the cottage itself, not beginning at a point some
hundred yards beyond.

"It walked here," Wetherby said.

"On two legs?"

Wetherby nodded.

Bell looked back towards the cottage. A uniformed
policeman stood by the door.

"Nothing could have jumped this far," he said.

"Nothing we know about."

"Could it have run to here, and only left the trail when
it began to walk?"

Wetherby shrugged.

"I'm beginning to think this creature can do anything."

"The dogs . . ."

Wetherby nodded grimly.

The dogs had followed the scent to the point where the tracks began. No farther. They had not followed where the tracks were obvious in the ground, where the scent, if it existed at all, should certainly have been. Even Bell understood that there were implications to that – implications that led to far-fetched and mind-staggering conclusions.

"But an animal – or a man – can't simply cease to leave a scent," Bell said. "Certainly not where it has left an obvious trail."

"That's right. But if the dogs had followed a certain scent to this point – the scent that they had followed from the cottage, a strong and noticeable scent – and that specific scent suddenly changed – "

Wetherby paused, not sure what he wanted to say, knowing what he thought, but hesitating to voice it.

"When the creature began to walk on two legs – "

Bell was watching him closely.

"If some change occurred – if it was, in some way, no longer the same creature that had run on all fours – "

"It's possible," Bell whispered. He hadn't meant to whisper.

"I know," Wetherby said.

But there were the tracks, commencing where the scent had ceased – where the dogs had lost the trail of the creature that had killed at the cottage, and where that creature had begun to walk like a man . . .

Wetherby could find no further tracks in that general direction, and once more he attempted to pick up the trail by following a circle with the cottage as the centre. Bell walked behind him in silence. The first circle was completed without finding anything, and Wetherby suggested that they move farther from the cabin and make another attempt. They both realized that it was futile, but there was nothing else to do, and they felt a great need to be doing something. They walked north from the cabin for perhaps half a mile, then turned in an arc to the west, circling and keeping the cottage as equidistant as unaided judgement could manage. The circumference of this path was thus about three miles, and they moved slowly. Wetherby paused to inspect the ground from time to time, spreading the grass and heather and pushing with his finger to test the resistance. They left no tracks themselves, and found none. The circle passed within a few hundred yards of Byron's house, turned back towards the east and skirted the lane, went on behind The King's Torso as far as the trees that bordered the secondary road and then curved back towards the starting point. They arrived back where they had begun and had found nothing. The sky was darkening and there was a smell of impending rain. They stood and looked helplessly at one another, then headed back towards the lane without speaking.

This course brought them to the line of tracks once more.

"I expect I'd better send a team out here to take casts," Bell said.

"Purely for routine," Wetherby said. "These tracks are the same as the others, the casts won't be different."

"I've been thinking about what you said," Bell said, looking towards the cottage. "If – if such a change were possible, how would it account for these tracks being plain here and then abruptly stopping?"

Wetherby, too, had been thinking. They were not thoughts that he liked, conclusions that fitted the facts but were alien to all his beliefs . . . more, they were alien to his disbeliefs. He pondered for a few moments before he spoke.

"Granting such a metamorphosis, which I don't . . . it seems obvious. A creature, a beast running on all fours suddenly undergoes a transformation. It becomes a creature that walks on two legs. Such a change would certainly have the strongest possible side effects. Perhaps even unconsciousness. And then, after a while, the creature, the changed creature, would stagger off in a stupor, perhaps not remembering how he had come to this place or suffering unbelievable horror and remorse. It might stagger away for a short distance in this half-conscious state before it realized the possible consequences of what it had done in its previous form. That would be when it might begin to cover its tracks, through instinctive self-preservation. This is all idle conjecture, of course. It isn't possible . . ."

"Not the remorse, anyway," Bell said.

Wetherby looked at him. Granted the initial premise, that had seemed valid enough.

"If it felt remorse it would want to get as far away as possible and try to forget what it had been responsible for, wouldn't it?"

Wetherby nodded.

"It wouldn't take the head with it, as a gruesome reminder."

"I guess not," Wetherby said, and they continued back to the lane. They came through the hedgerow by the police car. The driver had his hat pulled down and was sleeping. He snored slightly.

"I need a drink," Bell said.

Wetherby nodded. They walked past the car towards The King's Torso. They both needed a drink, although neither was thirsty.

Aaron Rose was suffering a conflict of conscience and ambition. He sat at the bar of The King's Torso with his notebook open beside his beer. The photographer sat beside him. He had his camera beside his beer, but had no conscience outside the frame of a lens. He drank quickly but Rose sipped at his beer and considered his plight. Not that he had any choice in the matter, there was no decision he had to make and no way he could influence the results. But Rose was a man who worried about everything, and at the moment he was worried because his hopes were divided. It was quite simple, really, although nothing is simple to a man who worries. As a man, with a conscience, Rose hoped that the killer would be captured or slain before he killed again. The last killing had particularly influenced him in this, because it seemed far worse than the others, there was something so tragic about a young woman dying helplessly and horribly in her own home. But, as a junior reporter on

his first big assignment, he hoped that the killer would not
be found before the weekend, so that his story would not
be obsolete for the Sunday edition. The report of a capture
would not be nearly as thrilling and sensational as the story
of these terrible unsolved crimes, especially the story he
intended to write. Even any hint that the police were on
the trail of the killer would dampen the shock value, for
that depended totally on the terror of the unknown. Rose
had the proper instinct and knew what sold newspapers.
But, because he was a worrier with a conscience, and
despite the fact that he could affect the result in no way,
Rose was suffering with his hopes, and because he was
basically an honest man he admitted his hopes even to
himself. He admitted that he hoped the killer would not
be uncovered before the weekend, provided of course that
it did not kill again. Of course. And his face twisted in
anxiety as he realized that a further killing would greatly
enhance the value of his story. That provided a new conflict,
far more terrible than the first, and his face provided the
battleground of his emotions.

Rose turned as the door opened. Wetherby and Bell went
up to the bar and Bruce moved down to serve them.

"You cops?" he asked. He looked very sad.

"I am," Bell said.

"I'm a reporter," Rose said, and mentioned his paper.

"Any luck?" Bruce asked.

Bell said, "I'll have a pint."

"No luck, eh? Can't you follow this animal's tracks or
something? I mean, you got to do something. You can't
have something like this running around killing people, can
you? Why aren't you out looking for clues or evidence or
something?

Rose slid his notebook up the bar, sensing a local colour
angle.

"We'll get it. In time," Bell said.

"Time? And what about the meantime? You gonna let
it kill more innocent people?"

"Don't you feel the police are doing enough?" Rose
asked. "As a local citizen, I mean?"

Bruce ignored him.

"Give me a beer, will you," Bell said.

Bruce shrugged and began filling a pint. He said, "Guess I didn't mean to snap at you, but Mrs Lake was a fine person. Her husband is a regular here. It was a terrible thing." He shook his head and shoved the pint over the bar. "Can't you get the Army down here or something? Organize a search? They'd find it all right."

"I'll consider your advice," Bell said.

"You ought to."

"Brandy," Wetherby said.

"Can I quote you? About the Army?"

"You can just shut up, for God's sake."

"My readers have a right to know."

"Readers? You think people read that rag you work for? They just buy it for the picture of naked women and the juicier divorce cases."

Rose looked hurt.

"He's right, you know," Bruce said. "That's the only reason I ever buy it."

"Can I quote that?" Rose asked, then frowned and thought better of it. He leaned sullenly on the bar beside Bell. Bruce set Wetherby's brandy down and Wetherby took a long drink, discarding the ritual of smell and taste. It went down well. Some of the tenseness left him, the mental construction of fact without belief. He took a second swallow and the door opened. Byron came in.

"Saw the car down the road," he said. He had a heavy walking stick and a tweed cap. He walked over to the bar and stood beside Wetherby. Bell turned slightly away.

"Are you pursuing your investigations here?" Byron asked.

Wetherby saw Bell tense. He said, "I suppose you've heard about last night?"

Byron nodded. Bell doused his anger with beer.

"Any tracks?" Byron asked.

"Some. Not enough to follow."

"No? That's a shame. I thought that by now your old skill might have returned."

"No one could have followed that trail." Wetherby said.

Byron smiled. He ordered a beer and leaned his stick against the bar. Bruce slid the beer over.

"You're welcome to try," Bell said.

Byron shook his head.

"But you're the man who's always right, aren't you? Well, this is a challenge for you. Wetherby says that no man could follow that trail. What about it?"

"Oh, doubtless he's right," Byron said, smiling again.

Bruce said, "Didn't you used to be a big-game hunter, Mr Byron?"

"I am a hunter. Yes. You misuse the past tense, my man."

"Can't you maybe find the killer?"

"I haven't tried."

Bruce looked from Byron to Bell.

"If you cops didn't want all the glory for yourselves – "

Bell said, "Mr Byron has declined to assist us. I asked him."

Bruce looked at Byron again.

"It's no concern of mine," Byron said.

"No concern – are you crazy? Don't you care that these people were killed?" He leaned on the bar, his thin face pointing at Byron. Byron placidly sipped his beer. "Haze Lake was killed last night," Bruce said. "Did you know her? She never harmed a soul, never did a bad thing in her life – "

"I expect she never did a thing. Full stop."

Bruce blinked. He looked like an angry badger. Blood flushed darkly into his face. "I don't want your custom," he said. "Drink up and get out of here."

Byron paused, the mug half raised. He was balanced between anger and amusement. Confronted by a man who did not understand his concepts, Byron hovered between scorn and rage for a moment. And then he laughed.

"Ah, you are angry," he said. He set the mug down on the bar. "That's good. I like to see a man in anger, with the courage to speak . . . courage in his beliefs, stupid as they may be. It is, at least, a living emotion."

"If I come over this bar, these cops will have to pull me off you," Bruce said. He was half Byron's size and he trembled with his sudden hatred.

"And what about you, Justin?" Byron asked. "Are you feeling anything? Does any semblance of activity begin to surge sluggishly behind that policeman's face? Or is it a policeman's mind that vegetates there?"

"What in hell is wrong with you?" Wetherby asked.

"Wrong? Nothing. Perhaps I'm a trifle outspoken. But don't you see? If people feel anything, even anger, or fear, even doubt, then at least they are alive." He stared at Wetherby for a moment. "If you are alive enough, then you will find your killer," he said.

Byron turned and walked out, tapping his stick along the floor. He didn't hurry. Bruce's eyes bulged after him, as though he wanted to send his eyeballs like bullets into Byron's back.

"That heartless bastard," he murmured.

Rose was gaping.

"Who was that?" he asked.

No one answered him. Byron was gone, and he had left a vacuum of black silence behind him . . . a vacuum which only their own thoughts could fill, and they were not pleasant thoughts and they led towards unspeakable conclusions.

Fear stood over the land.

It was a blanket of fear, invisible but oppressive and intense, and it covered the moors like an overcast sky, more ominous than an impending storm. The fear was all the greater because the people did not know what it was they feared, what the monstrous being was that had three times struck so terribly. They no longer spoke of it often, as they had at first, for the fear had increased with each killing and reached absolute intensity with the death of Hazel Lake, peacefully reading by her fireside. This was a people who had long regarded their home as their castle, sanctuary inviolate, and a new dimension was added to their terror. Nowhere was safe, this fiend might come at any time, to

any place, and anyone might be his next victim. It wasn't
death itself that brought such consuming fear, it was the
unknown quality of that death, the method of dying and
the agony of wondering if the creature would strike
again . . . where it would strike . . . whom it would kill.
Superstition, never far below the surface of civilized minds,
came bubbling up in globules of terror, bursting and
enflaming the brain.

The national newspapers played up the horror, capitalizing on shock, and sensationalism sold papers throughout
the rest of the country. But in those few square miles where
the creature had struck, it was pure fear that sold papers,
and trembling hands that held them opened to the headlines
of horror. The majority of the papers played with the angle
of doubt, the uncertainty whether it was man or beast, but
Aaron Rose's scandal sheet pulled out all the stops on the
lycanthrope line. The editor was immensely pleased with
Rose's story, and ran a companion piece dealing with the
supposedly recorded instances of werewolves, and ghouls
in the Balkans and, killing two birds with one stone, hinted
that the killer was obviously an immigrant or at least of
foreign extraction, since Englishmen were never werewolves. The editorial questioned police efficiency in no
uncertain terms, asking whether any attempt had been
made to establish a lunar cycle and whether the amount of
blood remaining in the corpses had been measured, on the
chance that it might be a vampire. No one connected with
the paper believed the story line, certainly, but that didn't
matter at all.

Aaron Rose was not as pleased with his success as he
might have been, however. He was closer to the killings
and farther from the editorial offices, and he felt the fear
surrounding him. He worried, thinking that his story might
have added to that fear, but justified himself by thinking
that it was just as well that the people were afraid, that it
would make them more cautious. When he was not worrying, he was planning his next story, intending to focus it
around local comment and opinion, but he found that more
difficult than he had imagined. People who would normally

have jumped at a chance to be quoted in a national newspaper looked at him solemnly and said nothing; they
resented being asked to comment about something so overwhelming, so tragic and so close to home. It was far beyond
the point of being a topic of conversation. Rose abandoned
the direct approach and went into the nearest market town
to mingle with the populace and overhear their private
words. It was a small village on the moors with narrow
cobbled streets and several cheerful-looking pubs, but when
he entered the pubs the pervading sense of gloom was
severe. Faces were pale in the gloomy interior and conversation was hushed and solemn. Rose settled himself in a
dark corner and listened. He heard one bold fellow
announce that this killer was a fiend and should be tortured
to death, but heard several whisper the question that plagued them all: what is this thing that walks among us in
the night? And when Aaron Rose looked into their eyes,
he knew that everyone shared the common thought: Who
is next? Who is next? And Rose felt a sympathetic twinge
of the freezing fear that closed its fetid talons on these
people; he felt it reach out to grasp at his own heart . . .

The police were helpless, and Justin Bell underwent
agonies of indecision, not knowing whether to concentrate
his search on man or beast, and beleaguered by dark concepts he hadn't known lurked in his mind – unspoken and
vague primordial fears that had been carried through the
aeons since man's ancestors crawled out of the slime and
began their ascent. He told himself that it was an ana-
morphosis, a deformed figure which would appear in pro-
portion if only he could view it correctly, but at the same
time he feared it was something that could never be shaped
by human logic, something beyond the understanding of
man because it was more than man and less than man,
some monstrous combination of man and beast from a
dimension apart from ours. At times, in the light of day,
he ridiculed himself for such fanciful thoughts, but in the
night the facts came tumbling back – it walked as a man
and ran as a beast, it possessed talons that could shred
human flesh and still open doors, the strength to tear a

man's head off and grisly desire to carry that head away to its lair. It could change its tracks and alter its scent, and was transmogrification beyond such a being?

Bell began to place more and more faith in Wetherby, perhaps with a subconscious desire to relieve himself of some of the terrible burden of helplessness and absolve himself of some of the guilt if it killed again . . .

And Wetherby failed.

Each night he walked the windswept moors and each morning he returned tired and drawn with more than physical fatigue. It had ceased to be a pleasure. Alone in the night, his shoulder-blades drew together across the icy bridge of his backbone, and he had a constant and terrible sensation that he was being watched; that the creature followed him and waited for him; that it had the ability to differentiate between a helpless victim and a dangerous opponent, and was waiting for Wetherby to make the fatal slip, the sudden irrevocable blunder through lack of concentration or failure of awareness which would transform him from hunter to hunted, opponent to victim. At times this feeling of being watched was so powerful that Wetherby halted abruptly and spun about, crouched and ready, positive that the creature was behind him. But he saw nothing. At other moments, loathing his own fear, he would shout aloud as a challenge to the unseen beast and stand tense and strained, listening for an answer that did not come, listening to silence on those anechoic moors.

Wetherby was not a man of fear.

He had never taken deliberate chances as Byron did, but he had never declined a necessary risk. He had followed wounded lions into thick bush and faced charging buffalo with steady nerves, but this uncertainty ate at his courage, the sensation of being watched from the dark devoured his confidence, and he knew he would soon begin to make mistakes; knew he could afford no mistakes; began to believe that Byron had been right, that he had lost his skill and grown soft. It was necessary to force himself away from the warmth of the hotel as night fell, and he had no willing determination left – only the lever of pride to keep him a his quest. And when another night's vigil was over, he had to admit the relief he felt at returning to his comfortable bedroom once more . . . the desire to crawl into his bed and sleep which went far beyond physical tiredness.

But he did not sleep well.

He drew the blinds against the dawn and went to bed, but when sleep came it was disturbed. He dreamed. Confused images danced through his mind, snatches from the past mingled with some uncertain future, a jumbled connexion between the two binding them together. He saw the dream image of himself, felt the heaviness of his limbs and knew he could not move quickly; heard a howling wind and felt a cold solitude, and then there was a rush, sudden and blinding, and he moved very slowly to face it, his rifle still and unmanageable in his hands. The creature was upon him, he felt its foul breath flow over his face, felt fangs sink into his flesh and fiendish haunches draw up for the fatal stroke. He looked into the creature's face – and awoke, sweating and writhing in his bed, with only a nightmare hint of what the creature had been, only a half-remembered glimpse of a near-human countenance; and half-awake, Wetherby wondered where he could have a silver bullet moulded . . .

Wetherby was sitting in the hotel lounge with Aaron Rose when Byron walked in. Wetherby had become rather fond of Rose. He realized that the reporter had depths beyond ambition, and found him pleasant company when he was not inscribing the conversation in his notebook. Ambition was not the same thing to Wetherby as it was to Rose, because he had never needed success in the same fashion, but he could sympathize with it, and tolerate it. Rose noticed Byron first, and remembered him from that rather violent conversation at The King's Torso. Byron was memorable. Wetherby was surprised to see him there, and for some reason could not remember whether he was angry with Byron or not. It was some paradox of the emotions that Byron inspired in him.

"Good morning," Byron said.

He smiled pleasantly. He was wearing shabby tweeds and had a fine pair of field-glasses slung over his shoulder. A metal badge hung from his lapel.

"I'm on my way to the races," he said. "Newton Abbot. Thought you might care to join me."

For a moment, Wetherby was tempted to agree. He would have liked to get away from this place, to forget all about the killings and his fruitless hunt. But he knew that the thoughts would accompany him.

"No. Thanks for asking, but I don't much feel like it now."

Byron pulled a chair up and sat down. Rose was watching him closely, with marked interest.

"You look worried, John."

"Certainly I'm worried."

"No results as yet, I take it?"

"No, nothing. I've been out there every night without a glimpse or a sound. Nothing at all. And yet I get the feeling that I've been very close to it many times. You know the sensation, Byron. The eerie feeling that I'm being watched. That it is waiting for me to blunder. The same way you feel when you're after a wounded buffalo and you know damn well that it has doubled back and is waiting beside the trail."

"Yes, I know the feeling," Byron said. He made it sound like a great pleasure, a sensation in which he took delight.

"If only I could be sure . . ."

"Sure? Sure of what?"

"If I knew for certain it was waiting for me, it would be better. I would be calmer. But I can't tell, I don't know if my sense is reliable or if my mind is playing tricks."

"Ah, John. You may lose your reflexes but you never lose your intuition. If you feel it is there, it is there. Uncertainty is a civilized trait, don't let self-doubt take command. When you stalked a wounded buffalo, you had no doubts. You knew it was waiting. You didn't know when it would come, or where it would come from, but you knew positively that it would come. And it did. You didn't have much time, John. A buffalo comes with its head lowered and the boss protecting its head and you had to shoot fast and well the first time. You did, of course, because you are sitting here alive. But in those days you knew it was coming. And now you tell me that you can't be sure, that you can't trust your sensations?" He looked into Wetherby's eyes and cold fingers walked up Wetherby's vertebrae.

"You've lost it all, John," he said, softly. "When this thing wants you, it will take you. It will wait and you will be too slow and it will take you. When it wants."

Wetherby and Byron looked at each other, and Rose looked from one to the other with his mouth open. Then Wetherby lowered his eyes. A thought that he didn't like at all had stirred in his mind.

"Perhaps," he said.

They didn't speak for a while. Then Byron, his tone matter of fact now, said, "The trouble is that you are too involved, John. You feel too strongly, your mind has centred upon what this creature has done, rather than what you intend to do. This isn't a hunt, as far as you're concerned, you feel you must kill this thing before it strikes again. But, you know, these killings may not be a bad thing."

Byron looked out the window.

"I've seen people alive with fear. Seen farmers carrying guns on their way to the barn, housewives looking over their shoulders in crowded streets. They are alert, they are alive because the possibility of death hangs over their minds."

"And that isn't a bad thing?"

"I think not. When is a man more alive than on his way to the gallows? What cigarette tastes as good as the last one, when the firing squad is waiting? These deaths may well turn out to be a benefit, in the end. When they can be viewed with proper distance and objectivity. A few useless lives snuffed out, and ten thousand people granted the awareness of their existence, the joy of their survival."

"You can't believe that, Byron," Wetherby said, but he knew that Byron did.

Byron shrugged.

"Oh, it's one point of view," he said. "Are you sure you won't come with me? Steeplechasing. A dangerous game and a fine sport. A National Hunt jockey has an awareness of life which is arcane in our jaded society. I would have liked to be a steeplechase jockey. Ride in the Grand National. Think of the fullness of feeling as Becher's looms up before you and horses are thundering on all sides . . .' Byron's mind had wandered, he shifted in his chair as though in a saddle, then returned to reality and laughed at his daydream.

"No, I won't go," Wetherby said.

Byron shrugged. Bell appeared at the doorway, saw Byron and screwed his face up in distaste as he crossed the room. Byron stood up.

"Well, I'll be off then," he said.

He moved away, passing Bell. They didn't speak.

"Is he mad?" Rose asked.

"I often wonder."

"There's something about his voice – his tone of voice – when he speaks of danger of death. I wonder . . ."

Bell sat down. He showed distaste for Rose, too, but not as greatly as he had for Byron.

"Any news?" Rose asked.

"I've decided to request a massive search by the Army," Bell said. He spoke to Wetherby, but Rose got his notebook out.

"And what will they be told to look for?" Wetherby asked.

"God knows," Bell said.

Rose wrote it down faithfully.

Wetherby had followed the same pattern in his nightly searches, following the stream at first and then cutting back over the ridge and across the lane towards the secondary road. He saw no reason to expand this area, since it encompassed the three places where the killer had struck, but he decided to vary it by starting from the other direction. He had no hopes that this would bring results, but it was at least a variation and might make him feel less helpless and, too, if the creature had indeed been watching him he might well surprise it by approaching from the opposite direction. But he had few hopes of this, either; he felt that the creature knew exactly where he was at all times, and would make no mistakes – an eerie certainty that he would never encounter it until the creature wished him to. Wetherby hated these thoughts, for they seemed to sum up all the failure of nerve and instinct that Byron had accused him of, but they dogged his mind relentlessly, ready to pounce the moment his conscious will relaxed for a moment, clinging despite his efforts to shake them away.

Wetherby was feeling the strain of his vigil.

He came out of the hotel at dusk. It was a pleasant evening, remarkably warm and cloudless and the moors rolled away in a patchwork of moonlight. Wetherby rather wished that he had gone to the races with Byron, that he had nothing more important on his mind than to study a form book and search for a decent-priced winner. He waited at the verge of the highway for a motor-car to pass, and Aaron Rose came running after him.

"Mind if I walk along with you for a ways?"

"Of course."

They crossed the highway and headed up the secondary road.

"That's a nice-looking weapon," Rose said.

"It will do the job. If I ever get a chance to use it."

"You sound discouraged."

Wetherby shrugged.

"Listen, any chance I could come with you tonight?"

"Absolutely none."

"I'm not frightened."

"It isn't that," Wetherby said. He was almost tempted to grant the request. It would have been much easier if he had a companion. But he knew that would defeat his purpose; that the beast would never show if he were not alone, and that he would be sacrificing whatever chance he had to his failure of nerve, his growing dread of being alone. He said, "I don't want to be responsible for anyone else, and this creature would be wary if I weren't alone."

"Yeah. I guess. I admire you, going after it alone. It takes courage, Wetherby. I'd like to do an article about it. Later, of course. When it's over."

Wetherby smiled faintly. They had come to the turning on to the lane, and followed it along between the hedgerows. An old man on a bicycle pedalled past, going home earlier than usual from the pub. No one stayed out late now. They walked on in silence until they were at The King's Torso.

"Want a drink before you start?" Rose asked.

Wetherby looked at the sky. There was still some light low in the east – as good an excuse as any for delaying.

"All right," he said.

There was only customer in the pub – Grant the ex-miner, sitting in the corner with a pint of beer. He didn't look at them as they entered, his eyes were turned to the past, towards the bowels of the earth. Rose had a whisky and Wetherby drank a brandy. It tasted good, and he wanted another, but he knew that would not be wise. There was no light left in the east and he set out with forced determination.

"Good man, that," Rose said.

"Hasn't done Hazel Lake much good," Bruce said.

"Who has? He's trying."

"Yeah, I guess that's right. If I had a gun, I'd get out after it myself. Don't have a gun. Read your story in the paper on Sunday. Load of old rubbish, you ask me."

Rose didn't argue.

"Werewolves! Ain't no werewolves. Leastwise, not in England. Might be an immigrant, though, you can't never tell. Or some animal that was sneaked in to avoid quarantine."

Grant looked up. His eyes were deep set in curiously hollow sockets, as if he had come to resemble the holes he had gouged in the earth.

"It's no animal," he said.

His voice was hollow, too, as though he carried his own echoes in his throat.

"What do you think it is, then?" Bruce asked.

"They're making a mistake, looking for it above the ground. That's all I'll say."

"You think it lives in a cave?" Rose asked, looking for an angle.

"Not in a cave. In the earth. None of you ever been down in the earth. There are strange things there."

"Like what?" Rose asked.

Grant looked at his empty mug.

"Will you have a drink with me?"

Grant nodded suddenly, taking no favours. He came up to the bar. Bruce filled his mug.

"You were saying?" Rose prompted, jotting the price of a pint on his expense account.

"Eh?"

"These subterranean creatures?"

"Oh, aye. Strange things. You can hear them moving in the shafts and tunnels. And in the rocks, too. They know how to move along the veins. Strange, slimy creatures, oozing through the earth. And stink! You can smell 'em for days after they've been in a tunnel."

"Have you ever seen one?"

"Not me. Once a man's seen one . . . they got him!"

He grasped Rose's jacket sullenly, pulling his face close and hissing the final words. Rose leaped in his strong hands.

"Once they got a man in their slimy claws, you never see him again. They suck him back into the rocks. Just like that. Slurp and he's gone. They hate men, because men have come down to their home, you see. Men disturb them with explosions and drills, and they get even by caus-ing cave-ins. We wake them up, tunnelling through their level, and they don't like it. Oh, we know all about them. We know."

"Why haven't the miners told anyone about these things?"

"We have. But it's all hushed up, you see. The mine owners won't let it get out. They're all in league with the politicians. If people knew what lurks down there, well pretty soon no one would become a miner, see. They're bloody clever, those mine owners. They don't give a damn how many men get slurped into the rock."

Grant stared intensely at Rose. Rose wriggled free from his hands.

"You think this killer comes from under the ground, then?"

"Where else could it come from? Eh? Where else? It figures, don't it? We dig down there, and pretty soon they were bound to start coming up here. And there are thousands of 'em, too. Millions, maybe."

"Are there any recorded instances?"

Grant smiled crookedly. He had said enough for one beer. He went back to his table without reply.

"You don't want to take no notice of him," Bruce said. "Crazy. Works for that mad bastard Byron, so I guess he's crazy, too. Contagious, maybe."

"Byron is surely unbalanced."

"Yeah. The bastard."

Rose sipped his drink contemplatively, his narrow shoulders twitching. He contemplated a subterranean approach in his next article, looked absently towards the window and started. He had suddenly realized that it was dark, and it startled him. It was a considerable walk back to the hotel, and Rose was a man who had never taken a chance in his life, who worried about the statistical chance of being struck by meteors as much as he did motor-cars. He was amazed that his preoccupation, even with the pursuit of success, had left him in his position.

"I'd better be off now," he said, sliding from the stool.

"Say, you on foot?" Bruce asked.

Rose nodded unhappily.

"Well, you better be careful."

"Yeah. I'll hurry."

"Don't do no good to be careful," Grant said.

Rose looked at him nervously.

"You won't see it coming. That's cause it don't come at you on the ground, see. It can suddenly pop up right under your feet. That's the way they get you. Pop! Just like that. One minute you're alone, the next it's got you. Slurp! And down into the ground you go. It's a horrible death."

Rose shuddered as he went out.

Grant moved to the bar to get a refill.

"Say, are there really things like that under the ground?" Bruce asked, looking towards his beer cellar entrance.

"Don't be daft. A beer's a beer."

Rose walked quickly down the lane. He kept his eyes forwards, resisting a temptation to peer back over his shoulder and even to glance suspiciously at the ground beneath his feet, and he told himself that his nervousness was absurd; that the likelihood of anything (a vague anything, he refused to make his dread concrete by giving it a name) happening to him was so remote that it was unimaginable. He worried, of course, but managed to limit his worry to the statistical averages that had always plagued him, as if he were worrying about being struck by a motor-car. The night seemed remarkably dark, although there was a bright moon and no clouds, and the moon cast shadows along the hedgerows and did not benefit failing nerves. Rose began to play a game, fixing his eyes on some point a little distance ahead and concentrating on it as it drew nearer, until he had passed it and then fixing on a new point, breaking the walk up by dividing it into a multitude of short walks. It preoccupied his mind and lessened the tension.

A huge shadow loomed up before him.

Rose gasped and jumped. The shadow jumped with him. He turned in terror, and let his breath out in relief as his heart began to beat once more. It had been his own shadow, thrown before him by the headlights of a silently approaching motor-car. He stepped aside to let the car pass, his heart still pounding, but already calming himself with the thought that there was certainly more danger from motor-cars on this unlighted lane than there could be from his nameless dread.

The motor-car drew past him very slowly. It was a police car. The driver looked closely at Rose, scrutinizing him with hard eyes, and Rose felt much better knowing that the police were patrolling the area. The car speeded up a bit, winked red brake lights as it came to the junction of the secondary road, then wheeled around the turning. Rose wondered why he hadn't asked for a lift; he supposed that he'd been too startled by that looming shadow to think properly. He began to walk again. He looked ahead, seeking his next point of division, and noticed the red phone box at the junction some hundred years ahead. That was a convenient point and he stared at it. It seemed to be moving away from him as his eyes played games of their own in the moonlight. He began walking faster. And then, gradually, he realized that whatever was walking on the other side of the hedgerow was walking faster, keeping abreast of him. He had so carefully shut his mind against his fear that the knowledge didn't register as a whole, but seeped into his mind in disintegrated bits. The terror did not come until he had actually turned and looked at the hedgerow; stared as the hedge parted, and he looked into the grotesque face of death.

Rose ran.

He ran as fast as madness could propel him down the narrow lane. He had looked into the face of the killer, but it made no impression on his mind. His mind did not function, he did not feel anything as his instincts took possession of his functions. Perhaps the soundwaves of the feet that padded behind him reached his ears, but his ears sent no impression to his brain. His brain was screaming too loud to hear. He stumbled, but was running too fast to fall; came crashing up against the phone box and yanked the door open; hurled himself inside this cubicle sanctuary of society and pulled the door closed behind him. Something slammed against the closing door with violent fury. Rose was still controlled by his instincts, and they were the instincts of civilized man. He had already jammed his finger in the dial and lifted the receiver to call for impossible salvation, when the door sprang open behind him, and Aaron Rose was drawn down with his finger still hooked in the dial . . .

Wetherby came to the top of the ridge beside a mound of rocks and stood there, looking down. The stream wound through the moonlight like the slimy track of a snail and the open land between was silver-filigreed by the slender shadows of the reeds. Wetherby stood very still and looked. If anything was moving down there, he would have seen its shadow beneath it. This was the first night that the moon had been his ally. But nothing moved, and he saw little sense in proceeding farther in that direction. He decided he would follow the crest of the ridge back to the secondary road, carefully circling each rocky mound . . .

Wetherby jumped with realization.

For a moment he quivered, taut and tight, and then he relaxed, cursing his stupidity. He had made his first blunder. He had climbed the ridge and stood beside that high peak of stone, hardly noticing it. He had stood there for several minutes. If the killer had been lurking in those rocks, Wetherby would have died beside them. It was unbelievable carelessness, a mistake he would never have made in the past, a routine that had been second nature to him until now.

Wetherby was sweating. He mopped his brow and drew his brandy flask out. Byron had been right, he knew, and the knowledge brought Wetherby as close as he had ever been to self-pity. The tension had got to him, and the blunders had begun. He took a large swallow and felt the heat of alcohol along his cold spine. He thought, deeply and objectively, weighing the possibilities and loathing the conclusions. Then he sighed. He knew that he should not be there, that his day was past and his skill was gone. If he continued, he was going to die, and Wetherby did not want to die.

Wetherby turned slowly and started walking back the way he had come. His shoulders felt heavy, he was tired. He was finished. He wondered how he would tell Bell . . .

Wetherby came out on the lane just east of The King's Torso. The pub had closed, the lights were off. It was just as well, because Wetherby did not want to see anyone; he felt that his failure was inscribed on his face, that any man

could decipher the runes of his defeat. He walked slowly
down the lane, keeping in the centre and looking to both
sides. He intended to make no more mistakes now, and
thought how ironic it would be if he were to die now that
he had given up the quest. All he wanted to do was to
return to the warm safety of his room, return to London
in the morning and close his mind to recrimination. But
to a man like Wetherby; a man like Wetherby had been
the knowledge of this was a torment far greater than death
and his emotions began to rebel against his mind.

Because he was watching the hedgerows with his eyes
and because his senses were directed against his mind
Wetherby did not notice the phone box until he was quite
near to it – near enough to see the heap inside, to see that
the door was slightly open. The door was open because a
leg protruded from the booth. The receiver dangled at the
end of its cord. Wetherby opened the door and looked in.
A shaft of wind blew past him and the receiver began to
revolve very slowly; turning just where the man's head
should have been. Wetherby recognized the man's blood-
spattered clothing with a cold lack of feeling.

It would make a splendid headline for the newspaper
which had employed Aaron Rose.

Wetherby's hand had already stretched out to lift the
receiver and telephone for the police when the savage hatred
sank a shaft into his brain. It was hatred of himself. He
stared at that hand that was so willing to seek help, and he
hated himself so much that it was unbearable, that the
hatred had to be transferred to save his mind. He stepped
out of the booth and let the door swing gently closed on
Rose's leg, moved away from the land and looked at the
ground. The tracks were there. He followed them. He was
not being cautious now. He was possessed, and caution was
there because it was part of his possession; not because he
was afraid, but because he must live to kill. He would make
no mistake this time. The hunter did not blunder when he
did not think.

The tracks ran beside the hedgerow, back the way

Wetherby had come. He wondered, without caring, if the creature had been crouched there when he walked past. The trail was plain for some distance before it stopped. But Wetherby paused for only a moment at the end of the tracks. Then he moved on. There was a broken stalk of grass, a crumpled shard of moss, the faintest imprint of a foot. There were all the things that he knew now, as a certainty, but he had failed to see before. He scarcely bothered to look at them now. His course was direct, and he knew with cold precision exactly where he was going . . .

Byron was waiting.

He was waiting beside the house, but Wetherby did not come up the walk. He came from behind the woodshed and the moonlight was running up the barrel of his rifle. Byron stood up and smiled. His smiled formed a curious pattern on his face; he looked in some way relieved

"You came silently," he said.

He carefully leaned his axe against the house.

"I thought you would never come," he said.

Wetherby said nothing.

"The races were excellent. A pity you missed them. There was a pile-up at one fence. Two horses killed and a jockey fractured his collar-bone. One horse had a broken back and they let it suffer until they could erect a tent around it, so that the people wouldn't see them kill it. That says something for our world, eh?"

"Where is it, Byron?"

"What, John?"

"I don't know what it is. I want it. I'm absolutely cold, Byron, and I can kill you if I must."

"That's good. You really should have recognized the tracks long ago, John. You should have followed it. I know, because I very carefully laid the trail. Did you follow it tonight, or did you guess?"

"I suppose I knew all the time," Wetherby said. His gun was pointed at the ground but the safety catch was off. "But tonight I realized something – perhaps it was something you

tried to tell me. It was like a magnet, drawing me here
tonight."

"No. It was a touch of your old skill. That's all. The
hunter's instinct." There was respect and genuine affection
in his expression. "Do you understand why I did it?"

"I know the purpose in your deranged mind."

"You still think I'm insane? But clever, you must admit.
And I succeeded in giving these rustic clods a reason to live.
Perhaps more than they deserve." Byron leaned against the
house. His hand played over the axe handle. "If they had
been brave, I might have let them live. Perhaps not. But
John, the fear! You should have seen the fear in their
eyes . . ."

"Was Hazel Lake supposed to be brave?"

"Oh, what does it matter? Her death made it more terrible for the others, that was all."

Wetherby's finger caressed the trigger. But he couldn't
kill yet, it was not resolved. He did not know himself yet.

"What do you think it was?" Byron asked.

"Which?"

"Ah, you'd realized that much. That's good. I made the
two-legged tracks, of course. A simple matter of borrowing
the claws from several different trophies and fastening them
to an old pair of boots. Quite simple, but clever. You were
certainly taken in by it. Half bear, half lion. But have you
forgotten seeing those other tracks?"

Wetherby was forgetting nothing now, because he was
not consciously thinking.

"Wolverine?" he said.

"Excellent, John. Excellent. Remember when we studied
those tracks together. Must have been ten years ago now.
You mentioned that a wolverine could never be tamed, I
believe. It wasn't easy. I was forced to breed one in captivity
to get any semblance of control. But then, I always did
have a rapport with wild animals. I didn't really tame it,
of course. I reduced myself and met it on its own level. It
knows I am necessary for its survival, and we hunt together
as equals."

"My God," Wetherby said.

"It gets in the cage willingly enough now," Byron said: "It's a bit more difficult after the kill, but I manage. See how simple it was, really? How effective?" Byron's hand had closed on the axe handle. Wetherby ignored it.

"But now, the question, John . . . what are you going to do?"

Byron was balanced, his knees bent. He was enjoying it immensely.

"You haven't a chance." Wetherby said.

"That isn't what I mean. You know I am immune to fear. In that respect, perhaps I am mad. A pleasant madness. But I've longed for you to come, John. You were perhaps the only man alive who had a chance with me. A slight chance. I was so disappointed when I saw how you had changed. How easy you would be. Are you going to try to kill me, John? Or will you try to inform the police? How much is left of the man I knew?"

"I don't know," Wetherby said. Then he said, "Enough."

"Come, I'll show you my bloodthirsty little friend," Byron said, moving suddenly away from the wall. He left the axe where it was, and the quick movement did not cause any reaction in Wetherby. Byron walked past him, close, and Wetherby regarded the space between his shoulders where the bullet would kill. He followed Byron. Byron swung open the angled doors that led to the cellar and went down into the dark. Wetherby went in behind him. It was very dark and for a moment he couldn't see Byron. Then Byron turned the lights on. The wolverine snarled from its cage, its stink filled the close room. Thirty pounds of claws and fangs and pure hatred, it turned its terrible eyes on Wetherby. He stared at it, a small monster that could inspire terror in a grizzly bear or put a pack of wolves to flight. Byron stood beside the cage. He smiled again. Wetherby raised his eyes reluctantly from the hypnotic gaze of the beast and looked at Byron. He looked beyond Byron and felt his stomach turn.

There on the wall, very effectively mounted on oak plaques, three human heads looked with glass eyes across the

room. The lips were drawn back in snarls. And hanging
from the ceiling, supported by a hook through the scalp,
swung a face that Wetherby knew, a man that Wetherby
had liked. Aaron Rose's head turned through a slow revol-
ution, until the countenance was full to Wetherby, the face
twisted in unspeakable horror and gore dripping from the
severed neck. A white glint of bone parted the flesh at the
throat. Byron made a sweeping gesture of presentation.

"My trophies," he said.

Then he was not smiling. He was crouched beside the
cage, his hand on the lock. The wolverine reached out with
curled claws, instinctively, then drew them back with slow
reluctance as Byron's fingers scratched its bristling neck.

"Well?" Byron asked.

Wetherby did not move.

"He comes fast, John. there will be time for one shot,
perhaps. But I come fast too."

"Not here," Wetherby said.

Byron's brow arched.

Wetherby knew what he had to do. What he absolutely
had to do, beyond right and wrong, beyond hatred and
fear . . . beyond self-preservation, if need be.

Wetherby worked the lever. The shells spun from the
chamber and clattered on the concrete floor. He counted
the clicks. Byron too, was counting. Wetherby worked a
bullet into the chamber and stopped ejecting.

"Two bullets, John?" Byron asked.

"Bring your friend."

"Ah. Quite so. I judged you badly, John."

Byron was still stroking the wolverine. It was impossible
to stroke a wolverine, uncanny and inhuman. but Byron
was more than a man. Or less than human. The wolverine
rubbed against him, but its eyes were on Wetherby and its
fiendish jaws dripped in anticipation.

"If I was wrong, John," Byron said. "If men are beyond
salvation, I have at least saved you." Again he smiled.

"Here?" he asked.

"No. Out there."

"Much better."

"I'll walk towards the tors."

"Excellent."

"Don't be long, Byron."

"No. Of course not."

Wetherby moved backwards to the stairs. Then he turned
and went up with his back towards Byron. Byron nodded
in approval.

"I'll see you soon," Byron said.

Wetherby was afraid.

But it was a healthy fear. It was not the strained tension
of the nights before, his senses were alive and tingling, his
blood pounded but his muscles were calm. He was smiling
in the dark at the crest of the ridge. Every detail of the
land was impressed effortlessly on his mind. A solitary
cloud was drifting towards the moon, slipping through the
sky. It was going to bring black night when it blocked that
moonlight, and Wetherby welcomed the shadows, because
he had no need for light. He wanted very much to live,
and he understood Byron at last. In that much, at least,
Byron had known. He wanted to live because he was alive,
and because the wind was blowing across the moors, and
because he had two bullets in his rifle . . .

Stephen Jones

Afterword: Bringing the Horror Back Home

The popularity of horror has always been cyclic: every decade or so we plunder the darkest recesses of our imagination as this most disturbing of all genre fiction enjoys a critical and commercial re-evaluation before being banished once again to the safety of the collective subconscious.

During the post-atomic years of the early 1950s, our fears found new expression in the guise of bug-eyed alien invaders from the depths of space, or the accidental discovery of monster *gigantis*, the latter invariably a by-product of radioactive residue. There was a brave new world awaiting the children of the Second World War, and with it new horrors for them to confront. Those traditional terrors, which once could be vanquished by fire, stake or silver bullet, were all but forgotten amongst the complexity and paranoia of the modern age.

Then in 1957, Britain's Hammer Films brought the horror back home with their garish colour remakes of the Frankenstein and Dracula legends. On screen, blood was significantly coupled with sexuality, and while some critics and defenders of moral behaviour were predictably outraged, the public lapped it up.

Ten years later Hammer received the Queen's Award to Industry for exporting horror, while the movie version of *Rosemary's Baby* (based on the best-selling novel by Ira Levin) convinced millions of cinemagoers that God was dead and, in New York at least, the Devil still had all the best tunes.

By the mid–1970s, Hammer Films had all but ceased

churning out their steady diet of adult fairy tales. Audiences wanted something more explicit, and William Peter Blatty's hit novel *The Exorcist* was turned into the most popular horror film of all time. Meanwhile, an advertising art director from London's East End had just written his first book: the graphic intensity of James Herbert's novel *The Rats* ensured it became an instant bestseller, with the initial print run of 100,000 copies selling out in a matter of weeks. And a young writer from Bangor, Maine, captured the reading public's imagination with his first three books: *Carrie*, *'Salem's Lot* and *The Shining* sold millions of copies around the world and made millions of dollars for their author, Stephen King.

Within a decade King's name had become synonymous with horror, his books reputedly outsold only by the Bible, while Herbert's insatiable readership made him the most popular and successful horror author in Britain.

But it was the turn of a new breed of writer to emerge, a group committed to pushing the genre to its limits. In the UK, Liverpudlian playwright Clive Barker made a bid for King's crown by revealing the stark reality of revulsion, and across the Atlantic a loose community of young authors calling themselves "splatter-punks" injected new blood into the genre, while pizza-faced dream-killer Freddy Krueger became the unlikely hero of countless cinemagoers' nightmares.

Today horror is once again doing business. Every new sequel creates the opportunity for greater box office returns, and for those writers at the top of the pile, horror fiction means Big Bucks.

Despite the vagaries of the genre over the past thirty years, *The Pan Book of Horror Stories* has consistently offered the aficionado the opportunity to annually unlock a Pandora's Box of terrors (no mean achievement in a field that has watched numerous anthology series come and go), making it the longest-running most successful horror collection in the world.

The first 300-plus page volume appeared as a "Pan Giant" in 1959, and it remains an exemplary collection, showcasing classic reprints by Jack Finney, C. S. Forrester, Nigel Kneale, Joan Aiken and Bram Stoker, to mention only a few.

The book was edited ("selected" it proudly proclaimed on the cover) by Herbert van Thal, who continued to oversee the contents of each volume until his death in 1983. For van Thal, editing a collection of "spine chilling tales" every year probably seemed at odds with most of his other literary endeavours: born in 1904, Herbert Maurice van Thal was a literary agent for most of his life. He wrote more than fifty books and is best remembered as the co-editor of *The Music Lover's Companion*; the compiler of Thomas Adolphus Trollope's autobiography; a book about Victorian travellers; and a two-volume work on Britain's Prime Ministers.

However, under his own publishing imprint, "Home and van Thal", which he established in 1945, van Thal edited *Weird Stories* by Mrs Riddell and *Twilight Tales* by Rhoda Broughton. Besides *The Pan Book of Horror Stories*, he was the editor of half a dozen similar anthologies, his first being *A Book of Strange Stories* in 1954. Van Thal's autobiography, entitled *The Tops of the Mulberry Trees*, appeared in 1971.

The Second Pan Book of Horror Stories was published in 1960 and the series became annual two years later. New stories began appearing in volume four and became the bulk of the contents from the fifth book onwards.

These early editions contained a remarkable breadth of stories, many culled from the classic *Not At Night* anthologies of the 1920s and 30s edited by Christine Campbell Thomson (who herself became a contributor to the *Pan* series). Van Thal's eclectic taste resulted in a body of fiction that ranged from the psychical to the psychological, from the supernal to the supernatural.

Over the year, *The Pan Book of Horror Stories* has showcased the work of established British masters of the macabre like H. G. Wells, Bram Stoker, Algernon Blackwood, William Hope Hodgson, Lord Dunsany and E. F. Benson. The American tradition, perhaps best exemplified in the pulp magazine *Weird Tales*, was represented by such exponents as Ray Bradbury, Robert Bloch, Seabury Quinn, Frank Belknap Long, August Derleth (under his "Stephen Grendon" alias), Joseph Payne Brennan, and H. P. Lovecraft (who collaborated – without credit – on Hazel Heald's memorable "The Horror in the Museum").

Newer names in contemporary horror fiction, such as David Case, Robert Aickman, Basil Copper, Alan Ryan, Christopher Fowler, Tanith Lee, Robert Holdstock and, of course, Stephen King, have been featured throughout the series; and it might come as a surprise to discover William Faulkner, Ruth Rendell, Patricia Highsmith, Muriel Spark, Ian McEwan and Paul Theroux listed on the contents pages.

In recent years the series has moved away from the more traditional tales of supernatural evil to concentrate on the excesses of the Grand Guignol. However, under the guidance of Clarence Paget, the popularity of the series has continued, with combined sales now totalling in the millions.

It should also be remembered that besides spine-chilling entertainment, *The Pan Book of Horror Stories* has something else to offer: in a rapidly diminishing market for short fiction, it still provides a welcome outlet for new and up-and-coming writers to break into professional publication. The next generation of James Herberts or Clive Barkers could well emerge from their ranks.

This present volume collects together thirteen of the most memorable stories to have been featured in the series over the past three decades, introduced by a selection of the finest practitioners working in the field today.

To celebrate this unique 30th anniversary, we have helped you rend the veil, peek beneath the shroud, and gaze into the darkside of your imagination to confront insanity, revenge, cannibalism, murder, lycanthropy and the walking dead.

Welcome, then, to *The Pan Book of Horror Stories* – and many happy returns!

Stephen Jones
London, February 1989

The Pan Book of Horror Stories
Index Volumes 1–30

The 7th Pan Book of Horror Stories (1966)
Selected by Herbert van Thal

The 30th Pan Book of Horror Stories (1989)
Selected by Clarence Paget

interzone

SCIENCE FICTION AND FANTASY

Bimonthly £1.95

- *Interzone* is the leading British magazine which specializes in SF. We have published the major names of the past decade — Aldiss, Ballard, Banks, Benford, Bishop, Brin, Campbell, Carter, Crowley, Disch, Gibson, Harrison, Kilworth, Moorcock, Pratchett, Roberts, Shaw, Sladek, Stableford, Sterling, Watson, Wolfe, etc. — but we are especially proud of the new authors we have discovered, or whose work we have encouraged from an early point in their careers:

S.M. Baxter	**William King**
Michael Blumlein	**Christina Lake**
Scott Bradfield	**Ian Lee**
Keith Brooke	**Paul J. McAuley**
Eric Brown	**Ian R. MacLeod**
Christopher Burns	**Lee Montgomerie**
Richard Calder	**Jamil Nasir**
Greg Egan	**Kim Newman**
Neil Ferguson	**Marianne Puxley**
Peter T. Garratt	**Geoff Ryman**
Nicola Griffith	**Alex Stewart**
Lyle Hopwood	**Charles Stross**
Richard Kadrey	**Steven Widdowson**

- *Interzone* also publishes illustrations, articles, interviews, film and book reviews, news, etc.

- *Interzone* is available from good bookshops, or by subscription. For six issues, send £12 (outside UK, £13) to: **124 Osborne Road, Brighton BN1 6LU, UK** Single copies: £2.30 inc p&p (outside UK, £2.50).

- American subscribers may send $22 ($26 if you want delivery by air mail) to our British address, above. All cheques should be made payable to *Interzone*.

- -

To: **Interzone** 124 Osborne Road, Brighton, BN1 6LU, UK.

Please send me six issues of *Interzone*, beginning with the current issue. I enclose a cheque / p.o. for £12 (outside UK, £13; US subscribers, $22 or $26 air), made payable to *Interzone*.

Name _____

Address _____

_____

Dan McGirt
Jason Cosmo £3.99

Jason Cosmo was a humble woodcutter in the village of lower Hicksnittle on the northern fringes of Darnk, where a conversation about mottled pig pox in the Festering Wart Tavern was a major community event.

But the arrival of a foppish stranger who promptly tried to kill him, made Jason realize that there was more afoot in the magical Eleven Kingdoms of Arden than he'd previously suspected.

In neighbouring Whiteswap, sipping carrot juice under the watchful eye of the Sanitary Police, Jason met the wizard Mercury Boltblaster – and learned some bad news.

The evil Dark Magic Society had placed a ten million gold crown on Jason's head – and bounty hunters Black Moon and Red Huntsman were on his trail. Was it a case of mistaken identity? Was there another Jason Cosmo? Or did he have something strangely wrong with his aura?

First British publication

All Pan books are available at your local bookshop or newsagent, or can be ordered direct from the publisher. Indicate the number of copies required and fill in the form below.

Send to: **CS Department, Pan Books Ltd., P.O. Box 40, Basingstoke, Hants.   RG21 2YT.**

or phone: 0256 469551 (Ansaphone), quoting title, author and Credit Card number.

Please enclose a remittance* to the value of the cover price plus: 60p for the first book plus 30p per copy for each additional book ordered to a maximum charge of £2.40 to cover postage and packing.

*Payment may be made in sterling by UK personal cheque, postal order, sterling draft or international money order, made payable to Pan Books Ltd.

Alternatively by Barclaycard/Access:

Card No. ☐☐☐☐☐☐☐☐☐☐☐☐☐☐☐☐

Signature:

Applicable only in the UK and Republic of Ireland.

While every effort is made to keep prices low, it is sometimes necessary to increase prices at short notice. Pan Books reserve the right to show on covers and charge new retail prices which may differ from those advertised in the text or elsewhere.

NAME AND ADDRESS IN BLOCK LETTERS PLEASE:

....

Name ————————————————————————

Address ————————————————————————

————————————————————————

————————————————————————

————————————————————————

3/87